KATIE'S FOREVER PROMISE

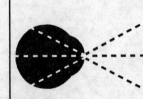

KATIE'S FOREVER PROMISE

JERRY S. EICHER

THORNDIKE PRESS

A part of Gale, Cengage Learning

GALE
CENGAGE Learning·

Detroit • New York • San Francisco • New Haven, Conn • Waterville, Maine • London

LIBRARY OF CONGRESS CATALOGING-IN-PUBLICATION DATA

Eicher, Jerry S.
  Katie's forever promise / by Jerry S. Eicher. — Large print edition.
    pages ; cm. — (Thorndike Press large print Christian romance) (Emma Raber's daughter series ; #3)
  ISBN-13: 978-1-4104-6177-3 (hardcover)
  ISBN-10: 1-4104-6177-7 (hardcover)
  1. Amish—Fiction. 2. Young women—Fiction. 3. Large type books. I. Title.
PS3605.I34K35 2013b
813'.6—dc23   2013033758

Published in 2014 by arrangement with Harvest House Publishers

Printed in the United States of America
1 2 3 4 5 6 7 18 17 16 15 14

KATIE'S FOREVER PROMISE

CHAPTER ONE

Katie Raber sat on the tall, swivel chair with a smile on her face. She was now mistress and queen of this one-room Amish schoolhouse for the term. Her hiring had been reaffirmed this morning by Enos Kuntz himself, the chairman of the school board. Enos had paid her a special visit, leaving with a friendly nod and a quick comment. "I think you'll do just fine with your new job, Katie. Let us know if you have any problems."

Katie swept the top of her teacher's desk clean with a shaky hand, pausing to replace the small plastic pencil holder she'd knocked over. On the other side of the room, pushed up against the window, sat a table loaded with the year's supply of schoolbooks. She was a little scared, but she told herself there was nothing to worry about. This world of learning called her, just as she was certain it would also beckon eager young students once school began next week. And then, in less than two months, she would be twenty-one, considered an adult in her Amish community. Her wages would be her own to spend how she chose instead of sharing them with her parents — *Mamm* and her new husband, Jesse Mast. How blessed Katie felt. It was still hard to comprehend all the changes that had occurred in the last few years.

Katie stood and looked out the window. Enos was driving away in his buggy, his bearded face still visible through the open door. Calm was flooding over Katie now. There could be only one reason he would take the time to drive all the way over here this morning, the week before school officially begins. And it wasn't because he harbored any doubts about her teaching abilities. The vote to hire her had been unanimous and given with pleased smiles on the faces of all three school board members.

No, Enos had stopped by to emphasize his approval one last time. Likely he thought she needed it — this being her first year teaching. But it was more than that. Enos knew the details of her past, as did all the Amish community. And they wished her well as she continued to put her life back together after the awful situation with Ben

Stoll. Even now Ben was sitting in jail, serving out the last few days of his sentence.

Katie had survived that disastrous time because *Da Hah* had been with her, just as He'd been with *Mamm* and her after Katie's *daett* died. And just as *Da Hah* had been with the two while Emma Raber raised Katie alone. Katie's *mamm* had an awful reputation for a long time. After a love gone wrong in her teen years, a marriage to a man she learned to love, and then being widowed at an early age, Emma had chosen to remain a single *mamm,* raising her daughter on the land her husband had left her. She'd gone against usual Amish practice by refusing offers of marriage until, by *Da Hah*'s grace, she'd accepted a marriage proposal by a local farmer named Jesse Mast. That marriage had created a new atmosphere of change and acceptance, and Katie's reputation had improved along with her *mamm*'s. After Katie fell in love with Ben and he'd turned out to be involved in the drug trade, part of her acceptance in the community came from how much she was admired for the way she'd handled herself since Ben Stoll's arrest and imprisonment.

She'd loved Ben with all of her heart. And he had broken and smashed her trust beyond repair. Now he was no longer part of her life. That had all happened over a year ago, when the news of Ben's arrest had reached Katie while she was in Europe with her Mennonite friends Margaret Kargel, Sharon Watson, and Nancy Keim. Only *Da Hah*'s healing touch a few days later had kept her from spending years in bitterness and sorrow. The miracle had happened the morning they'd gone up in a cable car high in the Alps to Schilthorn, where she'd seen the mighty works of *Da Hah*'s hands displayed in the mountain range around her. The tears had flowed freely that morning, washing the deepest pain from her heart. Afterward, she'd returned home and continued mourning her loss for a time, but without the crushing hopelessness that had first gripped her heart. Then last fall she'd made application to join the instruction class to officially join the Amish church, and this spring the *wunderbah* day had arrived. She'd been baptized by Bishop Jonas Miller himself! She was now a member of the church.

If anyone had entertained doubts about her, they'd been answered in how Katie had lived her life the past year. She still stayed in touch with her Mennonite friends Margaret and Sharon, but she saw them infrequently. The invitation to Margaret's wedding had arrived in the mail yesterday, and Katie would certainly attend. Beyond that, Sharon and Margaret understood that Katie had made the best choice for her — to stay within the Amish faith. And it was, Katie told herself. Her heart was settled on the matter. The Amish were her people, and this was her home. She'd seen the land of the church fathers in Switzerland, and now she'd chosen this faith for herself. This community in Delaware was the place where her heart could rest for whatever time *Da Hah* had for her on this earth.

Enos's buggy was already a black speck just before disappearing around the curve in the road. In addition to his interest in her success in the classroom, there was the suspicion on Katie's part that Enos had hopes she would be his next daughter-in-law. She could tell by the light that sprang up in his eyes when he spoke to her of his son Norman.

Norman Kuntz, though, wasn't like his *daett* at all. He was shy and withdrawn for the most part. The boy was handsome enough and came from an excellent family, so he ought to bubble with confidence, but he didn't. So far he'd lacked the courage to take Katie home from the Sunday-night hymn singing — although he did spend considerable time stealing glances at her in the meetings. He'd mustered up enough courage lately to send a few tentative smiles her way.

There was nothing in Norman that set Katie's heart pounding so far. Not like Ben Stoll had done. That had been another matter entirely. But Katie knew she shouldn't be comparing Norman with Ben. Her life had changed for the better now, and she wasn't going back to the past. Ben had been a terrible misjudgment, and she didn't plan to repeat the error.

This time whoever the man was who drove her home, Katie wanted *Mamm*'s full support. And hopefully Jesse's too, although he'd mostly care about whether the young man was a *gut* church member and knew how to work hard. Norman met both of those standards quite well. It helped, of course, that he would be a *gut* provider for his family, but that paled in comparison to the really important matter to Katie. Her main concern was that Norman would never do what Ben had done — break her heart.

Katie sighed, pushing the dark thoughts aside. Things were coming together well for her. This offer of a teaching job had been another blessing from *Da Hah.* One of the many she'd been given since Ben's betrayal.

Katie sighed again, allowing her mind to wander into the past. For years she'd dreamed of capturing Ben Stoll's attention. *Mamm* had warned her that such handsome boys were above her, and she shouldn't dream that way. And that was long before Ben even knew Katie existed. But *Mamm* had been drawing from her own experience of rejection, and the young man she'd loved had never even asked her home. So Katie had rejected *Mamm*'s counsel and hadn't drawn back when Ben finally noticed her at a Mennonite Youth Gathering. She'd ridden in Ben's buggy and held his hand. They'd even kissed — often and with great joy. How could she have been so wrong about him? Katie pondered the question and managed a faint smile. Even in this situation she could be thankful. The pain of that question no longer stung as much. She'd given the pain and hard questions over to *Da Hah.* He knew the answers, and He would forgive her where she'd been wrong.

Now she was being given a *wunderbah* opportunity by the community. They were entrusting her with the care of their children for a whole school year. This honor had been held by Ruth Troyer for the past few years, After chasing Jesse Mast before he'd married Katie's *mamm,* Ruth had finally found a man who asked to wed her — Albert Gingerich. He was an older farmer in the community whose wife had passed away last year.

Ruth had stepped down from consideration as a teacher this summer in preparation for her wedding, although she probably hadn't imagined in her wildest dreams that Katie Raber would be offered her job. Ruth might have hung on for another year if she'd known that. After all, she'd been rebuffed by Jesse in favor of Katie's *mamm,* Emma Raber, and the sting of the rejection and community talk surely still rankled in Ruth's mind.

Katie smiled at the memory of *Mamm* and Jesse's courtship. The two widows — Emma and Ruth — had faced each other down, and *Mamm* had won! The strange thing was that *Mamm* hadn't put up much of a fight — at least not out in the open. But maybe that was the allure that drew Jesse in. Katie decided she needed to allow that *Mamm* had more wisdom than she let on at times. Ruth had had all of Jesse's children on her side at first, and she put her best moves on Jesse by baking the pecan pies he loved. *Mamm,* on the other hand, had turned down Jesse's advances the first few times he came calling, which seemed to make him all the more determined. And when she finally came around, Emma offered nothing but herself. In the end, all of Jesse's children except Mabel, the eldest, had come over to *Mamm*'s side.

Mabel hadn't been the easiest person to live with after the wedding, but since Katie's return from Europe they were on decent terms. Mabel's heart had been softened last year by seeing the great heartache Ben's betrayal had caused Katie.

A rattle of buggy wheels in the schoolyard interrupted her thoughts. Katie walked to the window again. She gasped as Ruth Troyer climbed out of her buggy. What did *she* want? Had she forgotten some of her personal possessions? If so, she could have come in the evening after I'd gone home, Katie thought. But, there was no sense avoiding Ruth, so she might as well put on a brave front.

"*Gut* morning," Ruth said with a forced smile when Katie opened the door.

"*Gut* morning," Katie replied as she held the door and invited Ruth in.

"I thought I might catch you here this morning."

"*Yah,*" Katie managed to get out, her

15

smile gone now. "There's much to do before school starts."

Ruth pushed past her and bustled inside. "I thought I'd drive over in case you might want some advice, seeing this is your first term and all. And remember, I did teach here for three years so I know many of the students and the material. If you have any questions, I'd be glad to answer them."

Katie swallowed hard. "Did the school board send you?"

Ruth laughed. "*Nee,* I'm here on my own. Don't tell me you're too high and mighty to accept help? Just because you're a schoolteacher now doesn't mean we don't all remember where you came from, Katie Raber. After all, that man of yours is still sitting in jail."

"I have no connection with Ben Stoll anymore," Katie countered. "I haven't seen him since before he was arrested."

"Well, that doesn't matter now." Ruth breezed around the room, speaking over her shoulder. "I guess we all make our mistakes. But I, for one, would have seen that one coming. And I suspect your *mamm* did, but she was too busy stealing Jesse from me to warn you."

Katie turned and watched Ruth. This was after all her schoolhouse now, and she'd better act like it was. Katie kept her voice even. "*Mamm* did have reservations about Ben — just to set the record straight. And she didn't steal Jesse from you. Jesse made up his own mind."

Ruth turned around. "Things do turn out for the best now, don't they? Thank *Da Hah* Jesse didn't decide on me. Then I never would have been available for Albert's proposal. Did you know he farms more than 100 acres northwest of Dover? Some of the best black soil in the area. It's worth a fortune. He'll have a mighty *gut* heritage to hand down to his children."

Katie forced a smile. "I'm glad for you, Ruth. And *Mamm* has fallen deeply in love with Jesse, so everything *did* turn out for the best."

"It always does." Ruth glared at Katie. "And I guess you know *gut* and well why you got this job. Enos is expecting quite a lot out of his investment, if you ask me."

"I don't expect you know what you're speaking of," Katie said. She tried to still her pounding heart. How this woman could get under her skin! Enos might hope she'd date his son, but he hadn't made any requirement or suggestion for her to do so while hiring her.

Ruth laughed. "I don't think you're that

17

blind, Katie. Enos is a man of high standards. And your past hasn't gone away, believe me. He's just overlooking it right now. But if you turn down the advances of his youngest son, I doubt if things will stay that way for long."

Katie almost sputtered a denial, but she pressed her lips together instead. Nothing would persuade Ruth's mind. Not once she'd made it up. And there likely was some truth to the woman's statements.

Ruth smiled, apparently taking Katie's silence as victory. "Let me show you the books then, and I'll get out of here. I have a ton of things that need doing for the wedding preparations, but I told myself this morning that I owe you at least one visit since I was the former teacher. I'm aware you know nothing about teaching. I do hate to see you thrown into this situation and making a total mess out of it — to say nothing about all the decent learning from the past few years that could be lost. Let's look at the books for this term."

Katie walked toward the table by the window. Two of the books had fallen to the floor while she'd been going through them, but she hadn't noticed until Ruth's criticizing presence entered the room.

Ruth marched over and bent down to pick

up the books. "This is no way to treat new books! I always told myself, if I don't respect the school's property, how can I expect 'my' children to? Because they do, after all, learn more by example than by any lecture. But how would you know such a thing? Your *mamm* probably never taught you much."

Katie choked back her response. Ruth was trying to goad her into saying something she might regret. And Enos had just been here, and he'd said nothing about books lying on the floor. Everyone knew such things happened during unpacking. But Katie knew Ruth would only see more of Enos's scheming and favor in his silence, so she might as well keep quiet about that too.

Ruth's voice continued in lecture mode. "These are your first-grade reading books, Katie. Be sure to spend plenty of time with that age group. The children need to learn quickly because everything else is at a standstill until they learn how to read."

Katie nodded, forcing herself to listen. Ruth was telling her some *gut* things, and she did have much to learn. She even managed to keep a smile on her face as the former teacher droned on far longer than Katie had hoped. Over an hour later, Katie was more than ready to see Ruth leave. She summoned up her best manners as Ruth finally prepared to go. "Thank you for your time, Ruth. I do appreciate it."

"It's *gut* that you can listen," Ruth remarked. "I guess your *mamm* taught you something after all. Now, will you come out and hold my horse for me? He gets a little skittish when I take off. Albert promised me a decent horse when I move into his house after the wedding. Now that's a decent man, if you ask me."

Katie held her tongue as she walked outside. She held the bridle of Ruth's horse as the former teacher climbed inside the buggy.

"I hope you remember everything I told you," Ruth said as she took off with a slap of the reins.

Grinding her teeth, Katie watched Ruth go. That woman was the limit and then some. But Ruth was also a creature *Da Hah* had made, and her elder besides. And the woman had given her some useful advice.

CHAPTER TWO

That evening the whole family was seated for dinner when Katie slid her kitchen chair forward while *Mamm* brought the last of the food to the table. Katie hadn't arrived home from the schoolhouse until a few minutes ago — too late to help. Apparently this would be another privilege of school teaching. When she'd worked as a cashier at Byler's Store, coming home late hadn't been an acceptable practice at all.

"Let us pray," Jesse said.

They all bowed their heads as Jesse led out in prayer. "Our great and heavenly Father, blessed be Your name. We pause at this evening hour to give You thanks, and to beseech Your continued aid and care over our lives . . ."

Katie listened to the sound of Jesse's voice. It was soothing after Ruth's harsh tones just a few hours ago. That woman's words had stung more than Katie wished to admit. Still, it wasn't true that her job had been given to her so Enos could influence her to be his future daughter-in-law. How did Ruth dare say such things? She had to admit that Enos probably hoped she would say *yah* if Norman ever asked to take her home after a hymn sing. But the outcome of that certainly wasn't tied to her hiring in any way. Ruth shouldn't even be thinking such thoughts! If anyone had reason to entertain doubt about someone's character, Katie did. Didn't Ruth give plenty of cause for people to question her character. Yet *Da Hah* required that His people think only the best of others, even when they acted in ways they shouldn't.

"Amen," Jesse said, interrupting Katie's thoughts.

"Why's the stove still putting out so much heat?" Mabel asked.

Mamm leaped to her feet with a gasp and rushed over to turn the damper knob.

"Getting forgetful in your old age?" Jesse teased.

Mamm blushed. "That goes for you too, you know."

Katie smiled at their light banter. *Mamm* had blossomed since her marriage to Jesse. She actually appeared years younger than she had when they'd lived alone on their farm.

A shadow crossed Katie's face as the table chatter continued around her. She would have been married to Ben Stoll by now if he hadn't done what he did. Or at least they'd be talking of marrying next year. But what *gut* was it mourning what couldn't be helped? Besides, during and after Ben's trial had been a time of purifying for her, and now she felt settled about where *Da Hah* was guiding her. The brief time she'd spent associating with the Mennonite youth group now seemed like a dream, far off and distant — much like Ben himself.

"How did things go at school today?" Leroy asked from his place on the back bench.

Katie jumped. Then she quickly smiled. "Fine."

The eldest of Jesse's three boys from his marriage to Millie, Leroy had shown the most interest in Katie's work at the school. From the look on his face, the answer seemed to satisfy him. He nodded as he dipped a huge helping of mashed potatoes onto his plate before passing the bowl to his brother Willis.

Mabel, though, was staring at Katie. "Surely something exciting happened? You didn't sit there all day by yourself with just the books for company, did you?"

Katie shrugged. She really didn't feel like going into the visits by Enos Kuntz and Ruth Troyer.

"Come on, tell us," Mabel teased. "I can tell you're holding something back. Let's not start with secret things this early in the school year."

Leroy grinned from ear to ear. "I see what Mabel's after. She wants Katie spilling all the juicy gossip each night. Training her early so she'll have the inside track on what's going on in the community."

Mabel didn't deny the accusation. "Why shouldn't I know if Katie does?"

They all laughed.

"Katie shouldn't be bringing home news like that," Leroy said. "Gossip isn't good, so she won't. You might as well get used to the fact."

Mabel wrinkled up her face but didn't say anything.

Taking a deep breath, Katie began anyway. "Well, Enos Kuntz showed up to give me some words of encouragement. And after that, Ruth Troyer came along to help me with the books and see if I had any questions about teaching. So, nothing really exciting happened."

"Enos Kuntz?" Leroy was all ears now.

Everyone else laughed, and Leroy lowered his head. They knew Leroy had his eyes focused on Enos's niece, Lizzie Kuntz.

Without missing a beat, Willis piled on. "Of course Leroy finds that interesting. He finds even the passing shadow of Lizzie to be of great interest."

"You just wait!" Leroy muttered as laughter filled the room again.

Mabel made a face at Willis. "Ha! Someday you'll be the same way," Mabel said, defending Leroy. Then she dismissed the subject with a wave of her hand. "What I want to know is what Ruth came over for."

"Katie just told you!" Leroy blustered, obviously trying to recapture his dignity.

"That's why you should leave this kind of conversation to the women," Mabel lectured her brother. "We know how to see below the surface of things — unlike men who only see what they see."

"Now that's nasty," Willis said, back on his brother's side in a flash.

"But it's true," Mabel said. "Am I right, Katie?"

Mabel *was* right, Katie thought as she deliberately kept her face neutral. Mabel knew Ruth Troyer well and had been on Ruth's side back when Ruth had her *kapp* set for Jesse. Mabel had played her part in

25

passing along anything unpleasant she knew about *Mamm.* Still . . . Katie smiled a little. Mabel had changed since then, and she shouldn't hold the past against her.

"I'm right, am I not?" Mabel persisted.

"Maybe you shouldn't pry into Katie's business," Jesse said. "Katie might not wish to share everything she and Ruth spoke about. Perhaps it was information Ruth had about some of the children. That's a private matter between teachers, unless it involves Carolyn or Joel."

Carolyn sat up straight at her place at the table. "I didn't do anything wrong — *ever*! Plus I'm no longer in school. I graduated!"

"Neither did I!" eight-year-old Joel added. "And I'm still going to school."

"I doubt that either of you were trouble free," Mabel shot their way.

Katie struggled to speak. "I . . . really . . . Ruth had nothing bad to say about any of the children. I think she liked all of them very well."

"See, I told you!" Carolyn looked quite vindicated. "Ruth was a *gut* teacher."

"I'm sure she was," Katie agreed. "And Ruth wanted to share some of her wisdom with me. So she drove all the way over on her own time to help me out — even though she's busy with wedding preparations."

"I think you'll also make a great teacher," Joel piped up.

"I hope so." Katie said, lowering her head. That was the one uncomfortable thing about teaching in your own district. How would she handle giving orders to her brother? *Mamm* always did that at home.

"You'll be great!" Carolyn agreed.

Mabel turned to Carolyn. "Remember to keep thinking that when you hear that Katie has to boss Joel around. I believe in discipline, and I don't want to hear any reports floating around the community that my baby brother is getting special treatment."

"That's a *gut* attitude to have," Jesse said. "I'm hoping for the best for Joel this year again. And don't be all that hard on Katie. She's new at this and might need some time to learn the ropes."

"You can say that again," Katie murmured. Suddenly she was very glad she'd listened to everything Ruth had told her. The woman had a surprisingly large amount of wisdom behind that wagging tongue of hers.

"Guess what I heard today?" Willis spoke up. "You won't believe it!"

"That some girl consented to drive home with you?" Mabel shot at him.

Everyone laughed good-naturedly, but

27

Willis looked undeterred.

"Ben Stoll will be out of jail next week."

Katie gasped, and everyone turned to look at her.

Jesse spoke up at once. "That wasn't a nice thing for you to be saying at the supper table, Willis. Katie didn't need to hear the news dropped on her like that."

"I'm sorry," Willis said.

Katie caught her breath and tried to smile. "It's okay. That just came as a surprise, although I knew the time was getting close."

Leroy cleared his throat. "I'm surprised Ben's out so soon with all the charges that had been brought against him."

"We shouldn't talk about this at the table," Jesse warned.

Leroy shrugged. "The subject was brought up, and I'm curious, that's all."

"Willis can tell you later what else he knows," Jesse told him. "We shouldn't talk about this in front of Katie. She's suffered enough already."

"Thank you," Katie whispered, keeping her head down as the meal continued. She didn't join in the chatter when the subject changed to the day's events on the farm. She shouldn't have reacted like that when the subject of Ben Stoll came up. *Da Hah* had healed her, and she'd moved on. Per-

28

haps next time she would do better.

When supper was over, they bowed their heads in silent prayer. Then the menfolk scattered to the living room. Jesse would be calling for evening devotions before long, but in the meantime the womenfolk would clean the kitchen.

Katie went to run water in the sink for dishes.

"Mabel and Carolyn, Katie and I will take care of the kitchen tonight. Both of you helped me prepare the food, so you've done enough," *Mamm* said.

"Are you sure?" Mabel asked. "We can help."

"Get on now, and I mean it!" *Mamm* gave both girls a sweet smile that softened the order.

Mamm is being quite wise, Katie thought. This way no resentment would fester between them over her working late at the school. Katie hadn't thought of how this could be best handled, but *Mamm* was already finding a solution. And *Mamm* probably wished to talk, if Katie didn't miss her guess. Both matters would be taken care of this evening at the same time.

Mabel and Carolyn were no more out of the kitchen before *Mamm* asked her first question. "So what did Ruth Troyer really want today, Katie? I know she didn't drive all that way just to 'help' you."

"*Mamm,* please. The woman did offer some helpful advice."

"But that wasn't everything, was it?"

Katie looked down as she continued to wash dishes. "Well, no. She claims Enos Kuntz only gave me the job with the understanding that I'd be his daughter-in-law. And she rubbed in the fact that she's marrying again — and marrying rich at that. And she said something about you stealing Jesse from her."

Mamm smiled. "Some people are the limit, that's all I can say."

"You don't think Enos really gave me the job for that reason, do you? I know he'd like me to be open to Norman's attention, but hiring me would be going kind of far . . ."

"Of course he wouldn't do something like that." *Mamm* didn't hesitate. "Enos isn't that kind of man. And the entire school board had to approve your hiring."

"That's what I thought."

"I do approve of Norman." *Mamm* had a touch of teasing in her voice. "And Enos and his *frau* apparently approve of you. So on that point, Ruth is correct. All of us like the potential match."

30

"Oh, *Mamm*," Katie whispered, "do you think I can ever love again?"

"Love is a gift from *Da Hah*." *Mamm* looked pensive. "I was given it again, long after I gave up all hope. And twice at that — first for your *daett* and then Jesse. *Yah*, you can love again. *Da Hah* will see to that."

"But Norman . . . he's so . . . so . . . timid. I'm not used to that at all. He hasn't spoken a word to me yet, *Mamm*. Not one."

"You mustn't compare every young man to Ben." *Mamm*'s voice was low. "That will be your temptation, Katie."

Katie nodded. "I've tried to forget Ben. I really have."

Mamm continued as if she hadn't heard. "If Norman loves *Da Hah* and His ways, and if he loves you, then love can grow in your heart. You're now a church member, Katie, and so is Norman. In fact, he's been one for some time. That doesn't happen often — that young men make up their minds so quickly. You can't go wrong on this one, Katie. Even if the feelings don't come at once, they will in time. They did for me — with your *daett* and with Jesse."

Katie continued washing the dishes. *Mamm* was right, she was certain of it. After what had happened with Ben, she should be honored that Norman was even considering her for his *frau.*

They finished the dishes and found their way to the living room for the evening devotions. After Jesse read the Scriptures and they knelt in prayer, Katie slipped up the stairs.

Willis followed her, stopping her outside her bedroom door.

"Katie?"

"Yah?" Katie turned around and paused.

Willis glanced down the stairs before continuing. "I didn't say anything at the supper table, but Ben wants to meet with you when he's out of jail. It's urgent, he says."

Katie struggled to keep breathing. "I can't, Willis. You know that."

Willis shrugged, his slim shoulders barely visible in the shadowed stairwell. "I'm just passing on what I was told by Emery Graber."

Katie didn't say anything more; she just stared as Willis disappeared into his room. What did Ben want? It didn't really matter though. Meeting him was out of the question. Their relationship was over . . . *way* over.

CHAPTER THREE

The following Monday, Katie stood at the door of the schoolhouse as the first buggy full of students turned into the yard. They waved to her, and with a pounding heart Katie waved back. Should she go out and help unhitch? No, she couldn't do that — not for all of them, and presenting any hint of favoritism on the first day of school was unwise. She would wait inside. And from there she would make sure each child was comfortable as he or she entered. The older students would know their way around, of course, but the first graders might need a tender touch this morning to soothe their ruffled feelings. For some of them, this would be their first time away from home for an extended period of time.

Katie retreated into the classroom and brushed off her desk again. It was already spotless, but she couldn't stop cleaning. A sloppy desk was a sign of a dimwitted

teacher, Ruth had told her last week. The barb had sunk in deep, along with her other instructions. Katie gathered herself together. She could do this job just fine. *Yah,* it was different from working the cash register at Byler's, but still manageable and hopefully a lot more rewarding. From this school-house, she could touch so many young lives.

The door swung open, and Katie called out, "*Gut* morning!"

Three cheerful voices hollered back, "*Gut* morning, teacher!"

Katie walked to the back of the room to greet them. She helped the youngest take off his coat. Johnny Yoder handed it over with a whisper, "I'm glad you're my teacher this year."

His sister Elsie laughed. "Johnny's been saying that all week. I think he's scared more than anything."

Katie bent over and gave the little boy a hug. "Then we'll try to make it easy for you."

Johnny nodded, hanging on to Katie as Elsie and his older brother left for the out-side.

Katie tousled Johnny's hair. "Do you want to go out and play?"

"I guess so." Johnny looked up at her, his

eyes wide, before turning and running outside.

The schoolhouse door swung open as more students arrived. Katie greeted each one individually. They all smiled a greeting before rushing past her, putting their stuff on desks, hanging up their coats, and then rushing outside again. Katie held the door open for them. A game of softball was already in progress, the students wasting no time getting started. Katie liked that. It spoke of industriousness — using every available moment before she rang the bell.

Somewhere in that group of children would be Ben Stoll's youngest brother, Noah. He was in the third grade, if she remembered correctly. At least Noah didn't look anything like Ben, which was something to be thankful for. She didn't need the constant reminder of her past in front of her.

Thoughts of Ben had been swirling in the back of her mind ever since Willis delivered the startling news that Ben wanted to see her. What nerve Ben had, supposing they could resume their relationship. That must be what he wanted. He had more nerve than a fox in a henhouse! But then Ben had always been like that.

Katie forced thoughts of Ben away and

stepped outside to wave at more arriving children. Their parents pulled their buggies into the yard to drop off the students. The children waved back and climbed out of the buggies, pausing to grab their lunch buckets. Most of them ran across the field to join the ball game. The few who came on inside, she greeted at the door with a smile and a cheery "*Gut* morning!" All of them showed her nothing but friendliness. Katie quieted her beating heart. She was surely doing okay her first day.

She caught sight of a man tying a horse to the hitching rack. His back was turned, and he looked young. Had one of the parents decided to speak with her this morning? Perhaps to wish her well? Or maybe someone was sending a message through one of the older siblings? Katie caught her breath as the man turned and glanced in her direction. It was Norman! And he was heading in her direction. What could he possibly want beyond dropping off his youngest brother, Abram? Abram was racing even now across the schoolyard to join the ball game.

Stepping back inside the school, Katie took a deep breath. Norman must intend to finally speak with her. It was time they faced each other and got the awkward meeting

36

over with. Katie pasted on a smile as Norman came to an abrupt halt in front of her. He cleared his throat, looked at the ground, and then glanced back up.

"*Gut* morning, Katie."

"*Gut* morning, Norman. Is everything okay with Abram? I see you just dropped him off."

"*Yah,* he's fine. I need to speak with you about a matter."

Katie stepped back. "You're welcome inside, Norman — if you wish."

Norman didn't move. He just studied the ground. Finally he looked up again. "I'd like to take you home on Sunday night, Katie, if that's okay with you?"

Katie smiled. "I'd be glad to, Norman."

"You would?" Norman's face showed the first trace of a smile.

"Yah," Katie said, still smiling.

"Okay, then! Well, I'll see you on Sunday." He nodded, turned toward his horse, and left with cautious steps. He untied his horse and climbed into the buggy. He didn't look back as he pulled out of the schoolyard and drove down the lane.

Norman was different, but Katie already knew that, and it was okay with her. She didn't want a dashing man like Ben Stoll again.

What Katie wanted was stable and plain. Norman certainly fit that. But she mustn't think of such things right now — especially Ben. That was in the past, and Ben no longer fit into her new life. She'd outgrown the old image of Emma Raber's daughter and was now a schoolteacher. She was respected and looked up to in the community.

Da Hah had healed her heart, and she wouldn't look back. Norman might not be much of a conversationalist on Sunday night, but they would manage somehow. She would make apple pie for him or something else special. And Norman could go home early if they ran out of things to say. Eventually, with a little practice, she would draw Norman out of his shell. At least she didn't have to worry that Norman was dealing drugs on the side, like Ben had.

Walking back inside, Katie retrieved the bell from her desk. Opening the window on the side of the playground, she gave the bell a vigorous shaking. The clanging produced an instant reaction — just like she'd experienced during her school days. Children went running to grab their lunch buckets, dragging bats or ball gloves as they raced toward the schoolhouse.

In short order everything was stored in

the back closet, and the smiling children sat at their desks looking at her. It had taken them only moments to find their seats by following the little white name tags she'd stuck on the desks. They were an intelligent lot, and it would be a great pleasure teaching them.

"*Gut* morning," she greeted them, putting on her best smile.

"*Gut* morning!" they chorused back.

"I know who you are, and you know who I am," Katie began. Now that the moment had arrived, she was a little nervous — but not too much. "This is my first year teaching, but I've been given some *gut* advice from teacher Ruth. I think I'm ready to go."

The children looked at her expectantly, so she continued. "I may do some things differently from what you've been used to, but that happens with all new teachers. And maybe you've forgotten how things were done last year, anyway. What with the happy summer we've all just been through and you helping your *mamms* and *daetts* on the farm, I doubt if school was much on anyone's mind during those months."

A few laughs and plenty of smiles met her remarks.

"So why don't we spend just a moment this morning for our devotion time by tell-

39

ing what we did over the summer. We could include things we are especially thankful for."

Johnny was seated in the front row, and he stuck up his hand. Katie gave him a smile. What a brave little boy he was, risking a speech on his first day in school. She was going to like him, along with all the rest.

"Okay, Johnny," Katie said as she nodded to him.

"We had little chickens hatch in the henhouse, and little ducks swimming on the pond." Johnny's face beamed.

Katie returned his enthusiasm. "Were they all fluffy and cute?"

Johnny nodded.

Katie turned to the other students. "Is there someone else who had something happen to them this summer that they can give thanks for?"

Norman's brother Abram stuck up his hand.

"Yes, Abram?" Katie took a step closer.

"I heard *Mamm* and *Daett* talking about something this week which they are very thankful for." Abram grinned from ear to ear. "I don't think I was supposed to hear, but I was sitting on the couch, and they forgot about me."

"Ah . . ." Katie said, her smile fading. "Maybe you shouldn't talk about things you weren't supposed to hear."

Abram wasn't about to stop though. The words spilled out. "Norman told them he is finally asking a girl home on Sunday night. And *Mamm* and *Daett* are very thankful, since Norman is a little shy. I couldn't hear who it was though."

The whole room tittered, with even the first graders joining in.

Katie blushed, but took comfort that there was no way anyone knew she was the girl Norman had planned to ask home. And even if they did, this was nothing she should be ashamed of. It was an honor to have such an upstanding community member ask if he could take her home.

"I wonder who the girl is?" Leslie Yoder, a third-grader, whispered, falling into fresh giggles.

Now what was she going to do? Katie wondered. They would all know next Monday morning anyway, after Norman had taken her home. The whole community would know by then. Should she confess now? Katie paced a few steps. They would just have to wait. Couples fell in love with each other all the time, and they didn't announce things in public even if everyone

41

would eventually find out.

"I'd guess the girl would agree to the date," Katie said instead. "Norman's a decent young man."

There! She'd covered her bases, and she could face them without embarrassment when her secret was made known.

Elsie, though, was looking suspiciously at her, so Katie glanced away and moved on before the girl could ask further questions. "Anyone else want to tell us about your summer?"

One of the eighth-grade girls, Clarice Wagler, put up her hand.

Katie nodded at her.

"We had a little brother, Kyle, born in our house this summer. He came early but didn't have to go to the hospital, for which we're all thankful. Now he's the cutest little thing and doesn't even cry during the night. Not like some of us used to, *Mamm* said."

"I got to hold him the other Sunday," Katie added. "And I have to agree Kyle is a very well-behaved baby. But then I only held him for a little bit."

"He's like that all the time," Clarice insisted. "Dad claims there will be trouble cropping up elsewhere to make up for it because no one can be that *gut*."

Katie smiled. "Well, *Da Hah* will make that

decision. All we can do is accept what He sends our way. But we will hope for the best. Little baby Kyle is indeed quite cute."

A few more shared about their summer, and finally Katie said, "Well, let's have prayer and begin our very first day of school together."

As they bowed their heads, an interesting thought flashed through Katie's mind. Was it proper that she pray out loud? Women seldom prayed aloud in public, and they did it at home only in the presence of their children and when the *daett* wasn't present. But weren't these "her" children? No one had given her any instructions on the matter of praying aloud. Now it was too late to ask the children if teacher Ruth had led them in prayer.

Gathering her courage, Katie began. "Dear *Hah* in heaven, I want to thank You for each and every one of these dear, precious children. Be with us today, and bless us with Your presence. Give each one of these dear children strength to study hard. Refresh their minds from the summer break. And forgive us all our trespasses which we may have done, even as we forgive each other their faults. Help us live together in peace during this school year. Amen."

Opening her eyes, Katie glanced around.

No one was looking strangely at her, so these students must be used to hearing their teacher lead in prayer. Sending up her own quiet whisper of thanks to *Da Hah* for leading her right, Katie called her first class of the day up front.

CHAPTER FOUR

Ben Stoll sat at the family supper table the following evening with his head bowed. Around him the others ate in silence, occasionally stealing glances at him. This was his first night home after being released from jail. He couldn't blame his family for looking strangely at him. He'd do the same if he were in their shoes — and perhaps even more so if one of his brothers or *daett* had served time in jail for a crime. He'd messed up his life, that was for sure. How he would ever get back on his feet was beyond his comprehension. But then he'd told himself this a thousand times already while waiting out the slow days that crept by while in the county jail.

Sending a message to Katie through Emery Graber that he wished to speak with her had taken a lot of courage, but it was the right thing, Ben told himself again. He had to apologize to Katie. He couldn't rest until he did. That they could ever recapture what they used to have was only a wild dream of his mind — impossible and unrealistic, but he couldn't help having it. Saying sorry to Katie was the least he could do, even if she never wanted to be with him again. He certainly couldn't blame her for that.

He at least had something he was thankful for. His sentence could have been a hundred times worse. The prosecutor hadn't failed to remind him of that fact more than once.

"If you don't cooperate, the judge will place you in prison for a dozen years or more."

That was the sentence Rogge Brighton and his brother Lyman were now serving since they had been in charge of the drug operation. They were convicted due in large part to Ben's testimony.

"You self-serving snake!" Rogge had yelled at him at the trial. "You turned against your best friend just to save your own hide."

Ben hadn't quite looked at it like that despite the prosecutor's warnings and the deal he offered. What Ben confessed to had been because of the honesty built into him from years of Amish training. He'd also been driven by his guilty conscience for the things he had done wrong. So he'd told everything he knew to the prosecutor and testified to it in court even though testifying against another went against Amish tradition. The result had been favor from the law enforcement establishment and a lesser jail sentence. This had enraged Rogge Brighton, evoking threats hollered across the aisle of the county jail. Those threats ceased only when Rogge and his brother had been transferred to the state prison in Wilmington.

While he was relatively safe behind bars, Ben hadn't worried much about Rogge's threats, but tonight with the darkness falling, he wondered. Were the threats real? His own life wasn't that high of a concern, but the safety of his family was another matter. Would they be in danger? And did they even know about the threats from Rogge? He hadn't really thought about that before. What if someone did show up seeking revenge? They wouldn't show much mercy to his family if they got in the way. It was a troubling thought on top of all the other things that lay heavy on his heart.

"It's *gut* to have you home," Ben's *daett,* Leon, said, breaking the silence.

"Thank you." Ben kept his head bowed. His family was trying to make things comfortable for him, but they didn't know how to act. He didn't know either. None of them had ever been in this situation.

"Teacher Katie was awesome today," Noah announced, obviously trying to move the subject somewhere comfortable. "I think I'll like her a lot."

Mamm winced and reached over to pat Noah's arm. "*Yah,* all of us like Katie."

Ben didn't look up. Noah hadn't known much about his relationship with Katie, although *Mamm* and *Daett* and his older siblings had. Noah couldn't be blamed for bringing up the subject, but now the tension around the table was worse. They already felt sorry for his ruined life. They all knew his relationship with Katie was over. Katie had made that plain enough by never showing up at the trial or inquiring after him in any fashion since his arrest.

Yet Katie shouldn't be blamed, Ben thought. They'd only been seeing each other a few months, though it had seemed much longer with how much he'd enjoyed being around her. Katie had reacted the way any decent young woman would to the betrayal of her deep-rooted trust and love. She'd grown close to his heart, if truth be told. At the beginning, Katie had been more of a way out of what he was doing wrong. But

48

she'd become much more than that. He'd been a fool not to tell Katie of what he'd done and how he was getting out of his past life. But he'd told himself he was cutting all of that out, that he was quitting Rogge, and that Katie need never know. He'd been afraid she wouldn't believe his repentance and that he'd lose her. But he'd lost her anyway. Now it was too late for anything but regrets.

"Katie's going home with someone on Sunday night!" Noah sang out, obviously thrilled with this news concerning his new teacher.

Ben looked up. This was news he couldn't help showing interest in. Let them see the pain in his heart. There was no point in hiding it now.

"Now, how would you know something like that?" Brenda, the eldest girl in the family asked. "You're kind of a little tot to obtain such information."

Noah puffed out his chest and quickly added additional information. "I heard the older girls whispering out in the playground. They said Katie turned all red when Abram Kuntz announced that his older brother Norman was taking someone home on Sunday night. So there! Abram heard this from his *mamm* and *daett* when they thought he wasn't listening."

"Sounds like a bunch of gossip to me," Brenda muttered, stealing a sideways glance at Ben.

Ben knew Brenda really did feel sorry for him, and he hated it. That someone would feel pity for him. Still, this feeling was *gut* for him. The shame helped him humble his soul and cleanse it from the awful things he'd done. He'd never thought of himself as evil before being arrested, but now he saw things in a much different light. No one who was *gut* would sell or distribute drugs that destroyed people's lives.

"I think it's true too," Noah continued, sticking with his story. "And I think Norman is getting a very decent girl. Katie's swell. And we all think it's going to be a fun school year. Much better even than teacher Ruth, and I liked her."

"I'm glad to hear that news," *Daett* said, smiling.

Ben stood up, his food only half eaten. "I think I'll go to my room."

"You sure you don't want to finish your food?" *Mamm* looked alarmed.

"I'm okay." Ben gave her a smile. "It's not your fault. Maybe things will go better tomorrow."

They all — even Noah — looked concerned as he left the room. To *Daett*'s credit he didn't insist Ben stay for the evening devotions. They'd been having the family's Bible reading and prayer time without him for well over a year now, and they could see that it would take awhile for him to get back into the flow of things.

After putting his dishes near the sink, Ben opened the stair door, letting it shut behind him as he took the steps two at a time. Inside his room, he lit the kerosene lamp and rummaged around his dresser drawer for Katie's picture, taken when she'd needed a photograph for her passport. He'd left it here somewhere before his arrest — hidden under a stack of pants, he thought. And there would have been no reason for *Mamm* to open this drawer, much less find the picture. But if *Mamm* had, the picture would no doubt be destroyed. *Mamm* wouldn't allow a photograph of anyone in the house. That was the Amish way because it was considered vanity, and that was strictly forbidden.

Ben's fingers found the thin piece of paper. He pulled it out and lifted it to the flickering light of the lamp. Katie's face looked back at him, her eyes shining with love. He remembered leaning over the photographer's shoulder that day to distract

51

Katie as the woman took the picture. Those days seemed like years ago, the joy lost in the pain of his jail time. Destroyed because of what he'd done. Oh how he'd loved Katie — and she him! He was sure of it. Katie wasn't one to fake such things. That was no doubt why Katie was going on so well with her life . . . like he'd never even existed. That was the way she would go about things. Honestly and without thought to appearances. Not that anyone blamed Katie for loving him, especially since she'd joined the church and made peace with *Da Hah* and the community.

Ben laid the picture down with a sigh. He had no one to blame but himself. And now Katie would be sitting beside Norman on Sunday night. Norman, the shy, awkward guy. So unlike me, Ben thought. Was that what attracted Katie to Norman? She now wanted someone who was the opposite of his daring ways? Not that he could blame Katie for that either. Look how he'd turned out — a total disgrace to his family and the community. Walking to the window, Ben looked out at the barn and the road that lay on the other side of it. Lights from an *Englisha* automobile moved toward the north, having just passed the house. He watched the lights go, momentarily distracted from his troubled thoughts.

Out of the corner of his eye, Ben saw a flicker of light beside the barn. Just a brief flash, but it shouldn't have been there. Moments later it came on again then blinked off. Someone was outside. Perhaps *Daett* was checking on some last minute chores. But it couldn't be *Daett*. He'd be in the living room for evening devotions by now. Ben stayed by the window until a single beam found the house. It lasted only a moment. Someone was searching for something, and Ben was now sure it wasn't anyone in his family.

Rogge's threats echoed in Ben's mind. Was he imagining things even as fear pounded through his veins? His family shouldn't be placed in danger because of him. He needed to face whoever was out there. Slipping out of the room, Ben crept down the stairs. Everyone was seated around the living room when he appeared. They looked up with pleased expressions on their faces, thinking he was joining them for devotions.

"I'm sorry," he told them, "but I think someone is outside by the barn. I'm going to check."

"There's someone out there?" *Daett* was already standing.

Ben held up his hand. "There were threats

made against me in court and in jail. I don't want you to go outside until I've checked to make sure everything is okay."

"Threats?" *Mamm* asked, her face turning white.

"I will go with you." *Daett* stepped toward him. "*Da Hah* will protect us."

Ben forced himself to smile. "*Yah,* I hope so. You don't have to worry, *Daett.* I won't do anyone any harm. I didn't learn how to hurt people while I was in the *Englisha* jail."

Concern didn't leave his *daett*'s face. "I was also thinking of your safety, son. Let me go outside and look around with you."

Ben kept his voice firm. "I did what I did, and I want no one else with me. Not until I know if there is danger or not."

Daett sighed and sat down. "I hope it is nothing then, but we must pray."

"Who could it be?" *Mamm* asked, her hands on her cheeks.

Ben left them to their questions. He couldn't answer them anyway, other than saying what they already knew. That he'd done wrong first of all, that his confessions placed others in jail, and now he might have to pay physically through the hands of those seeking revenge.

Grabbing a flashlight, Ben slipped outside, comforted at hearing the soft prayers of his family in the living room. They must have skipped the Bible reading and knelt at once in prayer. Ben paused only long enough for his eyes to adjust before creeping toward the barn. There was no sign of the blinking light now, so maybe he'd imagined it. Still, he was certain he hadn't. The light beam playing on the house had been real enough. As he approached the barn, he hollered, "Hello! Anybody here?"

Silence.

Ben entered the barn and checked the horse stalls carefully, the light from his flashlight illuminating every corner. Everything looked okay. Longstreet greeted him with a soft whinny. He hadn't driven the horse in more than a year now. There hadn't been time since he was home, and he didn't have any place to go right now anyway. Katie had loved the name he'd chosen for his horse, he remembered with a pang. The only person other than Brenda who thought the name fitting.

A quick sweep of the flashlight beam into the back barnyard showed nothing out of the ordinary. The cows stood calmly chewing their cuds after the evening's milking. Finding his way back, Ben was closing the barn door when a rustle sounded behind him.

He turned around and a thin beam of light hit his face.

"Who are you?" Ben asked.

"This is from Rogge," a voice answered. "Just thought you'd like to know. Bye bye."

A loud boom rang in Ben's ears just as his chest seemed to explode. Pain filled his body and mind. Gasping for air, he collapsed on the ground beside the barn door.

CHAPTER FIVE

In what seemed like another place and time, Ben struggled to awake. He thrashed an arm, and someone grabbed his hand and held it still. Ben forced his eyes open, focusing on the forms standing around him in the dim light. They kept fading in and out of his vision. Where was he? His mind groped for understanding. What had happened? The memories came back in a rush. The loud noise, the pain, the feeling of falling. Had he been shot? But he must not be dead. This didn't look like he'd thought heaven would. And the pain in his chest was still present, dulled now to a steady ache from those first stabbing flames of fire.

"Hold still," a female voice instructed. "You're doing just fine."

An *Englisha* voice, Ben thought. "Am I in the hospital?" he managed.

"Yes," the voice replied. "And don't move

anymore or I'll have to strap your arm down."

Ben blinked as he tried to see better. More memories were coming back now. His *daett* leaning over him in front of the barn. Urgent voices calling his name. Sirens and flashing lights. The voice saying, "This is from Rogge." Ben's thoughts paused. He knew that voice from somewhere. It was a haunting piece of his past that he'd tried so hard to forget.

"How badly am I hurt?" Ben asked as the face of a woman in a white uniform came into better focus.

She smiled down at him. "Bad enough, but you'll make it. You were brought in last night. You're a tough fellow, huh? Taking a bullet for a good cause."

"I don't know what you mean."

Her smile dimmed. "There are two detectives outside waiting for you to wake up. They seem to have urgent questions about catching the person who hurt you. You can see them as soon as you're able or feeling up to talking. The doctor said it would be okay — considering the circumstances."

"What happened?"

"You were shot in the chest. You're lucky to be alive."

Ben winced in pain. "I thought it was

something like that. Where's my family?"

"Right over here," Brenda's voice piped up. Her face appeared within his vision a moment later. "Hi, Ben. I stayed here with you all night."

"Thanks." Ben closed his eyes. There was so much to absorb at the moment. So the threats Rogge made hadn't been idle, Ben thought. And his family had been in danger, to say nothing of himself. What if *Daett* had gone out to the barn instead of him? Would the shooter have threatened *Daett* — perhaps even killed him as part of Rogge's revenge?

"I'm going to let the detectives know you're awake," the nurse said, interrupting his thoughts. "No more thrashing about now."

Ben nodded.

The nurse vanished, and Ben heard the sound of a door opening and closing. Brenda's face came into his view again.

"How are you doing?" she asked.

"Rotten."

"We're glad you're alive, Ben."

Ben moved his arm and then stopped. "How's *Daett* taking this? That must have been quite a ruckus if the things I seem to remember really happened."

"It was a mess," Brenda said quietly. "But

Daett and *Mamm* and the rest of us are glad you're alive."

They would be, Ben thought. Even with the shame of having *Englisha* police on the farm. The police must have come after the shooting and stayed around like they did, asking questions of everyone.

Ben forced his eyes to focus on Brenda's face. "Was anyone else attacked?"

Brenda shook her head. She looked weary and the evidence of streaks from earlier tears marked her face. Her *kapp* was wrinkled, which was so unlike Brenda. She must have been up all night sitting watch with him. He didn't deserve any of this attention. He should have died like the shooter intended. Then his family would have been rid of him once and for all and they'd be safe.

"I'm sorry, Brenda," Ben whispered. "I didn't know it would go like this."

"That's what comes from sin, Ben." Brenda's voice was clipped. "It always gets much worse than we intend."

Ben blinked as the pain of her words cut deep, especially coming from Brenda. *Mamm* would say something like that — and *Daett* too. But Brenda? The shock from last night must have cut deep into her heart.

When he didn't reply, Brenda added

60

more. "We thought you were going to die, Ben. *Daett* found you in a pool of blood after we heard a gunshot. All of us ran out after him. Do you think that sight was easy to see? You lying there and not moving? Seeing your face so white and blood everywhere? It was awful, Ben. Worse than enduring the time you spent in jail."

"I'm sure it was." Ben looked away. The sorrow in Brenda's face was hurting him more than his chest. He'd known to some degree what his family must have gone through because of him. But seeing the pain on his sister's face and listening to her, he realized it was much worse than anything he'd imagined.

A door opened and two uniformed officers appeared within Ben's eyesight. They approached his bedside.

One of them looks familiar, Ben thought. Perhaps he'd met the officer during his time in court or prison.

"I'm Detective Barton," the first man said. "This is Detective Lessen. Are you able to answer questions at this time, Mr. Stoll?"

"*Yah,* I guess. But I don't know much about what happened."

"Anything will help. What do you remember before the shooting?" Detective Barton asked as he took out a pen and small note-pad.

Ben's vision blurred and he felt dizzy. He forced himself to focus. "I saw a light blink out by the barn from my bedroom window. Looked like a flashlight perhaps. And a light beam hit the house at least once. I didn't think it was anyone in my family. I didn't want my family to be in danger, so I went outside to check it out."

"You were expecting someone?"

Ben gathered his thoughts. "No. But last year I testified in a drug trial against Rogge Brighton, and he had made threats in court and in jail. I hoped he wasn't serious, but apparently he was."

Detective Barton appeared grim. "It appears that way. We reviewed that case before coming to see you. So you didn't see anyone before the shooting? Did the shot come out of the dark?"

Ben glanced away from the detective's face as the memory came into focus. "A light shone in my face, and I heard a voice. Then I heard a loud noise. I don't remember much beyond that."

"Did you recognize the voice?"

Ben winced. "*Yah,* but I don't want to say any more about this."

The two detectives looked at each other.

Then Barton said, "We understand how the Amish community feels about law enforcement. But it's important that this suspect be apprehended. If he tried to take your life once, there's no reason he won't try again. Tell us what you know, Stoll."

Ben met the Detective Barton's questioning gaze. "My family's safety is more important to me right now. I want to leave things as they are."

Detective Barton didn't back down. "They might come looking for you again. This won't be over until we arrest the gunman."

"I don't care about that," Ben said. "I can't draw attention to my family."

"You won't. And next time they might hurt someone in your family. Share what information you have, Mr. Stoll. Help us help you."

Ben tried to smile. "I can't . . . not right now. I need to think about this."

Detective Barton folded his notebook and put it in his rear pocket. He clicked the pen and placed it in his breast pocket. "I hope you get well soon, Mr. Stoll. The doctors said it won't be long. Just be glad you didn't take a bullet in the heart or some other vital area. That would have been a shame after the information you gave during the investigation of the drug ring a year or so ago.

We'll see if we can get you some protection at least until this thing blows over. And we'll be back . . . soon."

Ben's arm jerked up. "Protection? What do you mean?"

Detective Barton shrugged. "We'll see if the county can run a car past your parents' place a few times during the night. And I might even convince them to post a guard outside your hospital room door for a few days."

Ben stared at Detective Barton's face. "You can't do that — going by my *daett*'s place. Only protection from *Da Hah* through prayer is allowed by my people . . ." Ben's voice died out.

Both detectives frowned as they glanced at each other. "Religious beliefs again. Well, we'll have to see then. But we're not leaving you unguarded so someone can take a shot at you again. Dampens the spirit of the next informant who might come along. And you still have information we can use."

Ben let his head fall back on the pillow. "Is that what I am? An informant?"

Detective Barton smiled. "Don't look so down in the face. You did a great service for the county and community. Helps make up for what you did wrong. Isn't that a good thing?"

"I suppose." Ben closed his eyes. His head was swimming again, and their voices sounded miles away. Moments later he heard the door open and close. He opened his eyes, and Brenda came up to stand beside him. She held his hand.

"You did the right thing, Ben. *Daett* wouldn't have wanted armed men going by the farm. That goes against everything we believe in. And don't tell them anything more. You've already told them too much."

"I can't place the family in greater danger," Ben muttered.

"But what else can you do, Ben? We'll just have to trust *Da Hah*. He's protected you so far, hasn't He?"

Ben groaned. What was there to say? The shame was too much. He was bringing great evil on his family. First had come the jail sentence, and now there had been *Englisha* police on the farm. His family shouldn't be asked to bear this. What a price they were paying for what he'd done.

The door swung open again and the nurse reappeared. She glanced over the monitors and held Ben's wrist for a moment as she took his pulse. "Everything okay here, young man?"

Ben nodded.

"Are you up to more visitors? Not as taxing this time, I would say. Your parents just arrived."

Ben didn't hesitate. "*Yah,* please let them come in."

The nurse disappeared again.

Moments later Ben's *mamm* and *daett* entered the room.

Mamm rushed to Ben's side and looked him over carefully. "You had us all so worried!"

"I'm sorry," Ben said. "I didn't mean to bring this trouble on you and *daett.*"

"It's the price that sin causes, Ben," *Daett* told him. "But we will bear it with you. That is who we are as a people. When one suffers, we all suffer."

Ben blinked back the tears. He wouldn't cry in front of his parents, but their compassion was tearing him up. How could he have sinned so against them?

Mamm squeezed Ben's arm. "You must not make him feel worse than he already does, Leon. And we shouldn't be staying very long."

"How bad was it at the farm last night?" Ben asked, not looking at either of them.

His *mamm* glanced at his *daett* before she answered. "We were worried about you, Ben. That's all that matters."

Mamm would say that, but both of his

66

parents knew what he really meant. His *daett* spoke brave words about bearing the shame of his sin along with him. That was because there was real shame to bear. The community would not look lightly on the disgrace Ben had brought on all of them. They had obligations that his parents alone didn't have.

Mamm squeezed Ben's hand again. "No one can fault you for how you conducted yourself last night. You could have let *Daett* go out to the barn, but you didn't."

Daett cleared his throat. "Maybe it would have been better if Ben had. Whoever that was probably wouldn't have shot me. You'd better stop taking things into your own hands, Ben. You have to let others help carry the load. That's also what our people are about."

Ben glanced away from his *daett*'s gaze. "What should I do then?"

"You have to live at *Dawdy*'s for awhile . . . at the *dawdy haus.*" *Daett*'s voice was firm.

Ben's arm twitched. "And put them in danger?"

"It will take awhile for anyone to figure out where you're living. That will give everything time to settle down."

"But I don't want to," Ben managed to get out.

"You don't have any choice," *Daett* said. "It's already been decided. I've spoken with *Dawdy* this morning. They have the extra room in the back. It's small, but *gut* enough."

Mamm squeezed Ben's arm. "It'll be for the best, Ben. Trust us."

Ben leaned back before closing his eyes. There were rustlings in the room as he dozed off. When he opened his eyes again, his family was gone, including Brenda. It was just as well. He needed sleep. Closing his eyes again, he thought about one of the main decisions he'd made during his time in jail. Could it really happen now? He'd determined to join the church after his release from jail and work to make things right with his parents and the other people in the church. Katie too, but that might prove an impossible dream. Jail had changed him, breaking him in ways that nothing had before. He'd knelt by his cot many a night, repenting of his sins and reaching out to *Da Hah* in prayer. And for the first time he seemed to break through. Peace filled his heart. The flood of doubts he used to have about the faith no longer came rushing into his mind.

None of his family ever knew the depths of the questions he used to carry inside.

Only Katie had been told of the thoughts he'd had about the *ordnung,* the rules the church put such stock in. Questions about the community's separation from the *Englisha* world. About the founding fathers and their lives way back in Switzerland. Katie was supposed to have brought back answers for him from her trip to Europe, but he'd ruined that expectation by his arrest.

Even worse, he now had no contact with Katie at all. His life had turned into a shameful existence. He was even bringing a physical threat upon his family. How could someone so completely mess things up? He grimaced and turned away from the light coming through the window, accepting the sleep that drew him back in.

CHAPTER SIX

Katie paced the floor of her room. How could this be happening? She'd thought she was rid of Ben Stoll once and for all — and now she obviously wasn't. Well, it would only be for one day. Then things could go on like they had before.

Enos Kuntz had come driving in to the family farm early, well before breakfast with the news. He'd spoken with Katie out on the front porch after *Mamm* had met him at the door. She'd called Katie from her work in the kitchen, and then left Katie and Enos alone. Deep concern for the situation was written on Enos's face as he gave Katie the news about the Stoll farm events, expressing nothing but sympathy for her over the situation.

School had been called off for the day, he announced, because there'd been a shooting over at the Stoll farm late last evening. The school board didn't wish to expose the children to danger in case the gunman was still in the area. All the children were to stay at home.

He also explained that Ben was in the hospital, a gunshot wound to his chest. He was expected to survive.

Even in her shock, Katie realized that because of agreeing to let Norman take her home after the hymn singing this Sunday, she was already being considered a part of the Kuntz family. She should be thankful . . . very thankful. What a change this was from a few short years ago when she'd been known as Emma Raber's daughter — a backward and awkward girl. But no one was calling her that now.

Why was she so irritated over this situation about Ben? She should feel sorry that he'd been shot. And she did, Katie reassured herself. But Ben was like a burr from the summer hayfields that clung to your shoestrings and wouldn't go away. He'd even had the nerve to send word through Emery Graber that he wished to speak with her. She had a right to move on with her life without Ben's interference, didn't she? And she wanted to! Katie continued to pace. Was she being too hard on Ben, perhaps? But what did that mean? She had nothing to do with him anymore. She didn't want to! She knew he was sorry for what he'd done. That went without saying. She didn't need to hear it from Ben's lips — if that was why he wanted to see her. Beyond that, Ben had no claim on her. They never had a formal engagement or anything close to it. Her cheeks burned red with the memory of the kisses she and Ben had shared — and how she'd enjoyed them. She felt a twinge of guilt over liking kisses from a man who had betrayed her.

Norman's hesitant face floated before Katie's eyes. What would it be like to kiss Norman? She couldn't imagine that happening until after the wedding vows were said. Norman was that kind of man . . . upstanding and steady — exactly what she wanted in a man now more than ever. Katie let the thought hang in her mind. Norman would be no Ben. She was sure of that. She couldn't even imagine snuggling up to Norman in his buggy. He'd probably freeze up with fright and pull away. Ben, on the other hand, had moved closer, slipping his hand over her shoulder as if he had a right to have her close to him.

Katie shoved the thoughts away. She had no call to think these thoughts about Norman or Ben. They weren't decent — comparing one man with another. Still, the memories came back insistent and demanding. He had kissed her one last time, pulling her aside that evening at the airport before she flew out of Philadelphia bound for Zurich. Her Mennonite friends Margaret, Sharon, and Nancy had teased her plenty about her rosy cheeks and lips.

Katie flopped on her bed. Confound Ben for getting himself shot and bringing all these thoughts back! He was probably lying in the hospital bed in Dover right now, hanging on to the edge of life and looking helpless and sweet. How dare Ben's dealings reach all the way across the community and close her school? And here she was, thinking only about herself when Ben was so seriously injured and in the hospital. Well, she would pray for him. She could at least do that, Katie thought. She knelt beside the bed, but before she could get a word out, a knock came at the door. Katie leaped up, went to the door, turned the knob, and opened it to find Willis standing in the hallway.

"Yah?" Katie asked as she stared at him.

"I just heard," Willis said, a frown creasing his face.

"Enos said Ben's doing okay," Katie told him, as if that settled the matter. Why was Willis at her door? Was he trying to comfort her? She didn't need comfort or want to talk about Ben.

Willis seemed to understand her hesitation. "I . . . I thought . . ." Willis tried again. "It troubles me . . . that Ben wishes to speak with you and you haven't responded. I can imagine how he feels, especially now. He lost you after all, and now he's been shot — almost killed."

Katie raised her eyebrows. "What are you saying, Willis?"

"I think you should visit Ben today, Katie. Let him tell you in person that he's sorry for what happened. I'll go with you."

"But he's not dying," Katie protested, as if that were the perfect answer. Her heart pounded. Why was she having this surge of emotion at the thought of seeing Ben?

Willis didn't appear convinced. "You never know about such things."

Thoughts raced through Katie's mind. Could Willis be right? He did have a kind heart, and she might be blinded by her past bitter experiences with Ben. What if Ben did take a turn for the worse, and she'd denied him the opportunity to apologize? Forgiveness was more for the asker's benefit anyway. Katie looked into Willis's sorrowful eyes and gave in.

"Okay, I'll go. But you can't leave us alone

in the hospital room. You have to stay right with me."

Willis appeared puzzled, but he nodded. "Whatever you say. I'm glad you've decided to go."

Katie marched downstairs ahead of Willis and found *Mamm* in the kitchen. "Willis and I are going to visit Ben Stoll at the hospital."

Mamm gasped. "But, Katie, he's not your boyfriend any longer! You shouldn't go. It's not decent."

"I'm going with her," Willis said from the kitchen doorway. "I think she should, Emma. Ben should be allowed to say he's sorry in person to Katie. He needs to."

Mamm swallowed hard. "Well, I don't know what to say. You do have a tender heart, Willis. But this is going a little too far."

"*Daett* said we could go." Willis's words cut through the air and ended the argument.

Mamm wouldn't go against what Jesse said, and neither should she, Katie told herself. Bitterness had apparently crept into her heart, and she should be thankful that Willis was trying to help her deal with it.

Katie found her coat in the washroom, and *Mamm* came out to whisper in her ear.

"Katie, do be careful."

Katie nodded as *Mamm* stayed at the washroom door. When she turned her head to look back, *Mamm* was still watching as she followed Willis across the lawn.

Was she doing the wrong thing? Katie wondered. But how could this be wrong if Jesse approved? Willis pushed open the barn door, and Leroy glanced up from the harness he was oiling. Surprised, he commented, "Going somewhere, are we?"

Willis answered. "*Yah,* I'm taking Katie in to see Ben."

The surprised look changed to concern. "You wouldn't be doing something foolish, would you, Katie?"

"She needs to speak with Ben," Willis insisted. "And *Daett* said it's okay."

Leroy shrugged. A smile grew on his face as he helped them harness Katie's horse, Sparky. "I hope all goes well."

Katie nodded her thanks and followed Willis out of the barn. She held the shafts of the buggy as he guided Sparky in place. They fastened the tugs and climbed in. Willis slapped the reins gently against Sparky's back and they headed down the lane. They turned south at the end, eventually driving past Byler's Store, where Katie used to work. Sparky wanted to turn in, but Willis kept him on the road and clucked at him to keep up the speed.

Katie glanced into the store as they went past. Arlene was likely busy with the cash register as usual. Mrs. Cole probably had a new woman working by now, taking over where Katie had left off. Working here had consumed much of her life before *Mamm* had married Jesse. While at Byler's, Katie had dreamed of Ben. On some mornings she'd even passed him on her way to work. At first he hadn't even noticed her enough to wave. Her heart had imagined how *wunderbah* it would be for any girl who got to ride with Ben in his buggy. And then the opportunity had come her way, just like the miracle that it was.

But now she knew Ben wasn't who or what she'd thought he was. He had betrayed her and so many other people, including his family and the Amish community. She was going to visit him this morning just so he could find relief from the sorrow that must be heavy on his heart. It was one's Christian duty, wasn't it? Offering forgiveness even if it wasn't asked for? And Ben probably wanted to ask. Katie glanced at Willis sitting beside her in the buggy. Her new brother had been wise beyond his years to see this.

Katie hung on to the side of the buggy as

they approached Dover. Willis took Sparky down the many blocks until they reached State Street. Thankfully it was the middle of the day, and traffic was light. The Amish used the Bayhealth hospital, so a buggy being driven there shouldn't be anything unusual.

Arriving at the hospital parking lot, Willis stopped along a fence and climbed out. He tied Sparky with a rope kept under the seat. Now that they were here, the place looked much bigger than she remembered. Katie stayed close beside Willis as they found their way inside.

"*Gut* morning," Willis said to a woman sitting at a large desk. "Will you give me Ben Stoll's room number?"

"Certainly." The woman smiled as she punched in letters on her keyboard. "Third floor, room 320."

Moments later Katie and Willis stepped out of the elevator onto the third floor. A waiting room was off to the right. No Amish were present.

So Ben's family must have been here and left for the day. That was *gut,* Katie decided. The less people who learned of this visit, the better. Thankfully, *Da Hah* was helping her out, making the path smooth in front of her.

Approaching room 320 with Willis behind her now, Katie pushed open the door and peered inside. It was Ben on the bed all right, although his face looked quite pale against the white pillow. He must be sleeping, she decided. Maybe they needed to wait around until he awoke? If he was injured badly, Ben needed all the sleep he could get.

Suddenly Ben's eyes flew open, and he caught sight of Katie. His eyes grew large, and she saw hope mixed with joy swimming in them. She knew those eyes well. She clasped her hands together as she struggled with her emotions. She was here for a specific purpose only, and she mustn't forget that.

"You've come!" Ben whispered.

Katie forced herself to move closer. Thankfully, Willis was sticking right by her side or she would surely have turned to run out of this room. Her pounding heart was reason enough to flee. She mustn't fall for Ben's wiles again. Slipping over to the hospital chair, Katie sat down as calmly as she could and folded her hands on her lap.

"I asked Katie to come with me," Willis offered. "We're all sorry to hear about last night."

"Oh that," Ben said dismissively, his gaze

focusing on Katie's face. "I'm so thankful you've come. I don't deserve to see you, but I have to tell you how sorry I am, Katie, for what I did to you. It was so wrong of me. I want you to know I've changed my ways." Ben struggled to sit up, but he gave up at once. His head fell back on the pillow.

"Katie understands," Willis said, trying to help. "She forgives you or she wouldn't have come."

Katie knew she needed to speak for herself. She forced the words out. "I do forgive you, Ben, I really do. But things can never be the same between us. I hope you aren't thinking such thoughts."

Sorrow filled his face, but Ben nodded. "I will pray *Da Hah* heals your heart of what I have done."

Now why did Ben say that? Katie thought. Her heart was already healed, and she'd moved on. Obviously Ben had something else in mind when he spoke of healing. Well, Ben could pray. Prayer was always *gut* even when it seemed to go unanswered.

"How was your night?" Katie forced herself to speak again. "Are you going to be okay?"

Ben attempted a smile. "Difficult. But Brenda was here during the surgery. She stayed until this morning sometime. Yes, I'm going to recover."

Silence settled in the room. Katie glanced away from Ben's face and then back again. How helpless he appeared. So broken. He didn't appear evil at all. Not like she'd expected or built up in her mind. How could he not be evil after what he'd done? After he'd tricked her? Was she being deceived again by his charm? Katie took a deep breath and gathered herself together. "We'd best be going. There's no school today because of the shooting, but there's always work around the house."

"Take care then," Willis said, giving Ben a smile. "We'll all be praying for your quick recovery."

She should say the same thing, Katie thought. She did wish Ben well. But the words stuck in her throat. She wanted to give him a goodbye hug right now, but that was out of the question. Katie turned and quickly followed Willis out of the hospital room. Perhaps it would have been wise, Katie thought, if she'd visited Ben in jail. Surely there she would have seen the evil in him. Then she'd be spared the current of confusing emotions coursing through her. But she hadn't, so this was the way to get it done. Now, in a few days when Norman drove her home, he could have her full at-

tention. What a relief that would be —
finally putting Ben Stoll behind her for *gut.*

CHAPTER SEVEN

Willis drove Sparky out of town some ten minutes later, allowing the horse to settle into a steady trot. Katie sat beside Willis as wild thoughts rushed through her head. What in the world was wrong with her? Never in her wildest dreams had this been the expected outcome of this trip. She was thinking *gut* thoughts of Ben after seeing him in his hospital room. He'd appeared so humble and broken, lying helplessly on that bed. How could she feel this way? She was finished with him. He simply could not be trusted. He was a charmer and a bewitcher of the heart — of *her* heart. Nothing *gut* had come out of their relationship. How could anything *gut* come out of it from here on out?

Katie almost groaned out loud. What was she going to tell *Mamm* when she got home? *Mamm* would know how she was feeling. There was no hiding this from her discerning eyes. Willis didn't seem to notice as he casually held the reins while seated beside Katie. This was a breach of the highest order, Katie realized. Yes, she had to admit her heart was still pounding from the sight of Ben. How could this be? She'd even been tempted to hug Ben before they left! The shame of it burned up and down her neck.

What would happen if Norman found out she still had feelings for Ben? To say nothing of his *daett*. And Norman planned to drive her home on Sunday night! She couldn't change that. And she didn't really want to . . . did she? What a horrible mess! Why had she allowed Willis to talk her into this visit? If she'd just stayed home, everything would have been okay. Ben might eventually have come to church, but her reaction would have been different there. It was seeing him so helpless that did this to her heart. That was the answer. It had to be.

Willis drove past Byler's, and Katie glanced in. Perhaps she should ask Willis to stop for a minute so she could speak with Arlene. They'd always shared things during hard times. Should she? Katie almost spoke up when she realized that Willis would want an explanation. She couldn't tell him what was going on in her heart. Arlene probably wouldn't be sympathetic anyway. She was still in *rumspringa,* and she might delight in hearing that Katie still had feelings for Ben Stoll even after what he'd done. Reuniting with Ben would fit Arlene's sense of adventure and daring. Arlene had never once said anything negative about Ben since his arrest. Not even when Katie had expressed her bitter heartache.

Nearing the turnoff toward home, Willis pulled back on the reins, slowing Sparky to a steady walk. Another buggy was coming their way, and Katie forced a smile as Bishop Miller's *frau,* Laura, passed them. Laura smiled back, but Katie wondered if she'd be so friendly if she knew where Katie had just been. Or worse, if she knew how Katie felt after just seeing Ben.

What am I going to do? Katie wondered. And this time there was no fleeing to the Mennonites for relief. She was an Amish church member now, and she would have to face her problems straight on. Well, she would confess this matter to *Mamm* when she arrived home. That would be embarrassing, but the right thing to do. And *Mamm* wouldn't give her away, and she might even have some *gut* advice. Like how Katie was supposed to act on Sunday night with Norman when she knew her heart still thought it was attracted to Ben.

Minutes later Willis guided Sparky down their driveway. The horse broke into a trot as he neared the barn. Willis pulled up, and Katie climbed out to help unhitch. Willis was well able to put Sparky away by himself, but Katie followed him. Inside the barn, the bright noonday light shone through the dusty windows. Sparky jerked his head up and neighed, the sound ringing through the building. From the barnyard, one of the other driving horses answered, welcoming Sparky back.

Even the horses felt at home in this place, Katie thought. Just like she did. Never in her life had she felt the peace and happiness she'd experienced these last few months since her baptism. Ben wasn't going to rob her of this. He couldn't be trusted. Not after he'd torn her heart apart by selling drugs while acting like a decent man. Ben had been kissing her in his buggy while committing such a horrible sin! Katie shuddered.

"Here, I'll take care of Sparky," Katie told Willis when he looked at her questioningly, wondering why she was tagging along.

Willis shrugged. "I guess I'll get back to the fields then."

Katie jerked the harness off after Willis left and threw it up on the wall hook. She quickly rubbed Sparky down and then led him to the barnyard door. She turned him out with a soft pat on the neck. He raced outside and threw his head high in the air, prancing a bit. The other driving horses joined him for a quick dash around the lot. Katie smiled. They were happy like she was. And it would stay that way. Walking through the barn, she walked out the door, closed it behind her, and hurried across the yard. She pushed open the front door.

Mamm looked up, startled. "Is anything wrong, Katie?"

"*Yah,* there is!" Katie pressed back the tears. There was no sense hiding her turmoil from *Mamm.* She couldn't even if she wanted to. "It was terrible, *Mamm!*"

Mamm guessed at what was bothering Katie. "He didn't want to see you?"

Katie shook her head.

"Then . . ." *Mamm*'s concern deepened. "Has Ben taken a turn for the worst?"

"*Nee, Mamm.* It's my heart! Oh, *Mamm,* how can this be? How can I still have feelings for him?"

Comprehension dawned on *Mamm*'s face, and she came over to wrap Katie in her arms. "You poor thing. I would have kept you home if I'd known this would happen."

"It's not your fault, *Mamm.* Jesse thought

I should go, and Willis too." Katie collapsed on the couch. "And they were right in a way. But now what in the world am I supposed to do? I can't see Norman and let him bring me home on Sunday night when I feel this way."

Mamm sat down beside Katie and stroked her arm. "Feelings come and go, Katie. I wouldn't be too worried. At least you know better this time."

Katie groaned. "If you felt what I did, you'd be worried. What's wrong with me, *Mamm*?"

Mamm sat for a moment in silence. "Did Ben tell you he was sorry?"

Katie nodded. "And I told him I forgive him."

"Then leave it there," *Mamm* said. "Ben has learned a few things by now. At least let's hope he has. He knows your relationship is over. And I'm sure you've felt nothing in your heart that I haven't felt myself. The feelings I once had for Daniel Kauffman eventually left my heart to be replaced by a beautiful love for your *daett*. Now *Da Hah* has done the same thing for Jesse and me. And He can do it for Norman and you."

This is true, Katie thought. *Mamm* had told her often of the crush she used to have for the handsome Daniel Kauffman. For years she'd hung on to the hope that her love would be returned — right up to the wedding day when Daniel said the vows with his *frau,* Miriam Esh. The story had always fallen on deaf ears during the time Katie had dated Ben. But then *Mamm* had been proven right. And no doubt she was right this time as well.

"I'll try to remember," Katie whispered, glancing up as Mabel appeared in the doorway.

"You can send him my way," Mabel said.

Katie glanced at *Mamm,* who shrugged. So Mabel had been listening to their conversation. Oh well. They shouldn't keep secrets from her — not these kinds of secrets. When *Mamm* first married Jesse, they'd tried that approach and incurred Mabel's wrath.

Katie sat up on the couch. "Mabel, what do you mean by that?"

Mabel looked sheepish as she took small steps into the living room. Katie motioned for Mabel to sit on the couch. "What did you mean by that remark? Do you have a crush on Ben Stoll?"

Mabel's cheeks flamed. "I didn't say that."

Katie stared at Mabel. "Norman Kuntz? You like Norman Kuntz?"

Mabel said nothing as she gazed at the floor.

"But, Mabel," *Mamm* said, "Norman's bringing Katie home on Sunday night."

"You don't think I know that?" Mabel muttered, still not looking up.

Katie stood up and paced in front of the living-room window. She burst out moments later, "Well, then, you can have him! Right now I don't really care!"

"Girls, girls!" *Mamm* interrupted. "Let's be sensible about this. Mabel, I had no idea you felt like this. Obviously Norman doesn't share your feelings, so you shouldn't interfere like this."

"I'm not interfering." Mabel glared at both of them. "So don't blame me for that. I heard Katie say she was still in love with Ben, so why shouldn't I speak up? She can leave Norman to me. I'll get his attention."

"You would wish Ben on me? Even after what he's done?" Now Katie glared at Mabel. She'd thought her relationship with Mabel had grown, but it clearly wasn't very deep. Not if Mabel was willing to undercut her because of some infatuation the younger girl had. Anger rose inside her. Katie faced Mabel. "What happened to Mose? Have you forgotten about how much you loved him? And Norman is much too old for you."

A smile crept across Mabel's face. "You know *Daett* doesn't approve of Mose. He

90

does like Norman though. So why shouldn't I choose someone *Daett* likes? And lots of younger women marry older men. They're the mature ones, of course. Not like you and Ben. You didn't even know the guy was delivering drugs." And with that, Mabel retreated to the kitchen.

With her heart pounding, Katie sat on the couch again. Surely Mabel couldn't be serious.

Oh, if only she hadn't agreed to the visit to see Ben, she wouldn't be in this mess. Then Mabel wouldn't have heard that her feelings for Ben still lingered.

Mamm took a long look at Katie and then marched out to the kitchen. She returned a few seconds later with Mabel in tow. "Sit beside Katie," *Mamm* said as she pointed.

Reluctantly Mabel sat down.

What was there to say? Katie wondered. Obviously *Mamm* wasn't going to let this problem continue. And the responsibility lay with her as the eldest sister to make the first move. Katie glanced at Mabel. "I'm sorry I threw Mose into your face."

Mabel pretended to smile. "I'm sorry too. I shouldn't have spoken like I did."

"There now. That's much better." *Mamm* looked at both of them. "And let's not have any more of this foolish talk about liking men we have no right to. That's not the way of our people."

Katie nodded, and beside her Mabel did the same. But Katie knew her heart hadn't changed and neither had Mabel's. Not if all the blushing Mabel was doing was any indication. So now they'd driven the problem underground.

Oh, why had Ben ever come into her life? And why had she ever wished he'd notice her?

CHAPTER EIGHT

Ben awoke with a start, his eyes focusing on his surroundings. *Yah,* he remembered now. He was in the hospital with a gunshot wound. In some ways, it seemed like it had happened a long time ago, but that wasn't possible. He'd been dreaming that Katie was still here asking how he was doing. But that wasn't possible either. Katie hadn't made any contact with him since his arrest. A single card had arrived from Zurich after Katie had left on her trip with a sweet note scribbled on the back — obviously written before Katie had found out about the arrest. After that, only silence.

A nurse pushed open the door and peaked in. "Awake, are we?"

Ben hesitated. "Was someone here earlier?" he asked.

The nurse smiled. "Your girlfriend. You don't remember? She was here with her brother."

"I don't have a girlfriend," Ben whispered, but the nurse was already gone. So he hadn't been dreaming. Katie had really been here. Had that been a look of longing in her eyes he'd noticed? Or was it just his imagination? Could Katie ever consider repairing their relationship? If only he hadn't broken her heart what a blessed man he would be today. But he *had* broken her heart, and that couldn't be changed. It hardly seemed possible that Katie would ever trust him again. *Yah,* he'd dared hope, though, and he wouldn't give up that hope. He was even willing to accept this shooting as a good thing if it turned Katie's heart back toward his.

Ben held his throbbing head with one hand. What would it be like if Katie loved him again? Was that even possible? If he didn't stop these wild thoughts, his head was going to split wide open! The door of the room opened again, and the same nurse appeared, bringing in his lunch. As she set the food before him, she said, "The detectives are back. They wish to speak with you. Are you up to it?"

Ben looked at the meager meat loaf, smattering of peas, and Jell-O salad before him. "*Yah,* I suppose so."

The nurse left, and moments later the two

detectives entered.

"Mr. Stoll," Detective Barton began without delay, "we won't keep you long. We've made an arrest in your case. And things look good with the evidence. We thought you'd rest better if you knew."

"Who did you arrest?" Ben asked. He tried to appear interested, but what would really make him feel better right now was to have Katie beside him.

"Mr. Stoll, are you okay? You look a little pale."

The concern in Detective Barton's voice cut through Ben's thoughts. *"Yah."*

"We want you to look at some pictures. Tell me if you recognize the man who shot you. It would sure help us if you did."

Ben's hand went to his head again. "I didn't see anything. There was a light in my eyes, and it was dark outside."

"At least look at the photographs," Detective Barton insisted. "It might jog your memory."

Detective Lessen handed several black-and-white printouts to Detective Barton.

He held one in front of Ben. "Take a look, Mr. Stoll. Do you recognize this man?"

Ben focused and shook his head. Another picture appeared in front of him. This time Ben looked at it longer, but he shook his head again.

"I did hear his voice," Ben finally whispered. He was duty bound to tell the detectives the truth, even though there might be trouble down this road.

The detective looked relieved. "What did you hear, Mr. Stoll?"

Ben gathered his thoughts. It was time he said what he knew. He owed the detectives that much. "A man's voice said, 'This is from Rogge' just before he fired."

"Did you recognize his voice?" Detective Barton's voice was excited.

"I'm sure I did," Ben whispered. "His name is Martin Lap. I used to make drug deliveries to him. He was Rogge's best customer."

A quick look passed between the two detectives. "This is very helpful, Mr. Stoll. We'll be in touch. Thank you." And with that they were gone.

Ben picked at the food in front of him. He'd named the correct man, he was sure. He could tell by the looks on their faces. Martin Lap was already in custody. Now Ben really was in trouble because he knew he would never testify in open court again. And the police and prosecutors would surely ask him to.

While Ben struggled with his thoughts,

the nurse returned and checked his monitors, touching his head for a moment. Noticing his barely touched food, she said, "You need to eat. Give it another try, Ben."

Ben rolled his head away from the light streaming in through the window. "*Yah,* in a minute."

The nurse smiled and left the room.

Ben's troubling thoughts continued. He'd just identified the man who had shot him. This could lead only to one place. The last time he'd justified testifying on the basis of needing to be honest, hardly knowing what he was doing but realizing it wasn't the usual Amish practice. Now he knew better. His actions had endangered the people he loved; it had garnered the disapproval of the Amish community. He was sure his *daett* and the ministers would never agree to his testifying again. It went against a deep conviction of his people. They believed in forgiveness, in reaching out to those who had harmed them hoping to draw a lost soul into the love of the Savior. Punishing people for their crimes didn't soften hearts, the community believed. It usually only hardened them.

If he ever wished for a chance to be accepted in an Amish instruction class and become a member of the church, it was high time he started playing by the rules. And he firmly believed in Jesus now and in the Amish way. His doubts were gone. And he wished to win Katie's love again. He could never accomplish that outside the Amish church. *Yah,* he would answer the detectives' questions, but he wouldn't testify. Such a thing was out of the question regardless of the cost to him personally. Oh, how he loved Katie!

Da Hah would have to help him find his way through all of this. The first thing would be to submit to his *daett*'s decision. *Daett* wanted him to move in with Grandpa and Grandma in the *dawdy haus* once he was released. That would be embarrassing. His parents were treating him like a child who couldn't run his own life. But the truth was he couldn't run his own life. He'd done that and ended up in jail and placed his family in harm's way. And now the police wanted more testimony from him. What a mess he'd made. Ben groaned again.

The nurse returned and looked at the food tray. She clucked her tongue. "Mr. Stoll . . ."

"I'll try to do better with supper," he said unconvincingly.

"I hear it'll be a good meal. Chicken, they say." She offered a sympathetic smile.

Ben tried to return the smile as she

98

checked the monitors again and then left. The nurse might think the upcoming supper was good, but Ben knew better. At home he would get a real supper. Hospital food just couldn't compete.

In jail he hadn't thought of home more than he had to. The memories were held back by guilt and by the knowledge of how hard it would be to become part of Amish life again. And he hadn't been wrong about that. He couldn't blame his family for how tense they'd been the past few days. They were doing much better at handling the situation than he would have. And now they had this shooting to deal with on top of everything else. The community would have questions by the hundreds. He mulled them over.

"Why had Ben agreed to testify knowing the strong negative beliefs of the Amish community on the matter?"

"Why had Ben been involved in drug dealing to begin with?"

"Hadn't his *daett* trained him well enough?"

"What kind of example was his *daett* setting for the family and community?"

"What kind of example was Ben setting for the community?"

"Does Ben know how much his actions

cost the Amish community?"

And so they would speak and ask, going on and on, and the shame of it would mount ever higher. He ought to be thankful Brenda had sat with him at all last night and that his *mamm* and *daett* had visited this morning. Ben wiped away a tear and prayed silently.

Dear Hah, please forgive me for what I've done to my family and for what I've ruined with Katie. I don't deserve any consideration from You, but will You help Katie see I've changed? I don't know where to go anymore or what to do. The way is dark. I don't know what lies ahead for me, but I do know You're here with me. Will You please help me?

I've thrown things away in my pride, thinking I could handle life on my own. But I know now that I can't, and that I don't deserve anything from You. So I ask for Your forgiveness. Forgive me like I want to forgive others. Even this man who shot me — help me do the right thing when I'm asked to testify against him. Bring Martin to a saving knowledge of You, dear Hah. And please let Katie find a happy life, even if that isn't with me. She deserves all that and more. Amen.

Peace settled over Ben as he looked around the empty room. If any blessings were to be given from here on out, they would surely be way above anything that should rightly come his way. He would be content with whatever *Da Hah* chose for him.

CHAPTER NINE

Katie stood up after the hymn singing ended and walked past the few young people still sitting on the benches in Bishop Miller's living room. Sunday morning church had been held here, and now the hymn singing this evening. All morning the whispers had been about Ben and the shooting last week.

"He wasn't wounded too badly, was he?"

"Why did Ben get involved with such evil people?"

"Will he be home soon?"

"*Yah*, but he's going to live with his grandparents in another district."

"Will he bring further danger to his family?"

"You'd think going to jail was bad enough. But now this . . ."

"Did you hear they captured somebody? I hear they want Ben to testify again."

"That poor Stoll family! It seems their

troubles never end with that boy."

Katie had shut her ears as much as possible. She wanted to stop thinking about Ben and his problems. Norman was taking her home tonight, and she was moving on with her life — as well she should.

Norman had vanished out the front door some five minutes ago, and he would have his horse hitched to the buggy by now. Katie made her way to the walk to wait for him. Norman too had heard the talk about Ben. It was a wonder he still wanted to take her home because every time Ben's name was mentioned, everyone glanced in Katie's direction. Tongues were wagging, and Norman couldn't miss hearing what was being said. If he were to head straight home without her, Katie couldn't blame him. Then she'd have no way home tonight, since Leroy had left soon after the hymn singing — driving Lizzie Kuntz, Norman's cousin, home. Apparently Leroy had mustered the courage to ask the young woman home now that Norman was taking Katie in his buggy. Sort of riding the Kuntz family wave, she figured. If Norman bolted, she would never live down the humiliation. The community would certainly find out. This was, after all, their first date. Many eyes would be watching.

Willis had given her a sympathetic look before he left. Perhaps even he couldn't imagine how shy Norman was taking a girl home, let alone his sister who was part of the controversy.

Mabel had left with Willis without even a glance in Katie's direction. The girl hadn't said anything about her feelings for Norman since the blowup in the living room. Surely Mabel's attraction to Norman was only a passing thing. She'd gotten over Mose fast enough after Jesse had put his foot down.

Mabel's affections must not go that deep yet. Someday they might, but right now she was like a bee flitting among the flowers. If Norman showed any interest in Mabel, that might be another matter. But Norman didn't seem interested in her. He wanted Katie, and that was a great honor she didn't wish to ignore.

Norman would be a much better husband than Ben could ever hope to be.

A few girls lingered in the washroom and smiled as Katie gathered her wrap. They'd all figured it out by now. Since she hadn't left with Willis, they knew something was up. Their minds were whirling this very moment trying to decide which boy had gone out ahead of her. Katie gave them all a sweet smile. They would just have to wonder for a few more minutes. Making people curious was part of the fun of having a young man take you home.

With her bonnet on, Katie stepped outside and searched the line of buggies for a sign of Norman. She paused as several girls came out of the washroom too. They took discreet glances at the line of buggies before climbing into their own families' vehicles. Laura Mullet peered back to give Katie a little wave along with a bright smile. She no doubt had it figured out and was feeling triumphant in her guess. By tomorrow night the whole community would know that Norman Kuntz had driven Katie Raber home from the hymn sing.

This was the first time she'd been on an official Amish date, Katie thought, as she moved closer to the end of the walk. Ben had never driven her home from a hymn singing with the approving eyes of the community on them. They'd always been together at Mennonite youth gatherings.

It gave a person a warm feeling on the inside, Katie decided, knowing she was doing the right thing. She and Norman would make a *gut* couple. Everyone would approve of the match. And since she'd stood up to Mabel, Katie felt much better about Norman. It was almost as if the issue had forced her to make a claim on Norman — calling him her boyfriend in front of Mabel and *Mamm.* And wasn't that the case? Why else would he be taking her home?

As Norman's buggy pulled into the first place, Katie froze. Something about the shape of Norman's horse in the shadowy darkness stopped her. Norman's horse looked just like Ben's Longstreet! But that couldn't be. All horses were different. It must be the shadows playing tricks on her mind. Katie forced herself forward, her mind spinning. If this were Longstreet, then Ben would be waiting in the buggy. And she would snuggle up to him under the buggy blanket. They would kiss even before they arrived at the house. Celebrating this night for what it was — a special night of being together again.

Katie grabbed the side of Norman's buggy and pulled herself up the step, angry at herself for imagining such a thing. Ben had no right to intrude on this moment. She was done with him. Katie landed on Norman's buggy seat with a thump. She was about as graceful as a bag of feed tonight.

Seated beside her, Norman didn't seem to notice. His face twitched as he let out the lines. "*Gut* evening, Katie."

Katie forced thoughts of Ben out of her

mind. "*Gut* evening, Norman. I didn't want to keep you waiting."

"Oh, you wouldn't do that, I'm sure." Norman attempted to laugh.

The poor man was frightened half to death — and of her! The thought was ludicrous, but then Katie was used to Ben's confident attitude. He never blinked an eye at the presence of girls. Norman wasn't Ben. And most men probably weren't as confident as Ben had been.

"Are you cold?" Norman asked as he offered her part of the buggy blanket.

"Oh *yah.*" Katie took it, her hand going toward his.

Norman dropped the edge of the blanket, jerking his hand back. The blanket slid to the floor.

Please, I'm not deadly. You can touch my hand, Katie wanted to say. She smiled instead and bent down to pick the blanket up.

Norman took his horse around a turn, hanging on to both lines. "I hope I'm not driving too fast. Bonnie is a little skittish yet. I only got her at the sales barn a few weeks ago."

"Fast?" Katie laughed. "I like fast horses. And that's a nice name — Bonnie."

"You do?" Norman was looking at her as

107

if she were some strange creature from another planet. "My sisters are always complaining about my driving too fast. Susie just this morning even threatened not to come to church with me if I drove Bonnie. But I wanted her broken in some more before I . . . well . . . picked you up tonight."

Katie laughed. "I think your sisters don't know what they're talking about. There's nothing like a fast ride home in the dark. It's romantic."

"Ah . . ." Norman fell silent but he loosened the reins, and Bonnie raced through the night. The buggy wheels hummed under them at the steady pace of Bonnie's hooves on the pavement.

Norman seemed to relax, but he soon tensed again, pulling back on the reins. He glanced sideways at Katie. "I'm . . . I'm not used to . . . to driving so fast. *Daett* says something could fly off the wheels. And there's no fixing a buggy that slides along the blacktop, to say nothing of the people inside."

"I suppose so," Katie allowed, as Norman slowed down even more. She chided herself for allowing Ben to intrude again. Thinking about how it used to be . . . those evenings dashing home from the Mennonite youth gatherings. Fast living was now a thing of her past, Katie told herself. She was wrong to encourage Norman to live differently than he'd been brought up.

Minutes later they were turning down the driveway. Norman parked in front of the hitching post and jumped out with the tie rope to secure Bonnie. Katie climbed down and waited for him. She led the way to the house. On the front porch, the swing squeaked in the evening breeze, bathed in the soft light of the lantern *Mamm* had left on inside the house.

Katie paused. Why not sit on the swing at least for a few minutes? She gave Norman a sweet smile. "The swing. We could sit out here for a few minutes."

"*Yah,* maybe." He hesitated, but Katie had already sat down.

Lowering himself on the swing, Norman stayed on his side, a wide space between them.

"Norman," Katie said, "you don't have to sit way over there. I won't bite."

He laughed and moved closer, but he still kept plenty of space between them. It was clearly going to take awhile for Norman to get over his nervousness. She had to be patient.

Norman cleared his throat. "You used to date Ben Stoll, didn't you?"

"You know I did," Katie said. "That was a long time ago."

"Sorry. I didn't mean to . . . well . . . I just mean I'm sure you quit the relationship when you found out about . . ."

"*Yah,* I did. In fact, I haven't spoken to Ben since . . ." Katie let the words hang for a moment. Her visit to Ben's hospital room wasn't something she wished to discuss with Norman. "Well, let's just say the relationship is over."

Norman sighed, his relief evident. "I'm glad to hear that."

Apparently she needed to justify herself in Norman's eyes, so Katie continued. "I know what Ben did was a great evil. I had nothing more to do with him after I found out about it."

"I expected that of you, Katie. You're a decent girl," he said at once, although his tone wasn't very convincing.

Katie turned to face him. "Why would anyone expect me to do something else?"

Norman managed a smile. "We didn't, but *Daett* still thought I should ask where you stood."

Katie almost gasped. "Your *daett* must believe I'm committed to Amish ways. He hired me as the schoolteacher."

"That's different. Your joining the church

110

kind of took care of that doubt. But for dating, I guess one must be sure."

Katie settled back in the swing. What kind of strange conversation was this? Her character was still being questioned. What would Norman say if he knew she'd been to see Ben at the hospital? Thank *Da Hah* that had been Willis's idea and for a *gut* cause. Even Jesse had approved so who could hold that against her? But wasn't it possible Norman would find out about the visit? *Mamm* knew, as did the rest of the family. They had no reason to spread the information around unless Mabel had. Katie drew in her breath. Would Mabel do such a thing? Perhaps. If her feelings were strong enough for Norman — and if Mabel suspected Norman cared about the matter. Plus it was hard to keep things from the community.

"It's *gut* to hear that you agree," Norman was saying, seeming more relaxed now. "Our youth are open to so many temptations in the world today with wild living during their *rumspringa* time. There's also drinking and, in Ben's case, even worse things. You never did *rumspringa* either, did you?"

Katie's head was spinning. She hadn't expected this kind of questioning from shy Norman. She forced the words out. "*Mamm*

111

never allowed it."

Norman smiled. "Emma's a decent *mamm* then. I hope to keep my children out of such things." He fell silent for a moment before continuing. "After I . . . well, after I wed, of course. When *Da Hah* sees fit to open the door for my wedding vows."

"I understand, Norman." Katie touched his arm and he flinched. She pulled her hand back quickly. She would have to learn how to act more circumspect again after being around Ben. But that was a *gut* thing, no doubt.

Norman was looking at her. "I hope I'm worthy of love. I search my own heart many times, and I don't know. Keeping a wife and raising children can't be an easy thing."

Katie said nothing. She felt as if she weren't here, that Norman was lost in his own thoughts. Still, she was on a date with him, which meant they were headed toward the very thing Norman was wondering about.

"I hope I'm not boring you with these things," Norman said.

Katie forced a smile. "It's okay, Norman. We all wonder and doubt at times. I know I do. Shall we go inside where it's warmer?"

"*Yah,* let's." Norman stood.

Katie also rose and led the way inside. If

Norman knew what her doubts were or what she'd been thinking all evening concerning Ben, the shy man would surely have gotten into his buggy and driven home right away. That must not happen. She'd worked too hard to achieve a position of respectability in the community to lose it now.

CHAPTER TEN

Katie stood in the kitchen glaring at Mabel, who was smirking back at her. Norman was in the living room where Katie had left him. She'd promised him cherry pie and ice cream. She'd seen a flash of Mabel's dress vanishing into the kitchen doorway when they'd walked in, so she knew Mabel had probably been listening by the window.

"So we're back where we started, Mabel," Katie said. "I thought we were going to respect each other from now on. And what about being friends . . . you and me?"

"That was before I knew you were going to date Norman and get all high and mighty again," Mabel shot back.

Katie sighed. "I'm just trying to live a normal life, Mabel. Can't you understand that?"

Mabel didn't back down. "You know you don't love the man, Katie, so why don't you let me have a chance at him?"

Katie couldn't stop herself. "What do you know about love, Mabel? You kissed Mose out in the feed bin. That's about how far your experience goes. I've had my heart broken."

Mabel glared. "Just wait until I let it slip at the sewing that you were down at the hospital to see Ben. What do you think Norman and Enos will think about that?"

So Mabel *had* been listening and planned to use the information gathered to her advantage. "You'd better not Mabel," Katie warned. "Don't you dare!"

Mabel smirked. "And what would you do, Katie? Once they know, the damage is done."

Katie grabbed a thought. "And you think Norman will ask you home just by getting rid of me? There's not a chance in the world. The Kuntzes have higher standards than you."

Mabel laughed. "You don't have anything over me, Katie. You just think you do. At least I'm not stupid enough to still have feelings for a drug dealer. What if Norman finds that out about you?"

Katie turned away. The girl was impossible. And Katie was losing all the ground she'd thought she'd gained in their relationship in the last year. She didn't want to go back to those days of fighting with Mabel over every little thing. But on this point she simply couldn't — wouldn't — yield. Mabel was out of line. Besides, Norman didn't care for Mabel anyway.

Before she could decide what needed doing, Norman stuck his head in the kitchen opening, a puzzled look on his face. "Is something wrong?"

"Nee," Katie tried to smile. "I was just talking with Mabel."

"Well . . . then," Norman continued, "why doesn't Mabel join us for ice cream and cherry pie? That is, if there's enough."

Mabel looked at Katie with triumph.

Katie fumbled for the right words. "*Yah,* I guess there's enough. There's a whole pie and a half gallon of ice cream left from last night. We made plenty of extra knowing you'd be coming."

Norman looked quite pleased. "Then I'll go back to waiting in the living room."

When Norman disappeared, Mabel turned to Katie. "See there? He likes me!"

Katie pulled out the cherry pie and set it on the counter. If she did what she felt like doing, she'd throw the whole thing in Mabel's face. Instead she commanded, "At least help with the ice cream."

"Glad to." Mabel was clearly gloating. If

Norman swooned over Mabel once they arrived in the living room, Katie decided she would throw the pie after all — but in his face. Katie cut the pie and slid three pieces onto plates. Mabel was busy scooping out ice cream and scurrying around for bowls and spoons. Without a sideways glance at Mabel, Katie strode into the living room carrying two plates.

"Here!" She handed Norman his pie, and set the other plate on the footstool in front of the couch next to Norman. She sat down beside him. Mabel could get her own pie. Norman glanced at Katie out of the corner of his eye. His irritation regarding her display of temper was obviously showing, but she couldn't seem to help herself. Recent events were bringing out a nasty side of her that she hated to acknowledge. She was acting worse than she ever had back in the days when she was known to everyone as "Emma Raber's odd daughter." Now she had a well thought of boy bringing her home, and she couldn't even control her temper.

And to make things worse, Mabel appeared all smiles, the bowls in her hands brimming with pecan ice cream. She acted like she'd made it! And Katie had been the one who had toiled over the ice cream maker last night, preparing this treat for Norman. Mabel hadn't touched the handle once. Yet there she was, beaming as if she'd done everything. And clearly Norman, smiling ear to ear, didn't seem to know the difference or care.

"That looks delicious, Mabel," he said as he accepted his bowl.

"Fresh from last night," Mabel chirped, disappearing into the kitchen for her piece of pie. Now it looked to Norman like Mabel was doing all the serving, which would no doubt score extra points for Mabel in Norman's book, Katie thought. How had she gotten herself into this situation? Outfoxed by her temper and a teenager! Katie was truly irritated now.

"You're not eating," Norman commented, looking sideways at her.

"She wasn't feeling too well earlier in the day," Mabel offered, appearing like a ghost in front of them. She *was* a ghost, Katie thought. A haunting ghost she couldn't get rid of.

"Is this true?" Norman asked, concern evident.

"I . . . well . . . I did have a little headache after church," she stammered. "But it was nothing serious."

"You didn't say anything on the way

home." Norman was still looking at her.

Mabel gave another chirpy little laugh. "Katie's a secretive sort of girl. You have to dig things out of her."

"I am not," Katie snapped. She'd said it much too loud, displaying her anger again.

Norman looked puzzled for a moment before shrugging. "I hope you'll be okay. And I hope you don't hide things from those around you and from *Da Hah*. That is not something our people believe in."

"She has her moments," Mabel offered. "Most of the time Katie's honest around the family."

Norman looked like he might ask another question, but he smiled instead. "This is quite *gut* ice cream. Did you make it, Katie?"

"Yah," Katie managed to get out.

They sat in silence as the clock ticked loudly on the wall. Mabel's spoon clicked in her bowl. She jumped up. "I'd better get to bed so I can get my sleep. Lots of work ahead of us tomorrow."

In a flash Mabel was gone up the stairs, her footsteps lingering in the stairwell.

Norman's eyes lingered for a moment on the closed door. "Jesse has raised his children well, I see. Industrious, all of them."

Katie didn't say anything until Norman's

gaze jerked her out of her daze. She stumbled over the words. "*Yah*. Jesse's a *gut daett*. I have no complaints with how Mabel helps around the house."

Norman smiled. "I think Jesse has also had a *gut* effect on you. At least that's what *Daett* told me. Before your *mamm* married Jesse, you used to attend the Mennonite youth gatherings, didn't you?"

"I used to, but I don't anymore," Katie said much too quickly.

Norman didn't seem to notice though. He settled back into the couch with a sigh. He pushed his empty pie plate onto the coffee table. Any further questions about her former days seemed forgotten at the moment. Mabel had put him in a mellow mood, Katie noticed. He was more relaxed than he had been all evening, especially on the drive home.

"Do you want more ice cream?" Katie asked as she picked up his bowl.

"*Nee*." Norman smiled. "I had enough — and plenty."

Katie took the plates into the kitchen and set them on the counter. She returned to the living room. Norman was looking at Jesse's copy of *The Budget*, flipping through the pages.

"Anything interesting?" Katie asked, attempting a sweet smile.

"Not really. Just the usual. Do you think this week's news will make it in?"

He had to mean Ben's *kafuffle,* Katie thought. "I hope not."

"Me too." Norman appeared vexed, the level of his voice rising. "The community doesn't need the added shame. It's going to carry far enough the way it is. I mean, what Amish community has had such a scandal ever? Ben should be thoroughly ashamed of himself. In fact, he should leave and never come back. He should move to some other community where they don't know him."

"I heard he's moving in with his grandparents," Katie offered.

"That's not nearly far enough." Norman grunted. "He'll still be around. And what if another attack comes, and his grandparents get hurt? I say Ben should leave for good."

"But surely there won't be another attack?" Katie said, hoping her concern didn't show through.

"The police want Ben to testify, I heard," Norman said. "I guess Ben can identify the man who shot him. It's going around that he heard the shooter's voice before he blacked out. If Ben testifies again, that will be another scandal we'll have to live down."

"Maybe he has no choice?" Katie said, realizing she sounded like she was defending Ben.

Norman stared at her. "No choice? We all have choices, Katie."

She might as well go on. It wasn't right that Norman was being so hard on Ben. "They might be able to make Ben talk. I don't know . . . somehow . . . by their *Englisha* laws."

Norman didn't appear too happy. "No one can make anyone talk, Katie. Not when it's not right. Our forefathers withstood fire and torture rather than betray the faith or each other. The least we can do is stand up for some principles in this peaceful land we live in."

He was right of course. Katie gave Norman a quick smile. Apparently it hadn't occurred to him yet that she'd defended Ben. Well, even the worst people needed a little defending. Wasn't that also the belief of their people?

"How's school going?" Norman asked, changing the subject.

"Okay, I guess. Maybe it's too soon to tell."

"A little overwhelming perhaps?"

"No, well, *yah,* perhaps. It is after all, only my first year."

"You're doing okay though. At least from

122

what I heard. *Daett* said he's getting very *gut* reports from the parents."

"Did your *daett* take a big risk then by hiring me?" The words burst out, and Katie looked away. Where was this insecurity coming from? School was going fine. She already knew that.

Norman smiled. "It's *gut* to see that you're a little nervous about the subject. Pride and overconfidence are deadly sins."

He hadn't answered her question, so it must be true. She wouldn't ask again. At least she must have passed the test of meeting Enos Kuntz's high standards despite the risk.

Norman continued without looking at her. "I thought for the longest time you were a little full of yourself, Katie. Especially after you came back from your trip overseas and gave all those talks at the sewings. *Mamm* used to come home with the stories. She retold them to us around the supper table. But *Daett* told me you came from humble roots which had given you a *gut* heart — and a deep and religious one. That's a rare combination in a girl, Katie."

"Thank you," Katie choked out, trying to catch her breath. Norman had been thinking this about her?

"Well, I'd better be going." Norman was

on his feet now and moving toward the door. "Thanks for the *gut* evening. And for the food. Tell Mabel I enjoyed her company also. Maybe we'll have her join us again next Sunday night. That is, if you'll let me come back again?" Norman paused with his hand on the door. He didn't really look like he expected her to say *nee* so he must be much more confident of himself than he let on.

"*Yah . . .*" Katie replied.

Norman smiled. "And I hope you can make plans to be with my family this Thanksgiving day. *Mamm* and *Daett* would both love that. And so would I."

"I . . . sure . . . why not?" Katie clasped her hands in front of her. So Norman was serious about their relationship. That was a *gut* sign.

He was gone in an instant, softly closing the door behind him.

Through the window, Katie watched his form move across the lawn in the darkness dimly broken by the lantern light spilling out the window. Out by the hitching post he untied Bonnie and climbed into the buggy. He drove away, and as the lights went down the lane Katie turned to walk to the stair door. It had been a *gut* evening, she told herself. And a proper one too. So why was she seized with a great desire for

124

something . . . someone . . . who had been banished from her life once and for all? Truth be told, she wanted Ben's arms wrapped around her shoulders and holding her tight. She wanted them . . . him . . . badly. Catching herself, Katie turned her thoughts away as she opened the door. How could her heart so betray her after she'd spent the evening with a decent man like Norman? She must not think of Ben like that again, Katie resolved as she walked up the stairs in the dark with care.

CHAPTER ELEVEN

Katie leaned against the schoolhouse windowsill and watched the buggies discharge their young occupants. As usual, most of them made a dash for the ball field to get in precious playing time before she rang the bell. They were all *gut* children, and just as energetic with their schoolwork as they were playing softball. Katie knew she should be happy with her lot, and yet she felt dreary for no *gut* reason.

On their second date, Norman had seemed a little more confident. The evening spent with him last night had been okay. At least Mabel had the decency to keep herself scarce when they'd arrived home this time. Other than a cheerful smile to Norman, she hadn't said anything or hung around before dashing up the stairs. And Norman didn't mention his interest in eating pie and ice cream with Mabel present. Perhaps his interest was now centering totally on Katie like it should be.

Ben had seemed a distant thought all week. That was after she'd cried herself to sleep thinking about him after Norman left that first Sunday night. She didn't want Ben back — *nee,* not after what he'd done. That wasn't the issue. Her heart hadn't sunk that low. But the good memories were still painful, even with the healing *Da Hah* had done. Perhaps dating again was stirring her wounds that needed further healing. She would make it through this with *Da Hah*'s help.

Katie caught sight of Norman's buggy racing into the schoolyard. His sister usually dropped off their youngest brother, Abram, but this morning it looked like Norman was driving. At least a black hat filled part of the buggy's windshield. Was Norman going to stop and talk to her? If so, what could he want that would have him driving so much faster than usual? Or maybe he was driving because his sister was busy this morning? In that case, Norman would just give her a quick wave before turning to leave. Katie opened the window and leaned out. A few of the children in the playground turned her way, smiling and waving. She gave them a little wave back, her eyes still watching Norman's buggy.

He came to a fast halt as both doors burst open. Little Abram leaped out and tied up Bonnie. Norman marched earnestly toward the schoolhouse. Katie's smile vanished. The man looked mighty grim. What could be wrong? She'd just seen him last night, and everything had seemed fine.

Racing to the schoolhouse door, she held it open with a smile on her face. Norman paused a few feet away. "I need to speak with you, Katie. Right now!"

Never had she seen him so disturbed. Katie stepped back inside, still holding the door open. "It's almost time to begin school, Norman. What's wrong?"

He brushed past her into the schoolroom. She caught her breath and followed. Had she done something wrong? But what? And since last night?

Norman turned to face her. "Is it true you visited Ben Stoll in the hospital?"

Katie swallowed. "*Yah,* I did. Willis took me."

"So it is true!" His eyes were blazing. "Did you expect this to stay a secret? How could you, Katie?"

"I . . ." She looked away. She hadn't expected this level of anger from him. "I'm sorry you're taking this so hard, Norman. But Willis insisted I go. He told me Ben wished to apologize to me face-to-face for what he'd done. Willis thought he should be given that chance, and Jesse concurred. Ben was injured severely, you know. And one never knows when *Da Hah* will call a person home. Ben wanted to make peace with me and *Da Hah,* and I needed to give him that opportunity. Surely you can understand that."

"How do I know what you say is true?" Norman snapped. "Am I supposed to ask Willis what happened when you spoke with Ben? And besides, that's not the issue. It's how things look. Now I'll be seen as dating Ben's ex-girlfriend who can't seem to stay away from him. That's how it appears to the community. You're making a fool out of me, Katie Raber. Is this what Mabel meant by your sneaky ways?"

Katie paused. This seemed so unlike the Norman she knew. "Is this your way of telling me you're not going to see me again? That you're ashamed of me?"

Norman glanced up for a moment, taking in the tears on her cheeks. "Katie . . . Katie . . . please . . . of course I'm not saying that. I don't start something without finishing it. But I needed to know whether this was true, and I needed to hear again that you are over that drug-dealing Ben Stoll."

"Well, it *is* true I went to see him in the hospital . . ." Katie let the statement hang.

Norman hesitated before drawing himself up to full height. "I don't want you speaking with Ben Stoll ever again, Katie."

"I wasn't planning to, Norman. I won't be seeing him."

"Still, you must promise me."

"But what if I see Ben in church? I have to say *gut* morning to him. It wouldn't be Christian not to."

Norman frowned. "That's something you won't have to worry about. *Daett* is going to speak with Bishop Miller this morning. Ben will be asked to leave the community at once, before he can bring more shame on all of us."

"He's leaving? But where is he to go? We can't just drive him away. He's not in the *bann*. That takes a vote by the church members."

"Don't worry about Ben, Katie. He's not your responsibility. Others who know better will take care of him. I can only say that on my part I'm just glad he'll be gone."

He moved a step away, her need to promise apparently forgotten. He suddenly turned on his heels. Glancing over his

130

shoulder, he said, "I'll see you Sunday then, Katie."

"But Norman!" Katie stopped him mid-stride. "What about us? You can't just come in here, yell at me, and then leave. What am I supposed to think?"

He gave her a weak smile. "Everything's okay, Katie. At least you didn't lie to me. And Ben will soon be gone."

Everything was not okay, Katie thought as she watched him walk out to his buggy. She ached in her heart over this. It was even more painful as she realized she couldn't imagine Ben walking out like that — not after chewing her out over some matter. In fact, she couldn't imagine Ben talking to her in that manner at all. But Norman wasn't Ben. And Norman wasn't deceiving her by hiding some awful sin as Ben had done. She ought to feel thankful for Norman's care. Yet the truth was that she didn't.

How had things come to this awful state? By Ben's actions, of course. And now everyone involved with him was reaping the bitter harvest. If Ben had to leave the community, there was no one he could blame but himself. And she had no reason to hold anything against either Norman or his *daett* for wanting that. No doubt they were trying to deal with things as best they knew how.

They were trying to stop evil from doing even more damage. If their methods seemed harsh, she would have to refrain from judging.

A soft step coming from the closet area turned her around. "Well, Noah, where did you come from?"

Had Ben's brother overheard the conversation? He appeared troubled, but surely he hadn't been inside while Norman was here.

"I was playing ball, and I bent my finger in my glove." Noah held up the offending body part.

"How bad does it hurt?" Katie took his hand and turned it over. Redness spread from the joint to the fingertip, but it wasn't bleeding.

Noah tried to smile. "It's not too bad, but I didn't want to continue playing. Not until it feels better anyway."

Katie let go of his hand. "We'll pray it gets better really fast, okay? And you need to be more careful with those fast balls. Was it one of the big boys batting?"

Noah nodded and added, "It was Lester. But it's worth playing ball even if you get a little hurt once in awhile."

Katie smiled and rumpled Noah's hair. How like life, she thought. It was worth living even if you received a few bruises along the way. And Norman would be worth it in the end. But she'd have to get used to his anger. What a surprise that was. Did he have these outbursts often? If he did, this might be something she could work on with him. Perhaps she could help Norman get over them.

And tonight she would have to temper her own anger when she spoke with Mabel. Mabel was certainly going to get a talking to. This tale-spreading from Mabel couldn't be allowed to pass without a strong rebuke. Passing around family information to aid one's own position was not Christian. What did Mabel expect from her actions? That she'd break up Norman and Katie's relationship? *Mamm* and Jesse should probably be brought in on this too.

Noah was pulling on her sleeve with his uninjured hand. He interrupted her thoughts. "What did Norman want this morning? He looked upset when I walked past him."

"He just needed to speak with me." Katie smiled down at him.

"He's your boyfriend, isn't he?"

Katie's smile broadened. "Don't tell me you're jealous, Noah."

He grinned. "You're a little too old for me. But you used to date my brother."

"*Yah,* before your brother got into so much trouble."

He looked away for a minute before continuing. "We visited Ben a couple of nights ago at the hospital. I heard him tell *Mamm* you stopped by."

"*Yah,* I did."

Noah shrugged. "I think Ben still likes you."

"Well . . ." Katie tousled his hair again. "It's about time for school to start," she said, hoping to end the conversation.

Noah wasn't deterred. "You ought to stop by again sometime. Ben's really feeling low. I'd like to see him cheered up some."

"*Nee,* it wouldn't be right for me to do that, Noah. I'm dating Norman now."

"But you could still stop by. Ben is quite blue."

Katie forced a smile. Noah had only his brother's welfare on his mind and meant no harm. "It's time for me to ring the bell, but thank you for the invitation. It's kind of you to think of your brother's well-being."

Noah nodded but he looked quite sorrowful.

Katie left him to grab the bell and lean out the window. She rang the bell vigorously. The students came pouring in, finding their way to their desks. When things quieted down, Katie opened the Bible storybook and read a short piece, followed by leading the class in prayer.

She was still thinking about Ben when the five first-graders came to the front. They sat down with their readers open on their laps. Katie stared at them vacantly. She was seeing Ben's pale face lying on the hospital bed pillow. His eyes were closed, and he was alone. The children's rustling feet interrupted her thoughts, and Katie jerked back to the present. She gave them all a quick smile. "Are we ready to learn more words today?"

They looked hesitant but tried to smile.

Katie forced herself to focus. "You're going to do great today! I know you are. All of you! Before long you'll be able to read so well you won't even have to think about it."

"I know what the lesson is about," little Johnny piped up.

"Okay! You can tell the class," Katie said.

"Be kind to all," Johnny said at once.

"That's right. And how did you know?'

Johnny looked sheepish. "*Mamm* told me."

Katie still gave him a warm look. "That's okay. Now does anyone wish to begin? Maybe one word at a time, making the sounds like we learned."

Johnny launched right in. "Kind."

Katie glowed with approval. "Okay, that was good. Now, moving on to the next in line, what is the picture?"

"Bird," another student ventured.

"And what is happening? Can you tell even though all the words aren't there?"

"The little birdie has fallen out of the nest," Karla Miller said. "And it can't fly away yet. And there's a snake coming to eat it."

"That right, Karla. And what is the little boy doing that is kind? Look at the next page and tell me the word."

"Nest," James Troyer read. "He's putting the bird back into its nest."

"That's right! Let's say all those words together a few times to see how they're sounded out."

Katie waited as they chanted together: "kind . . . bird . . . nest." She kept smiling, leading them through the rest of the lesson but every word seemed associated with Ben. She saw the way he'd looked that last time at the airport before her trip to Switzerland. Ben had been so full of life and joy. His face had been aglow with love for her. And now his brother Noah wanted her to stop by the hospital again and cheer him up. But she couldn't do that. The hospital was way out of the way. Ben had gotten himself into this mess, and she was dating Norman. It wasn't her fault Ben was lonely. And Norman would never understand her going to see Ben twice for whatever reason. And she couldn't blame Norman one bit.

When the first-graders had completed the reading assignment, Katie dismissed them and called up the next group. Hopefully they would have a different kind of story. Katie didn't need another reminder on kindness. When she opened the reader with the second-graders seated in front of her, Katie smiled. This story was on bravery. The story was of a young boy who needed to confess lying to his parents.

Katie listened as the two students read their way through the story, halting often at difficult words. In the story, little Robert Helmuth had forgotten to shut the gate to the calf barn, and during the night his *mamm*'s garden had been raided. In the morning, Robert had denied his actions at first, claiming he had shut the gate. Only after his *daett* believed him had Robert found the courage to tell the truth, say he was sorry, accept the punishment he deserved, and know he was forgiven.

With the story completed, Katie dismissed the class and called up the third-grade students. She almost groaned out loud at the title of the story: "Emma's Compassion." Pushing thoughts of Ben out of her mind, Katie forced herself to listen as the students read the story of how Emma stayed home from school for a whole week to take care of her younger sister while her *mamm* was down with the flu and caring for a sick baby on top of that. Emma had to work extra hard the next week to catch up with her schoolwork, but she did. This great act of compassion helped make Emma a more gentle and loving person.

Noah glanced at her when they were done. He's probably thinking about Ben, Katie decided. She dismissed the class without meeting the boy's eyes. She was a kind and compassionate person, and she would practice her kindness tonight on Mabel.

CHAPTER TWELVE

With a sigh, Katie glanced at the clock on the schoolroom wall. Two more minutes and she would release the children. This day had been a difficult and troubling one — not from anything the students had done, but from the thought of facing Mabel tonight. Should she let this problem pass? It would allow for a more peaceful atmosphere at home tonight. When the clock read three o'clock exactly, Katie stood in front of the students and said, "Time to go home. See you all tomorrow!" Most of the students were already prepared to leave, their books tucked inside their desks.

Oh, to be young again and carefree like her students, Katie thought. They had the whole world lying like a clean sheet in front of them while she felt like an old woman, her life soiled and dirty. Even the fresh start with Norman didn't look all that *gut* right now. But maybe tomorrow would be different. She really needed a thankful heart for all the blessings she had, most of them had been sitting right in front of her eyes all day. They were "her" children. She had a *gut* teaching job, and her standing in the community was the best it had ever been. And tonight *Mamm* and Jesse waited for her at home with their acceptance, and Leroy, Willis, and little Joel were the brothers she'd never had. And Carolyn certainly cared for her. All of these things had been absent not so long ago. She didn't deserve any of these recent blessings from *Da Hah*'s hands.

Katie walked to the window and waved as she watched the students scurry in the schoolyard. Several buggies were already waiting in line to pick up passengers.

Katie smiled as the first buggy left. The others soon followed except for one. The driver was climbing out of the buggy instead of taking off. Katie looked closer. It was Leon Stoll, Ben and Noah's father. He was heading her way, his face looking drawn. What could the man want? Was Ben okay? Forcing her feet forward, Katie pasted on a smile. She was a schoolteacher now, and she needed to act the part. That was maturity, wasn't it? Katie walked over and opened the door.

Leon stood there, holding his hat in his

hands, for a few moments before he spoke. "Katie, you need to come with me to the hospital. Ben is calling for you. I waited until school was out to come. Ben's had a serious setback."

"A setback? What do you mean? He was doing well when I saw him."

Leon bowed his head. "He's developed an infection, and the antibiotics aren't doing much good."

"But I can't come. Norman, the man I'm seeing, he won't understand."

"Katie, please! Our people understand such things. I know this is hard, and I wouldn't ask if I didn't know how much this might help Ben. We're worried, Lavina and I. Hearing you speak words of comfort might give Ben strength and hope. Knowing you've forgiven him could encourage him to want to get better."

"But I did forgive Ben. I was down there the other day with Willis. I told him then."

Leon nodded. "I know, but at times we need to hear those things again. He's mighty bad off, Katie. We need you to help us give him the courage and hope to fight to get well."

Katie pulled in a deep breath.

Leon reached out and took her arm, steadying her.

What should she do? Katie wondered. Wasn't it her Christian duty to go? And she hadn't promised Norman this morning not to speak with Ben again, so she wasn't going back on her word. If Ben's *daett* thought it was important, then she should go. Norman would just have to understand, that's all there was to it. Katie made her decision. "I will come then. But I must go home and tell *Mamm* first."

Leon nodded. "Thank you, Katie. This will mean so much to Ben . . . and to our family. I'll head back to the hospital then. Thank you again, Katie."

Fifteen minutes later, Katie rushed toward home, her thoughts scattered. Though she'd forgiven Ben, she knew they had no future together. Yet she surely didn't want him to die. But he wouldn't die. Infections were common in hospitals, weren't they? And they were giving him antibiotics. Still, the idea that Ben's life might be in danger kept Katie moving at a rapid pace.

As she suspected, when she dashed into the house to tell *Mamm* where she was going, she was met with disapproval. "You can tell me all the reasons I shouldn't go when I get home," Katie said. "I promised Ben's *daett* I'd be there, and I'm going." With that she hurried back to her buggy and headed for the hospital in Dover.

In the parking lot, Katie tied Sparky to a lamppost and rushed inside. Going past the receptionist with only a quick nod, Katie used the stairs and rushed into room 320. Ben's *mamm,* Lavina, was standing beside his bed.

"Thank *Da Hah* you have come!" Lavina said.

"It really is that bad?" Katie stopped short of the bed. Ben's face looked even whiter against the pillow than it had the last time she'd seen him. He moaned, his lips moving but his eyes stayed closed.

"*Yah,*" Lavina whispered. "We wouldn't have called you otherwise. They're treating him for a staph infection with antibiotics. It's all happened so fast. If he doesn't fight, he might not live."

Katie moved closer, her heart pounding. She reached out to touch Ben's hand. The fingers that had once brushed her face were now pale and frail. The lips that had kissed her were colorless.

"Ben," she whispered gently. "Ben, I've come. Can you hear me?" Katie repeated her call leaning closer to Ben's ear.

Lavina moved away from the bed and sat down. "I'm sorry, Katie. We were hoping he'd recognize your voice and respond. We

143

thought it might help."

"Shall I stay the night? I can if you want me to and you think it might help."

Lavina voice caught. "You would stay? Speak to Ben some more? I'm told they can hear sometimes, even when they're like this."

Katie managed a smile. "*Yah,* I have heard that myself. I will speak to him for awhile. Maybe it will help. What can it hurt?"

Lavina nodded, and silence fell between them.

Katie hesitated. It would feel strange talking to Ben in front of Lavina. And what was she to say? Ben and Katie had said so many things while they'd been together. Loving thoughts, tender words, and joy-filled hopes. Now none of those could be said. Still, Ben needed words of comfort, and she was duty bound to say them if she could. Katie took a deep breath and began in a whisper. "I loved you once, Ben. But you already know that. Everything I ever told you in those days was true. It came from my heart. I knew I'd never find another man I admired more. So what you did hurt me deeply. Yet I have forgiven you with the help of *Da Hah.* And I've done that with all my heart. And now I want you to go on living. *Da Hah* can't be done with you down here on earth,

Ben. He loves you — just as He loves all of us. And *Da Hah* also forgives. He gave us His dear Son, Jesus, to die for our sins. How can there be a greater love than that?"

Katie glanced over at Lavina, who smiled through her tears and nodded.

Katie took another deep breath. "You wanted to see if our faith was worth it, Ben. Remember the trip I took to Switzerland? And all the doubts you used to have? I don't know if you had your questions answered, but I found plenty of reasons to believe while in that country. Our people come from a great faith, Ben. They believed in their faith enough to die for it, and they were not mistaken. We saw the place where Felix Manz was drowned in the Old Town of Zurich. We saw the house where the first baptisms were performed. We stood by the fountain where the water might have been dipped from. We drove through beautiful towns perched on the hillsides where our people had to leave their farms behind and flee.

"It broke their hearts, Ben, and yet they counted the faith worth the price. We sang in a cave back up in the mountains where our people used to gather and sing and worship. This was the only place they were safe from arrest. We climbed into a hiding place

145

inside a barn where they took temporary
shelter before fleeing further into the mountains. We saw the castle where many of them
were kept prisoner. Some were held there
for years until their bodies wasted away.

"I wanted to tell you all of that when I
came home, Ben. I wanted to help you
believe and take courage. But then what
happened, happened. I know you didn't
plan things that way or wish them to be so.
But that's how sin works, Ben. I'm sure you
know that by now. I'm not trying to make
you feel bad. I'm trying to encourage you. I
cried tears by the buckets when I heard the
news of what you'd done. I didn't know if I
could go on. I wanted to lie down in that
foreign country and die. That's how much I
loved you, Ben.

"I thought joy would never come back to
my life. Then I thought maybe it could, but
only after years and years. But *Da Hah*
touched me a few days later, Ben. High up
in the mountains of Switzerland, up in the
Alps. We almost didn't take the cable car up
that morning because it was so foggy. But
we did anyway on the chance that things
might open up. And as we approached the
last leg of the journey, the weather lifted.
Those mountains were unbelievable!" Katie
stopped to wipe her eyes. "They were like

nothing I'd ever seen, before or since. They stretched from the right hand to the left as far as the eye could see. All laid out in a glorious splendor which shouted out the wonders of what *Da Hah*'s hands had done. The words were so loud in my ears, and yet there was perfect silence.

"I cried that morning, Ben. I soaked in all that glory. I saw what *Da Hah* had created. He's a great *Hah,* Ben. There is none like Him. While we go about messing up our lives, He goes around making beautiful things — things unlike anything we can imagine or think. I wish you could have seen all of that."

Katie paused. "My heart was healed that morning, Ben. *Yah,* I've cried many times since. And I still wish things had turned out differently. But *Da Hah* touched me with His glory. I remembered His promise that He would work all things for the best. And He'll do the same thing for you, Ben. He can . . . and He will, Ben. Don't doubt Him." Katie paused. She was out of breath. And she wondered what Lavina was thinking about her words. Was she being too emotional? Too personal?

Before she could look at Lavina, a nurse came in and checked the monitors. When she'd gone, Lavina came up to stand beside

Katie. Ben's *mamm* hugged her with both arms. "That was so beautiful, Katie. Thank you." She then turned to Ben. "My son, can you hear me? We love you more than we can say."

She *does* love him, Katie thought. And I must still have a little love for him too. But the fact remained that she was here because it was the right thing to do. Tomorrow she would be at the school again. Norman would still be the man who would love her and, unless she missed her guess, marry her.

CHAPTER THIRTEEN

Katie awoke and rubbed her hand on her neck. What time was it? There was no clock in the waiting room, but it felt like early morning. A nurse walked by in the hallway, and a woman she'd seen last night was sleeping on the chair across from her. There hadn't been time last evening in the brief glimpse they'd had of each other to find out what her trouble was. The concern on her face had been indication enough that someone she loved was facing a serious crisis.

Rising, Katie found her way down the hallway to Ben's room. Lavina was awake and standing by the window that had the drapes pushed back. She didn't look back when Katie walked in, apparently deep in her thoughts.

Two chairs sat beside Ben's bed. One of them had Lavina's shawl draped over the back. She should have slept in here with Lavina instead of staying in the waiting room, Katie thought. But that might have been too forward. Her mission was to help the family and Ben, but she wasn't his girlfriend any longer.

"Is he sleeping?" Katie asked as she stepped beside Lavina. The first signs of dawn were creeping into the sky outside.

"Yah." Lavina smiled. "Peacefully now. The doctor was in earlier. He thinks the worst is past, but I'm staying here for the day."

"So he's going to make it? That's great news. I'm so glad!" Katie gave Lavina a brief hug and glanced at Ben's still face. It would be so *wunderbah* to see a smile creep across his face right now. But she shouldn't be thinking such thoughts. Katie quickly added, "Is Leon still having the *Englisha* driver come for me?"

"Yah," Lavina replied as tears brimmed in her eyes. "I'm sure it was your speaking hope to Ben last night that pulled him through, Katie. We can never thank you enough."

Katie shook her head. "You had more influence than I did. A *mamm* is close to her boy's heart. But I'm glad if I could help."

"You'll never know how much you did." Lavina wrapped Katie in a tight hug. "Do you want to wait for the driver outside in

150

the waiting room?"

Katie's gaze moved back to Ben's face. "I think I will."

"Perhaps it would be for the best."

Lavina seemed to understand, much to Katie's relief.

"You won't tell him that I was here if he doesn't remember, okay?"

"Not if you don't want me to. Oh, Katie, I'm so sorry for what Ben did to you. I can never say how much. And I know Ben sorrows deeply himself. The boy has suffered more than you can imagine. What he did was a great sin, and I'm afraid he's not through suffering over it."

Katie pressed back her tears and slipped into the hallway. Perhaps it wasn't over for Ben, but it must be over for her. Now it was best if she went home and continued with her current life. She'd done her duty; no one could fault her for that. Back in the waiting room, Katie settled into a chair. The woman across the room was stirring, her eyes bleary. Katie was ready to ask who in her family was ill when Leon came in, his face drawn from stress. He didn't waste any words.

"Are you ready to leave, Katie?"

"*Yah.*" Katie rose and followed him down the stairs and past the receptionist desk. In the parking lot, Leon led the way to an *Englisha* car and tapped on the window. When the woman rolled it down, he motioned toward Katie. "This is who you'll be driving home. Katie can tell you where she lives. And if you would come back afterward, I'll be needing a ride home myself."

"I'll do that," the woman replied.

"Thank you for taking Sparky home last night," Katie told Leon. "And thank you for arranging this ride home." She smiled at Ben's *daett* before climbing into the passenger side of the vehicle. "*Gut* morning," she offered to the driver with a tired smile.

"Rough night, huh?" the woman asked. "So you're Katie? I'm Angela. Neighbor of the Stolls. Just trying to help out a little myself. It's awful what's been going on over at their place. A man getting shot in our neighborhood! Thank God they caught the guy."

"*Yah,* it was terrible." Katie gave directions to her home and then settled back into the seat as Angela drove out of town.

"Are you Ben's girlfriend?"

Katie sighed. "Well, I used to be. But now I'm just trying to help out, I guess. Ben was calling for me last night."

"Oh, that's darling," Angela cooed. "Did the two of you have a falling out?"

152

Katie nodded, a lump rising in her throat. "Something like that."

Angela winced. "Oh, that's rough, sweetheart. And hard to get over, I'm sure."

"I'm dating someone else now."

"Oh . . ." Angela forced a smile. "Moved on, huh? Well, it does happen. And I can't say I blame you." Angela paused, as if she'd just thought of something. "The new boyfriend didn't object to you spending time with the old one?"

Katie kept her eyes on the road ahead. "After I spoke with Ben for awhile, I spent the night in the waiting room. We weren't sure if he was going to recover. And his *mamm* was with us the whole time we were together." Katie struggled for words. "Ben . . . he was . . . in danger last night. He still is. When I left, he hadn't regained consciousness."

Angela reached over to touch Katie's arm. "I didn't mean to embarrass you, dear. It's okay. This just shows your tender heart. And you Amish people are so good at helping each other."

Katie gathered herself together. "We try."

Angela slowed down for Jesse's driveway. "And all of you do a great job. I'm glad I can do my small part this morning. Guess I'll get some more chances to help out."

Katie got out of the car after Angela pulled to a stop. "Thanks for the ride. I'm sure the Stolls will be very grateful for your help."

Katie stepped back, and Angela waved as she left. Katie suddenly realized she'd had nothing to eat and was starving. She made a beeline for the house, hoping she was in time for breakfast. Then she paused and switched direction. First, she had to see if Sparky was okay. Leon had found an Amish driver last night to bring him home so the horse wouldn't have to stand in the parking lot all night. She wanted to make sure he'd made it home and to rub his nose in thanks for the *gut* fast ride he'd given her to the hospital last night.

Katie pushed open the barn door to the sound of Jesse and his boys busy with the chores. She paused a moment to blink in the bright light of the lanterns.

"It's Katie!" Leroy hollered from the back of the barn. He came toward her at a fast walk, followed by Jesse and Willis, both of whom left their milk buckets sitting in the middle of the aisle.

"Is Ben still alive?" Leroy asked as they gathered around Katie.

Katie nodded and smiled. She was suddenly so tired she could fall asleep right here. But there was still the whole day of school in front of her.

"Did Leon request that you visit the hospital?" Jesse's voice rumbled in the morning stillness of the barn. "Or did you offer?"

Katie's eyes jerked open and she stepped back. "He asked, of course. He came to the schoolhouse right after we'd let out. He said Ben had taken a turn for the worse, and they hoped Ben would respond to my voice."

Jesse's face broke into a smile. "*Gut.* Emma told me that's what you'd told her, but Mabel thought you probably had called at Ben's house first and sort of invited yourself to the hospital."

"Why would Mabel say something like that?" The words flew out of Katie's mouth, as anger rose inside her. Mabel must be up to her old ways again!

Jesse shrugged. "That's Mabel. Well, I'm sure glad about Ben. The boy's made a mistake, but I didn't want to see him pass on so young. Now, boys, let's get busy."

They scurried off, and Katie made her way over to Sparky's stall. She reached through the slats to rub his nose that he'd extended toward her. Sparky nudged her hand, and Katie smiled. "Thanks for the fast ride last night. You did real *gut,* and I

155

hope someone gave you extra oats when you got home."

After a nicker from Sparky, Katie left, heading out of the barn and across the lawn. Her thoughts turned to Mabel and the probable confrontation ahead. That girl needed a *gut* chewing out and then some. Sticking her nose in where it had no business being.

Mamm met her at the door and wrapped Katie in her arms. "It's so *gut* to see you again. We were so worried. Is everything okay? Is Ben still alive?"

"He made it through the night," Katie shared. "Lavina didn't think I needed to stay any longer."

"Then Ben will be okay?"

"The doctors think so." Katie glanced around *Mamm* for any sign of Mabel. Faint clinking noises came from the kitchen, but Mabel hadn't appeared. The girl was thoroughly embarrassed, no doubt.

"Have you had breakfast?" *Mamm* asked.

"*Nee,* and I'm pretty hungry."

Mamm nodded. "Then go get cleaned up. You must feel like a cruddy mess after sitting in that hospital all night. We'll have breakfast ready in no time."

"I need to speak with Mabel first." Katie marched around *Mamm* without waiting for an answer. *Mamm* might try to calm her down, but she didn't want that right now. The furor inside was rising again, and she decided she might as well have it out with Mabel now.

Mabel looked up with a sweet smile when Katie rushed into the kitchen. "*Gut* morning, Katie. How is the little sweetheart?"

Behind Katie, *Mamm* stopped suddenly and gasped, but she didn't say anything further.

Katie stood a few steps away from Mabel. "I want you to hear me *gut,* Mabel. I've had enough of your interfering in my life. This spreading of rumors has to stop. And no more insinuations in an attempt to make me look bad! You have to stop, Mabel!"

"Rumors? Like what? Did I say something that wasn't true?" Mabel kept her smile pasted on. "You *did* go to the hospital that first time. And from the looks of you now, you spent the night with Ben at the hospital. What more is there to say?"

Katie couldn't keep the words in her mouth. "And it was all quite innocent and aboveboard — and you've made it sound like something's going on that isn't. You're spreading lies by the sin of deliberate omission, Mabel. You have a wicked mind, and you ought to be ashamed of yourself. I don't want you to go around to Norman again to get him all upset and rushing over to the schoolhouse thinking I'm forsaking him."

"I didn't say anything that wasn't true." Mabel put on a pout now. "And you *are* forsaking him. I heard you say so myself not that long ago. Your heart is still going pitty-pat, pitty-pat for Ben Stoll. And now you've spent the night in Ben's hospital room. If I were Norman, I'd drop you like the hot potato you are. Why should he wreck his life with a *frau* like you?"

Katie glared. Her temper was still boiling, but she obviously was getting nowhere with Mabel. Just like the Scriptures said, the wrath of man didn't work the righteousness of God. How often had she heard those words from the preachers on Sunday? But right now she couldn't help herself. "So what are you offering Norman? You? You hope to be his *frau*?"

Mabel smirked. "The thought has crossed my mind. I know I'd make a better *frau* for him than you ever could."

Katie could hardly think. Her head was throbbing and she was so hungry she thought she might faint in a moment. And Mabel was totally, completely impossible. "I'm not giving you a chance to steal Norman," Katie whispered. "Put that in your *kapp* and pin it fast."

Mamm moved between them, and Katie stepped back and sat on a kitchen chair.

"I want both of you to apologize right now." *Mamm*'s voice was firm. "Your *daett* will not tolerate this kind of disharmony in his house. You two girls will — and I mean it — you *will* get along. And Mabel, you will stop saying things that aren't true."

Katie groaned inside. *Mamm* was trying to be neutral, but Katie knew she'd done nothing wrong. She did get angry, though, so perhaps she should apologize for that.

Mabel spoke up first. "Sorry. I'll try to get along more. And I'll try to watch my words."

"And you, Katie?" *Mamm* turned toward her.

"I'm sorry I got angry."

"There!" *Mamm* bustled around the kitchen finishing up breakfast.

Mabel glanced at Katie with a broad smile on her face.

Obviously Mabel didn't feel defeated in the least, Katie thought. Nor did Mabel plan to cease her scheming.

CHAPTER FOURTEEN

The following Sunday evening after the hymn singing was over, Katie pulled herself into Norman's buggy. Norman slapped the reins before Katie was seated, so she was thrown against the seat back. Katie hung on and glanced at Norman. What was wrong with him tonight? The action had obviously been deliberate. Come to think of it, Norman hadn't appeared too happy during the entire hymn singing tonight. Only once had his gaze drifted her way, and even then he'd quickly looked away. She had at first written it off to his usual shyness, but, *nee,* it was more than that. Katie ventured to speak. "Is something wrong, Norman?"

He grunted but didn't say anything as he gripped the reins. Perhaps she was reading something into his actions that didn't belong. Yet Norman hadn't said nothing was wrong.

Katie tried again. "Maybe you'd better tell

me what's wrong."

"Nothing's wrong. Everything is just peachy keen."

Katie stared off into the darkness as the shadowy forms of trees whizzed past. What was this — a guessing game? Clearly Norman was upset. But about what? She hadn't done anything wrong. Everyone knew about her night spent at the hospital with the Stolls. Both Leon and Lavina had been profuse with their praise after the Sunday service this morning. They even credited her with being the inspiration for Ben's recovery. They'd made it clear to everyone that they'd asked her to visit Ben, and that Katie had been circumspect in her attitude and behavior. Lavina even pointed out that Katie had spent most of the night in the waiting room. Ben's parents had been a little overboard with their praise, Katie thought, so maybe that was the problem. Norman must think her proud. But that wasn't reason enough for this kind of coldness and treatment.

"You might as well tell me, Norman." Katie hung on to the buggy door. "I won't stop asking until you do."

Norman gave her a brief glare. "I said there was nothing wrong."

Katie sighed and settled back into the

buggy seat. Norman was acting worse than Mabel, and that was saying a lot.

They drove in silence until Norman pulled into Katie's driveway and parked in front of the hitching post. The lights from the house spread out onto the lawn. As usual, they were the last ones home. Norman always took his good old time in leaving the hymn singing. That was his right, and Katie wasn't about to try to change him. A *gut frau* didn't do that.

Katie cleared her throat. "I'm not leaving this buggy until you tell me what's upsetting you, Norman. If you don't talk, you can drive me on home to your parents' place and explain to them why I'm still sitting in your buggy."

Norman gave her a full stare now, his eyes fierce in the soft lantern light. He looked ready to throw her out of his buggy by force! He wouldn't though. For one thing, Norman had a thing about touching girls. She'd figured that out by now. "Well, are you going to tell me or not?" she persisted.

Norman exploded. "I'll tell you this, little Miss Goody Two–shoes! You've been hanging around that rotten Ben Stoll again. You even dared spend the night with him at the hospital. All so holy, of course, and full of sympathy and compassion. You even fooled

Ben's parents, but you're not fooling me. Now I see what Mabel warned me about. And I thank *Da Hah* in heaven that I've seen the light before I asked you to say the wedding vows with me. You are a disgrace to any man's love, and a shame and blight on anyone who ever weds you. And I hope it is Ben Stoll. You two deserve each other."

Norman stopped to catch his breath.

Katie clutched her pounding chest. From somewhere the words found their way to her lips. "None of that is true, Norman. I did go, yes, but I was only doing my Christian duty. I wouldn't have gone to the hospital if Leon hadn't come and asked me himself. He said Ben was calling for me, and that he might not live through the night. They wanted to do anything they could to help Ben survive."

Norman launched into his tirade again. "And why do you think Ben was calling for you? What reason would he have for that? What did you tell him the time you visited his hospital room before? Something obviously that stirred his passion. Did you kiss him like you used to? And don't tell me that's not true. I can see how you can't keep your hands off boys. You've been wanting me to kiss you ever since you first climbed into my buggy. What decent girl has those kinds of feelings, Katie? None! None, I say!"

Katie forced herself to keep breathing normally. "You don't really mean this, Norman. Have you listened to yourself? You're not making sense, and you're totally out of line."

Norman grabbed her arm hard. "I mean every word I said. How dare you act like you're so holy when you have such impure thoughts about me? Go find yourself a boyfriend who's like you. It certainly isn't going to be me." Norman let go of her arm. "Now, does that make you feel better? I *touched* you. Get out of my buggy. We're through."

Katie didn't move. "You can't really mean this, Norman. I've tried to love you. You know I've tried. You make it so hard . . ."

"And you're also a liar, Katie. You promised at the schoolhouse never to speak with Ben Stoll again. I'm not having a *frau* like you. Go now!"

"I didn't promise, Norman. I didn't." Katie groped for the handle of the buggy door, tears streaming down her face. There was no reason his words should hurt so deeply because they weren't true, yet they cut like the edge of a hot knife. She glanced up at Norman's face, but he was staring straight off into the night. Katie jumped

164

down and fled toward the house. Behind her, Norman's buggy whirled out of the driveway, Bonnie's hooves churning in the night air almost as if she were flying.

Mabel was standing inside the front door when Katie burst in. A smile spread over the teenager's face as she took in Katie's tears and demeanor.

"Well, well," Mabel said, relishing the moment.

Through her tears, Katie managed to say, "You're a schemer, Mabel. This will come back to haunt you. How do you expect to benefit from this anyway?"

Mabel's smile broadened. "Don't you worry about that, Katie. Just stay out of my way."

"I wouldn't get in your way in a thousand years. You're welcome to him. He's an immature boy."

"Boy?" Mabel smirked. "He's quite a man, if you ask me."

Katie took a deep breath. She felt great anger toward Mabel, but it wouldn't be right not to give her some warning. "Norman's someone you don't want to mess with, Mabel. He's got a dark side. You don't know what you're getting into."

Mabel tilted her head. "That's just sour grapes talking. Norman's just dumped you, if I don't miss my guess. You're bound to point the finger of blame at anyone except yourself."

"Okay then. Have it your way." Katie brushed past Mabel and headed up the stairs. "But don't say you weren't warned."

In her room, Katie collapsed on her bed. She muffled her sobs with a pillow. After a few minutes, she tried to pull herself together. Why was she crying? She really didn't love Norman, if it came right down to that question. And after his performance tonight, she was well rid of him. What if she'd agreed to marry him before knowing what he was really like? She shuddered. Still, the tears welled up again. She had so hoped this was the answer for a new start. A man who fit in with what she'd already accomplished — joining the church, teaching school, becoming more accepted in the community. But now the man she'd thought was sent from *Da Hah* had spoken words that stung her like fire. And the words were all false . . . so completely false and yet Norman chose to believe them.

Didn't the preachers say on Sundays that no one's word was to be totally discounted? That was how the community lived with each other, by looking for the truth within people's words and actions. Katie sobbed into the pillow some more. But what Norman accused her of couldn't be true, could it? That she was high and mighty? That she acted like a holy person? *Nee,* she was only trying to do what was right. And now here she was torn and bleeding, and she had no one she could turn to. Even *Mamm* wouldn't understand. And Mabel certainly wouldn't be supportive. Apparently she had plans to move in on Norman. How the girl would manage that was beyond Katie's comprehension, but Mabel had certainly shown herself quite resourceful.

Right now Katie needed someone to speak with or her heart was going to bleed all night. And tomorrow was another school day. She couldn't arrive all bleary-eyed and tear-stained. She owed the students and the community a decent day's work. The only one she could talk to was *Mamm.* Katie would have to try to talk to her even if she didn't understand. After what Norman had said, even words of rebuke *Mamm* might say would be like drops of honey on her wounded heart.

Katie crept downstairs and peered into the living room first and then the kitchen. No sign of Mabel. Creeping up to Jesse and *Mamm*'s bedroom door, Katie tapped. A floorboard creaked, and moments later the door opened and *Mamm* appeared.

"May I speak with you?" Katie whispered.

Mamm opened the door and followed Katie out to the living room. A bathrobe was wrapped over her nightgown.

"What is it, Katie?" *Mamm* found a seat beside Katie on the couch.

"Norman just told me he didn't want to go out with me anymore." Katie looked away. "I need someone to pray with me . . . or something because my heart hurts."

"Oh, Katie . . ." *Mamm* scooted closer and wrapped Katie in her arms. "Is it permanent . . . or just a spat?"

Katie grimaced. "Quite permanent."

"Did Mabel have a hand in this?"

"Yes, but not directly this time. Norman's upset that I spent the night at the hospital with Ben and his parents."

Mamm was puzzled. "But Leon and Lavina both approved, Katie. They said so at church today. They said someone was with you the entire time, and that they'd asked you to come. And Jesse thought it was okay too."

"I know, but Norman doesn't care about that."

"Did he say things that . . . hurt you?"

Katie choked back a sob. "Yes."

"Do you want to tell me?"

168

"I'd better not. Norman looks at things differently than I do. And I'm probably not what I should be, either."

"Don't be too hard on yourself. According to Lavina, you helped Ben pull through. That counts for a lot."

Katie managed a thin smile. "It really doesn't make much difference now. I'm not sure why I'm so upset about Norman. I know I didn't love him yet. Talking to you has helped in the past. I didn't want to lie awake most of the night crying so I knew I needed something."

"Then let's pray." *Mamm* got down on her knees and reached over to hold Katie's hand as she followed suit. "*Da Hah* knows what needs doing now."

Katie nodded. For once *Mamm* didn't have any lectures to give. Katie continued to weep, letting go of *Mamm*'s hand to cover her face. This must really be a serious problem for *Mamm* to have no ready answer.

Mamm's soft voice began. "Dear *Hah* in heaven, hear us tonight, we pray, in this moment of our sorrow. You know what Katie just went through. You heard the words that Norman spoke to her. And You know if they were right or wrong. Let Katie now take them to You for healing or repentance if she has done anything she shouldn't have. And forgive us all our sins even as we forgive all others tonight, including Norman and what he has done."

Katie sobbed even harder, pressing her face into the couch. *Mamm*'s words were cutting deep, but they were also providing a healing balm. She would accept all of them — and whatever else *Da Hah* chose to send her way in the days ahead. *Yah,* even if it meant living single the rest of her life. No young man would ask her home anytime soon with this blight on her record. Norman would see to that, and Mabel would be only too glad to help him.

"Are you able to forgive Norman?" *Mamm* asked, holding Katie's hand again. "And Mabel? Even though you think she had no great hand in this, I know she's caused trouble before."

Katie nodded. "I think so." She forced herself to pray. "I'm sorry, dear *Hah* for anything I've done wrong. I forgive Norman and Mabel for what I think they did wrong. Please heal this hurting heart of mine because I don't know what I can do about it."

Katie and *Mamm* stood. *Mamm* turned and gave Katie another tight hug. "Are you okay now?"

"Maybe." Katie managed a slight smile.

"Thank you for praying with me."

Mamm followed Katie to the bottom of the stairs. "You have a *gut* night's sleep now."

"I'll try," Katie whispered before turning and slipping up the stairs. And she would — as hard as that might be. She would trust *Da Hah* to make sense and good come out of this mess. She certainly couldn't.

CHAPTER FIFTEEN

Two Sunday nights after the breakup between Norman and Katie, Willis drove Sparky home from the Sunday night hymn singing, Katie seated beside him. She wanted to stay home or crawl into a hole somewhere, but when Willis offered to go with her, she'd accepted.

She also knew Norman left the hymn singing right behind them. With Mabel at his side. Somehow Mabel had contrived a way to get Norman to ask her home. How had the girl managed that feat? Katie wondered. Now Mabel would have to deal with Norman's temper and other eccentricities.

"It'll get better after awhile." Willis's voice oozed compassion. "And, besides, you didn't really want him anyway."

"I thought he was *Da Hah*'s choice for me. I was going to marry Norman — if he asked. And Mabel knew it. Now she's riding in his buggy."

Willis was quick to reply. "Sometimes things don't work out — and that's not always for the worst."

Katie shot a quick glance at Willis. "You don't seem to carry a very high opinion of Norman."

Willis laughed. "Norman's okay, I guess. He just never seemed to fit you very well."

"Maybe you're right." Katie let out another long sigh. "How did Mabel do it? That's what I want to know. It took forever before he asked me."

"Well, Mabel's my sister, so don't spread this around . . ." Willis chuckled before continuing. "From what a little birdie told me, Ruth Troyer told Norman's *mamm* what a great match Mabel would make for the grief-stricken Norman. I'm guessing Mabel put Ruth up to it. I'm sure you can guess the rest from there."

"I hope Mabel likes what she gets." Katie turned around in the seat to look at the buggy lights behind them. *Yah,* from the gait of the horse, it was Norman and Mabel. Katie sighed. Would Mabel dare hold Norman's hand on their first date? Even if she didn't, Mabel wasn't such a saint herself. The girl had spent plenty of time getting experience by kissing Mose Yutzy out in the feed bin when she was sneaking around.

173

Katie rebuked herself. She shouldn't be thinking such nasty thoughts about Mabel or Norman — or anyone else. She was even a bit ashamed of the smile that came to her face when she thought of how the two schemers deserved each other.

"I think Mabel's got herself a deal this time." Willis was also watching the buggy lights behind them via his rearview mirror. "Norman's going to be serious about getting married, considering how you broke his heart. It might help him save face to do it quickly."

Katie snorted. "I'm the one who should be talking about a broken heart."

Willis didn't laugh. "Do you know what Norman's spreading around the community? I don't want to hurt your feelings, but I want you to be aware of what's going on."

Katie sighed. "*Yah,* I know. Norman says I'm sneaky, that I stretch the truth, that I betray hearts, and that I have a hard time keeping decent thoughts in my head about guys."

"Whoa, Sparky!" Willis stopped the buggy at a stop sign and turned to stare at Katie. "Have you heard all that already?"

Katie sighed. "No, but I used to date Norman, remember? I know how he thinks. I also know Mabel and what she told him about me — most of it untrue. And I know what both of them are capable of. Norman is saying such things, isn't he?"

"Yah." Willis didn't look at her.

"Willis, I hope someday you have better success with love than I do," Katie said.

Willis touched her arm. "It'll get better. Tonight's the worst, Katie. Just remember that."

Willis clucked to Sparky, and the buggy lurched forward. "There will be someone out there for you, Katie. I know it. Someone who doesn't sell drugs or dump you because you do what you think is right."

Katie snorted again. "The chances are getting slimmer, that's all I can say. And worse than that, can you imagine who's going to ask me home? What with the reputation I now have?"

"Like I say, it'll get better."

Willis was trying to comfort her, but it wasn't working. She still felt quite low — and not without reason. The evening ahead of her with Mabel and Norman spending time together downstairs wouldn't be easy.

"I'm finished, Willis." Katie moaned. "Finished with love and everything else."

Willis touched her arm again, his voice comforting. "When the heart hurts, it often says things it doesn't mean. You'll feel better tomorrow. You still have your teaching job, and the children love you. And so do we — your family — even Mabel, I think."

"You are the sweetest thing, Willis. Did anyone ever tell you that?"

Willis laughed. "*Nee,* but thanks. Now, if a certain someone would just see things that way, my life would be nice."

"Oh!" Katie cooed. "Have you asked her home yet?"

Willis's face fell. "*Yah,* and she turned me down."

Katie sat up straight. "Tell me who it was, and I'll speak with her. I'll tell this girl what an awful mistake she's making."

Willis laughed again. "You'll do nothing of the sort. She'll come around. And if she doesn't, then it wasn't meant to be."

"Stop being such a saint," Katie told him. "I want to weep and howl and go to bed in sackcloth and ashes tonight. Instead I'll have to deal with those two lovebirds sitting on the porch swing or in the living room. Do you think I could make a wild dash for the upstairs and get out of sight before they see me?"

"*Nee.* I think you'd be better off speaking to them." Willis pulled into the driveway and stopped beside the barn. "It won't get any easier, and the problem has to be faced sometime — especially if Mabel has designs on marrying Norman. And you can depend on it that she does. A *gut* start tonight between the two of you would go a long way to smoothing things over. I know it will be hard, but try, Katie. For the rest of the family, if nothing else."

Katie caught her breath. "Is this why you offered to drive me tonight, Willis? To help smooth things over for the family?"

Willis smiled as he climbed out of the buggy. "*Nee,* Katie. I came because of you. But it will be for the best — even for your own sake — if you accept this situation graciously."

Katie opened the buggy door. "Then I will do what I can. And thanks for driving home with me, Willis. You're a real gentleman. Tell me something else quickly though. Do you have suggestions for a storybook I could read to the children at school?"

"That's a sudden change of subject," Willis said, as he unfastened the tug on his side of the buggy. "But, in fact, I do. I'll get it for you tomorrow morning."

"Thanks!" Katie climbed down and they finished unhitching in silence. Willis vanished into the barn with Sparky in tow. Waiting beside the buggy, Katie forced a smile when Norman and Mabel drove in. Norman pulled up to the hitching post and climbed out to secure Bonnie. Without a glance in Katie's direction, he marched toward the house with Mabel beside him.

Katie was sobbing into her hands when Willis returned.

"Will you be all right?" Willis asked as he shifted on his feet in front of her.

"*Yah,* I think so. I'm ready to go inside. It's just hard, that's all."

The two walked across the lawn and entered through the washroom door. Katie splashed cold water on her face, but her eyes still looked red and teary. Willis waited until she shooed him on. "Go in. I'll come in a minute." Katie soon heard Willis's cheerful voice coming from the living room. Whatever his comment, it was followed by laughs. Willis was trying hard to keep everyone happy tonight. And she would have to play her part for the good of them all.

The sound of Willis closing the stair door soon came, and with her head held high, Katie stepped into the living room. Norman glanced up and just as quickly looked down at the floor again. Mabel, though, had a smile on her face as she stared at Katie. "There you are. I was wondering where you'd gotten to. Willis just went past. Was that you standing beside the buggy when we pulled in?"

Katie pasted on her best smile. Mabel knew where she'd been. She wasn't blind. But bringing up that fact wasn't going to help. She managed to keep her voice friendly. "*Yah,* that was me. Waiting on Willis to come back from the barn."

"Willis was so nice tonight," Mabel cooed. "Bringing you home. I couldn't ask for a better brother."

"He was a real gentlemen," Katie agreed and headed toward the stair door. She'd done her duty and was getting out of there.

Mabel though wasn't finished. "Katie, please, let's not fight on this my special night. Can't you see that things are so much better this way?"

"I'm glad you think so," Katie said, not turning around. They had been over this last week after Mabel announced that Norman was bringing her home. Why rehash it now? Likely for Norman's benefit.

"I really hope there are no hard feelings, Katie." Mabel's voice oozed like honey. "Norman and I were talking on the way home, and he sees it now himself. I don't know how we both could have been so blind. Me . . . blending in so well on that first night when Norman brought you home. Don't you remember, Katie? How it went with the ice cream and cherry pie? It was already *Da Hah* showing us what really ought to happen. Aren't you glad everyone listened before it was too late?"

The girl had more gall than seven foxes in a henhouse. Katie turned around. "Norman, do you agree with this . . . this version of events?"

"Of course he does," Mabel chirped.

Katie waited. If Norman were going to marry into the family, he might as well face her on the first night. "I'd like to hear him say it."

"It was for the best." Norman finally looked up, meeting her gaze. "Things weren't working out between us, Katie. You know that."

"Then I hope there will be no more false words spoken around the community about me from either one of you." Katie knew her temper was rising, but this needed saying. "I apologize for anything I did wrong during our brief courtship, Norman. And I hope you can forgive and leave things at that."

"Of course he can," Mabel said. She turned to Norman with a smile. "You certainly can, can't you, Norman?"

"I can." He managed a few more seconds of eye contact with Katie before he looked down at the floor.

"Then I will hold no hard feelings." Katie turned toward the stair door.

"Oh, this is so sweet," Mabel cooed behind her as Katie left. She'd noticed that Mabel wasn't sitting too close to Norman. She must have figured that out already. The man had more problems than a person could shake a stick at, Katie thought. In a way she should be happy she wasn't sitting on the couch with him. But it still stung — being thrown aside like a used rag. Twice that had happened now, though for different reasons. Was there something wrong with her? Something deep inside that she couldn't see? Why else would Ben so easily despise their relationship, risking it on such an evil thing as drug dealing? And now Norman. He had his reasons, which were simple enough to understand. She wasn't *gut* enough for his high standards.

Katie flopped down on the bed and lay there for a long time. Tears wouldn't even come anymore. They were all dried up inside her. How could she ever trust her feelings again? First, she'd loved Ben, and look what came of that. Then, she'd hoped to love Norman as *Mamm* had come to love Jesse. What was so wrong with her that she couldn't find happiness with someone? Was

Da Hah punishing her? If so, for what sin?

If she was so awful, should she just flee and find solace in her friendships with the Mennonite youth group again? *Nee,* that wouldn't work this time. She was a church member now. And so much had changed even with Margaret and Sharon. Sharon was dating now, and Margaret's wedding was coming up soon. Maybe the wedding would cheer her up . . . give her hope for herself — if she wasn't so far gone as to be beyond hope.

Katie groaned and slid down on her knees. "Dear *Hah,* help me or I'm going to go mad — if I haven't already."

CHAPTER SIXTEEN

Ben eased himself up on his elbows to glance out the front-room window. It was Saturday afternoon, some three weeks after his setback with the infection. The buggy that had just driven into his parents' driveway looked familiar. Moments later Deacon Elmer climbed out of one side and Bishop Miller out of the other. Ben sighed. He'd been expecting something like this. Both the deacon and the bishop arriving together meant something serious was going on.

Obviously he was causing great concern for the community with his recent incarceration and now the shooting. If he were a member of the church, the *bann* would be used on him for sure. But since he wasn't a member, there was little that could be done. And yet both men were here so they had something up their sleeves.

Mamm stuck her head out of the kitchen. "Who is it, Ben?"

"The deacon and the bishop."

Mamm gasped as she rushed to the window. "I didn't expect this. I wonder if Leon heard anything about what might be going on."

"I'm sure *Daett* would have told me if he knew," Ben responded. And his *daett* would have, if nothing else but to lecture him on how he ought to conduct himself for this visit. Instructions Ben already knew. "Act humble and don't talk back." He'd been told that dozens of times in his life, but *Daett* still repeated the words whenever he knew the ministers were involved.

"*Ach,* the house is in a total mess." *Mamm* wiped her hands on her apron and rushed back into the kitchen.

That was the least of Ben's concerns right now, he figured. The ministers wouldn't even notice the condition of the house. If *Mamm* fed them some of the blackberry pie she'd made this morning, sliding ample pieces onto plates, the two wouldn't see a speck of dirt. *Mamm* no doubt knew this and was preparing the plates even now. Ben couldn't stop a smile from flitting briefly across his face at the thought. Then he frowned again. The ministers probably wanted to make sure he didn't testify against the shooter the police had captured.

The detectives had been by again just yesterday, urging his full cooperation in the upcoming trial. With his recent illness, his mind was still foggy but he'd told them he wouldn't be testifying. That much he knew. But they still made their points in favor of him testifying: another criminal would be placed behind bars, his family would be safe, and Ben could rest easier knowing he was doing what was right. Those were their *Englisha* arguments, anyway.

But Ben had shaken his head. "We Amish believe in turning the other cheek and practicing forgiveness."

"But what about justice?" they'd asked. "Forgiveness isn't all that's necessary for people to live peacefully with each other. And you've testified in court before."

Ben knew the answer to that point, even if he hadn't told the detectives. True believers risked all in the hopes of touching the heart of the transgressor, even as Christ had given all to reach lost and dying sinners. This time Ben was staying with the beliefs of his people. He would not testify. He realized this was taking the hard road. The easiest decision would be to go along with what the detectives wanted. He had a place of shelter at his grandparents' place. In fact, he'd already be there if it hadn't been for his setback. His family would be out of danger. That someone outside the community would trace him to his grandparents' place was a possibility, but not a large one. But he couldn't testify, even in the face of the police's disappointment.

Mamm interrupted his thoughts by rushing out of the kitchen again and heading for the doorway. He'd been watching the bobbing black hats draw closer to the house and now *Mamm* opened the door and stepped out on the porch. Ben listened to the low murmur of voices as she spoke with the ministers. Soon *Daett*'s voice joined in, and *Mamm* opened the door again. Ben sat up straight on the couch, as the two ministers followed *Mamm* inside, holding their hats in their hands.

They nodded. "*Gut* afternoon, Ben."

"*Gut* afternoon." Ben tried to sit up even straighter, but the discomfort was too much.

Mamm set up chairs, and when the men were seated facing Ben, she vanished into the kitchen again. *Daett* sat near the window waiting, his gaze turned toward the floor. Whatever the ministers had told him outside must be a heavy load to bear, Ben figured. He turned toward Deacon Elmer when the deacon cleared his throat. "Are you getting along okay, Ben? With the latest . . . setback?

We heard it was pretty serious."

Ben shrugged. "I'm still on antibiotics, but the doctors think the worst is past."

"We missed you at church on Sunday again," Bishop Miller said, his eyes kind but sorrow hung behind them.

Ben wished they'd just come out and say what they'd come to say. But there would be no hurrying these two. "Thank you." Ben smiled back. "I miss attending church."

Bishop Miller didn't answer as *Mamm* came out of the kitchen carrying two plates holding huge slices of blackberry pie. "I know you two have to be hungry. And I had fresh pie from this morning just sitting right out there on the table."

Both ministers smiled and leaned back in their chairs.

Mamm held out the plates. "Do eat all you want. I have plenty where that came from."

"Do I get some?" *Daett* teased, and they all laughed.

"Of course!" *Mamm* joined in the laughter. "And I'll be right back with glasses of milk."

Ben watched *Mamm* leave and return moments later with *Daett*'s pie and the milk glasses on a tray. No one offered him pie, but *Mamm* knew he wouldn't be able to eat any.

He *did* miss church, Ben thought, his

mind going back to the prior conversation. But what he missed worse was seeing Katie. She was more and more in his thoughts of late. Katie was even drifting in and out of his dreams. His recent illness had made things even worse. He would almost declare at times that Katie had been near him during his delirium, but he knew that wasn't possible. Katie had come once to accept his apology, but she wouldn't have come again.

Still, he thought he'd heard her voice. The sound had seemed to fall in and out of his hearing like waves of the ocean ebbing and flowing over his soul. He had called to her, reaching out for her with all his might, but nothing on his body had moved. And his voice didn't escape his mouth. He'd mentioned hearing Katie while he'd been in and out of consciousness to his *mamm* after he felt better, but *Mamm* had just given him a weary smile. She probably thought he was losing his mind thinking such things.

Now the voice of Bishop Miller jerked Ben out of his thoughts. When he forced himself to focus, the bishop was in the middle of saying something to *Daett,* and he'd only caught the last words: "*Yah,* perhaps there will be rain tomorrow."

Daett smiled briefly. "The threshing crew will make much better progress this fall if we don't have a wet one."

"They'll be at my place next Thursday," Deacon Elmer offered. "It's a pretty good crew this year, if I must say so myself."

"That's because you're on it," Bishop Miller said with a laugh.

Daett smiled. "One of these days an old man like you will have to find easier things to work on."

"When I can't totter to the barn, then I'll stay off the threshing crew," Deacon Elmer declared.

Ben felt a smile creep across his face. Deacon Elmer's determination to hang tough on his threshing-crew spot was a well-known story in the community. One which everyone played along with, likely because they hoped to earn an easier handling when it came time for Deacon Elmer to call at their places on Saturday afternoons. But Deacon Elmer was a jolly man in his own right and easy to befriend. A strange characteristic for a man who often had difficult calls to make for the church. But then a man's calling wasn't of his own choosing. *Da Hah* made that choice by use of the lot. At least that was how Ben had been taught. Recently he hadn't spent much time questioning his faith. He'd made a pretty decent mess of his life without adding unbelief to his list of sins.

Deacon Elmer put aside his empty plate. "Well, we're taking up these people's time on a sunny afternoon, so why don't we begin?"

"*Yah,* I agree." Bishop Miller set his empty plate on the floor. "Let us pray."

They all bowed their heads as Bishop Miller led out. "Now dear *Hah* in heaven, we come again at this hour to ask Your guidance. Give us grace. Give us wisdom on how to say what needs saying. And give us all tender hearts to respond to Your will. Amen."

"Amen," Deacon Elmer echoed.

"You go on." Bishop Miller nodded toward Deacon Elmer. "I'll join in if something else needs saying."

Deacon Elmer looked down for a moment before he began. "There have been quite a few complaints among the community concerning what has been happening in your life, Ben. We all know, of course, about your arrest and imprisonment."

"I deeply regret my past actions," Ben said. "I've asked *Da Hah* and my family for their forgiveness."

With a nod, Deacon Elmer continued. "We wish to express our heartfelt sympathy for your recent illness, and even for the time

190

you spent in jail. But you must realize that the way of the transgressor is hard, and that *Da Hah* will not be mocked. What a man sows, he will also surely reap. This the Scriptures teach most clearly." Deacon Elmer looked directly at Ben.

Ben nodded. He didn't disagree with any of this, but he knew there was more to come. There had to be.

Apparently satisfied with his reaction, Deacon Elmer continued. "We know you've repented of your involvement in illegal drugs and suffered the *Englisha* punishment for your involvement. You say you've repented before *Da Hah,* and that's *gut.* Ben, there's another issue to consider. A year ago you testified against others, which resulted in heavy jail sentences for them and a lighter one for you. Is that true?"

Ben nodded again.

Deacon Elmer frowned. "Testifying against someone is not our way, Ben. How did you get involved in such a deal? In placing your welfare before others? That is not what we believe. We are to reach out to those who do wrong so we can draw them to a saving knowledge of Jesus Christ. We are to love those who hate us and do us ill, just as we are to love those who are dear to our hearts."

"I didn't plan things to turn out the way they did," Ben said. "I knew my actions were wrong, and in my repentance and sorrow, I wanted to confess what I'd done. I was lost and confused and didn't seek godly counsel. And for that I am sorry. I was wrong in so many things back then. But I've changed. I want to embrace the Amish faith and ways."

Neither of them looked convinced.

Bishop Miller took over. "And now we hear that you are being asked to once again testify. Is this true also?"

Ben looked at both Bishop Miller and Deacon Elmer before answering. "*Yah,* that is true, but I've told the detectives I wouldn't testify because it's not the way of the Amish."

"Did you perhaps protest the last time also, but you eventually gave in?" Deacon Elmer asked. "You've known how we feel about such things."

Bishop Miller didn't wait for Ben to answer. "This testifying cannot be allowed, Ben." His voice was firm. "Our beliefs should not be disgraced in this way. To have done this once is bad enough. Our testimony is to be held up like a light on a hill for all to see. That is not happening in your situation. We must forbid you to testify if you want to continue to be part of our community, Ben."

Ben nodded. "I understand. I have already decided not to testify, and I will keep to that decision to uphold our ways."

Deacon Elmer took a deep breath. "We are thankful to hear this, Ben. But we believe we must take further measures in light of what you've done in the past and until this trial has finished. We know these detectives won't be easily turned aside and the *Englisha* have many legal rules. We are asking you to voluntarily leave the community for a time, Ben. Even going to your grandparents' place isn't *gut* enough now. When the flock of *Da Hah* is in danger, we must not think of ourselves. As shepherds we must do what we can to keep everyone safe."

Ben winced. "Even if I promise not to testify?"

Deacon Elmer looked out the window for a second before looking back to Ben. "We wish this could be otherwise. And we don't want to doubt you, but you have testified in the past and brought danger to our community. We will continue to pray for you, of course. There is also another matter we considered." The deacon paused and looked at Bishop Miller.

"I thought so." Ben cut in as he leaned back against the couch. "Perhaps you'd better tell me everything now instead of beating around the bush." From the corner of his eye, Ben noticed that his *daett* had turned pale. Ben realized he'd broken one of his *daett*'s primary rules: "Act humble and don't talk back." He looked away. He might have spoken out of order, but his head was pounding and he wanted to know the rest — he needed to know. His thoughts went to Katie. Was she the "other matter"?

"There is . . ." Bishop Miller hesitated. "There is the matter of Katie Raber."

"What has she to do with any of this?" Ben asked.

Bishop Miller held up his hand. "Let me finish, Ben. It is known that Katie spent the night with you at the hospital recently."

Mamm gasped and *Daett* sat up straight. Concern was etched on both their faces.

Sympathy crossed Bishop Miller's face, but he continued. "I know what your parents said at church on Sunday. And I don't say that we doubt their story, but there is also another version of what happened that we've heard."

Ben was confused. "You'll have to explain this to me. Katie came to see me, *yah*. She came with her brother Willis when I was

194

first shot. I sent a message to her, asking her to come so I could say I was sorry in person. But she did not stay long, much less overnight."

Bishop Miller looked at Ben's *daett* and then his *mamm.*

"Bishop Miller, Ben wasn't awake when Katie came to the hospital the second time. He was delirious from the infection. He called repeatedly for her, and when we thought he might die, we hoped Katie's presence would help him find the courage to fight to get well. Leon went to the schoolhouse and asked Katie to come. And she agreed — which helped Ben recover! But let me say at once that Katie did not spend the night in Ben's room. She slept in the waiting room. She insisted on that. Even when I offered the chair next to mine in Ben's room, she wanted to make sure there would be no misunderstanding with Ben or the community."

"And Ben was unconscious the whole time Katie was present," *Daett* added. "We weren't even sure if Ben could hear her voice or if he knew she was present."

"That's very helpful to know," Deacon Elmer said. "Still it wasn't decent, if you ask me. Even under the special circumstances. Katie is a church member in *gut* standing, and she shouldn't have gone to speak with Ben."

"Then it was our fault," Leon stated. "Ben was calling for Katie, and we hoped she'd help him want to live. You shouldn't blame Katie. She came very reluctantly. I'm sorry if we did something you consider wrong, but Ben's life was in danger, and we thought anything that might help should be tried."

Bishop Miller held up his hand. "Then we will say no more about the matter."

Ben stared at everyone. He moaned as he held his head. "I'm not sure I understand. Katie spent the night at the hospital?"

"Ben knew nothing of Katie's visit," *Mamm* repeated, choking back a sob. "That is why he's having such a hard time understanding this."

"I see." Bishop Miller stroked his beard and looked perplexed. "We just want to protect a church member from any danger. This new knowledge adds further confusion to the matter. Even though the situation is innocent enough when it's told in detail, many people won't hear the entire story. Considering the current circumstances, I believe it best if Ben still separate from the community until his legal issues are cleared up and he chooses to set things right with the community and church."

196

"Then I will leave when I'm well enough to travel." Ben stood up, still holding his head and swaying slightly. "Early next week, perhaps."

"Where will he go?" *Mamm* wailed to the bishop. "He's our son."

"I can find a place in town," Ben responded.

"I'm sorry this has to happen like this, Ben." Bishop Miller reached over and placed his hand on Ben's shoulder to steady him.

"I understand," Ben said. "I'm not feeling well, and I need to lie down. I will do as you ask." He turned and made his way to the staircase. He felt his way up the stairs, taking each step slowly and carefully. Heavy silence hung over the living room. They can straighten out the details themselves, Ben figured. He wasn't going to make any more trouble for Katie, but hearing that she'd been at the hospital when he was delirious was turning his world upside down. She cared enough to come! It was her voice he'd heard! Did that mean she possibly still cared for him? That couldn't be, could it? Not after what he'd done.

Ben finally made it to the top of the stairs and turned into his room. He held his head as he gently sat down on his bed and then gingerly laid back and swung his legs up.

CHAPTER SEVENTEEN

Ben packed the last of his clothes in a suitcase on the following Thursday morning, stuffing in one last shirt before closing the lid. *Mamm* was waiting in the living room downstairs, her face still tear-stained. She was ready to drive him to his new apartment in town. *Daett* had been nice enough to find a place for him and pay the first two months rent. Ben assured his *daett* he'd be back on his feet and working by then, able to pay his own way. He wouldn't and couldn't work for the Amish carpenter crew again. Not just because of his jail record, but because of the church troubles. Deacon Elmer had been over on Tuesday night, checking up on things. He'd made it clear to Ben's *daett* that the ministry hadn't changed their minds about Ben. After all, something needed to be done because of the uproar he'd caused. The community wouldn't rest unless they knew their leaders were taking a strong stand.

Ben now realized that Enos Kuntz was behind most of the effort. After the ministers' Saturday visit, this knowledge had fallen into place. Katie had been dating Enos's son, Norman. That much Ben had known, but he hadn't known that Norman had quit dating Katie because she'd come to the hospital to see him. At that news, Ben had wanted to rush over to Katie's house. Hope had risen strong. Would Katie consider a renewal of their relationship now that Norman was out of the way? But when he'd asked *Mamm* about it, she'd thought otherwise.

"Katie's heart is still torn," *Mamm* informed him. "She came to the hospital out of Christian duty. In fact, Katie requested that if you didn't remember she was there, you not be told."

Ben was sure Katie knew that request couldn't be kept, especially considering how everyone in the community eventually heard about everything. But it showed where Katie's heart was. She didn't consider a full healing of what had been lost possible — and she was probably right. Nothing could ever be the same. Ben paused. At the very least, he should thank her. But how? Going over to her house was out of the question.

Grabbing a pen and paper from his dresser, he jotted down his thoughts:

Hi, Katie. Please hear me out. I don't know what to say or how to say it, but I'll try. First, thanks so very much for coming down to the hospital that night I was so sick. I just found out today that you came! I can tell Mamm thinks most of the credit for my being alive belongs to you. And you obviously didn't expect any benefit. It shows how great and beautiful your spirit is.

I've heard you lost your boyfriend over that visit. I'm sorry about that — and about a hundred other things I did wrong. I know there's no hope of ever healing the hurt between us. I don't deserve you, and you don't deserve someone like me. I had so much with you, and I lost it through my own foolishness.

Perhaps you won't believe me, but I need to say this anyway. I wanted to tell you while we were together, but then I'd have to explain, and I thought I could just quit and no one would ever know. Katie, you were the reason I wanted to leave the secret life I'd been living. At the time of my arrest, I had quit working for Rogge for several weeks. I know that's small comfort. Thank you for helping me do it though.

You touch people's lives for the better, Katie. I hope you never doubt that. I hope Da Hah uses you to touch many more people in the world for His good. I'm one of those you've helped, and I will forever be the better for it. May you have a fulfilling life, Katie.

Thank you again,
Ben

Ben folded the paper, pushed it inside an envelope, and sealed it. There! he thought. He felt much better. This wouldn't do any good other than perhaps encourage Katie while she went through this troubling time, but at least it was something. This much, at the very least, he owed her. He went down the stairs dragging the suitcase.

Mamm rose when he entered the living room, attempting a smile. "So you're all ready and packed?"

"*Yah.*"

"Will we be seeing much of you?" *Mamm* asked, her eyes glistening.

"I'll come home when I can," Ben said softly. "But I don't have a place in town to keep Longstreet or a buggy."

Mamm hugged him. "It's not that far, Ben. Your *daett* and I can drive in to visit every once in awhile."

Mamm was grasping at straws, but they both knew that the Amish who were asked to leave the community rarely came back.

"Shall I get the horse and buggy ready?"

Mamm nodded. "*Yah,* and I'll be out to help hitch up. I think your *daett* has Longstreet harnessed in his stall."

Brenda came out to the kitchen and gave Ben a tight hug. "You take care of yourself now."

"I will." Ben's smile was weak as he gave his sister a kiss on the cheek.

He turned, opened the front door, stepped through it with his suitcase, and closed the door behind him. He made his way to the buggy and slid the suitcase under the backseat. Going into the barn, he led Longstreet out and to the buggy. *Mamm* was waiting, holding the buggy shafts up so he could maneuver Longstreet into place.

When they finished hitching, *Mamm* climbed in, and Ben threw her the lines. Once he was on the seat beside her, Ben took the reins. Waving to Brenda standing by the livingroom window, Ben turned Longstreet down the drive. He could tell Brenda was crying. His own eyes were dry, but he knew the tears would come tonight when no one was around. This was a lot more difficult than he'd anticipated.

Mamm and son rode silently, listening to Longstreet's hooves beat a steady tattoo on the blacktop.

Mamm broke through Ben's thoughts. "Perhaps the ministers will change their minds. You know they do sometimes, and then you could come back home."

Ben shook his head. "It's not going to happen, *Mamm*. You know that. We'll have to see how things go with the *Englisha* police and court before we can cross that bridge. And there's Katie, of course. My staying away should make her life much easier. I don't want to make more trouble for her."

Mamm wiped her eyes. "I'm sorry about you and Katie, Ben. She's a jewel. She'll make someone a very *gut frau* someday."

"You don't have to tell me that. I know what I lost."

Mamm didn't say anything for a few minutes. "I've never heard one of our women speak to you like Katie spoke beside your bed, Ben. She shared words of faith and hope. Of course, she thought you might not live, but still her words and thoughts moved me very deeply. You ought to mend

204

your relationship with her, Ben. You should at least try."

Ben's laugh was hollow. "And how exactly am I supposed to do such a thing? I did a very bad thing. I've been arrested and spent time in jail. And now I've been shot and have detectives calling at my door. And who knows whether someone won't come after me or those I love again? What Amish woman deserves something like that?"

"I suppose it does seem impossible," *Mamm* allowed. "But then you didn't hear the young woman speak to you. Katie still loves you, Ben. I'm sure of it. You shouldn't throw that away. *Da Hah* can do amazing things when we trust Him and ask Him for help."

"*Mamm,* come on now. I'm your son. You are a little biased, you know. And I know you don't want me to leave. Stop saying things like that. If the ministers heard you say Katie was interested in me, they might place her in the *bann.*"

Mamm smiled. "They're not hearing me right now, are they? And you won't tell them, I'm sure."

Ben smiled. "*Nee,* I wouldn't do anything more to hurt you or Katie."

Mamm's voice trembled. "I worry about you being in town, Ben. So near to the people and things that led you astray. You've always been attracted to the *Englisha* things. I pray that you don't fall for them again. And watch the books you read in town. Look what reading those war stories brought you. I should never have allowed those books in my house."

"I've changed, *Mamm,*" Ben said quietly. "I'm going to be all right, and I'm going to keep our faith."

Silence fell between them until *Mamm* ventured a question. "Where did you get the name 'Longstreet,' Ben? I've always wondered."

"I think I'd best not tell you."

"That's what I thought. Oh, Ben!"

"I got it from a book on the Civil War. Katie loved that name when I told her about it. And she's sound in the faith, *Mamm.*"

Mamm sputtered a bit. "Katie doesn't have any sense on that point. And she was in love with you. We'll change your horse's name when I get back home, that's for sure. What if the ministers ever found out?"

Ben shrugged and pulled the envelope out of his pocket. "You can do what you wish, but would you give this to Katie after things have died down a bit? I wouldn't want either of you to get into trouble."

Mamm held the envelope. "What did you

write, Ben?"

"I thanked her for coming to the hospital that night. And I wished her well with the rest of her life."

"Do you think this is wise? To send a letter to her?"

"*Yah, Mamm.* It needed to be done. Just give it to Katie sometime later. No one will care after I'm gone for a bit."

"Then you really are cutting all ties with us . . . with the community?"

"I don't plan to, *Mamm.* But we don't know how this situation will end."

"Don't become bitter, Ben," *Mamm* begged. "The ministers are doing what they think is best."

Ben looked away. "I know."

Mamm slipped the envelope into her dress pocket.

Ben turned toward her. "I love you and *Daett.* I'm sorry for everything — for the hurt I've caused. Thank you for taking such good care of me these last few weeks. I know it couldn't have been easy."

Mamm pulled her handkerchief out. "You're our son, Ben. Of course we'll take care of you when you need it. Even when the way looks dark for us we'll do it because we love you and *Da Hah* loves you."

Ben nodded. "Thank you. And tell *Daett*

I'm sorry. He's done more for me than I deserve. I can't imagine the shame and pain I put the family through by breaking the law and being sentenced to jail. I know I didn't say it very often, but I really am sorry. I'll never do something like that again."

Mamm smiled through her tears. "You know the door at home is always open, Ben. So don't be forgetting that. Visit us as much as possible."

"I'll try. And don't forget the letter to Katie. It's important to me."

As the outskirts of Dover approached, they fell silent as they listened to the steady drum of Longstreet's metal shoes hitting the pavement. They were pounding away like the minutes of a person's life, Ben thought. The sound of life moving forward with a power of its own that no person could stop. The Amish surrendered to its flow, giving in willingly. He didn't feel like giving in right now. He felt like fighting, like trying to get back what he'd lost.

"How are you going to get around?" *Mamm* asked, interrupting his thoughts.

"I'm going to get a bicycle."

Mamm smiled and looked relieved. She was probably glad he wasn't thinking about getting a car. But now he'd have to buy a bike even though he'd meant the comment as a joke. He hadn't really thought about the matter much, but maybe riding a bicycle was a good idea.

"*Yah,*" Ben said, forcing a smile. "That's what I'm going to do."

CHAPTER EIGHTEEN

Katie drove Sparky toward the Mennonite church house on the other side of the community. The October leaves were beginning to change into their first touch of deep reds and gold. She was wearing her nicest dress, and the wedding present of a quilt she and *Mamm* had worked on for Margaret was wrapped and safely stashed behind the buggy seat. This was a mighty strange feeling, Katie thought. Going to a wedding in the afternoon and on a Saturday was very different from the Amish tradition. But that just went to show how many differences there were between her faith and that of the Mennonites. Most of those differences were found in practices like this. Neither of them exactly wrong theologically, but a bridge difficult to cross nonetheless. Thankfully *Da Hah* had settled Katie's heart about joining the church she'd been brought up in. Even during the difficult days she'd not doubted that guidance.

In spite of her commitment to her Amish community, Katie didn't want to miss Margaret's wedding or be late. Katie wouldn't attend any more Mennonite youth gatherings, but going to her friend's wedding was a different matter. Her friendship with Margaret and Sharon had been a *wunderbah* thing, healing her heart and offering her support and encouragement when she'd badly needed it. Now things were different. Her love for her people and faith was more settled. There would be no thoughts of joining the Mennonites this time.

Mamm had had a worried look in her eyes when Katie had left the house twenty minutes ago. She was still worried Katie might stray into the Mennonite fold. Well, *Mamm* had nothing to worry about, as Katie had assured her many times. Mabel, on the other hand, didn't seem to care either way. She'd made no sharp jabs like she had last time, going on and on about the scandal of Katie consorting with Mennonites.

Instead, this morning Mabel had been all flustered about Norman's visit tomorrow night. She'd rushed about the house until the living room and kitchen had been cleaned again from top to bottom. The floor had been scrubbed at least twice — by

211

Mamm the first time and then again by Mabel when it didn't meet her specifications. What those were, neither *Mamm* nor Katie could figure out. Mabel declared the floor totally unacceptable, produced a fresh pail of water, and did it all over again.

As far as anyone could tell, things were going well for Mabel and Norman. It still seemed a little strange to hear their voices murmuring downstairs until late on Sunday nights, especially considering that not that long ago it had been Katie sitting beside the young man. But Katie was getting used to it. They hadn't really dated that long, and she still felt well rid of Norman and his hidden dark side.

Ben was living in town somewhere — at least according to the news that had spread across the community. A couple of the older schoolchildren had chattered endlessly about the matter during recess, oblivious to how much interest she had in the matter. They said he'd left because of the ministers, although no one was quite sure in what way they'd been involved. Clearly they'd seen a danger in either Ben's life or in its effect on the life of the community.

There was even talk that Ben planned to testify against the man who had shot him, and that his testimony would send the man to jail for a very long time. Whatever the reason, not having to see Ben at church was a relief really, Katie thought. She'd been dreading it. How would she explain to Ben the night at the hospital if he were to speak to her about it? Lavina had tried to respect her wishes to keep her visit secret, but Katie knew news of the trip would eventually get out, if it hadn't already.

Katie pulled back on Sparky's reins as she approached the Mennonite church house. Cars sat everywhere — and no buggy was in sight. A few vehicles were turning in the driveway ahead of her. Where was she supposed to park? Along the fence? But the ditch there was too deep.

As Katie approached, a young boy waved his hands toward the back, hollering out, "There's a light pole over there you can tie your horse to."

His eyes were big as Katie passed him. Apparently he hadn't expected a buggy to arrive, but at least he knew where to send her. Several boys were busy directing cars. They glanced at her with amused expressions. When she stopped by the light pole, she noticed that one of the boys had followed her.

He held out his hand. "I can secure your horse for you if you give me the tie rope."

"Do you know anything about horses?" Katie asked.

He laughed. "Enough to tie them up."

Giving him the rope, Katie climbed down and found her way to the front door. Glancing back, she noticed Sparky was looking around, like he was trying to figure out why he was tied in the middle of all the *Englisha* automobiles. Well, he'd be okay in the strange surroundings, just like she would be. Even though they were different, the Mennonites were nice people. That much she knew.

An usher inside the door greeted Katie with a smile. "Relative or friend of the bride or groom?"

"Friend of the bride," Katie replied. She wanted to say *gut* friend, but he probably wouldn't have understood. How could anyone understand in just a few words what Margaret and Sharon had meant to her back in the days when she was considered strange by her own people and largely ignored? Not only had the two befriended her, they'd invited her along on a trip to Europe with their friend Nancy.

"Over here then." The usher put out his arm.

Katie looped hers around his elbow and let him lead her down a side aisle to a seat about halfway back. When she'd settled in the pew, the woman next to her turned and whispered, "My name is Florence Miller. How do you know Margaret?"

"I'm Katie Raber. I'm a *gut* friend of Margaret's. I know her from the youth gatherings."

"Welcome then!" the lady said.

The service began with what Katie guessed was traditional wedding music for the Mennonites. Katie watched closely, trying to take everything in. First, a little girl came down the aisle spreading flowers on the floor. Katie thought that was cute. The Amish would never do that. Even flowers on the table would be considered a vain thing. Celery and fruit was about as far as decorations were taken at Amish weddings. But here it seemed right, even *wunderbah*. Maybe her friendship with Margaret was coloring her opinion. Katie shrugged. It was *gut* that no one else from the community was here to see her pleased reaction. She was a member of the Amish church now and was expected to uphold the community's standards. Well, this was Margaret's wedding, and there was no harm in enjoying it. In a few hours Katie would be back in her community.

Following the flower girl came the bridesmaids. They marched slowly down the aisle wearing the most *wunderbah* long and flowing, dark-blue dresses. Katie smiled to think that *Mamm* would pass out flat out on the floor if Katie ever wore something like that. No wonder the preachers warned all the time about the dangers of worldly weddings. She'd never known that worldly could look so tempting.

Fresh music began, and Katie gasped when Margaret appeared in a light-blue dress even more flowing and ruffled than the bridesmaids. She almost looked like an angel as she leaned on her *daett*'s arm. Everyone stood up, and Katie followed their lead.

Margaret made her way slowly and gracefully up the center aisle, coming to a halt in the front where she was met by a handsome young man in a shiny black suit — obviously Margaret's groom, Lonnie. He was smiling from ear to ear, clearly very happy and satisfied with his choice of a *frau*.

As he should be, Katie thought. Margaret was a very nice person.

While the couple stood still, a beautiful solo was sung by a young woman Katie didn't recognize. Then the preacher prayed, and Margaret and Lonnie stepped up to stand in front of him. Margaret was lined

on her side by her bridesmaids, and grooms-
men flanked Lonnie's side. The preacher
asked everyone in the audience to sit down,
and then he gave a short sermon. Katie was
surprised that all the people up front remained standing. When he'd led in another
prayer, the preacher started the wedding
vow questions right then and there, without
any more sermons being preached, as would
have happened at an Amish wedding.

Katie listened to the vows, all of them
asked in *English*. That was unexpected.
They sounded so different. Yet Margaret
was married at the end, just like her people
were when they were married. When the
vows were completed, candles were lit by
Margaret and her husband. Then the two
turned around to face everyone while the
preacher announced, "And now it's my
pleasure to introduce to you Mr. and Mrs.
Lonnie Brinkman." Then the couple came
sweeping down the aisle again. Smiling as
she went by, Margaret caught Katie's eye
and waved. Katie waved back, turning her
head to follow Margaret and her husband
as they walked out the church house door.
That's it? Katie wondered. It was nice, but
from an Amish point of view, way too short.

"May I have your attention?" The preacher
was speaking above the conversations buzz-

ing in the church house. "The bride and the groom have prepared a lovely meal in the fellowship hall right next door. Let me direct your attention there, and remind you to head over right away after the ushers dismiss you and find your seats. On behalf of Lonnie and Margaret, thank you all for coming."

As the ushers directed each row of people, the guests moved down the aisle.

"Are you staying for the meal?" Florence asked.

"Certainly! I want to see Margaret, and I haven't spoken with my friend Sharon yet."

"Then you have other friends here?" Florence asked.

"Just those two. But they're *wunderbah* friends."

"Believe me, hang on tight to those you have. People have way too few friends!"

"I will," Katie said as Sharon caught her attention from across the room by waving. She was making a beeline to reach her. They embraced to the accompaniment of their happy squeals.

"You must be great friends!" Florence commented.

Sharon gave Florence a quick hug. "That we are. Katie and I go back a few years and quite a few miles traveled together. How are you today, Florence?"

"Just fine and happy to be here. What about yourself? Is that Toby fellow still hanging around your place?"

Sharon laughed. "He sure is — and seems to do so more all the time."

"Well, the best to the both of you."

Katie cringed on the inside. Any moment now the two were going to ask if she had a boyfriend. And then she'd have to admit to the sorry tale. Being dropped by your boyfriend for whatever the reason wouldn't look *gut* even in a Mennonite community.

Sharon pulled on Katie's elbow. "Come on, let's go see Margaret!"

Katie followed Sharon through the crowd, stopping a few times to smile and nod as Sharon spoke with her friends. They eventually arrived at the fellowship hall, and Sharon headed straight for the receiving line where Margaret and Lonnie were greeting people.

Margaret was even lovelier up close, her flowing wedding dress sparkling and her face glowing. Katie gawked the whole time it took to reach her. Sharon didn't give Margaret a hug when they arrived, Katie noticed. Probably because of the dress. Margaret grabbed both of Katie's arms though. "Oh, Katie, I'm so very glad you could come! I know I've said that to a hundred other people already, but I mean it from the bottom of my heart. I'll never forget our trip to the Old City of Zurich."

"Hello," Lonnie interrupted, offering his hand. "So it's you who went to Europe with Margaret and Sharon and Nancy? I'm glad to finally meet you."

"Yah," Katie replied. "And you have gotten yourself a very good *frau.* Margaret's a *wunderbah* person. She's been a great friend to me."

"As she has been to me." Lonnie linked his arm with Margaret's, and the two gazed into each other's eyes and smiled sweetly.

"So how are you coming along?" Margaret asked. "Any wedding bells ringing yet?"

"Nee." Katie tried to keep a smile on her face. She really wanted to grab Margaret and cry on her shoulder, but that wasn't the thing to do, especially on Margaret's wedding day.

"Oh, I'm sorry." Margaret's face fell. "Troubles? I'm sure you'll find the perfect man someday. I'll pray for you, okay?"

"Yah," Katie said as she nodded. "That would be *gut."*

"I will too!" Sharon took Katie's elbow again. "Come, we have to keep moving."

Already Margaret was greeting other

guests, Katie noticed as she glanced over her shoulder. Just like in life, relationships had to move on. But she would always thank *Da Hah* for the opportunity He'd given her to know Margaret and Sharon. She'd been blessed indeed.

CHAPTER NINETEEN

The late Saturday afternoon sun shone across the open fields as Katie guided Sparky into the driveway. It was hard to imagine that Margaret's wedding was already over, but she'd seen the couple leave on their honeymoon with her own eyes. They'd roared out of the church house parking lot in Lonnie's car, streamers flying. All they needed to make the scene fancier was Esther's dark-blue Corvette. Katie smiled as she remembered the times Esther drove her to the Mennonite youth gatherings.

My, how different things had been today from what she was used to at Amish weddings. Katie brought Sparky to a stop beside the barn. She smiled at the memory of Margaret leaping into Lonnie's car while people threw rice and birdseed at the couple. Margaret was married, all in her own way, and that's what counted. But Katie knew she wouldn't share many of the details of this wedding with *Mamm* or anyone else.

Unhitching Sparky, Katie had him out of the shafts when Willis appeared with a broad grin on his face. "Back again, I see. Did the happy couple get sent off safely?"

"Yah!" Katie returned his smile. "A little differently than we're used to, but they're off."

"Fancy wedding, huh?" Willis apparently knew more than she did about Mennonite weddings. But then maybe he was guessing.

"Yah," Katie said. "Are you going to put Sparky up for me?"

"For my darling sister? Of course!" Willis grinned over his shoulder as he marched off with the horse.

"Thanks!" Katie hollered after him. Apparently Willis was still trying to soothe her wounded heart. Likely he figured the wedding had stirred up thoughts of her lost wedding hopes with Norman. Well, it hadn't. Now with Ben . . . that was another matter. But she wasn't going to admit that.

The barn door slammed as Willis disappeared with Sparky and jerked Katie out of her thoughts. She turned and headed across the lawn toward the house. As she entered through the front door, she stopped at once. Why was it so quiet? There should be noises coming from the kitchen or some-where else, but there weren't. Had *Mamm* and the others left for a visit? But Willis would have told her if that were the case.

Peering into the kitchen, Katie quickly pulled her head back. *Mamm* and Mabel were sitting at the table across from each other just staring at the ceiling. What in the world was wrong?

"You can come in," *Mamm* called out.

Katie advanced, stopping beside the stove. It didn't look like Mabel was crying, and neither was *Mamm.* In fact, Mabel looked quite pleased with herself now that Katie could see her face clearly.

"You'd best tell Katie," *Mamm* said. "It's not more than right Katie hears this from your own lips."

Katie pulled out a chair and sat down, her knees weak. From the look on *Mamm*'s face this couldn't be *gut* news.

Mabel smiled, apparently not sharing that opinion. "Norman has asked me to wed him this fall yet. He wants me as his *frau.*"

"Wed you . . . this fall?" Katie knew her mouth had fallen open.

Mabel's smile grew even broader. "Nor-man doesn't wish to wait another year for the next wedding season since he's older already and time is slipping away. And he feels quite certain about our relationship. In fact, he says I'm the first girl he has had such strong feelings for."

Mamm looked all sympathy now. "I would have tried to make this easier for you, Katie. But I didn't know how."

"It doesn't matter, really, *Mamm*. It's just so sudden. Couldn't you marry in the spring? It's not like that hasn't been done before."

Mabel glared now. "That's what someone like you would say, Katie. But I want Norman to have his proper time — not having to marry out of season. Besides, it won't do any *gut* for you to object, Katie. You have no hold on Norman. And you've gotten over your feelings for him by now. And if you haven't, you can just try harder."

Katie's mind spun. Mabel's barbs were stinging, but she had it wrong. "My feelings are not the problem, Mabel. I was thinking of you. Are you sure about this? Norman has a dark side you know."

"Katie!" *Mamm* exclaimed. "You shouldn't be saying that about him. Norman is not your boyfriend anymore."

"See?" Mabel tilted her head. "There'll be no sour grapes from you, Katie. You might as well get used to it."

"You shouldn't marry him, Mabel!" Katie

persisted. "Not this soon. You hardly know him."

"Come on, Katie." *Mamm* stood and pulled on Katie's arm. "I need to talk to you."

"You can talk about it right here." Mabel looked quite smug. "I can guess what you're going to tell her. 'Control yourself, Katie. Don't interfere in what's not your business. Mabel's old enough to make up her own mind.' "

Mamm sighed and sat down again.

Apparently Mabel had taken the words right out of *Mamm*'s mouth, Katie thought. Why Mabel didn't trust her was easy to understand, but *Mamm* should know better. Norman was a disaster waiting to happen.

Mabel folded her arms and looked triumphant. "So, Katie, are you going to help me with the wedding or are you going to mope around like a castoff piece of rumpled clothing?"

Before Katie could answer, *Mamm* leaped up. "Mabel, you need to show Katie respect and be more compassionate. That being said, the matter is settled. Katie will cooperate. Her heart might be a little wounded yet, but she will get over it. Now, all of us have more work than we can imagine — that is if we're to pull this wedding off. And we will, Mabel. You have my promise. This is an exciting time for you. I still can't understand why you didn't tell us earlier. Every extra day would have helped."

"I didn't know myself until last Sunday night. And then, well, I guess I needed to get my courage up. With how Katie's been acting, you can see why I was dreading this moment. And I did know this was a little unusual, but Norman wants to marry and soon."

"We will make this happen." *Mamm* smiled. "Are you going to speak to your *daett* about this tonight? Then we can start making plans."

Katie rose from the chair and left without a backward glance as Mabel and *Mamm* continued their conversation. She took the stairs up to her room. *Mamm* and Mabel probably wouldn't even miss her presence, and Katie knew she'd probably just get another lecture if she stayed around.

In her room, Katie sat on the bed as her head throbbed. She didn't care that much about Norman anymore. She never had, if she were honest about it. What was hurting was the shame of the rejection. This short time between Norman's dropping her and his asking Mabel to wed would not escape the community's attention. Clearly the community would think the problem between Norman and her hadn't been Norman's doing. At least if one looked at appearances — which was, of course, exactly how most people would look at it. Likely this had played a part in Norman and Mabel moving so quickly. They both wanted to add insult to her injury. Yet she mustn't think ill of what she wasn't sure of. The reasons Norman had for the quick wedding did make sense. He was older and way past the normal age when Amish men married. Besides, maybe Norman was afraid Mabel would catch on to his character flaws, if the truth be told. She closed her eyes and tried to clear her mind and calm her soul.

A loud knock came on the bedroom door. This couldn't be *Mamm;* the knock was much too rough. It must be Mabel, but what would she want? To give further words of rebuke?

"Yah?" Katie finally said.

"May I come in?" Mabel's voice seemed hesitant.

"Yah," Katie answered. What else could she say?

Mabel came in looking sheepish and sat down beside her on the bed. "I'm sorry for my harsh words downstairs. I really had no reason to speak to you like that."

"That's okay," Katie replied. "I got a little carried away myself."

"We do have to live together in the same house, Katie." Mabel was chirpy again. "We'd best try to get along. I just wish you wouldn't say such horrible things about Norman even if you feel them in your heart. And I will try not to think worse of you than what things really are."

Apparently *Mamm* had given Mabel a lecture about her attitude. Warring sisters weren't going to make *Mamm*'s life any easier in the weeks ahead, especially with all the wedding preparations suddenly thrust upon them.

Katie sighed. "You'll be leaving in a short time to be Norman's *frau*. I'll try to do my part." Katie didn't feel she was to blame for any of the problems with Mabel, but peaceful relationships often begin with taking more than one's share of the load. That her people believed in, and so did she.

Mabel stood. "Good. I'm glad that's settled. And I'm glad you're going to help. I really do want you by my side on the wedding day even though you used to date Norman. I'm not holding that against you. In fact, I want you as my bridesmaid, Katie, for my side of the family. Norman's sister will represent his side."

Katie gasped. "Mabel, I don't think I can do that."

Mabel's face turned into a pout. "Why not? Norman thinks it will be okay. He said he has no hard feelings at all. So why can't you feel the same way?"

"Because it's not right. Not this soon after we broke up."

"Oh, people will forget about all that. And you'll be seen with someone else — one of Norman's attendants. It might even help with your reputation — letting the community see you with another man."

Katie swallowed hard, angry thoughts racing through her mind, which she managed to hold back. None of those words rushing forward would help the situation right now.

Mabel was waiting, so Katie knew she needed to say something . . . anything . . . but what she was really feeling. "So why did you speak so harshly to me downstairs if you knew you were going to ask me this? Didn't you consider how I would feel?"

Mabel shrugged. "I do get a little carried away with my emotions sometimes. But I did say I was sorry. I'm so worried about you, Katie. Your life has taken such a bad turn lately. And being involved with my wedding would help you, I think. I thought of you right after Norman asked me last

Sunday night if I would be his *frau.*"

"Mabel, I just don't think I can do it."
Katie rose. "Now I have to change out of
this dress. Then we should go help *Mamm*
with supper."

Mabel's pout returned, but her face was
also turning red. She glared at Katie before
dashing out of the room and slamming the
door.

CHAPTER TWENTY

On a Saturday morning during the first week of November, Katie drove her buggy to Bishop Miller's. She parked beside the fencerow where a long line of buggies had already been left. She'd come to join the others in helping out with Mabel's wedding preparations. *Mamm* and Mabel would come later, but Katie was anxious to join the other women who had volunteered their help. The community women seemed to understand Norman's need to marry this fall. He was older, and if he'd finally found a girl he liked why should he wait — even if his bride was only eighteen. Well, going on nineteen, as Mabel so often reminded them.

Katie still wasn't convinced something more sinister wasn't going on with Norman's quick marriage proposal. But she'd mentioned it once, so why risk Mabel's wrath mentioning it again? Things were going well enough at home right now. If they could keep their relationship half decent, Mabel would be moving out before long.

After much debate with *Mamm*, Mabel had settled on Mahlon Bontrager as Katie's partner for the wedding. They'd both calmly ignored Katie's objections to being a bridesmaid.

Katie decided if she had to do it Mahlon wasn't all that bad a choice. He was a young widower, alone for a year now. Part of Mabel's purpose in this exercise was, no doubt, to present Katie to the community as someone's suitable *frau*. But to Katie, that didn't matter. She couldn't care less if any man from the community ever asked her home again. And she doubted if Mahlon would be tempted to think of her as a prospective *frau*. Not that she wanted him to. From what she'd heard whispered among the women after church, Mahlon had only accepted the request because Norman's *daett* was so well looked up to in the community. It was a confused mess, and only *Da Hah* could make final sense out of it all. For her, the easiest thing was to go along and keep her mouth shut.

"*Gut* morning!" Bishop Miller's wife, Laura, called as she came out of the house. "I see you're out bright and early."

Katie returned Laura's smile. "I wanted

to get here even earlier, but I was a little slow. I see the others have arrived."

Laura laughed. "*Ach,* you know how it goes. Most of them will be leaving early, but I expect you'll be around all day."

Katie nodded. "*Yah,* I plan to be. By the way, thanks for giving us the use of your place. I know Mabel is very appreciative."

"We're happy to help, Katie. Someday we'd love to do the same for you."

Katie let the words flow past her and just said, "Thank you. Now, where can I begin?"

"Most of the women are still in the house cleaning the upstairs and basement. The men will be around in a bit pulling the machinery out of the pole barn. That's where I suggest you go. Wait a few minutes and start there. In fact, that's where I'm going right now. You're welcome to tag along."

"I'll do that." Katie fell in step with the energetic Laura. She might be getting on in years, but she sure hadn't slowed down since *Mamm's* wedding had been held here.

"I hope that Ben Stoll hasn't been bothering you." Laura gave Katie a quick, sympathetic look. "*Da Hah* knows life has been hard enough on you without him hanging around."

Katie looked away. Must Ben come up again? Why couldn't people help her move on by forgetting the past? "I haven't heard anything from him or his family since the night I spent with his *mamm* at the hospital. Well, except for what his little brother shares at school."

"Ben's living in town now," Laura offered. "The ministry thought it for the best."

"I see."

Laura wasn't finished yet. "And don't worry about those rumors going around right now. I told Jonas not to believe what he hears about you. I told him I'd spoken personally to Lavina, and she made it clear to me you were acting out of your Christian duty and that you were never with Ben without someone else present."

"Thank you," Katie responded as they walked into the pole barn. At least she had the bishop's wife on her side.

Behind them *Mamm* and Mabel came driving in, and Laura left to greet the two women. Bishop Miller came out of the barn about the same time and greeted Katie. "Here to help, are we? We'll have to make sure you have plenty of work then."

"I certainly wouldn't want to stand around idle all day," Katie said, smiling.

"So where are the men Laura promised would be here? I've seen nothing but women driving in."

"I wouldn't know, but I can help push machinery," Katie offered.

"An old man and a young woman?" Bishop Miller laughed. "That would be the day. I don't think the world has come to such a sorry state yet. Let's see what Laura has to say for herself."

Chattering away, the three women approached. When they came within earshot, Bishop Miller asked Laura, "Where's my help, my *frau*?"

"Coming right there!" Laura replied as she waved her arm toward the road. Sure enough, when Katie looked up a buggy full of men was pulling into the driveway.

"Should have looked before I asked," Bishop Miller said. "Happens every time a man doubts a woman."

Katie smiled at his humor. He was a kindly old soul, and he watched well over the spiritual health of the community. She could be thankful *Da Hah* had supplied such leaders she could trust.

"How are things going for you?" Bishop Miller asked as he glanced at Katie.

"Fine. I'm all right, although I guess my heart is still a bit troubled."

Bishop Miller nodded while stroking his long, white beard. "*Da Hah*'s ways are not always ours. But we will find they are always

236

the best." A twinkle flickered in his eye. "I hear you might have someone special on the hook at the wedding."

Katie laughed. "Believe me, that's Mabel's doing, not mine."

"One never knows." The twinkle didn't go away. "Just keep your heart open, Katie."

Katie was sure her face was turning red with such plain talk from the bishop. He must highly approve of Mahlon Bontrager to say such a thing. And the bishop must also approve of her — at least enough to think she was a worthy *frau* for Mahlon. That thought was enough to turn her face flame red if it already wasn't.

"*Da Hah* works in mysterious ways," Bishop Miller smiled at her and then turned toward the driveway as the men climbed out of the buggy and drew near. "Don't ever forget that, Katie."

"So what have we going on here?" one of the men hollered. "Surely you weren't planning on keeping all this work for yourself?"

"I was waiting for you to settle your breakfast and get here," Bishop Miller retorted.

"John was catching his late-morning winks out on the porch swing when I picked him up," another man added.

Laughing together, they moved into the

pole barn and started pushing the machines and dragging the tools out, parking and placing them along the edges of the yard.

Katie waited until the men had a section cleared before going in to clean. By then Laura and *Mamm,* along with several other women, were ready with brooms and dustpans. Ben's *mamm,* Lavina, had also arrived and greeted Katie with a gentle nod. Bishop Miller soon had a hay wagon brought in with the help of the other men for the women to use as a platform. By late morning they'd swept the upper cross ties of the pole barn, reaching the roof by standing on the hay-wagon racks. As each section was completed, the women pushed the wagon around to the next spot. It took a little doing, but with everyone's aid the wagon moved easily enough.

When they were done, Laura hollered to the men, "We need your help. Anyone with some muscles?"

This produced plenty of laughs, and the men quickly moved the wagon out. Showing off, Katie figured. Men were men, always liking to show off in front of women.

By twelve o'clock they had the pole barn floor washed; the concrete almost spotless. Rosanna Yoder, who had stayed inside the house, opened the washroom door and hollered across the lawn. "Dinner's ready! Come get it!"

"That's about time," one of the men commented.

Katie followed everyone inside to enjoy a meal of sandwiches and chocolate milk that had been set out on the table.

"Not much to eat I know," Rosanna announced. "But we were busy."

"It's more than enough," *Mamm* spoke up. "And we want to thank all of you for coming today. This means so much to us, especially on such short notice."

"We're glad to help," Bishop Miller said. "Now let's pray before someone faints from hunger."

They all bowed their heads with smiles playing on their faces. Bishop Miller was *gut* like that, putting everyone at ease.

"We give thanks today for what You have given us, dear *Hah*," Bishop Miller prayed. "Bless all the willing hands who have come to help today. Bless also this food which has been prepared. It is far above anything we deserve, even in this world of plenty that we find ourselves in today. We pray for those in other parts of the world where many are still persecuted for their faith. Help them and comfort them, dear *Hah*. Leave them not without the presence of Your Holy

Spirit. Amen."

"Okay, fall to!" Rosanna waved her arms about. "Don't be wasting any time now."

The men laughed and got in line at once. Katie moved to the back of the line behind the men, *Mamm* right behind her. When they got to the front of the line, Katie took a sandwich and glass of chocolate milk and went out on the front lawn to sit on the grass. The living room already looked full, and so did the front porch.

Lavina followed her. "I hope I'm not disturbing you, Katie."

Katie hid her astonishment. "*Nee,* not in the least. Please sit down."

"*Yah,*" Lavina said, as she sat on the ground, her legs tucked under her like a schoolgirl.

Lavina looked younger out here with the sun on her face and the breeze blowing through her hair. She'd often appeared so weary the past few months. Of course, she'd had plenty of reason, with Ben's shenanigans weighing on her heart.

"How are things going for you?" Katie asked.

"Okay, I guess." Lavina took a bite of her sandwich. "I'm sorry for the trouble you got into for coming to the hospital that night. But at the same time I can never thank you enough for coming. I think your presence really helped Ben."

"I'd do it again," Katie replied without hesitation. It had been the right thing to do, and she had no regrets.

Lavina dug into her dress pocket and pulled out an envelope. She hesitated only for a moment. "I have something for you. Ben said to give this to you when things had died down a bit. So here it is."

"What is it?" Katie didn't move as she stared at the white envelope.

"It's Ben's thanks, he said. I don't think he means any harm by this."

Katie hesitated. She really shouldn't take it. Ben was in her past, and she didn't want it stirred up again. Still her arm reached out, almost as if acting on its own, and took the envelope, slipping it quickly into her dress pocket.

CHAPTER TWENTY-ONE

The next afternoon Katie paced her upstairs bedroom with Ben's letter clutched in her hand. She'd already read it last night after the supper dishes and the evening prayers were over. She'd excused herself early, and no one had paid her much mind. The day had been full of hard work at Bishop Miller's place, and Jesse always encouraged an early bedtime on Saturday night so everyone would be fresh for the Sunday morning church services. Only she hadn't gone to bed early. Instead, she'd sat up and read and reread Ben's short note. Emotions she thought had been conquered had risen again, even worse than they'd been that night at the hospital. It was past midnight before she dropped off to sleep.

Then today, especially during church — through the singing and the sermons — she'd thought about Ben and what he'd written. Now the words swam in front of her eyes again. Katie held the page away from her. No tears must splatter on the page and mar the words. Ben was trying to release her from her affections, she was sure. Only it wasn't having that effect at all.

He'd written his thanks for her sacrifice of time and reputation by coming to the hospital that night. Only she knew it really hadn't been a sacrifice. She'd gone because it was her Christian duty, *yah,* but the words she'd spoken to Ben had flowed from her heart. They had been tender words, and she'd meant every one of them. She'd said them even while she was planning to wed Norman. It seemed that her heart had known even then what she was unwilling to admit aloud. She still loved Ben — and apparently she always would.

Yah, Ben was willing to set her free. He had, in fact, set her free with this letter. Only it had the opposite effect. Now her heart was flying back to him, seeking what she'd lost against her better judgment. She knew the situation her heart wanted could not have a *gut* ending. The past was gone. What Ben had done could be forgiven, *yah.* Had not worse sins been washed away from the lives of her people? There must have been, although she'd never heard much about that type of thing. *Rumspringa* wasn't exactly a holy time in many Amish people's lives. They were supposed to try out the things of the world. And, *yah,* Ben had gone way too far into the world. But what had really shattered her heart? Ben's sin? Or was it that he wasn't quite as perfect as she'd wanted him to be? That he had feet of clay?

Yet what was she supposed to do now? Ben was living somewhere in town. And she was a church member, which meant she needed to be circumspect in everything she did. She was scheduled to be a bridesmaid with Mahlon Bontrager as her escort at Mabel's wedding. Bishop Miller even thought Mahlon would be a good match for her. Life was becoming normal again, at least on the outside. If she simply left things alone, Ben would never know how she'd longed for him, and neither would anyone else. *Mamm* didn't even know she had this letter from Ben, and Katie was sure Lavina would never mention it.

Could she risk the loss of what she'd gained so far? Any contact with Ben would certainly lead in that direction. She'd arrived where she once thought everyone had walked. Accepted, loved, part of the community. But now she knew there was more to it. Norman had shattered the vision of what "normal" might be. He'd shown her the inside of the life she'd dreamed of for so long. It was no more beautiful or virtuous than the one she'd come from. Norman, and likely his family too, was capable of spreading rumors about her that were untrue. And Mabel too. And all because Katie had done something that at first look appeared suspect but had been perfectly reasonable and virtuous. And she was certain that Ben being asked to leave home could be laid at Enos's door too.

Bishop Miller and his *frau,* Laura, had hearts of gold. They intended only the best for her and everyone else. But what if the bishop and other men in the ministry hierarchy were wrong? What if Ben was redeemable, and they couldn't see it? What if Ben was ready to believe, and no one was ready to trust him or give him the opportunity? *What if . . .* The questions wouldn't stop, and Katie finally flopped on the bed. She was going to drive herself mad obsessing about what could never be.

And that was how it had been in the beginning with Ben. Oh, how her heart had throbbed with the longing to ride in his buggy with him, to be with him, to be noticed by him. She'd longed for just one friendly glance from him. And when it happened, she'd lived with passion, with feeling, with desire, with love.

How different that was from how she was today. Drifting along. Not caring what happened. Accepting what crumbs were thrown her way. She didn't even stand up to Mabel when the teen had clearly been in the wrong. She was even willing to humiliate herself by being Mabel's bridesmaid after all Mabel and Norman had done against her.

What was she to do, Katie wondered. Would she have to accept Mahlon, should he ask her, and try to be the best *frau* she could be while she loved another? *Mamm* would say she'd done this to herself — got herself into the mess. She'd say *Da Hah* would give her a love for her husband . . . eventually. After all, *Da Hah* had done that for *Mamm* . . . first for Katie's *daett* and then for Jesse. And *Mamm* hadn't been looking for love after being so rejected by the man she'd been infatuated with.

Katie got up to pace the floor again. But this was different. *Mamm* never had the opportunity to be with David Kauffman. To be loved by him. He'd never even asked to take her home or invited her to ride in his buggy. Daniel hadn't kissed *Mamm,* and *Mamm* had never snuggled up to him under a buggy blanket. Daniel had never written

Mamm a note saying he was so very sorry for any wrong done and wishing her well in her life. Nor had Daniel ever been sent away even though his heart was still with the Amish. And that was exactly what had happened to Ben, Katie decided. And Ben loved her. She now knew that for sure.

Katie would go to him. She'd tell him thank you for the note. She'd ride into town, they would talk, and all would be well again. She would fly into his arms and kiss him, and they could be as they once were — two people in love and living in a world that was right for them.

Only it wouldn't be right, even if they both wished it so. Even if they both overlooked the wrong done by the other. And what would it accomplish to go to him? Without the community's acceptance, the world she knew would fly apart. Then what would she have left? But if she did nothing, what did she really have? And would Ben move away and begin a new life without knowing she still loved him?

Katie clenched her jaw. She would go see Ben this very afternoon. If she didn't go, she'd always wonder if she should have. *Yah,* she must do the hard thing and show *Mamm* the note and tell her she had to go to Ben to thank him and talk to him. *Mamm* would

247

object, but Katie would be strong and deal with it. Besides, Ben wasn't in the *bann*. There was no rule against seeing him.

If she was late for the hymn singing tonight, that couldn't be helped. This was her moment, her hour of decision. If she let it slip away, the opportunity and courage might never return.

Katie slipped the letter into her dress pocket and walked downstairs. Jesse was sitting in the living room eating popcorn and reading *The Budget*. He looked up with a smile, but then went back to his reading. Katie continued to the kitchen. *Mamm* was pouring glasses of apple cider.

Mamm glanced up with a pleased expression. "You're just in time, Katie. I had thought you were stuck up in your room all afternoon. Shall I get you a glass too?"

"*Nee*, I have to do something this afternoon . . . make a trip into town. If I'm not back in time for the hymn singing, don't worry."

"Katie?" *Mamm*'s mouth tightened into a straight line. "What are you going to do?"

"I'm going to see Ben."

Mamm gasped and the glass of apple cider that had been in her hand crashed to the floor.

"*Mamm*, please." Katie reached for Ben's

letter. "I'll clean up the mess. Read this and you'll understand."

Taking the note, *Mamm*'s eyes moved over the page as a trickle of apple cider on the kitchen floor ran toward the stove. *Mamm* lifted her eyes from the page. "I still don't understand why you need to see him. He's not planning on coming back, Katie. You can tell by this letter that Ben knows it's best if you cut off all ties. At least he's an honorable man in that regard."

Tears swam in Katie's eyes. She grabbed a rag from the closet and bent down to sop up the cider. "That's why I must see him, *Mamm*. You might as well know. I've never stopped loving him."

"Oh, Katie." *Mamm* found another rag and joined Katie on the floor. "You were doing so well. I can't bear to see you hurt again — not by Ben and not by anyone else either."

Katie met *Mamm*'s eyes. "Is one really doing well when her heart aches all night?"

"Healing takes time," *Mamm* insisted. "I know."

"*Yah,* but your love was never given the opportunity to grow or be restored. I'm being given that chance. I can't walk away without giving Ben and me a chance. You just said that Ben has done an honorable thing. Don't you see what that says about his heart? That he's changed and grown?"

"What's going on?" Jesse asked from the kitchen opening. *Mamm* and Katie took last swipes at the cider and leaped to their feet.

"The cider . . . I dropped the glass and spilled cider all over," *Mamm* explained.

"I can see that. Is something else wrong?" Jesse obviously wasn't satisfied with such a simple explanation.

"Katie is going in to see Ben this afternoon," *Mamm* said. She picked up the letter on the table and handed it to Jesse.

He read it before looking up. "Come, I think we need to talk."

Katie glanced at *Mamm* as Jesse disappeared into the living room. Then she looked down at the shattered glass still on the floor.

Mamm shook her head. "I'll take care of that later, Katie. This is much more important."

Katie followed *Mamm* into the living room and seated herself on the couch. *Mamm* sat down next to her. Jesse was sitting in his chair looking over the letter again. "When did you get this, Katie?"

Katie looked down at the floor before answering. "Lavina gave it to me yesterday at Bishop Miller's."

"And you want to see Ben?" Jesse's hand fell to his side, the letter hanging above the floor.

"*Yah,*" Katie said. "I must speak with him."

"You know where this action will lead?" Jesse asked, looking directly at Katie.

Katie shrugged. "*Yah,* but I guess I don't care about that right now. I need to talk to Ben. I still love him, Jesse."

"Every time you're with this young man you get in trouble." Jesse shifted on his rocker. "Don't you think you should let him go? Nothing *gut* seems to come out of it. The last time he broke your heart. Then his *mamm* and *daett* asked you to help out during his illness, and your actions cost you a boyfriend and, in a way, your job. What could happen next, Katie?"

"I don't know. I only know I must follow my heart on this. I need to give Ben a chance. I need to know. If it doesn't work out, it doesn't work out, but at least I'll know for sure."

Mamm stepped in. "One should not be so sure of oneself, Katie. Please reconsider."

Jesse smiled. "Sometimes life is the best teacher, Emma. I don't like this any more than you do, but I believe we must not stand in the way. Katie is old enough to make her own choices and to live with the conse-

251

quences. We will trust *Da Hah* to teach her and guide her and be with her through whatever happens."

"Katie, do you know where Ben lives?" *Mamm* asked.

Katie shrugged.

Jesse spoke up. "*Nee,* she probably doesn't, but Leroy or Willis might know."

Katie jumped up and raced for the stair door. Taking the steps two at a time, she got to the top and ran down the hall toward the boys' bedroom. Jesse was a *wunderbah daett*! She'd known that, but she knew it in a deeper way now.

CHAPTER TWENTY-TWO

Willis drove Sparky through the outskirts of Dover toward the address that was supposed to be Ben's. Katie's heart was pounding at the thought that she would be seeing Ben in just a few minutes — if he was home, that is. But why shouldn't he be home on a Sunday afternoon?

When Katie had asked Willis and Leroy if they knew Ben's address, Willis had glanced at Leroy and then said, "*Yah*, I know." He'd agreed to tell her the address only if he could go along.

So protective, Katie thought. Just what a brother should be. Katie had planned to go alone, but when Willis insisted, she had no choice but to accept his offer.

Willis was being a very good brother, and it was probably just as well he'd come along. She'd realized this when they'd driven past Bishop Miller's place. Laura and the bishop had been on the front porch swing eating their Sunday afternoon popcorn.

Willis made a point of waving harder than she did, clearly sending the message that they were out on an innocent jaunt. Perhaps going to a friend's house for a few hours before the hymn singing that evening. The smiles on Bishop Miller and Laura's faces brought an ache of sorrow to Katie's heart. She'd be disappointing so many people when they found she'd gone to see Ben. But she wasn't turning back now. She must speak with him!

"His place is right over there." Willis pulled onto a side street and stopped across from a nice, two-story house. "I'll watch from here."

Katie gave a nervous laugh. "I'm not in any danger, Willis."

He didn't join in the laughter. "Just saying, that's all. Don't do anything stupid now."

"I won't," Katie said as she climbed out of the buggy.

Katie knocked on the front door and waited. She soon heard footsteps and the door cracked open. Ben's face was troubled when he looked first at her and then at the buggy across the street. "Katie?"

"*Yah.* May I come in?"

He hesitated. "You shouldn't be here. I'm

not even to speak with you. Didn't you get my note?"

Katie nodded. "That's why I'm here. I want to thank you for the kind things you said."

"Okay, but you shouldn't come in. Who is with you in the buggy?"

"Willis. I want to come in, Ben."

"You shouldn't," he repeated, but he opened the door and stepped back.

Katie stepped in and took in the living room with a quick look. He didn't have much furniture, just a couch and a chair. The kitchen was equally sparse, with only a small table and two chairs. Ben wasn't living high on the hog, that was for sure.

"Do you want to sit?" Ben motioned toward the couch.

Katie sat down, and Ben pulled a chair close and sat down too.

Katie cleared her throat. Now that the moment had arrived, the words were sticking in her throat. "I came . . . I came to tell you, Ben . . . that . . . that I really appreciated your note."

Ben nodded but didn't say anything.

Katie took a deep breath. "I caught a glimpse of your *gut* heart in that note. I'm not here to simply thank you, Ben. Perhaps . . . well, I want to ask . . . could we be friends again?"

Ben was silent for a moment. "Bishop Miller . . . does he know of this visit?"

"Nee."

"You're under his authority as a church member, Katie. They told me I'm here partly because of my relationship with you."

Katie sat up straighter. "I know . . . well, I figured that. But, oh, I don't know what to do, Ben! I'm so confused. Why did you write that note to me?"

He hung his head. "I never expected to see you again, Katie. At least not like this."

"Ben . . ." Katie clutched her hands together. Silence fell and long moments later Katie looked up to see Ben rise and then move to sit beside her on the couch. His face was etched with sorrow, and his hand trembled when he touched her arm.

"I'm so sorry, Katie. So very sorry for everything."

Katie placed her hands on Ben's shoulders and pulled him closer to her.

He tried to speak.

She pulled him even closer and kissed him gently.

Ben responded by embracing her and returning the kiss.

Katie never wanted this to end — this moment with his face slightly above her, his

fingers tracing her face after he moved his
head back to look at her. She pulled away
and nestled against his shoulder just as the
tears came.

"Katie, it's okay. I love you. I suppose I
always will. I'm so sorry that I ruined
everything for us. I thought I'd lost you —
the most precious thing in my life."

She turned her face up toward his and
kissed him again. At last she pulled away.
"Ben, I don't ever want to lose you again.
Not ever. This has been the most awful
thing I've ever gone through."

"I'm so sorry, Katie." Ben's fingers stroked
hers.

"Don't say that again, Ben. I've forgiven
you, and the past is behind us."

He smiled. "When I heard you were seeing Norman, I really thought it was over . . .
that I'd really lost you forever."

"Norman means nothing to me. I don't
know what I was thinking."

He drew her close. "When the heart is
broken, who is to say how it will be mended?
If Norman could have made you happy, I
wouldn't have objected. I know I've brought
you little but sorrow."

"And love." Katie looked up at him.
"Don't forget that. I love you, Ben Stoll.
More than you know."

He sighed. "That leaves us in a grand pickle, doesn't it? Where do we go from here?"

She nestled against him again. "I've missed you so."

"And me you." He stroked her face again. "But there's a world out there that doesn't feel like we do, I'm afraid."

Katie sighed and sat up. "I guess dreams can't go on forever. But can we at least enjoy this afternoon?"

Ben glanced out the window. "There's Willis out there. He's going to get tired of waiting."

"Oh, Willis! I forgot him!" Katie took both of his hands in hers. "Tell me quickly then what has happened since we . . . since we broke up. The arrest, the sentence, going to jail — I want to hear it all even though I know it will be hard."

Ben's face fell. "I'd rather not. Those are dark days, and I'd rather forget them. But I will tell you what I thought of during the time. That's worth the telling. I thought of you. Of how you looked, so happy and carefree, your eyes so full of love, and how I'd been so stupid . . . such an idiot to lose it all. I thought of what you might tell me about the things you were learning in Switzerland."

"Ben, I couldn't . . ." Katie said, but he silenced her with a finger on her lips.

"What a fool I was, Katie, to ever risk losing you. But please understand that when I began distributing the drugs for Rogge, I hadn't known you yet — other than you were just a girl named Katie Raber who lived with her widowed mother. You weren't part of the community very much. And back then my life was so empty. I think that's what led me to get involved with Rogge and drugs. The money was good too, I admit that. But then you came into my empty life and made it full. You brought in the sunshine and laughter. I'd never felt such things with any other woman."

"Ben . . ."

He silenced her again by holding up his finger. "It really is true that I stopped delivering drugs because of you, Katie. I just didn't know how to get out of it any faster."

"Ben, are you the one who gave me the money for the trip?"

He looked down. "I know it wasn't *gut* money — honest money — but I wanted to use it for a *gut* cause. I wanted to help you."

"It came from a *gut* heart, Ben. Thank you for making my trip to Europe possible."

"You're welcome, Katie. I'm so glad I

could do something good with the money."

"What do we do now?" Katie asked.

"I'm not sure, Katie. Have you given it much thought?"

"No, I haven't." Katie leaned forward and kissed him.

Ben soon pulled away. "Katie, when folks find out about this visit, you're going to be in a lot of trouble."

Katie stood up. "Well, I'll face that when it comes. For now all I care about is when I'm going to see you again. When, Ben?"

He shook his head. "I don't know, but not too soon. We have to take this slowly. We still have a long way to go before everything can be made right. The effects of my sin will not be done away with so easily."

Katie hung her head and then reached out to find his hand. "Okay. Just don't doubt me, Ben. I love you. I came down to the hospital that night because of my Christian duty, *yah,* but my heart would have been willing all on its own — duty or not. Norman had that right, at least."

"The only thing Norman did right was leaving you for me," Ben declared. "And for that I will thank him someday. But for that only."

"Then you don't doubt that we can love each other even after all that's happened?

Can we believe *Da Hah* has brought us through this, and that He will take us onward?"

"*Mamm* always said you were a woman of great faith," Ben said as his fingers touched her forehead and then twirled the hair that hung out from under her *kapp*. "She was right. Now I see it for myself. But there is still the matter of my faith. I need to make things right with the church. And I want to, Katie. I believe in the Amish way now."

"Then you will make things right, Ben. I know you will. We belong to a great faith."

"I know, Katie. Mostly because that's where you come from."

Katie shook her head. "*Nee,* Ben, that can't be the only reason. It also has to be where *your* heart lies."

Ben nodded and led her to the door. "You really should go. I'll find a way to come by and see you. I promise." He opened the door.

"I'm holding you to that." Katie gave Ben a quick kiss before turning and running across the lawn. When she climbed into the buggy, Willis clucked to Sparky, and they took off for home.

"I think you've been doing something you shouldn't have," Willis said as they were pulling out of town.

Katie didn't answer, but she kept her eyes on the road. If Willis didn't want to witness things like that, he should have stayed home. Still, she was thankful he'd brought her. And this was probably what Willis had been wishing for all along. Why else would he have insisted she see Ben right after he was shot? And today, Willis had come along quite willingly. Tilting her head up at him, she gave him a sweet smile. "I appreciate you, Willis. I really do."

CHAPTER TWENTY-THREE

"You did what?" Mabel's shriek echoed off the kitchen walls on Monday morning as she collapsed into a chair. "Katie, what is wrong with you?"

"There's nothing wrong with Katie," *Mamm* said as her hands fidgeted with her apron. "She went down to see Ben yesterday afternoon, and . . ."

Mabel was on her feet again. "You know this isn't right, *Mamm!* What about my wedding? Katie is supposed to be my bridesmaid. How can that happen now?"

"Nothing has changed." *Mamm* reached over to rub Mabel's shoulder. "You'd better calm down. This isn't becoming for a young bride."

Mabel flopped down on the chair again and glared at Katie. "About Ben, I don't care. The two of you deserve each other. But you would have to do this now, wouldn't you? If nothing else than to torment me. To get back at me because I won Norman's affections. I thought you were low, Katie. But this is really, really low."

Katie winced. "I've told you before that I don't care about Norman. So don't be making this into something it isn't." She'd been expecting a negative reaction from Mabel, but this was over the top even for her dramatic sister.

"I'm not buying any of her excuses." Mabel spoke to the wall, as if it needed an explanation for the outburst. "But I can't have Katie be my bridesmaid under these conditions."

"But you have to, Mabel," *Mamm* declared. "You've already asked Mahlon to be her escort and told everyone. How will it look if you change your mind? Everyone will know you're at odds with each other. That's not how it should be."

"That's better than the option of having people think I approve of Katie sneaking around to see that criminal," Mabel muttered.

"She wasn't sneaking around," *Mamm* replied. "Jesse and I talked with her about it before she left. And not very many people know she visited Ben. How would people find out before the wedding anyway?"

Mamm was obviously grasping at straws,

Katie thought.

Mabel's face turned even redder. "I can't believe you're joining Katie in this . . . this sneaking around! Think about what you just said! People will find out, and they'll know we knew. *Nee!* I'm having none of this."

"Fine. I won't be your bridesmaid. I'm okay with it." Katie shrugged. She could feel the shame of it burning inside of her, but she wasn't going to let Mabel know it. Sitting in the unmarried girl's section on Mabel's wedding day with everyone knowing she'd been rejected again, albeit in a different way, would be painful. But she wasn't going to apologize for seeing Ben. Not with the love *Da Hah* had stirred up in their hearts.

Mabel turned to Katie with a hopeful look on her face. "If you confessed to the church that you visited Ben and you know it was wrong, maybe everyone could be convinced to overlook your indiscretion again. *Yah,* if the proper things were said to the right people that might work. They'd understand that you're troubled right now, Katie."

Katie shook her head. "I'm afraid I can't do that. I don't regret visiting Ben."

Mabel's face turned stony. "You've made a royal mess for me, Katie!"

Katie tried to think kind thoughts about

Mabel. This wasn't going to be easy for her. Mabel would have to give some explanation for why her sister wasn't sitting in the bridesmaid's place during the ceremony. And Mabel had Norman to deal with. Likely when Norman found out, he wouldn't even want her at the wedding. If there was even a hint of scandal in the air, Norman would balk. Mabel must know that much about Norman by now.

"Please, Mabel," *Mamm* said, trying to help. "What harm can be done by Katie sitting beside you? People will be thinking of you — not Katie — that day."

Mabel didn't even hesitate. "It's out of the question!"

Katie turned and went into the living room. Carolyn was sitting in there, tears running down her face. The poor girl. What a shame that she had to listen to this family meltdown. Katie sat down beside her and slipped her arm around her teenaged sister's shoulder. "I'm so sorry that you had to hear that."

Carolyn looked at her with big eyes. "Will you still be teaching school? If you're running around with Ben Stoll, will they make you stop teaching?"

Katie managed a laugh. "My relationship with Ben has nothing to do with my school teaching. Mabel just doesn't like it when people might misunderstand a situation. She's getting married, so she wants everything just right on her wedding day."

Carolyn looked a little comforted. "Well, I'm glad to hear that. Joel would hate it if you had to quit. He loves you as his teacher."

"That's *gut.*" Katie gave Carolyn another hug. "I have to go now or I'll be really late for school. I expect Joel is waiting outside with Sparky already. He probably wonders where I'm at."

"I could be the bridesmaid," Carolyn offered. "If you can't, I could do it."

Katie smiled. "I'm sure Mabel would appreciate the offer, but you're not old enough at fifteen."

"That's right," Mabel agreed as she stuck her head through the kitchen opening. "Katie has left us all in an awful mess."

Katie grabbed her coat and headed out the front door before Mabel could fire off another missile. Just as she expected, Joel was waiting for her beside the buggy, and Sparky was already hitched.

"Where have you been?" he asked. "I thought you got lost in the house or something."

"I did get detained," Katie said as she

climbed into the buggy. "But I'm ready to go now."

Joel didn't seem to notice her dark mood, as he climbed up, picked up the reins, and clucked to Sparky. Katie usually let him drive because it made him feel grown up.

As Joel chattered away, Katie mumbled responses at the proper places. Thankfully, he'd been spared the outburst in the house. Hopefully he'd remain ignorant of the problem while it was being worked out. As they approached the schoolhouse, Katie stared at a buggy already parked near the schoolhouse. The horse was tied to the hitching post. It couldn't be one of the children because there was no one playing on the school grounds. She guessed it could have been one of the older girls riding in alone this morning, but then the horse would have been unhitched by now.

"It's Enos Kuntz's buggy," Joel said and glanced up at Katie as he turned into the lane. "Are you expecting him? Did you do something wrong?"

Katie smiled. "Not that I know of, Joel." She was worried though. Why was Enos here? There's no way he could know about her trip to visit Ben yesterday.

"Whoa, Sparky!" Joel called as he brought the buggy to a stop.

Katie hopped out, and Enos's bearded face appeared in his buggy's window.

"*Gut* morning, Enos," Katie said, trying to sound chirpy. Surely Enos was here with some positive news. Perhaps he wished to compliment her for all her hard work over the past few months. She could sure use a morale boost this morning after that run-in with Mabel.

"*Gut* morning."

Enos sounded cheerful enough as he climbed down from his buggy. He stood by as she and Joel unhitched Sparky.

Katie walked up to Enos after Joel led Sparky to a nearby corral. "How are you doing this morning?"

"Oh, *gut* enough," Enos replied and tipped his hat. "Is there a place we can speak? Inside, perhaps? Before the schoolchildren arrive?"

"*Yah,* of course. There's no one inside yet." Katie's heart was pounding now. This wasn't going to be a friendly visit, she could tell. But what could it be about? She hadn't done anything — at least that was school related.

Enos followed her inside, pausing in the foyer to leave his hat on a hook. Katie went in and placed her lunch and books on the desk. She headed toward the back and sat

269

down in one of the student chairs. She invited Enos to sit nearby.

The head of the school board took a seat on top of a student's desk, his long legs hanging over the side. He cleared his throat. "I've been wanting for some time to speak with you, Katie, but I've been putting it off. There's the wedding coming up, of course, in which you have a major part, Norman tells me. I didn't want to disturb things, you know. And I was hoping things would get better as you gain more experience. But I could no longer wait after what I heard yesterday."

"Oh? And what did you hear?" Katie stared as Enos stroked his beard.

A smile softened his features. "I knew you would take this hard, Katie. So that's why I hesitated to say anything. But as the head of the school board, it's my responsibility to bring the concerns of the parents to your attention."

"What is this about? You've heard a complaint? I haven't noticed any misbehavior in the children. When they do, I try to correct them at once."

Enos shook his head. "I haven't heard anything on that matter. But I've heard you are apparently bringing in some books from home that you're reading to the children.

Books of a questionable nature. I was told you started such a book last week. *Tom Sawyer* by Mark Twain, I believe."

Katie swallowed. "*Yah,* that is true. I didn't think it was wrong. If it is, I will stop reading it at once." She hadn't once thought to question the book. She had asked Willis for his opinion on what to read next for the story hour. Willis had pronounced *Tom Sawyer* a *gut* book and one the children would like. And they had liked it so far. Enos was nodding his approval at her words, but Katie could tell he wasn't finished yet.

"That's all well and *gut,* Katie. One is always glad to see that a person is quick to repent and see the error of one's ways. But we expect a high degree of *gut* judgment from our teachers. You are, after all, with our children every day for most of the week. And it's hard enough to keep the ways of the world outside without people they respect offering it to them in school."

"I'm very sorry. I should have asked someone on the school board or the ministry about the book before reading it aloud to the children."

Enos shrugged. "I suppose these things happen. I'll be expecting more care from now on, Katie. And there are other things also that concern the parents. Little things, *yah.*"

"What little things?" Katie asked, truly perplexed.

"Well, some say you seem a little light on discipline." Enos hesitated and then started again. "And you must know there are concerns that remain about . . . well, about your past. But I'm sure those concerns amount to nothing. And perhaps with Mahlon Bontrager showing interest in you at the wedding, well, that will surely help your reputation with the community."

How had she ever imagined this man as her father-in-law? Katie wondered. She'd thought he was a pillar of the community, and yet here he was concerned about rumors and half-truths. And he had yet to find out about her visit to Ben's house yesterday. What would happen when that was known? She decided she'd better tell him right here and now since he'd brought her past up. But the words stuck in her throat.

"Well, you have a *gut* day," Enos said as he stood.

He nodded to the students coming up the steps and was gone.

Katie forced a smile as she greeted the students. "*Gut* morning, children. Isn't it a lovely day?"

"*Yah,* it is . . ." one of them said. They all

smiled back at her, obviously thinking nothing strange about Enos being here to talk to their teacher. And that's how it would stay. She would change what needed changing at school, but she would never shut her heart to Ben again.

CHAPTER TWENTY-FOUR

Katie paced the kitchen floor, the late-afternoon sunlight flooding through the window. Now she was the one distraught while Mabel sat as calm as a cucumber at the kitchen table. Well, Katie decided, at least she wasn't shrieking like Mabel had been this morning — though she felt like doing so.

"Norman is bringing Mahlon Bontrager over here? Tonight? To speak with me? How did you finagle that so fast?"

Mabel looked quite pleased with herself. "I went to speak with Norman right after you left this morning. It's the only way, Katie. Someone has to talk sense into your head. And Norman agrees that you are savable, so he's making the effort."

Now she was going to shriek and screech all at the same time. Norman thought she was savable? From what? From the wreck he'd help make of her life? Was he trying to make himself feel better? Likely he was so full of himself he couldn't see straight. Helping her out — after what he had done? Right.

Katie calmed herself down. "I don't need any help, Mabel. I'm doing just fine."

"Is she?" Mabel asked, sending a contemptuous look in *Mamm*'s direction.

Mamm sputtered, "Ah . . . well . . . I'm still trying to think this all through."

"There's nothing to think through!" Mabel turned up her nose. "Katie doesn't know how to run her own life, and so we're trying to help."

Katie couldn't hold the words in any longer. "You steal my boyfriend out from under my nose. You let him spread rumors all over the community that aren't true. Now you're getting ready to marry a man who has a terrible temper. You're as blind as a bat about his problem. And you wonder why I don't trust you?"

"See?" Mabel shrugged. "What did I tell you? You're all messed up inside, Katie. And bitter too. No wonder you go sneaking around with that no-good Ben Stoll. You wouldn't know a good thing if it ran smack into your face."

"Girls, please!" *Mamm* begged. "None of this is Christian talk at all. You are to love

275

each other even as you disagree. And say what's needed with kind words, okay?"

"At least I'm not yelling," Katie defended herself.

Mabel was glaring at her now, and Katie muttered. "I'm sorry. That wasn't necessary."

"Okay." Mabel took a deep breath. "So why don't you stop fighting what's best for you, Katie? Norman's coming right after supper, and he'll have Mahlon with him. Beyond that no one can help you but yourself."

Katie couldn't keep the words back. "And will the good man have his marriage proposal with him? Is this what this is about?"

Mabel huffed. "Don't turn smart aleck on me now, Katie. Mahlon doesn't know why he's here. Other than he thinks it's to talk about the wedding. But we want you to see him up close. Then we think you'll change your mind. All you have to say is that you'll see him again at the wedding. Just be thankful we're trying to help, Katie. You should be thankful I've relented and allowed you back in my wedding at all!"

"I've never seen the likes of this. I'm not talking to the man." Katie stood by the kitchen window, both feet planted firmly on the floor.

276

"Yes, you will." Mabel's eyes blazed. "You won't make a fool out of me like that."

Katie glared back.

"You will talk to him. Won't she, *Mamm*?" Mabel said, turning around for reinforcement.

"I think you should," *Mamm* said. "It can't do any harm to speak to him."

Mamm was still grasping for straws, and Katie knew she should at least cooperate. If for no other reason than keeping a peaceful atmosphere around the house. "I'll speak with him, but it won't change anything."

Mabel looked triumphant. "Just forget about Ben for one night, Katie. And your bitterness. You'll see clearly what a great opportunity this is. I'm sure you'll drop Ben by the time Mahlon leaves."

Katie shut her mouth tightly and turned to go up to her room. She took her time going up the stairs. Not only did she need to collect herself, but she knew some of the bitter feelings needed to go. Harboring such things, even with how nasty Mabel was acting, was no excuse. She would explain the situation to Ben when she saw him the next time. He would understand. Their love had already weathered so much, it could also handle this, hard though it might be. Oh, how she wanted to fly into his arms this very moment and bury her head in his chest. How comforting that would be. Already the memory of being with him seemed distant, though she'd seen him only yesterday. Would Ben come visit soon? He hadn't said when, only that he would come. That's what she would think about tonight while speaking with Mahlon. And if her face turned red, he would probably take it as a compliment even as she explained that there never would be a serious relationship between them — if Mahlon even brought the subject up. Likely he was ignorant of Norman and Mabel's scheming.

Changing into her everyday dress, Katie went back down to the kitchen. *Mamm* was busy with the food, but Mabel was nowhere in sight.

"May I help with something?" Katie asked.

"The soup needs preparing." *Mamm* motioned toward a pile of vegetables on the table. "The recipe's on the third page."

Carolyn came in to help soon after that, but Mabel didn't make an appearance until just before the men came in from the barn. She was dressed in her Sunday best, which provoked an immediate reaction from Leroy. "What's all the lavishness about?"

"I just have on my usual dress I wear when

Norman visits," Mabel shot his way.

Leroy looked perplexed. "The wedding's not yet, for crying out loud."

"You're all so confused," Mabel said. "Don't even try to straighten out that muddled head of yours."

Leroy huffed. "Is it me or has Mabel turned into a crabapple lately?"

"It's the wedding," Willis said, as if marriage explained all of life's woes.

"Norman and Mahlon are coming to talk about the wedding plans tonight," *Mamm* said.

Leroy and Willis looked even more perplexed as everyone sat down at the table. Jesse led out in prayer. With the "amen" spoken, food became the focus, and platters were passed around at a rapid pace.

"So why is Mahlon coming over?" Willis brought the subject up with Katie as they walked into the living room for the evening devotions.

"You wouldn't believe it," Katie said, which drew a glare from Mabel. Katie wanted to say more, but that would only create additional conflict.

"Why are you in your everyday dress," Willis asked, giving her a quick glance, "while Mabel's in her best outfit?"

"Because Mabel's getting married, and

279

I'm not."

Mabel glared again, and Katie shut up. It was useless anyway.

Jesse cleared his throat, and everyone fell silent. He began reading, "I will praise thee, O Lord, with my whole heart; I will shew forth all thy marvellous works. I will be glad and rejoice . . ."

Katie listened to the words of Psalm 9. They were *gut* words for her tonight. She had so much to praise *Da Hah* for. Truly, how great was *Da Hah* even when enemies gathered around, just like the psalmist was saying. She felt like that — surrounded by enemies. But this, of course, wasn't true, she corrected. Mabel and Norman and even Enos were doing what they felt was the best for her, wrong though they were. *Da Hah*'s hand would see her through this. And the love in her heart for Ben would survive . . . and his love for her.

Jesse had just finished reading when Norman's buggy could be heard coming down the lane.

"He can wait," Jesse said. Kneeling, they prayed even as footsteps sounded on the front porch. Norman must have seen what they were doing through the living room window because he didn't knock until after they had all risen to their feet.

Mabel raced to the door, opened it, and rushed outside.

Katie couldn't hear the conversation, but Mabel soon stuck her head back in the doorway and motioned for Katie to come out.

Katie had her plan ready. It had come to her while Jesse was praying. This situation wasn't Mahlon's fault, and she should be nice to him. He probably didn't even know what was going on.

Mabel was all smiles when Katie stepped outside. "Norman and I have some plans to make, so if the two of you would sit on the porch swing, we'll be back before long." Mabel didn't wait for an answer as she led Norman through the front door with a gentle tug on his hand.

"Hi!" Katie greeted them, giving Mahlon a warm smile.

He turned quite red.

"Do you want to sit on the swing?"

"Ah, *yah*, I suppose," Mahlon said.

Katie sat on the swing as Mahlon also found his seat.

"So how was your day?" Katie asked.

Mahlon hesitated. "Okay, I guess. I worked on the farm."

"Is your fall plowing done? I've heard you're pretty industrious. I figure you're one of those early ones, you know, someone who always gets things in on time. My guess is you never get your hay cutting rained on now, do you?"

Mahlon turned red again. "I . . . well . . . I . . . I mean . . . well, that's a little much to say, really. I'm not that *gut* a farmer. But I do try to get things done on time."

The poor man was way out of his depths, Katie thought. Mabel was meaner than she'd even imagined.

Katie kept smiling. "Now don't be modest, Mahlon. You've got all your fall plowing done, don't you?"

He finally grinned. "*Yah,* I finished last week."

"And how many hay cuttings have you had rained on this year?"

Mahlon didn't hesitate now. "None. But that might have been an accident . . . or the blessing of *Da Hah.* I pray hard about such things."

Katie nodded. "I suppose all farmers do. I expect Jesse does, and Leroy and Willis. Farming keeps one close to *Da Hah* through prayer."

Mahlon showed a greater interest now. "Did you grow up on a farm?"

Katie shrugged. "I don't know if you'd call it a farm. *Mamm* had five acres or so left by the time I was old enough to help with the chores. We kept two cows, but it wasn't really farming."

Mahlon smiled gently. "Your *daett* died when you were young, didn't he?"

"*Yah,*" Katie replied. Did Mahlon remember her as "Emma Raber's odd daughter"? she wondered. Likely not. He probably had others things on his mind back in those days.

Mahlon was gazing across Jesse's fields. "I've always been on a farm, from little on up. I don't know any other way of earning a living. Lydia was born on a farm too. Lots of acreage. Her *daett*'s one of the best farmers around. Sort of in our families on both sides, I guess. I wouldn't have it any other way."

"She was your wife, *yah*? You still miss her a lot, don't you?" Katie reached over to give Mahlon's hand a quick squeeze.

Tears sprang to Mahlon's eyes. "More than I can ever say. I didn't know how much I loved her until she was gone. But I guess it's always that way. And now I'm left wishing I had loved her better. Lydia deserved so much more than anything I ever did for her."

Katie touched his hand again. "But she's in the arms of *Da Hah* now. Don't blame yourself, Mahlon. We all do the best we can."

He wiped his eyes. "We always wanted children, but I suppose that wasn't *Da Hah*'s will either. It was related to her illness, it turned out. Those were short years we had together. All of them are treasured greatly in my mind."

"I'm sure they are." Katie gave his hand another quick squeeze. Mahlon was a nice man. Perhaps some *gut* could come out of their time together in spite of Mabel. They spoke on into the evening — about Mahlon's farm, the corn harvest, the coming silo filling.

Finally Mabel and Norman appeared at the front door. She took in the two of them chatting away, and her smile grew broad. "Well, Norman's ready to go. I see you two are getting along just fine."

"Yah," Katie said, giving Mahlon another warm smile. Let Mabel draw the wrong conclusion.

"Then let's go," Norman said, leading the way off the porch.

"Now that was easy, wasn't it?" Mabel smiled at Katie while the two men were climbing into the buggy.

"It's not what you think," Katie replied.

Then she turned and headed inside and up the stairs for bed.

CHAPTER TWENTY-FIVE

On Thursday afternoon of that same week, after school had been dismissed, Katie sat behind her desk as the clock on the wall ticked the minutes away. Had she done the right thing today? The question wouldn't stop whirling in her mind. Noah Stoll, Ben's brother, had been caught cheating. He'd been copying answers from Abram Kuntz's arithmetic book. At least that's what Abram claimed when he ran in to report the infraction during the first recess. Abram said he'd spotted Noah peering over his shoulder and writing down the correct answers immediately afterward. This was a charge that sounded perfectly possible, since the temptation could be strong for those pupils struggling with arithmetic.

Her first inclination was to believe Abram, until she thought of the fact that Noah had never shown any signs of cheating before. Nor was he having a hard time learning the arithmetic they were studying. Noah could work out the early introduction problems in fractions blindfolded. In fact, she'd caught herself thinking just yesterday of how proud she was that Noah came from such a smart family. The thought was very sinful, of course, and one she should never have entertained. She might be in love with Ben, but that was no excuse for such loose thinking.

In the end, she'd called in Noah from the playground for a quick conference at her desk. Noah had come in frowning at being interrupted from his precious minutes of playtime.

"Tell Noah what you told me," Katie directed, while looking at the stony-faced Abram.

"I saw you looking over my shoulder and copying down arithmetic answers," Abram accused.

Horror flashed over Noah's face. "I did no such thing. I know how to do fractions better than you do."

Abram shot back, "I saw what I saw! You were cheating."

"I did not!" Noah declared.

Katie motioned to Noah. "Go get your tablet."

He did, opening it to the last page full of

fraction problems. Katie studied them. Several had been erased, so she flipped back several pages. The same pattern existed there. Noah must correct his answers frequently, which might be part of the reason he received such *gut* grades. Which could also be what Abram had noticed him doing. This was a trait that shouldn't be reprimanded but praised.

Katie checked several more pages, finding the same pattern.

"He cheated!" Abram declared. "Didn't he?"

"I'm afraid it's not conclusive." Katie closed the notebook. "I see no evidence to back up your claim, Abram."

"Do you think I'm lying?" Abram's face was red again.

"*Nee,* I think you might have been mistaken. I don't think Noah was cheating. He often erases his answers and corrects them."

Abram huffed. Apparently he wasn't giving up so easily. "Then check my two answers where I saw him cheating, and see if they are the same."

Katie shrugged. "That might work if you have the wrong answer. But if you both have the right ones, then they would be the same."

Abram thought long and hard on that

before going back to his seat. He returned with his notebook. "Check them anyway."

Katie did, and the answers in both notebooks matched. They also matched the answer key. She showed both boys the matches. "See, this proves nothing. So I think we'd better just let it go. And from now on, Noah, don't look over Abram's shoulder during school time. Okay?"

Noah nodded and was gone, racing back toward the playground. Abram didn't move.

"You can go now," Katie said, waving her hand toward the playground.

"It's because he's Ben Stoll's brother," Abram said. "That's why you're protecting him."

Katie's heart sank. She'd honestly not even considered that angle, but now it was out in the open staring at her. It wasn't true, but such accusations didn't have to be true to create trouble. They just had to *look* true. And now this looked very suspicious.

"It's true, isn't it?" Abram was obviously waiting for the answer he wanted.

Katie took a deep breath. "It is not, Abram. You are mistaken. And you are out of line saying such things to me. I won't allow thoughts like that in my classroom. Do you understand?"

Abram glowered for a few moments before

retreating to the playground. Nothing more was said all day nor would it be said tomorrow, Katie decided. At least not by Abram. But that didn't mean he wouldn't tell his *daett* the story, and that might mean another visit from Enos. And then most of the community would hear the tale. People would cluck their tongues and shake their heads. If a teacher was capable of bringing an inappropriate book like *Tom Sawyer* to school, she might also play favorites regarding her former boyfriend's brother. *Yah,* that's what they would think, Katie decided. It would make perfect sense to them.

What a mess! And she had no one to blame but herself. *Tom Sawyer* was out of the schoolhouse and back in Willis's hands. Following a brief explanation and apology to the students, she'd started reading aloud a "safe" book, one written by Christmas Carol Kauffman. But the damage had been done, and such a blunder wasn't easily undone. To say nothing of the accusation that she was too easy on students who transgressed. Now this situation with Abram and Noah might add fuel to the fire.

And there was Mabel's wrath that still had to be faced at home. She hadn't said anything all week to anyone but *Mamm* about the visit from Norman and Mahlon on

Monday night. Mabel assumed, no doubt from seeing how Katie had engaged Mahlon all evening in conversation, that her plan was working.

Well, sitting here worrying about things wasn't going to help, Katie told herself. The music might as well be faced. And she couldn't think about schoolwork anyway with all this on her mind. At home *Mamm* would have work which needed doing in preparation for Mabel's wedding. That would be much more profitable than doing nothing here.

Locking up the schoolhouse, Katie brought Sparky out of the barn. She was glad Joel had gotten a ride home with a friend so she could have some peace and quiet. She hitched her horse to the buggy and climbed in. Minutes later she was on the road, heading homeward. An *Englisha* car pulled up behind her. Instead of passing, the horn blew. Katie pulled off to the shoulder, yet still the car didn't go around. Her heart pounding, Katie quietly assessed the situation. She was on an open stretch of road, and there were plenty of houses around. No harm was going to come to her here.

Just as she was ready to pull out on the road again, the car pulled out and came alongside the buggy. The man on the passenger's side waved. Katie clutched the reins and gasped when she caught sight of his face. It was Ben! What was he doing flagging her down right out in the open?

Katie leaned out of the buggy door.

"Hi, Katie!" Ben called out.

"Ben!" She couldn't overcome her astonishment.

"I was hoping to catch you still at the schoolhouse."

"I left early." A great desire to speak with him overcame her. Whoever was driving Ben surely wouldn't mind spending a few minutes more of his time. Not if they'd been hoping to catch her still at school. She shouted, "I'll turn around and go back. Meet me there."

Ben nodded. The car raced forward and turned around in a driveway.

Katie turned Sparky around at a broad sweep on the road, urging him back toward the schoolhouse. She soon turned in the lane, entered the schoolyard, and tied up Sparky at the hitching post.

Ben jumped out of the car parked nearby.

Katie waited for him. If someone saw them, well, so be it. Besides, she was partly hidden by the buggy, so what did it matter? She reached out for his hand.

Ben laughed, taking both of hers in his. "My, my, what a greeting. I think I should come more often!"

Katie grinned. "That you should! Is something wrong?"

"*Nee,* I just had to see you." Ben pulled her close and gave her a long kiss.

Katie clung to him. "Hold me tighter, Ben."

"Why?" His fingers brushed the hair dangling under her *kapp.* "Is there something going wrong for you?"

Katie said nothing, but she didn't meet his gaze.

"That's as I expected," Ben whispered.

"They don't mean to make it so difficult," Katie said as she raised her eyes to his. "They just don't understand, that's all."

Ben sighed. "What is it, Katie? Tell me."

"Enos . . . and Norman . . . and Mabel, and now Mahlon Bontrager," Katie blurted. "And now there's children cheating at school."

Ben raised his eyebrows. "All that? Will you be okay? I can stay away if that will help you."

"Not that, Ben! I can take anything as long as I can see you."

He smiled. "That's nice to know, but it's not nice that I'm causing you trouble." A shadow crossed his face. "I'm sorry, Katie. I guess I'll have to say it a hundred times more before this is all over."

"I've tarnished my reputation with the Kuntz family," Katie admitted as she grimaced. "And that's causing trouble too."

"Because of me?"

Katie tried to smile. "Because I love you, and I didn't love Norman."

"That's no laughing matter, Katie. Enos is a powerful man in the community. Is there anything I can do to help?"

"I'm afraid it wouldn't do any *gut,* Ben. It goes deeper than that. I offended Norman, and there's little that can be done about that. And it's not going to help that your little brother was accused of cheating today by none other than Abram Kuntz — and I think Abram was in the wrong, so it came across as though I sided with Noah. So I'm deep in trouble, and nothing you can do will really help."

Ben's brow had furrowed. "I've been expecting something like this, but there's no reason I can't do my part. The issue of my testifying in court again seemed like the last straw to Bishop Miller. I wish he'd believed me when I told him I wasn't going to do that. Perhaps if I visit him tonight again and assure him I have no plans to testify — that I'm sticking with the traditions of our people, he can make it easier for you."

"But what about the danger of the man who attacked you being on the loose? He could harm you again!" Her fingers stroked his face.

"It doesn't matter, Katie. Not testifying is the right thing to do. It's our way."

She gazed up at him. "The right thing to do for me. Isn't that what you're really saying?"

He held her face with both hands. "Aren't you worth it, Katie?"

"Do you really want me to answer?"

"*Nee,* just give me a smile. Your sorrow is tearing my heart out."

They held each other for several minutes until Sparky's loud whinny interrupted them.

Ben let Katie go. "I have to be going."

"When will I see you again?" Katie clung to his hand.

"We have to be careful," he said, touching her cheek. "But I'll try to stop by as often as I can."

Katie nodded.

Ben turned and was gone. In what seemed like seconds, his friend was turning the car around and pulling away. She watched until they were out of sight before climbing back into her buggy. Swinging Sparky around, Katie drove down the lane and turned onto the main road. She hugged herself as she drove, remembering Ben's tight embrace. He was worth it! she told herself. Whatever trouble she had to go through, she wasn't going to lose Ben again. They would be together someday as husband and *frau*. That was *Da Hah*'s will, was it not? Pulling into their lane, Katie hadn't even come to a stop beside the barn before Mabel came racing out of the house. She screeched at the top of her voice, "You sneak, you! Katie, what a low, rotten trick! How could you?"

Katie noticed Willis stick his head out of the barn doorway. He grinned and pulled it right back in. So what's happened now? Katie wondered as she climbed out of the buggy.

Mabel came to a halt inches away, her face red. "Now I know you're the sneakiest girl in the whole community, Katie. Your *Mamm* even finally admitted it today. You've known all week that you're not dropping that Ben Stoll, and yet you let me think you were. I don't want you at my wedding."

"That would be a sight, wouldn't it?" Katie said with a smile. "I'm afraid you're stuck with me."

Mabel threw her hands in the air. "You're hopeless, Katie. Don't blame me for your mess. I tried my hardest to help you out." Mabel turned and marched off toward the house, giving one last screech toward the sky before disappearing through the washroom door.

Chapter Twenty-Six

On the Thursday before Thanksgiving, Bishop Miller was in full cry, his beard lifted toward the ceiling as he preached. Mabel and Norman were being married today, and Katie shifted her seat to get a better view of her sister. She looked happy enough — glowing, in fact. She stole brief glances at Norman, who was seated across from her. Mabel wasn't paying attention to Bishop Miller. Obviously the bride-to-be was interested in other things than the lesson being presented.

Katie sighed as she looked around. If she'd agreed not to see Ben again, she would be sitting beside Mabel as her bridesmaid instead of being stuck here in the unmarried girls' section. She shook herself mentally. This was Mabel's wedding — a day that should be all about joy and gladness. The happy couple would soon be beginning their new life together within the community. Katie pasted a smile on her face as Bishop Miller began telling the familiar story of Jesus attending the wedding feast in Cana where He turned water into wine.

"Weddings are that way," Bishop Miller said. "They are places of miracles. They are places where love grows, where two can become one and create a new home together. There the next generation is born and raised in the fear of *Da Hah*."

Katie listened and kept smiling. The embarrassment this morning when she wasn't at Mabel's side wasn't quite as bad as she'd expected. Most people didn't seem to notice she was sitting in the unmarried girl's section. Maybe they thought Mabel wanted an immediate family member by her side, not a sister by marriage.

Wanda, Mabel's cousin, had immediately accepted the last-minute offer to be bridesmaid. So she was now seated up front with a young man — someone she liked and had suggested. Mahlon had declined to take part after he was informed of the switch. Likely Mahlon knew he'd feel awkward sitting next to such a young girl, Katie thought. And people would wonder why he'd even been asked — not all of them knowing the original plans. Mahlon had made a wise decision, in her opinion. But then she'd expected that of him. The man was decent, and she hoped he'd find someone to stand by his side before long. Mahlon deserved a *gut* wife since his beloved *frau,* Lydia, had died.

Bishop Miller was now wrapping up his sermon, asking Mabel and Norman if they still wished to promise their lives to each other. Katie sighed with relief. Not that long ago she'd planned to be the one sitting in Mabel's chair today, promising her life to Norman until death parted them. How mistaken she'd been! Listening to her head instead of her heart. Thankfully *Da Hah* had intervened in His own way — a way that was too *wunderbah* to believe. That the love she'd once had for Ben had all come back . . . and even a little more if that were possible — was a miracle.

She hadn't seen Ben since that afternoon he'd stopped in at the schoolhouse. He would have loved to be here today, she was sure. But that wasn't possible. Maybe someday after the trial things would settle down to normal. Then Ben could come back home.

Norman and Mabel were now standing up. Katie watched as the last questions were asked and answered by first Norman and then Mabel. Bishop Miller joined their hands and pronounced them husband and *frau.*

Mabel's face was flushed with excitement. For all her fights with Mabel, Katie was still glad that Mabel was so happy. With Mabel married, maybe things would settle back to normal around the house. Without the rush of wedding preparations and Mabel's frequent outbursts over perceived transgressions, life had to be more peaceful. Katie grimaced. Maybe their relationship could settle to a more even keel now that Mabel was married. She'd thought that had happened after she came back from Europe — and it had . . . until Norman came along.

The last song had been sung, and the service was dismissing now. Norman led the way out to the pole barn where the noon meal would be served.

Katie suddenly thought of *Mamm*'s wedding at this very place not so long ago. In her mind's eye, she could still see the dashing figure Jesse had made that day in his new black suit. *Mamm* had been blushing as they left the house, just like Mabel was now. But Norman didn't look much like Jesse.

Someday soon she'd probably be heading out this very door following Ben after they'd said the vows together. That would happen when they had solved their problems with the community. And they would, eventually.

Someone tapped her on the shoulder, and Katie turned around to see the smiling face of Jesse's sister Sarah. "Beautiful day for a wedding, isn't it?"

"*Yah*," Katie agreed and smiled back. "I'm glad Mabel had such a nice one."

"You're not sore then . . . about Norman? I've been wondering about that."

Katie laughed. "*Nee*, it was for the best."

"That's a *gut* attitude to have," Sarah said. "And it might have been a little too much if you'd been bridesmaid. I understand perfectly. I was just curious, I guess, since Wanda was asked to be bridesmaid at the last minute."

Katie kept a smile on her face. "Let's just say . . . that also worked out for the best. And there are no hard feelings."

"That's a girl." Sarah patted Katie on the back. "I hope things work out the best for you also. And with that teaching job of yours."

Katie glanced up. "Why did you bring up my teaching job? Have you heard something I should know?"

Sarah looked down for a minute. "I probably shouldn't have brought it up. I suggest you speak with Enos Kuntz — and the sooner the better, Katie."

"But how can I today, a Sunday and a wedding day? How do you know something is amiss?"

Sarah shrugged. "One hears things. If I were you, I'd call for a board meeting. Tell them you're having trouble. It'll make for a more sympathetic hearing from the parents that way."

"But . . ." Katie stopped. There was no use showing her ignorance to Sarah. Obviously Sarah knew something. Maybe the tale of Noah's alleged cheating had made the rounds already.

"I don't want to spoil your enjoyment of the day," Sarah said and squeezed her arm. "Don't worry. I'm sure tomorrow will be plenty soon enough to head off trouble. That's what I always tell myself anyway." Sarah left then, melting into the pressing crowd of women moving toward the barn.

Katie moved with the flow of human traffic, but her heart felt like it was dragging on the ground. This was all she needed. More trouble ahead . . . trouble she didn't know how to deal with.

An usher at the pole barn door directed Katie to a seat among the other single females from Mabel's side of family. *Mamm* was already seated across the room in a choice spot near the corner table. Katie waved before she sat down and forced herself to smile. *Mamm* waved back, looking quite cheerful. Mabel was absolutely glowing with happiness now, hanging onto Norman's arm as they spoke with well-wishers passing in front of them. Norman was trying to look happy, Katie thought. But then he never looked very happy.

Bishop Miller soon stood and silence fell over the crowd. "We wish to thank everyone who has come here today on behalf of Norman and Mabel. This is their joyous day when they begin life together. We wish them *Da Hah*'s greatest blessings until He should see fit to call one of them home. And now let us pray and give thanks for this delicious meal we're about to receive."

Katie listened to Bishop Miller praying and wondered what he'd say if he knew she still loved Ben. She'd strayed far from what the ministry hoped would occur. Not that long ago the bishop had openly expressed his approval of Norman's relationship with her and then later of a possible match between her and Mahlon. Bishop Miller didn't approve of Ben. That much she knew. And he was likely saddened by what he was hearing right now about her from the parents in the community. A failed school-teacher would long be remembered, and

Katie's shame would reflect in some measure on Bishop Miller himself.

Katie sighed as Bishop Miller said "Amen." The food was passed around. After filling her plate, Katie pushed aside the dark thoughts and tried to enjoy the meal the women had worked so hard to prepare. Baked chicken done to a golden perfection, corn, green beans, various salads and Jell-Os. The young serving couples dashed about, making sure plates stayed full and food was kept moving along the tables.

Katie had heaped a large amount of food on her plate. She shouldn't indulge like this, what with the hymn singing coming up tonight when an "eligible" girl should look slim, but she was depressed. And Ben wasn't here anyway — he was the one person she really cared about and wanted to be eligible for.

Pies soon followed: cherry, apple, and blueberry. Added to that were big bowls of date pudding and sliced fruit. Mabel had gone all out, Katie thought. But that was only natural. A girl usually only had one wedding day in her lifetime so the most should be made of it. She continued to eat in silence. There were cousins sitting on both sides of her, but they seemed more interested in taking in the sights and sounds of the wedding than chatting with her, which suited her dark mood just fine. Food was the only thing cheering her spirits right now.

Bishop Miller stood and led the closing prayer. After that, the crowd spilled into the yard. Katie knew she should get in line to shake hands with Norman and Mabel and wish them well, but she didn't feel like it in the least. She almost left for the house but forced herself to stay. Once the line had thinned out, Katie approached the new couple. The greeting turned out easier than she'd imagined. She didn't even have to paste on a smile — it came on all by itself once she arrived in front of them. Katie offered her hand to Norman. "Congratulations to the two of you. And best wishes on your wedding day. It sure was a nice one."

Norman actually managed a decent smile back. "Thanks for coming, Katie." He bent low to whisper, "I'm sorry about the problem with the bridesmaid thing. I hope you're not too sore."

"I'm fine," Katie assured him. She then turned to Mabel, who reached out to squeeze her hand. Mabel was still glowing with happiness.

Katie moved on and found her way outside. All was forgiven and forgotten now.

And there was actually a *gut* feeling inside of her. Mabel would move on with her life, and the bad things from this day would soon be forgotten. Only the *gut* would remain, just as it should be.

CHAPTER TWENTY-SEVEN

The upstairs bedroom of Bishop Miller's house was filled with teenaged girls whiling away the afternoon of Mabel's wedding. They sat on the bed, along the floor, and leaned against the walls with their feet tucked under. Their low chatter had fallen silent as soon as the red-haired Stephen Graber stuck his head through the doorway. A grin spread over his face, and the rest of his short, stocky frame soon came into view. He was holding a clipboard in one hand and a pen in the other.

"What do you want?" one of the younger girls, Claudia Glick, snapped.

Stephen didn't say anything as his grin grew wider.

They all knew perfectly well what Stephen wanted, Katie thought from her place on the floor in the back of the room. But acting disinterested was part of the game. In fact, most of the girls in this room had been gathering here for the last hour in anticipation of Stephen's appearance. Well, they didn't know it would be Stephen, but they knew some boy, along with a sidekick, would come marching up the stairs looking for them. The two were assigned the gleeful task — from the boys' point of view — of making sure every unmarried male and female at the wedding was paired up for the evening's festivities.

"Hi, there!" Alvin Hochstetler joined Stephen in the doorway. He gave them all a little wave. "How are you all doing? Ready for the big night?"

He was a regular tease, Katie thought, smiling in spite of herself. He was also a natural for this assignment. At least the powers that be hadn't assigned some boy so nervous he couldn't look the girls in the eye. That always produced painful moments above and beyond the one that lay ahead of them. And today Katie was back in the game.

She knew none of the boys wanted to pick her. She'd already come to terms with that. It was common sense, what with how tattered her reputation was right now. She'd be left till the very end, when the leftovers were paired at random — usually by the two boys in charge, since no one cared much by that time. Right now, though, the interest level crackled. Every eye inside the room was fixed on Stephen and Alvin.

"So let's see," Alvin said as he peered over Stephen's shoulder. "We have the steadies all taken care of." Alvin rattled off a long list of names that had nothing to do with the occasion. He was dragging things out and obviously enjoying it. There were no steadies in the room. Most of them were either chatting with their boyfriends out in the yard or helping with the lunch cleanup. The only girls here were the ones whose fates hung in the balance.

"Just get to the point!" Claudia snapped again.

"Oh?" Alvin raised his eyebrows. "In a rush, are we?"

"Let's see, Alvin, we have Claudia down as your choice, don't we?" Stephen deadpanned.

A nervous twitter ran through the room. Some of Alvin's teasing was rubbing off on Stephen.

"Just pay attention to what's written down," Alvin countered without cracking a smile. Apparently he couldn't take a joke as well as he dished them out.

"Okay . . ." Stephen grinned. "Let's begin with Esther Gingerich. We have a request

310

from Joseph Yoder."

A squeal came from the bed where Esther was sitting, which was followed by bright red streaks running up and down her neck. Apparently Esther had been hoping for that choice. Katie smiled with amusement. It was nice when things worked out that way — but they didn't always. And from the smug looks on Alvin and Stephen's faces, someone had pulled strings on that one. Likely Joseph had done something to make sure his request was read off before everyone else's. Katie imagined Joseph had held a private conversation with either Alvin or Stephen. Otherwise some other boy's request for Esther could have come first, and requests were turned down by the girls only in exceptionally onerous situations.

"I'll take that as a *yah.*" Stephen moved on with a grin. "Next is Anna Hochstetler, who has a request from Leland Graber."

This one was greeted with a groan, but none of the girls were fooled. Anna too had been waiting on that one.

"So far so *gut.* Another *yah.*" Stephen looked pleased. "And now we have Katie Raber, with a request from Mahlon Bontrager."

Katie froze. *Mahlon?* Why would he do that? Did he feel sorry for her? That must be what it was. And she couldn't say *nee*. Not that she wanted to, but this was so early on the list . . . and so unexpected.

Alvin was looking around. "Katie?"

"Here!" Katie squeaked out.

"I'll take that as a *yah* then." Stephen moved on, reciting the names and going faster as the excitement level dropped. Soon it was simply a matter of pairing off the girls and boys who were left over.

Katie's head was still spinning when Stephen and Alvin finished. Would anyone think this strange? Mahlon taking her to the supper table? Most probably didn't know about the *kafuffle* with the bridesmaid issue. They might not realize why Mahlon was taking pity on her. And what if Ben found out? He probably wouldn't understand either. Well, she would just have to explain. And Ben would understand after all, she decided. He knew how people were paired for meals after a wedding. And their love had gone through so much already. It could handle a little thing like this. Before long they would have their lives straightened out, and Ben would be here at her side. Katie stood and stretched her legs. The room began to empty of girls, and Stephen and Alvin were long gone now, apparently ending their matchmaking list on a satisfactory basis. Following the girls downstairs, Katie veered off and went into the kitchen. A few women were working at the sink. They gave her smiles as she went past. They seemed friendly enough, just as everyone had been to her all day, which was strange, considering what was going on underneath the surface. But maybe things weren't quite as bad as Enos made them out to be. He might be blowing things out of proportion. Katie walked outside where the men were sitting on benches under some oak trees and then passed an area where more people were visiting. No one paid Katie any attention as she went by, especially the couples who were engrossed in each other's company. At least she had someone to sit with her tonight at dinner, even if it couldn't be Ben. That was better than being left to the last pick or, even worse, having no one. That was what she'd expected would happen.

Mahlon was a decent man. He really was. And thoughtful and considerate too. He hadn't said anything the other night about wanting to spend more time with her, so he must be trying to make her feel better after Mabel's rejection. That's all it was, and the least she could do was make this a pleasant evening for him.

Katie arrived at the tables in the pole barn

and busied herself with straightening out the tablecloths and other small chores that needed doing before supper. Bishop Miller soon appeared, obviously ready to begin the evening. Katie scurried back to the house. Since she had a man taking her to the table, it wouldn't be proper to meet with him before the official time. Arriving at the house, Katie mingled with the other girls who were peering out of the windows as the unmarried gathered. Bishop Miller was hollering something, and they were hollering back. Both parties soon dissolved into laughter.

Katie smiled as she watched the scene. These were her people, and their traditions warmed her all the way down to her toes. How nice of Mahlon to ease her mind about the dinner so she could enjoy the evening fully. Now that she thought of it, the Kuntz family was probably hoping to see her in disgrace tonight. Maybe Mahlon even knew that and had set out to foil their plans. Katie almost laughed out loud. She really had an imagination the size of the Empire State Building! Likely the Kuntzs were overjoyed today with the addition of Mabel to their family, and they weren't even thinking about her. But it was still nice of Mahlon — taking her to the table and all.

Moments later Stephen and Alvin came up the walk and opened the front door. Alvin was smiling. "Are all of my girls ready to go?"

"Shut up!" Claudia told him as she brushed past him. The rest of them followed her down the sidewalk and out to the pole barn. As each girl arrived, her steady date or partner of the evening positioned himself to fall in beside her.

Katie gave Mahlon a warm smile when he arrived next to her. "Hi, Mahlon. This is nice of you."

"I didn't want you lonely and crying all night."

"I wasn't doing anything of the sort, but thank you."

He chuckled. "Just making sure, that's all."

"I hope the *kafuffle* about this morning didn't bother you too much. Mabel has her ideas. Well, actually, it's probably more the Kuntz family that has their ways."

Mahlon smiled. "I guess we all do. But I understood — once Norman explained."

Katie glanced at him as they sat down. "Did Norman mention Ben?"

"*Yah.* I find your loyalty a *gut* thing, really. Regardless of what Norman says."

"You do?" Katie straightened her dress

315

"That's not what everyone else seems to think."

Mahlon shrugged. "So how is Ben doing? I hear he's living in town now by the ministry's orders. I'm sorry to hear that."

"Hopefully that will all be straightened out soon." Katie smiled. "Ben told me the other day that he was going to Bishop Miller. One of the ministry's concerns is Ben has been asked to testify at the trial of the man who shot him. Ben said he's not going to do that, but he wants to tell the bishop that he's serious about not doing it. He testified at a trial last year, and that was a big problem, of course."

Before Mahlon could respond, Bishop Miller cleared his throat. "Now that we have gathered here tonight, let us pray and give thanks once more for this food which has been prepared for our bodies."

They all bowed while Bishop Miller led out in prayer. The buzz of conversation picked up quickly once he finished. Katie noticed that a few of the younger couples were still silently sitting and watching. Conversation wasn't coming easy for them. In their nervousness, a few words might be all they managed most of the evening. Thankfully she wasn't having that problem.

Mahlon leaned toward her. "It may not be

that easy, Ben not testifying."

"Why not?" Katie was looking at him intently.

"The police or court might, well, you know — *make* him testify. I think the law can do that with a subpoena."

"Are you sure?"

Mahlon shrugged. "*Nee.* I'm not a lawyer, but that's something I've heard *Englisha* people talk about. They have more experience with these matters since they seem to do things they shouldn't sometimes and end up having to go to court."

"What would happen if Ben refuses to testify?"

"The judge can put him in jail, maybe even for a long time. But don't let me scare you. I could be wrong. I'm not sure how the justice system works out there in the world."

"That's just what I need," Katie muttered, as the first plate of pork chops came around.

"I'm sorry I mentioned it." Mahlon held the meat plate for Katie before taking a pork chop for himself.

"Let's not make this a conversation about me tonight." Katie said with a smile. "I'm tired of thinking about my troubles. Tell me what's happening in your life."

A smile flitted across Mahlon's face.

"Well, my best cow had twins last week. That's an accomplishment — for her of course. And a great gift from *Da Hah*. Both of them are heifers at that and healthy to boot."

"Oh!" Katie cooed. "I'll have to see them sometime. Jesse's cows haven't had any calves for some time now. I suppose calving season is coming up though."

"All part of a farmer's life." Mahlon held the gravy bowl for Katie while she dipped some out. "You said your *Mamm* and you had cows when you lived by yourself, right?"

Katie laughed. "*Yah,* we had two — Bossy and Molly. Do your cows have names?"

Mahlon smiled. "Maybe on their papers. Other than that, it's whatever I call them when they don't cooperate."

"I can't imagine you getting angry with a cow."

Mahlon smiled. "I've been known to twist a tail or two, but that's about it."

A vision of Norman's angry face when he was ordering her out of his buggy flashed through Katie's mind. Mahlon wouldn't ever be like that, she was sure of it. She couldn't come close to even imagining him angry. Twisting a cow's tail wasn't exactly anger in her estimation. Katie reached under the table to squeeze his hand. "I'm sure it wasn't quite like you describe it."

"A man's anger is not from *Da Hah*," Mahlon said, his face serious. "We must always fight against it."

"I couldn't agree more," Katie assured him. "But enough serious stuff. There must be plenty of *gut* things we can talk about."

He smiled and nodded. It was going to be a *gut* evening, Katie thought. Mahlon was being more than nice to her, and she was quite thankful.

CHAPTER TWENTY-EIGHT

The Monday after Mabel's wedding, Katie came home from school and was sitting at the kitchen table with *Mamm* seated across from her. *Mamm* had told her that Jesse's sisters, Sarah and Barbara, had been there earlier in the day to help clean up the last of the house. Katie had expected to help in the kitchen, but *Mamm* was insisting they take a break from the supper preparations. The house seemed quiet around them, almost as if it were holding its breath for the next outburst of trouble. Katie's news would likely bring it.

Let it not come, dear Hah, Katie breathed quickly.

Still, the look on her face must have hinted at impending trouble because *Mamm* asked, "What is it, Katie? You'd better tell me."

"Ben stopped by after school today. He wants to take me out tonight. He says his *daett* will allow him to use Longstreet and his buggy if he doesn't stay at the house very long."

Mamm was staring. "Stopped at the schoolhouse, Katie? Has this happened before?"

"Once. Ben was with an *Englisha* friend in a car. We stood outside and talked beside my buggy." *And stole a kiss,* Katie thought, but that didn't need mentioning right now.

Mamm sighed. "I'd hoped you were beginning to think about Mahlon as a possibility for dating, Katie. He was so nice to you at Mabel's wedding."

"*Mamm!*" Katie gasped. "Mahlon was just being kind to me. He never mentioned a word about seeing me, and he knows I love Ben. We talked about it, and Mahlon understands. He's not like some people in the community."

Mamm's face fell. "I had hoped you would come to your senses eventually. Ben isn't *gut* for you, Katie. Can't you see that?"

Katie sighed. "Really, *Mamm.* We've been over this so many times. Even before I went to Europe I loved Ben — and I still do. I've told you that. *Da Hah* has restored our hearts. You wouldn't stand against that, would you?"

Mamm looked away. "It's your life, Katie,

just like Jesse says. You'll have to do what you think is best."

Katie smiled. "Please don't look so glum, *Mamm.* Ben is just taking me out to eat. We'll come right back. I won't be out late."

"But that's what the *Englisha* do, Katie. They go out to eat. Since when have you started those kinds of customs? That's worse than running around with the Mennonite youth, in my mind."

Katie was silent. She hadn't thought of that angle before. Ben's invitation to spend time with him had been too exciting to think of much else. But *Mamm* did have a point. Going to an *Englisha* restaurant wasn't something Amish dating couples did, even if they drove their buggies into town on an errand.

"Ben could stay here for supper." Hope gleamed in *Mamm*'s eyes. "I can't see that Jesse would object to that."

Katie swallowed hard. That was an option indeed. And it would look much better to Jesse, *Mamm,* and the community. And right now she needed all the sympathy she could garner. *Mamm* might even see Ben in a different light if he stayed for supper. Katie nodded. "I'll ask him when he comes."

Mamm smiled. "I appreciate that. And you can talk with him out on the porch later.

That should be private enough for you."

"Thank you!"

Mamm might think the swing was private enough, but Mabel had listened to enough of Katie's conversations on that very swing so Katie knew better. Words carried easily into the house. And even though Mabel was gone, Katie was still nervous about talking there — unless everyone had gone to bed.

"Then it's settled." *Mamm* was all smiles again, jumping up to continue the supper preparations. Katie joined her and listened for sounds of Ben's buggy pulling into the driveway. Carolyn had just come down from upstairs when the sounds of buggy wheels carried into the house.

"Who's that?" Carolyn asked.

Katie didn't stop to explain; *Mamm* could do that. Right now she wanted to reach Ben's buggy before Jesse or one of the boys did. The conversation that might occur was too risky without her there. Ben's visit was going to be quite a surprise for them.

Panting, Katie arrived at Ben's buggy. Longstreet was such a welcome sight that she almost paused to give him a hug around his neck. Instead, she rushed up to the opening buggy door.

Ben appeared quite pleased. "It's *gut* to get such a welcome from the woman who loves me."

"Stop it, silly!" Katie said before pausing to catch her breath. "There's been a change in plans. *Mamm* wants you to stay for supper. She . . . well . . . I . . . we thought that might be better than going out to an *Englisha* restaurant."

Ben appeared surprised. "You don't want to go out? There are nice restaurants in town."

"*Yah,* of course that would be nice, Ben. But things are a little . . . shall I say . . . touchy right now? And I'm a church member now, so I have to watch myself."

Ben smiled. "Okay, I understand. I'll be glad to eat with your family tonight. In fact, it would be an honor."

She could have kissed him right out there in the open, but that had better wait until later — once she could get Ben away from the front porch swing to someplace where they could have some privacy.

"Hello!" Leroy called from the barn door. "Who's here, Katie?"

Katie pulled her head out of the buggy door. "Ben! And he's staying for supper."

"Okay." Leroy appeared perplexed, but he disappeared back inside the barn.

"He looks friendly enough," Ben commented. "How's the rest of your family?"

"Okay now that Mabel's gone." That wasn't totally true, but it was true in the way Ben meant it. They would be nice to him tonight. "Come in. We can sit in the living room until supper's ready."

"I think I'll do that." Ben climbed out of the buggy and secured Longstreet to the hitching post. Katie took his hand as they walked across the lawn. Everyone might as well see where her heart lay. And she wasn't doing anything wrong.

Ben seemed to understand, and his fingers wrapped around hers.

Mamm met them at the door with a smile on her face.

She's trying, Katie thought. *Mamm* really was a dear.

Carolyn stuck her head out of the kitchen. "Hi, Ben!"

"Howdy," he said in reply.

"Sit down here." Katie motioned Ben toward the couch. They'd never had a formal date. Their relationship this far had always been conducted in buggy rides and meeting at the Mennonite youth gatherings. But that wouldn't always be so. Eventually Ben would be able to bring her home after the hymn singing, proper like. They could sit on the couch on Sunday evening and eat pie. In fact, why not do so right now? Katie thought. It would be like a little sip of the delicious time ahead of them.

"Aren't you sitting?" Ben asked and motioned toward the empty seat on the couch beside him.

"*Yah,*" Katie whispered, settling herself beside Ben. "I have something I should tell you."

"Okay."

Katie looked around. "I've changed my mind. Let's go out on the porch."

Ben shrugged, but he got up and followed her out to the porch swing.

"This is better." Katie settled in again. "No listening ears, I hope. Carolyn's busy in the kitchen, and I hope she has better sense then to eavesdrop anyway."

"You sounds serious." Ben looked concerned.

"Not really, so don't get worried." Katie held his arm. "I just want to keep you up on what's been going on."

"So give it to me then."

"Well, at Mabel's wedding Mahlon Bontrager took me to the table. He felt sorry for me, I think. And it was sweet of him to help out since I would have been left alone for the evening, my reputation being the way it is in the community right now."

"That's okay." Ben's arm came around

326

her shoulder and pulled Katie tight. "I'm not worried."

Katie leaned against his shoulder. Ben was so understanding. Most people would go by how things appeared at first glance, but not Ben.

"How are things going with you?" Katie asked. "Did you make it over to Bishop Miller's like you planned?"

Ben's face darkened. "I did. But Bishop Miller said things still are the way they are. He'd rather wait until the trial is over before anything changes. And now the prosecutor claims he can force me to testify. I don't know how all this will turn out."

"That's what Mahlon said — about them being able to make you testify."

"Then he's a smarter man than I am."

"*Nee*, he's not Ben." Katie clutched his arm. "Stop beating yourself over the head. It won't do any good."

Ben sighed. "The truth be told, I don't know what else to do."

"Maybe Jesse knows the answer. You could ask him tonight."

"Jesse?"

"Maybe that's why we're here tonight instead of in town?" Katie suggested.

Ben still looked skeptical. "There's not much anyone can do. I'd rather not talk about this stuff with your family."

"Then we won't." Katie took his hand. "Supper must be about ready. You look hungry."

Ben smiled. "Starved, in fact. I have to live on my own cooking, remember?"

"Then we will stuff you full tonight!" Katie led the way to the kitchen.

Mamm was just putting food on the table. "Sit down, Ben. The men will be in from the barn soon."

Ben sat down with a pleased look on his face. "Thanks, Emma, for inviting me." The table was steaming with delicious food — mashed potatoes, gravy, peas, roast, and salad. On the counter several pies sat waiting. "This sure looks awfully *gut*."

"Ben's starved for home cooking, *Mamm*," Katie said. "Thanks for suggesting we eat here tonight."

"It's always *gut* to eat at home," *Mamm* said. "There's no place better really."

"I can agree with that." Ben's smile faded. "I never thought I'd miss home like I do."

Mamm appeared troubled. "Well, hopefully this will all soon be passed."

"I hope so," Ben said. "I hope you don't think ill of me about what's happening. I'm trying to do what's right and best for Katie."

Katie touched his hand. "You don't have

to explain, Ben. *Mamm* understands."

The stair door burst open and Carolyn rushed in, leaping into her chair at the table.

"You are an energetic young woman!" Ben said with a smile.

Carolyn didn't say anything, but she was obviously pleased by the attention.

Jesse and the two boys soon came in, water still clinging to their hair from washing up.

"Leroy said you were here," Jesse said, offering his hand to Ben. "Good to have you."

Ben stood and shook Jesse's hand.

Leroy and Willis grinned as they slid into their places on the far side of the table.

"Let's pray." Jesse bowed his head and led out in prayer. After the "amen," Leroy wasted no time in passing the food around. He made sure Ben got first choice though, minding his manners for once.

Katie leaned back in her chair. This was an evening she was going to treasure for a long time. Ben was eating at their table. This was surely a *gut* sign of what was yet to come.

"Are you about healed up from your wounds?" Jesse asked. "I haven't heard anything for awhile."

"Pretty much." Ben paused from dishing out the gravy. "I still suffer some aftereffects from the staph infection, but the doctor thinks even that will go away with time."

"And the gunshot wound?" Carolyn asked, her eyes shining with curiosity.

Ben laughed. "It's doing okay, Carolyn."

"How did it feel getting shot?" Carolyn pressed.

"Don't ask things like that," Katie said, trying to shush her.

Ben shook his head, smiling. "It's okay, Katie. Well, I remember a big bang and then a burning in my chest. I don't remember much after that."

"Did it feel like you were *dying*?" Carolyn asked.

"Don't be morbid," Willis said.

At least someone in the family besides her has some sense, Katie thought.

Ben sobered. "I can't say that I even thought about that."

"It's best if we are prepared for dying at all times," Jesse said. "Then we don't have to think about it in times of danger, but we can safely leave such things in *Da Hah*'s hands. We're glad you're still with us, Ben. And that you're doing well."

"Thanks." Ben nodded.

Katie found his hand under the table.

"You will come for Thanksgiving dinner, won't you?" *Mamm* asked after a quick glance toward Jesse for his approval.

"I would be honored," Ben said, his voice a whisper.

Katie squeezed his hand as the chatter continued. Thankfully the topics were on much safer subject — the day's events on the farm. Katie was almost beside herself with joy that Ben would be coming for Thanksgiving. *Mamm* must be softening her heart toward him. Oh, she was so blessed! And this after all they had gone through already. "Thank You, dear *Hah,*" Katie whispered, letting go of Ben's hand to pass the pie plate around the table.

CHAPTER TWENTY-NINE

It was Tuesday afternoon the week of Thanksgiving, but Katie wasn't thinking about the holiday as she drove Sparky into the Kuntz's driveway. Her hands were trembling so much that the lines shook. If there were any other option than being here, she'd be doing whatever it took right now. But she was the schoolteacher, and this was her problem to face and solve. She would not run from it.

Joel had told her at the noon hour what he'd seen, and she had confronted Abram during the last recess. Abram had denied the charge of cheating, but he did admit that he'd been snooping through Noah's tablet. Abram claimed he was checking whether Noah was cheating again — not copying answers as Joel reported seeing him do.

Abram had done a lot of glaring at Joel, but Joel had stuck to his story. And a check of several answers in both Abram and Noah's tablets had produced two wrong answers that matched, sure evidence that some cheating was going on. Abram agreed, but he claimed it was Noah who was cheating. Katie had questioned Noah after school for a few minutes, having asked Abram to wait by her desk. Noah denied any knowledge of either copying answers or of having seen Abram near his tablet. She'd thanked Noah and dismissed him.

Cheating was punishable by spanking. In the community, that was the only acceptable punishment. Any lesser response might be taken by the student and the parents as a serious neglect of her duties. She should have spanked Abram as soon as Noah was out of the schoolyard. But in the face of Abram's continued, vigorous denials, her courage had failed. Yet she couldn't ignore the problem. So here she was, on her way to talk to Enos about the situation. Perhaps he would be sympathetic, and her courage would return. Enos might even spank his son himself. If not, she would do the deed first thing in the morning at the schoolhouse. Katie groaned as she pulled to a stop beside the hitching post. She didn't need this *kafuffle* right now. Thanksgiving was this week. *Mamm* and Carolyn were feeling overwhelmed at home with preparations for the big dinner. And that was work she should be helping with instead of chasing down problems caused by Abram Kuntz. At least one bright spot remained. Ben was still coming for Thanksgiving Day! And he hadn't needed any persuasion from *Mamm* to accept the invitation. Ben had told her when they parted that he'd fully enjoyed the meal and getting to know the family better.

Thankfully, *Mamm* wasn't too up on the talk that continued to float around the community about Ben. It would die down after the trial, no doubt. Ben had told Bishop Miller that he wasn't going to testify, and he meant it. It wasn't Ben's fault that the prosecutor had threatened to force him to appear in court.

Mabel would have a fit on Thursday when she found Ben at the house, but she would have to deal with it. No one was asking for her opinion now that she was Norman's *frau*. Mabel could fume and fuss as much as she'd like.

Katie tied Sparky to the hitching post as she heard a door open behind her. She whirled around to see Enos shutting the barn door and approaching at a fast walk. Abram must have told his *daett* by now because it seemed that Enos had been expecting her.

"*Gut* evening," Enos said as he tipped his hat in her direction.

"*Gut* evening. I guess you know why I'm here. Is that correct?"

"*Yah,* I do." Enos's face was sober. "Abram told me. I'm sorry to hear of this trouble."

"So am I." Words rushed out of Katie's mouth. "Do you want to hear the full story? I believe the situation is rather serious."

"Obviously, otherwise you wouldn't be here."

"I have strong reasons to believe Abram is cheating at school."

Enos cleared his throat. "I also understand from Abram that he reported Noah Stoll was cheating some time back. He told me you refused to deal with the problem."

"*Nee,* that's not true. I did handle that situation."

Enos ignored her. "That is why Abram thought he needed to take matters into his own hands. He was checking up on Noah because you weren't doing your duty. Remember, Katie, that every teacher we've ever had has always been quick to deal with cheating problems."

Katie tried again. "I dealt with that problem, Enos. Noah was not cheating. Abram was mistaken."

A slight smile of disbelief crept across Enos's face. "That's because you are too blinded by Ben Stoll's charms to see clearly, Katie. It's plain enough to see. The corruption from Ben is spreading to his brother. And that's nothing more than what we would expect. *Da Hah* says He will visit " 'the iniquity of the fathers upon the children to the third and fourth generations.' "

Katie was stunned by the accusation but not surprised. She struggled to respond calmly. "Ben is not Noah's father. And I was not biased when I looked into the cheating situation."

Enos regarded her with pity. "Ben is Noah's brother, Katie. It's close enough. The problem is that we have a schoolteacher who brings corruption straight into the schoolhouse. If she would be willing to admit and forsake the evil, that would be one thing. But now you insist on accusing the one person in your school who dares to stand up to the corruption you encourage. I'm very disappointed in you. I had such high hopes for you at the beginning of the school year."

Katie tried to keep breathing steadily. "I

see. This has to do with Norman too. Is that what's going on? I need to be proven wrong and be punished so that Norman's actions are proven right?"

Enos's face darkened. "You will not accuse my eldest son for your own wrongs, Katie! He was right in cutting off his relationship with you. I would think your recent and continued contact with Ben Stoll proves all that needs proving about your judgment. You are the one refusing to see the truth."

"I'm sorry, Enos. I shouldn't have brought Norman into this. I'm here because of what has happened at the school."

Enos nodded. "I can understand why you did. I suppose your heart was completely broken. That still doesn't give you an excuse for renewing your relationship with Ben or for refusing to see what's happening right in front of your eyes."

Thoughts raced through Katie's mind, but none should be spoken out loud. Why was the Kuntz family filled with bitterness regarding her? Asking that would make the current situation worse. Enos had obviously made up his mind that Abram was telling the truth, but as the teacher, she needed to reason with him to get at the truth. That much was her duty. Katie kept her voice even. "Why not consider looking at the two tablets for comparison like I did? Then you will understand why I believe Abram is the one who has been cheating."

"I thought it was Joel who accused Abram?"

"It was originally, but I looked into it, and I'm standing by *my* decision to bring this matter up with you."

"Did you tell Joel about the trouble with Noah? Maybe even tell your entire family around the supper table? Did you want to make sure you had someone on your side?"

Katie's heart raced at this fresh accusation of treachery. "I did nothing of the sort! And you are in the wrong to even suggest such a thing."

Enos raised his eyebrows. "I see you suddenly find principles to stand on — when it suits you, of course. I'll tell you what we'll do. I'll call a school board meeting on Friday morning, the day after Thanksgiving. School will be out that day so we'll have plenty of time to look into this."

"I don't think that is necessary," Katie protested. "This is between you, as the parent, and the teacher."

Enos smiled. "I'm sure that's what you hoped it would be. But it's not, Katie. This is fast becoming a community matter. We now have our schoolteacher dating her old boyfriend again — a man who has been convicted of a crime and spent time in jail. A man who is planning to testify in a legal courtroom against a man accused of wounding him. A thing *Da Hah* forbids. And this is after you have made a commitment to *Da Hah* and His church. That's what really needs dealing with, Katie. Your relationship and support of someone who has been asked to leave the community. If I give in to you on this matter, how many more of our children will suffer from your poor judgment?"

Katie pressed her fist against her chest. "This is so wrong, Enos. Ben has nothing to do with this matter. Besides, he's told the bishop that he is not going to testify even if the court attempts to force him. He is going to follow his faith — *our* faith — and not participate in the trial."

Enos appeared grim. "I see you know plenty about his business, but do you know anything about his character? *Nee,* I say you do not. Ben will be put in jail again. He's already been there once, so he should be used to it."

Katie choked back a sob. "I don't think it's right that your family hates me like this. Norman got what he wanted — a better *frau* than I could have been for him. Why are you doing this?"

Enos shook his head sadly. "No one hates you, Katie. It is *gut* that you have some humility in seeing that Norman is much better off without you. I thank *Da Hah* that Norman saw this in time — before he said the marriage vows with you. I was taken in by you once, but that won't happen again. If you hope to keep your teaching job, it would be wise for you to retract your accusation of cheating against Abram."

"And if I do, would you drop the matter?"

Enos thought for a moment. "I'm afraid I'd still have to call the school board meeting. They need to hear about this and decide what needs doing."

"I'll be going then." Katie turned and walked to her buggy as slowly as she could make herself.

"We'll be expecting you Friday morning at the schoolhouse. Ten o'clock!" Enos hollered after her.

Katie untied Sparky and, blocked by Sparky's body, wiped away her tears so she could see to climb into the buggy. Her vision was still a blur as she urged Sparky down the lane. He seemed to catch her urgency and raced down the blacktop.

It was useless, running away like this, Katie told herself. But it was also useless staying and talking anymore with Enos Kuntz. The man had his mind made up, and nothing was going to change it. Her goose was cooked. That was the truth of the matter. Enos would have his story told to the other school board members long before she recounted hers on Friday morning. With her continued relationship with Ben hanging in the background, there was no way she would gain a sympathetic hearing.

With a flurry of gravel, Katie turned into her driveway, bringing the sweating Sparky to a stop by the barn. She leaped out, and unhitched him. *Mamm*'s face appeared for a moment in the kitchen window and then vanished.

Katie was long overdue from school, so she figured *Mamm* had probably been worried. And *Mamm* was already overwhelmed with work, without her adding more trouble to the load, Katie thought. Well, she just wouldn't tell anyone. Only how was that possible with the tears pouring down her checks and the sobs she couldn't control? Maybe if she stayed in the barn for a few minutes she'd gain more control.

Leading Sparky to the barn, Katie pushed open the door and stepped inside the cool darkness. It was like being swallowed by another world. Even the dim cobwebs seen in the rafters seemed quiet and friendly, beckoning her home. She pulled the harness off Sparky and tied him up. She grabbed a towel and dried him off, talking to him the entire time about what a good horse he was and how much she appreciated him. Then she got out a curry comb and soft brush and gave him a thorough work over. Sparky nudged her gently as he enjoyed the attention. Then Katie turned him into his stall and measured some oats into the feedbox.

"Dear *Hah,* help me," Katie whispered as she stepped back outside into the sunshine. When she made her way across the lawn and entered the house, *Mamm* was still in the kitchen with Carolyn. Both of them were in dough-covered aprons and baked goods were spread across the table.

"How did your day go?" *Mamm* asked.

"It wasn't the best. Did Joel say something about today?"

"Yes, he did. So I figured you were spanking Abram. I'm sorry you had to deal with this today yet."

Katie burst into tears and collapsed onto a kitchen chair. *Mamm* rushed over and draped her moist hand over Katie's shoulder. "I'd hug you dear if I wasn't so floury. Was it that bad? But you'll get used to it.

I'm sure it's not that different from having to spank your own children."

"I didn't spank him," Katie wailed. "That's the problem."

"You didn't spank him?" Both *Mamm* and Carolyn were staring at her.

"I went to Enos's place. I wanted to talk with him. And now it's a big, big mess. Enos is calling a school board meeting on Friday morning after Thanksgiving to complain about me."

"You should have spanked Abram," Carolyn murmured. "Abram's a spoiled little brat."

Katie shook her head. "I'm glad I didn't. It wouldn't have made the least bit of difference either way."

"Can we do anything to help?" *Mamm* asked.

"I'm going to change and help you." Katie jumped to her feet. "I need to do something to forget about Enos and Abram and school for awhile."

"Are you sure you'll be okay?" *Mamm* had moved back a step.

"As sure as I can be," Katie said over her shoulder as she moved toward the stairs. And that was about the truth. Her head hurt and her emotions were torn to bits, so how sure could one be in this state? She knew she loved Ben and that he was coming for Thanksgiving dinner. Now that she was sure of, and it brought a smile to her face.

CHAPTER THIRTY

It was Thanksgiving morning, and Ben was due any moment. The last of *Mamm*'s holiday meal was being prepared in the kitchen. To Katie it had seemed like years since she'd seen Ben. All last night she'd comforted herself by thinking about Ben and what it would feel like to have his strong arms around her again. Not that she would dare embrace him when he arrived. She wasn't that brave in front of her family, nor would it be considered decent. Expressions of such love were only appropriate in private. Perhaps they could slip outside after dinner and go for a long walk. It didn't look like snow was in the forecast, even though it was deep into November. The reports said the Delaware coast appeared to be in for a mild winter this year.

Too bad it couldn't snow by tomorrow so the meeting of the school board could be cancelled, Katie mused. It was clear what was going to happen. The men would likely take Enos's side, especially with her continuing to see Ben. Thankfully, Jesse and *Mamm* were willing to spend time to get the truth about Ben instead of jumping to quick conclusions or listening to rumors about Ben's character.

Hearing a buggy arrive, Katie took another quick glance out of the kitchen window. It was only Norman's buggy. Mabel and Norman must have decided to still come today even though they knew Ben would be here. Mabel also had to know about her visit to see Enos and the upcoming meeting at the schoolhouse. Such matters weren't long hidden between families, to say nothing of the community at large.

Perhaps Mabel was homesick, with the newness of her marriage to Norman last week already wearing off. Katie hadn't seen much of Mabel since the wedding. It was best that way, the feelings being the way they were. Eventually they would heal, but it would take some time. Today, though, was a *gut* day to begin the reconciliation, it being Thanksgiving and all. They would gather and give thanks for the blessings they had. Families had to get along on a day like this even if things weren't so smooth beneath the surface.

"Is that Mabel and Norman?" *Mamm* asked as she came over to look out the kitchen window. "Should you go help them unhitch?"

Mamm was being peacemaker again. Katie knew Norman wouldn't want her help with his horse. Someone should welcome the couple in though. Katie smiled. "I'll run out and see if Mabel might have something I can carry in for her."

Katie hurried out the washroom door. The chill in the air caused her pause, but she kept going. She should have grabbed a coat, but it was too late now.

Katie approached the buggy and offered a cheerful, "*Gut* morning!"

"*Gut* morning." Norman was clearly grumpy from the look on his face. Mabel was in tears and making no attempt to hide them.

Katie tried to cover her surprise. "May I help carry something in?" she asked.

Norman didn't look up. He was working on taking the tugs off. When that was done, he led Bonnie out of the shafts and hurried toward the barn without a backward glance.

Katie turned to the tearful Mabel. "What's wrong?"

Mabel climbed down, sobbing. "Oh, its awful. I can't say how awful it is. What am I going to do?"

"Going to do? What happened?" Katie hugged Mabel and then held her at arm's length to look into her eyes.

"Norman . . . his temper . . . it flares up for no reason at all. I know you warned me, Katie. But I didn't know it was like this. He's blaming it this morning on Ben being here . . . and on him having to come with me. But I had to come home. I couldn't stand not being here on our first Thanksgiving."

"Has he . . ." Katie hesitated and searched Mabel's face.

"*Nee,* of course not. He wouldn't do that. But his temper . . . I've never seen anything like it."

Katie bit back the words she wanted to say. Instead she took a deep breath. "Maybe *Mamm* has some advice for you. I've never been married so I can't offer any advice on this."

Mabel clung to Katie's arm as they went up the sidewalk. The barn door opened behind them, and Katie glanced over her shoulder. Norman didn't look all that happy as he followed them toward the house. If he was half the man he thought he was, he'd come and comfort his *frau* instead of leaving it to others.

"Maybe we should stop and talk with Norman," Katie whispered into Mabel's ear, "before we get to the house. You shouldn't take this quarrel inside where the others will see it."

"Maybe . . ." Mabel didn't sound convinced, but she did slow down a little. Katie pulled back even more until Norman caught up with them.

She turned toward him. "I think you owe your *frau* an apology for your actions, Norman. So spit it out, and we can go on with this day."

Norman smirked. "She's come home to cry on her family's shoulder. I expected as much. If I did what I should have done, we would have stayed home."

This produced a muffled wail from Mabel. "How can you say that, Norman?"

"I'll say what I wish," Norman shot back. "You're my *frau* now, and you will listen."

Katie searched her mind for what she could say. Perhaps something that would get through Norman's thick skull. She gave him a steady glare. "Do you really want Jesse to hear about your problem? That's what will happen if we go inside with Mabel in tears. And I don't think you want that to happen. Fathers have a way of getting upset when their daughters come home with bad tales about how their husbands are treating them. So why don't you say you're sorry, and we can go on in good humor."

Norman glared. "She's just a crybaby, and you're one to talk. I can't believe you're bringing Ben Stoll today. I ought to go straight home, Katie."

Katie became serious. "Then why don't you, Norman? We'll have Mabel to ourselves today, and we'll all have a good time."

He thought about that for a moment before nodding and clenching his teeth for a minute. Then he forced out, "I'm sorry, Mabel. Maybe I was a little out of line. Will you forgive me?"

Mabel gasped and threw her arms around Norman's neck.

"Well, *gut.* That's settled. Come in now." Katie pulled on Mabel's arm. "Let's get inside. You two can finish making up to-night."

Mabel wiped her eyes and followed Katie, already smiling by the time they entered the front door, Norman tagging along behind. Carolyn was standing just inside with a strange look on her face. Katie ignored her and figured Carolyn could think what she wished.

Mamm rushed out of the kitchen to give Mabel a hug as Norman snuck in behind them with a sheepish look on his face. He sat on the couch.

He should look more than a little ashamed of himself, Katie thought.

Mamm had to notice that Mabel had been crying, but Katie knew she wouldn't ask any questions. She wouldn't want to stir things up, even if there was trouble — especially not with the Kuntz family.

"I'm so glad you two could come today," *Mamm* gushed. "Jesse has some kind of problem with his cows in the back fields, and Leroy and Willis are with him now. They'll be back soon."

"I can go help," Norman offered.

Except for leaning forward, he hadn't moved, Katie noticed. Mabel loved the man even with his faults, and the rest of the family must do the same if they wished to all get along.

"*Nee*," *Mamm* waved her hand in a dismissive gesture. "Jesse has plenty of help with the two boys. Don't bother yourself. They'll be back before long."

Norman looked quite pleased with that answer and settled back onto the couch.

Katie avoided his gaze as the sound of buggy wheels came in the driveway again. Ben had arrived! Now it was Norman's turn to practice Christian charity. Hopefully he

351

had enough to avoid a scene. She made her way out the door and ran across the lawn to Ben's buggy. He had the door open by the time she arrived. It was all she could do not to fly into his arms, but Norman would probably have a sharp eye out for any possible indiscretions. Work wouldn't get him off the couch, but catching her in a misstep would certainly be motivation enough. He was probably peering out of the living room window right now.

"Hi!" Ben greeted her. "You look bright and chirpy this morning."

"And so do you." Katie stopped a few feet away. "I'm so glad you could come."

He seemed to understand about the lack of a hug, taking a quick glance toward the house. "And I'm glad to be here. Will Norman have me for lunch, do you think?"

Katie laughed. "I don't think so. He already had his temper fit for the morning. He'll get over it."

"I don't have to be here, you know," Ben said. "I know I'm not making you look the best right now."

"And miss Thanksgiving dinner with you? I wouldn't think of it!"

"I guess I could use a *gut,* home-cooked meal." A smile flitted across his face. "Although *Mamm* and *Daett* would have let me join them at Uncle Abner's place. That's where they are this morning."

"Not a chance!" Katie said. "You can unhitch and put Longstreet in the barn. There's an empty stall where he'll be comfortable."

"That sounds good," Ben said. He walked to the far side of the buggy and undid the tug.

Katie undid the tug on her side, and then held the shafts as Ben led Longstreet forward. Then Katie walked with them to the barn and showed Ben where he could put Longstreet and the harness. Taking Ben's hand, she said, "Well, let's get started. Let's go in and you can meet the lion himself. Norman was down to a whimper when I left the house."

"Is it that bad?" Ben asked. "I didn't know Norman had that kind of temper."

Katie snorted. "He saves it for the ones who can't do anything about it. He has his reputation to uphold, you know. And to think I once dated him."

"I guess I have nothing to say when it comes to faults," Ben admitted.

"At least you don't have that one. Let's be thankful."

Ben paused by the front steps. "The court date is set for some time after the first of the year, Katie. Maybe things will quiet down for us after that."

"So you're going to jail rather than testify?" The question slipped out, and Katie looked away.

Ben sighed. "That's what they're threatening me with."

"Is there no way the judge will consider our beliefs?" Katie implored, as if Ben could do anything to change the judge's mind.

"I asked the prosecutor that very question. He asked me if I'm a member of the Amish church."

"And you're not," Katie answered.

"*Yah,* and there's nothing I can do about that right now."

"Will you . . . afterward . . . join the church, Ben? I was hoping you might join next spring's baptismal class. I know that might be expecting a little much."

Ben winced. "I'll try, but I have to get all this behind me first, you know."

Katie beamed. "I know. But it will work out. I just know it will."

He nodded. "I still struggle with my faith at times, Katie. I always have. But I truly believe now. I want you to know that."

"We'll make it." Katie pulled on his hand. "Come. They'll be wondering what's keeping us so long."

"Is everyone here?"

"There's only you, Mabel, and Norman. *Mamm*'s having a small Thanksgiving dinner this year. But there'll be plenty of food, so don't worry. *Mamm* and Carolyn have been working hard in the kitchen. Jesse and the two older boys are working on some problem in a back field, but they should be in soon. Leroy didn't have enough nerve to ask Lizzie Kuntz over."

Katie approached the porch. Letting go of Ben's hand, she pushed the door. Norman looked up as if in surprise, but he wasn't *gut* at faking sincerity. Either that or Katie knew him too well.

"*Gut* to see you, Ben." Norman stood up and held out his hand.

"And you too." Ben shook it and then took a chair beside the stove.

"You two don't eat each other now." Katie wagged her finger at both of them. "I'm going to help *Mamm* in the kitchen."

"Who's she talking about?" Norman joked as he laughed.

"Must be us," Ben said as he joined in.

They would be okay together, Katie thought. At least for the day. How men could hide their feelings so easily was beyond her.

CHAPTER THIRTY-ONE

Katie held Ben's hand as they walked across the back pasture. Thanksgiving dinner had been finished over two hours ago, and she hadn't kissed Ben yet. And she couldn't here, either. Sharp eyes might be peering from any direction over these open fields just waiting to catch her in a discretion that would be quickly spread around the community. Not that kissing a boyfriend should concern anyone that much. But doing so in public at this point would add to her already long list of alleged transgressions. Enos would see to that.

"You've been troubled all day," Ben commented as he squeezed her hand. "What's wrong, Katie?"

Katie glanced at him. "I don't want to think about my troubles. I just want to be with you and enjoy the weather. Isn't it balmy for a Thanksgiving afternoon? Very unseasonable."

"Yah," Ben allowed. But he clearly wasn't going to drop the subject. "You really should tell me what's wrong."

Katie smiled up at him this time. "Mabel arrived this morning after a fight with Norman . . . or rather after an explosion of his temper."

Ben regarded Katie steadily. "You told me he had a temper. It's serious then?"

"Serious enough. Mabel wouldn't believe me before the wedding, but she does now."

"They'll work it out." Ben shrugged. "There's more than that going on, isn't there?"

Katie turned to face him. "You have enough problems without mine being added."

"But your problems . . . aren't they mine also? If I love you?"

Katie blushed. "You shouldn't say such things, Ben."

He smiled. "Come on . . . tell me. What is it?"

Katie sighed. "Enos Kuntz is determined to get me kicked out of my teaching job. And I've given him the perfect excuse. I caught his boy, Abram, cheating. Now he's called a school board meeting first thing tomorrow morning to accuse me of being unfair."

Ben took a minute to think about this. "I'm assuming you have proof of his cheating. And there are other people on the school board besides Enos. They'll listen to you, Katie."

"Perhaps." Katie dropped her eyes. "If there weren't more."

"*Yah?*" Ben waited.

"Enos has been sore ever since Norman broke up with me. I think it's still over that night I spent at the hospital with you and your *mamm.* I don't know what all his reasons are, but the fact that I'm with you now . . ." Katie looked away. "Well, Enos isn't going to let the court situation run its course. He's already judged you. And he's judging me because you and I are still seeing each other."

"So I'm a big problem?"

Katie clutched his hand. "You can't do anything about that, Ben."

"I can't let this hurt you, Katie. I've already hurt you enough."

Katie forced a smile. "Don't worry about me. I'll make it."

Ben gave Katie a stubborn look. "I *will* worry about you. And I will do what's best for you and me. If you get kicked out of your school teaching job because of me, you'll never live that down. And how will I feel about that?"

Katie gathered her courage. "It won't happen, Ben, so stop worrying. I said Enos was *trying.*"

"Then why are *you* worrying?" Ben raised his eyebrows. "It's because you know what Enos is capable of. And so do I."

Katie didn't answer.

"I'm going over to Bishop Miller's tonight to talk to him about the situation."

Katie's grip tightened on his hand. "Ben, please don't. It's not going to help. And it'll look like you're interfering."

He stroked the length of hair that had fallen across her forehead. "And so I am, Katie. I love you. But you're right, I suppose. I should concentrate on fixing my situation. Getting things straight with those detectives would make everything so much easier for both of us."

"You mustn't worry about me, Ben." Her voice broke. "You really mustn't."

"I know you're right. It's just hard for me. It has always been. But I wouldn't be here if it weren't for you."

She leaned on his arm when they both stumbled over a small ditch. Ben held her steady until they'd both righted themselves. "I think we need to watch where we're going!" Ben joked.

"That's hard to do with you around."

Ben laughed. "I wonder what Enos would say if he heard you talking like that?"

Katie grimaced. "Throw me right out of the schoolhouse at once, I suppose."

"Maybe Norman could be spoken to about this problem?" Ben suggested. "He seems nice enough today. And he has his *daett*'s ear, no doubt."

Katie shook her head. "I wouldn't try. It won't work, and I'll only look weak. Enos would probably love to hear that I'm begging for mercy."

"Then I will speak with Bishop Miller on the way home tonight. It's the least I can do."

Katie smiled up at him as they approached the barn. "Thanks, but you don't have to."

"I want to, Katie!"

She pulled his arm toward the barn door. "Just a few minutes, Ben. Where no one can see us."

He followed her as the darkness of the barn fell around them. Katie paused just inside the door, her hands searching for his face. She pulled him toward her, and he kissed her. Long moments of silence followed, with his hands on her shoulders.

"You're sweet, you know." Ben lifted his head.

"And so are you," Katie murmured, resting her head on his chest. "But I suppose we better go in before someone catches us."

He chuckled and led the way out into the sunlight. "We'll have to do that more often."

A shadow crossed her face, which Katie replaced quickly before Ben noticed. "I'll be seeing you soon again, won't I?"

Ben gave her a quick glance. "You know I can't come often, Katie. I'm already harming you enough."

"It wouldn't be any worse than it is now. And I'd get to see you."

"I'm sorry, Katie, but these are also my people. I know them well. It can get a whole lot worse for you . . . and for us."

"Then hurry, Ben. I can't stand being away from you. I want to see you every week like other dating couples do."

Ben squeezed her hand. "We're not like the others, Katie. It's different for us. It's always been different."

She looked up at his face. "But you too . . . you feel what I feel, don't you? That we belong here in spite of the differences? That these are our people. That this is our faith. And that we're filled with the same longing to be in the will of *Da Hah* as they are?"

"*Yah,* Katie. I feel it in my heart. My mind gets in the way sometimes, but I'm not turn-

361

ing back now."

"Thank you, Ben." Katie smiled. "I thought you felt that way, but I needed the encouragement."

"Katie, do you think believing is more than not seeing?"

"Ben." Katie held his hand for a moment. "I think it's about choosing right regardless of what you see. That and being helped along by people who care, like *Mamm* and Jesse for example. And like Bishop Miller and Laura do. He's one of those whose heart touches others easily."

"Your faith shames me, Katie." Ben smiled. "Come, I think we'd better go inside before they all wonder where we've gone."

Katie led the way this time, and they entered the living room.

Mabel looked up from her seat on the couch. "Looks like someone's been having fun," she said.

"You should try taking a walk out back," Katie said. "It's a nice day."

Mabel's face brightened. "Let's do, Norman. That would be fun."

Norman shook his head, his face sullen. "I think it's time we go home."

"But Norman . . ." Mabel protested.

Norman was already on his feet and grabbing his hat.

"The afternoon's young!" Ben called after him, but Norman never stopped walking. He opened the front door and walked out.

"I'm so sorry." Katie gave Mabel a quick hug. "I know it's hard, but *Da Hah* will give you grace, Mabel."

"You shouldn't be comforting me," Mabel said, wiping her eyes. "Not after the way I used you before the wedding. And then I wouldn't let you be my bridesmaid. I'm very, very wicked, Katie. I can see that now."

"Hush, Mabel. That's nonsense. You had to listen to what Norman said."

Mabel hung her head. "But I was in full agreement with him, Katie. I'm not excusing myself."

"It's okay." Katie gave Mabel another hug. "But you'll have to tell your *daett* if this gets much worse. Promise me, Mabel."

"It won't!" Alarm flew into Mabel's face. "It just can't!"

"Norman has a problem," Katie said. "You can't ignore it."

Mabel burst into sobs and clung to Katie. *Mamm* must have heard because she appeared in the kitchen doorway. "What's wrong, girls?"

"Norman's leaving early," Katie offered, quickly pasting on a smile. There was no sense in worrying *Mamm*. Jesse was the only

363

one who could help Mabel in this situation. And Mabel wasn't willing to accept that yet or she would have said something to him already.

"Oh, that's too bad," *Mamm* cooed. "It's still early."

"Thanks for having us over." Mabel put on her coat and gave *Mamm* a pained smile and quick hug. "Norman probably has Bonnie hitched up by now. I'd best be going." She gave everyone a quick wave and then headed out the front door too.

At that moment, they heard buggy wheels as Norman drove Bonnie in front of the house.

"Is something going on between Mabel and Norman?" *Mamm* asked, walking to the living room window to watch Mabel climb into the buggy. Norman slapped the reins against Bonnie's back, and the buggy lurched and then headed down the driveway.

"They're having some trouble," Katie admitted. "Mabel is finding out that Norman has quite a temper. I'm sure Mabel will talk to Jesse if she feels it's necessary."

Mamm's face fell. "I was hoping I'd imagined things today. I sensed she was troubled."

Quick, bitter remarks about the Kuntz

family wanted to burst out of Katie's lips, but she sealed them inside.

"We will have to pray for Mabel," *Mamm* said as they watched the speck that was Norman's buggy disappear in the distance. "He comes from such a *gut* family."

Ben made a choking sound from the couch, and Katie gave him a quick glare.

"I think I should be going myself," Ben said, rising. Katie nodded and followed him to the front door. *Mamm* was still looking out the window as they walked across the lawn to the barn. After harnessing Longstreet and bringing him outside, Ben and Katie hitched up the buggy.

"I'll be seeing you as soon as I can," Ben said as he climbed up into the buggy seat.

"I hope so," Katie said. She waved as he drove off. If only they could be happy together forever . . . starting right now.

CHAPTER THIRTY-TWO

Katie pulled up the blinds at the school-house Friday morning, allowing the early morning sunlight to pour into the room. Enos and the rest of the board members would soon be here. Those three men had the power to decide her teaching fate. But perhaps she was being dramatic about this. Enos might have changed his tune by now. Or he might not be able to persuade the others to his point of view.

Katie stepped back from the window as the first buggy came into the school lane. Enos was arriving early, likely to make sure she didn't spend any time in conversation with the others before he got his words in. But there she was going again, thinking ill of Enos when she had no proof. He was her elder and well respected in the community. She would have to make a major effort this morning to see his point of view.

The problem was that she couldn't. Try as

she would, Mabel's weeping face wouldn't leave her memory. Norman was misusing her, and Norman was Enos's son. And Enos seemed a lot more interested in disciplining her than in admitting the sins of his two sons. Katie sighed but went to open the door for Enos. They were all fallen human beings and full of error. She would have to keep that in mind.

"*Gut* morning," she said as she opened the door with a bright smile. "I hope your family had a nice Thanksgiving."

Enos looked surprised, but he nodded as he entered the room. "It was okay." He squeezed himself into one of the larger desks. "Katie," he continued, "I hope you understand that we have your best interests in mind. That and the community's interests, of course. That's the way of our people. We don't live or die to ourselves, but for each other."

"I'm sorry you think I've failed."

Before Enos could respond, the sound of another buggy arriving reached them. Katie left Enos squashed in his seat and waited by the door. The third buggy arrived just seconds later, and Katie opened the door and peered outside. There would be a longer wait now, she figured. The two men would exchange a few words outside before they

367

came in together. She decided to retreat for a moment. That was a better option than fidgeting by the front door where Enos could see her. If the men got to the door while she was gone, they could find their way inside.

After a few minutes, Katie gathered her courage and opened the door a crack. She could hear the murmur of voices in the classroom. The two new arrivals were Samuel Miller and Ray Mast. Ray was a younger, married man who's first child was in school. He was well thought of in the community in spite of his youth.

Samuel Miller was older and the father of Jane, who was in the eighth grade. At the Sunday meetings he appeared quiet like Jane.

Katie didn't know him that well, and she expected they wouldn't be hearing much out of him today. That probably wouldn't serve her well. She needed a strong, independent-minded man who could stand up to Enos. Ray Mast was her hope. That and *Da Hah,* who would surely be by her side during this difficult time.

Katie fussed with her *kapp* to make sure it was straight, took a deep breath, opened the door wide, and walked up the hall into the classroom.

"Hello, Katie," Ray greeted. "I hope my boy Troy is doing okay. He says he likes the first grade."

"He's doing fine," Katie said. "He's a good boy. I'm glad he likes school."

"*Gut* morning, Katie." Samuel also gave her a smile. "I hope we're not disturbing your morning too much."

Katie shrugged. "It's the day after Thanksgiving. Nothing's really happening at the house. And I will help *Mamm* with the cleanup later in the day."

They all nodded and smiled as if this were not the serious occasion it was.

Enos finally cleared his throat. "Let's get on with this then, and not take up more of Katie's time than we need to. Would you perhaps lead out in prayer, Samuel?"

"*Yah,* this would be well." Samuel bowed his head. "Dear *Hah,* we give You thanks again this morning for this day and for Your mercy and grace. Thank You also for Katie, and for the work she's doing here at the school. Give us wisdom today. Guide our hearts into Your eternal will and ways. Amen."

Katie wiped away a tear. Samuel's prayer had touched her heart deeply. It was like a balm on a hurting sore. Perhaps there was hope that things would turn out okay.

Enos wasted no time. He opened Abram's notebook and addressed the other two men. "Here is the problem that Katie has brought to my attention. She feels that Abram has been copying answers from Noah Stoll's book. Abram strongly denies this. When we could come to no *gut* agreement on the matter, I suggested we call for the rest of the school board to judge this matter."

This was no "suggestion" from Enos, Katie thought. He'd demanded this meeting. She kept quiet and managed to smile as he continued to speak.

"Katie, will you show us the tablet from which you think Abram copied the answers?"

Katie jumped up and retrieved Noah's tablet from its usual place in his desk.

Why did Enos have Abram's tablet? she wondered. Abram usually left it here like the other children did. Their school lessons didn't require homework.

Katie handed Noah's tablet to Enos with a puzzled expression on her face. "Abram took his tablet home to you?"

Enos gave her a sharp look. "Yes. He wanted to show me what was going on."

That was likely Abram's lie, Katie figured. That boy had something up his sleeve.

Ray interrupted Katie's thoughts. "Explain

to us what the problem is, Katie."

Katie took a deep breath and began. "Joel, my brother, came to me and said he'd seen Abram looking at Noah's tablet during recess and copying down answers."

"Do you think he could have been mistaken?" Ray asked.

Katie nodded. "Of course. That's why I looked through both of their tablets and checked the answers with my answer key. The two problems Noah had wrong were also the two that Abram had wrong. It's not likely that something like that would happen by chance."

Ray thought for a moment. "Noah could have done the copying and not the other way around. Is that Abram's story? And didn't Abram, in fact, accuse Noah of cheating a few weeks ago?"

"*Yah,* he did. And I looked into it at the time," Katie said.

"And you decided not to believe Abram?" Ray asked.

So Enos had gotten to Ray, Katie thought. Her heart sank, but she refused to give up now. Truth was on her side. "That is true. But there were no matching wrong answers that day."

A smile crept across Enos's face. "And why would Abram be so stupid as to cheat now, knowing what you were going to look for? He's not dumb, Katie. And look here." Enos handed over the tablet. "Doesn't Abram have the problems worked out below here? Just like Noah does. It looks to me as if they both made the same mistake. If that's the case, how can you accuse one student of cheating under those circumstances?"

Katie scanned the page quickly. Her voice faltered. "I guess they are worked out. But they weren't before. This has been done recently."

Enos cleared his throat. "So on top of your charge of Abram's cheating, you think he has now tried to cover his tracks by working on the problems after the fact? That's highly unlikely."

Why should they believe her? Katie wondered. There was no way to prove either side, so it would be her word against Abram's . . . and against Enos's too. She glanced at Ray and Samuel. They looked skeptical. Enos had obviously influenced them before she came in the room, possibly even before this morning.

"Did you talk about Abram's accusation at home, Katie?" This question came from Samuel, confirming in Katie's mind that Enos had fed the two men information prior to meeting.

Katie shook her head.

"Maybe you should be more careful in the future," Enos said, as if she hadn't denied the charge. The other two men were looking quite serious.

"This is the worst kind of mistake a young teacher can make," Enos continued. "Involving family members in school problems. You may have something against Norman, Katie, for cutting off his relationship with you earlier in the year. But that is not an excuse."

"But I didn't talk to anyone in my family about this," Katie sputtered.

"It's an easy thing to do," Samuel countered. "When one's heart is broken, it's easy to make mistakes. We wouldn't hold that against you, Katie."

Ray spoke before Katie could catch her breath.

"I hear you have resumed your relationship with Ben Stoll. I have to concede that your judgment is very troubling, Katie. To so quickly change your heart's affection from one man to another. In fact, Enos said Norman told him that's why he broke off the relationship — because your heart was attached to Ben all along. Even with the disgrace Ben brought on the community with his crime and jail term, you support him. And Ben is now separated from the community and considering testifying again in a court of law against the *Englisha* who shot him. Our people have been greatly shamed by his actions, Katie. You shouldn't have anything to do with Ben Stoll."

Katie looked away. She was going to burst into tears at any moment. Why was it any of their business that she loved Ben?

Samuel's voice was sympathetic but his words cut deep. "This is looking worse for you, Katie. You must surely see this."

"He's not going to testify," Katie finally stated. "Ben told me so, and he has told Bishop Miller the same."

The men looked at each other for a moment, and then Enos shrugged and broke the silence. "If this is true, then Ben has chosen well. But that still doesn't change the question of your judgment, Katie. We can't have our schoolteacher associating with a man who has made a serious break with our traditions. And we know Ben has done so. I'm surprised you can't see the situation without someone telling you."

"Perhaps Katie is willing to cut off her relationship with Ben Stoll now that she's been rebuked for her error?" Samuel asked.

Katie figured he was trying to give her a chance to rectify the situation. At least he had a heart.

Enos didn't appear pleased by this offer, but he waited with the others for her response.

Katie didn't keep them waiting long. "I can't do that. *Da Hah* has brought our hearts back together, and I will not deny my love for Ben."

"Then I would say our response is clear." Enos almost looked delighted. "Katie is making serious errors in judgment, both in school and in her personal life. It can't help but affect her students, and perhaps bring an even greater shame on the school and the community."

"What are you proposing, Enos?" Samuel asked. "We usually give our first-year school teachers a lot of understanding."

Enos wasn't backing down an inch. "This is not exactly a normal situation we are dealing with, Samuel. You must see that for yourself."

Samuel hung his head. "*Yah,* these are serious charges. But still . . ."

Ray looked ready to say something, but Enos barged in. "I say we compromise then. I was going to propose trying to get Ruth Troyer — I mean Ruth Gingerich to return, perhaps next week." Enos gave a sheepish smile. "But perhaps we could keep Katie on through the start of Christmas vacation.

She's probably already working with the children on a Christmas program. After that . . ."

Katie turned away to hide the tears that crept down her cheeks. She'd forgotten about doing a Christmas program, but she wasn't going to admit that now. It would be taken as more incompetence on her part.

"Something must be done," Ray finally said. "And I'm sorry about this, Katie. I did hope things wouldn't happen like this today."

"How am I supposed to keep going with the schoolwork," Katie asked, "knowing you're going to fire me after Christmas?"

A smile leaped to Enos's face. "Are you offering to quit then? I suppose we could see if Ruth could come on Monday. She hasn't been married but a few weeks, so that might impose some hardship on her, but she might be willing."

Katie hardened her voice. "We wouldn't want to do that, now would we?" She wasn't giving Enos the satisfaction of seeing her leave before she had to. "*Nee,* I'll continue my work as long as possible."

"We'll be praying for you," Samuel said. "And I too am sorry things have come to this, Katie."

They all stood up, nodded at each other,

and found their way out. Katie waited until the last buggy wheel was gone from the schoolyard before returning to the schoolroom, sitting at her desk, putting her hands on her face, and sobbing until there were no more tears.

Chapter Thirty-Three

Katie drove Sparky toward home, working hard to not take her anger out on her horse. If Ben would only come this afternoon so she could speak with him! But that wouldn't happen. She'd just seen him yesterday. Perhaps she should dash into Dover and cry on his shoulder? But *nee,* that wouldn't help anything in the long run. And Ben would worry more than he already did. They would have to weather this storm separately the best they could. Ben would come when he thought it best. In the meantime, she would suffer this sorrow alone.

Katie decided she would share with *Mamm* and Jesse though. They would surely find out soon anyway. Oh, what sorrow would smite *Mamm's* heart at this news. She'd suffer great disappointment and possible shame at her daughter's failure. The whole community would know by next week. How could things have fallen this low? She'd been so close to success, to acceptance, to being loved by everyone. Now it was all going to disappear.

Partly from her mistakes, but Enos, Norman, and Mabel bore their own fair share, to say nothing of Ruth Troyer Gingerich. Ruth would be preening her feathers in high glee on receiving word that her help was needed to rescue the school's reputation after Katie's failure.

Katie pulled into the driveway and saw Mabel's buggy parked near the barn. Why would she be here this morning? Had she come back to smooth things over from leaving so early yesterday? That must be what this was about. No doubt Mabel would be inside even now, making her apologizes to *Mamm* for Norman's sudden departure.

Katie stopped beside Mabel's buggy and unhitched Sparky. She wasn't going anywhere else today, in no way, shape, or form. There was housework that needed doing, and her heart was heavy. Sparky might as well enjoy some freedom by being let out into the pasture. Leading him into the barn, Katie pulled off the harness, brushed him down quickly, opened the back barn door, and shooed him outside.

Katie paused to glance around inside the barn. There were clumps of manure tossed about, forming a rough trail leading toward the back barn door. Peering outside, Katie caught sight of Leroy and Willis unloading the manure spreader in the back field. One of them sat on the seat while the other ran the levers holding a pitchfork. The men must be taking the day to clean the horse stalls, she figured. There was no sign of Jesse. Maybe he'd gone into town for supplies.

Leaving the barn, Katie went up the front porch steps, pausing at the sound of soft crying coming from inside. Looking through the window, she saw Jesse's hat tossed on the rocker while he paced the floor. Mabel, tears streaming down her face, was sitting on the couch beside *Mamm.*

Katie hesitated. Should she enter? Was this even her business? But she was family, and Mabel was her sister.

Mamm looked up when Katie walked in. Jesse didn't say anything; he kept up his pacing, clearly agitated.

"What's happened?" Katie approached Mabel and touched her shoulder gently.

The response from Mabel was louder sobs.

"What is it?" Katie turned to *Mamm.*

Mamm shook her head and looked away. Maybe they weren't going to tell her, Katie thought. Should she go upstairs then?

"This." Mabel seemed to have made up her mind to speak. She pulled up her dress sleeve. A long, red mark circled her upper arm with smaller ones on either side. "Norman did this."

Katie gasped.

Mabel was sobbing again as she slid her sleeve back down.

"She has others," *Mamm* whispered. "On her hip from falling when he pushed her."

Katie sat down beside Mabel. She would surely collapse if she didn't. No wonder Jesse was pacing the floor. She stole a glance at his face. It looked like a thundercloud. She'd never seen him so worked up.

"Oh, Mabel!" Katie wrapped her arms around her. "How absolutely awful. I'm so sorry."

"I'm going over there right now to talk to that young man," Jesse stated.

"Please don't," Mabel begged. "He'll only get worse. I didn't tell him I was coming here, and Norman will be even angrier if he finds out. He'll say I'm worthless and went home crying to my *daett*."

Jesse's words shot out of his mouth. "No man is treating my daughter like this!"

"Jesse," *Mamm* interrupted, "Mabel may be right. What are you going to do when you get there? Mabel has to live with him."

"Ignoring this kind of problem doesn't make it go away," Jesse turned on his heels. "Come, Mabel. I'm following you home."

"Norman's not home, *Daett.* I told you. And I don't want you coming. I'll leave now, and I won't bother you any longer."

"This is not a bother, Mabel," Jesse said.

"Jesse, at least wait until you cool off," *Mamm* said. "You're too angry right now. Wait awhile."

Jesse looked at *Mamm,* let out a sigh of exasperation, but nodded.

Mabel rose and put on her coat.

Mamm and Mabel left the house together, walking across the lawn. *Mamm* held on to Mabel's arm the whole way.

Jesse walked over to the window to watch them go, and Katie joined him. When the two reached the buggy, Mabel climbed in. *Mamm* undid the tie rope and handed it to Mabel. *Mamm* stood and wiped her eyes as she watched Mabel leave.

"I'm sorry you had to see this, Katie," Jesse said, still looking out the window.

Katie's voice trembled. "You will do something for Mabel, won't you? I feel so sorry for her."

"I'll talk to Norman. This behavior has to stop."

"I never thought he'd go that far. Not really."

Jesse's voice cut through air. "Was he like that when you dated him?"

Katie nodded. "Not that bad, but I knew he had a temper. He put on quite a tantrum the night he cut off our relationship."

"I would have thought better of the Kuntz family."

Jesse doesn't know the Kuntz family that well, Katie thought. But probably most of the community didn't. She decided to keep her opinion to herself. "I did talk to Mabel before the wedding, but she didn't believe me. She thought I was just upset about her marrying Norman."

Mamm came back in still crying, and Jesse gathered her in his arms.

Katie walked upstairs to change out of her school dress. Maybe she could bury herself in work today and forget everything. But it was the day after Thanksgiving, and the only work planned was cleaning the house from the Thanksgiving festivities.

Carolyn's bedroom door had been closed when she came up, so Carolyn must be in her room, no doubt shooed there by *Mamm* when it became apparent what Mabel's story had been. Joel was probably sent up to his room too. What a Thanksgiving season this was turning into. Normally this was a time to give thanks, and yet all around her there seemed to be so much *not* to offer the least bit of thanks for. How strange. And yet *Da Hah* was allowing it. And He must know what was best, even though it made no sense in human terms.

Katie knocked on Carolyn's door. "Carolyn, may I come in?"

"*Yah.*"

Pushing open the door, Katie stepped inside. Carolyn had the dark drapes drawn. She was lying on the bed reading a book. She didn't look up, and she'd probably been crying from the looks of the wetness still on her cheeks.

"Is Mabel gone?" Joel asked from his seat on the floor. He had nothing in his hands, so he must have been watching Mabel leave through the slit between the drapes.

Katie walked over and jerked them open. "*Yah,* Joel. And you two should be outside on a day like today."

"*Mamm* made us come up here," Joel objected, getting to his feet.

"Well, you can go outside and play now." Poor Joel. How was she going to explain to him about her not being his teacher after Christmas?

"What happened with Mabel?" Carolyn asked.

Should she tell her? Mabel would be shamed, but that couldn't be helped. Besides, it wasn't Mabel's problem, it was Norman's. Katie sat down on the bed. "Don't *ever* marry an angry man, Carolyn. Especially after you've been warned."

"Don't worry, I won't. What did Norman do?"

"He must have grabbed her very hard. Her arm has red marks on it. I don't know if Mabel fell down or Norman pushed her, but *Mamm* said Mabel also has bruises on her hips."

"Norman's a beast!" Carolyn minced no words. "*Daett* should have let Mabel marry Mose. He wouldn't have done that to her."

"Maybe Mabel didn't love Mose like she loves Norman."

"Oh, she loved Mose all right," Carolyn said. "I had to try to sleep through her crying at night."

"Mose could have come back once Mabel was of age," Katie said. "But he never did."

"I wouldn't have either." Carolyn sat up on the bed. "Mabel isn't the nicest person in the world."

"She's your sister, Carolyn. Don't say such things."

"I suppose I shouldn't," Carolyn allowed. "So what are we doing for the rest of the day?"

Katie's face brightened. "We have to clean the house first, but afterward maybe you can help me with ideas for the Christmas program at school. I haven't started a thing yet."

"Okay!" Carolyn said, obviously pleased at being included in such an important project. Not every day did one get a chance to help the schoolteacher with a presentation the whole community would see.

"Let's get started on cleaning the house," Katie said.

When they arrived downstairs, *Mamm* was staring out the living room window. Katie grabbed a broom from the closet and began working. The house had been cleaned from top to bottom the week before Mabel's wedding, so it didn't take that much effort to restore things to normal after yesterday's celebration. Carolyn pitched in, and after awhile *Mamm* joined in. They finished in no time.

Katie then got out a tablet and several books from the desk. Then she went into the kitchen and called Carolyn. They spread everything out on the table and were just getting started when they heard the sound of buggy wheels moving down the driveway away from the house. That must be Jesse driving over to Norman and Mabel's place. No wonder *Mamm* was standing by the front window again. Her heart would be deep in prayer, crying out to *Da Hah* for wisdom and mercy.

Few families in the community had this type of marriage problem. And for *Mamm* and Jesse to have this happen to Mabel would be a matter of deep shame. Jesse was taking a big risk in even going over to speak with Norman. But such was his love for his daughter — both deep and passionate. He wouldn't stand by and do nothing even if it brought disgrace on his own head.

"So where should we start?" Carolyn asked, looking at Katie with expectation.

Katie forced herself to concentrate. "Let's see, we need something to open up with, I guess."

Carolyn stared at the ceiling for a few seconds. "I'd want to open with a bang. Maybe by announcing the birth of Jesus right from the start. Wouldn't that be fun and different?"

Katie pasted on a smile and tried to concentrate. Right now she really didn't care about putting on a program. But *yah*, that did sound like a *gut* idea. "Carolyn, I knew I asked you to help me for a *gut* reason."

Carolyn beamed as they continued to work, laying out a rough sketch of poems and Scripture readings which would be memorized by the students. Since Carolyn had been a student last year, she knew the pupils well enough to help match the parts with the right children.

"Jane and Clarice should each say a long poem," Carolyn declared. "Clarice's piece could be on the hope of the coming Messiah, and Jane's could be on the dark times before there was a Savior born. Don't you think so, Katie?"

"That's fine with me," Katie said. "But shouldn't that come before the opening about the birth of Jesus?"

Carolyn shook her head. "Everyone knows the story, Katie. It doesn't matter. The effect is what will carry the day. You have the first graders announcing the birth of the Jesus in their little squeaky voices — hopefully getting them to smile a lot. Right after that, you have Clarice and Jane stepping out with their parts. People will follow with no problem at all."

Katie couldn't help asking, "Did Ruth do this any of the years she taught school?"

Carolyn laughed. "*Nee.* That's why I'm

interested in something different. She always followed the story from the beginning to the end without fail. Every year the same thing."

"Then it's fine with me," Katie declared. If Ruth never did this, then that was exactly the thing she wished to do. That was a contrary attitude and quite unchristian, but right now that was how she felt.

They worked through the afternoon, and *Mamm* came to join them until she heard Jesse's buggy come down the driveway. When Jesse walked in, Carolyn and Katie heard some whispering. Carolyn looked away, holding her ears with both hands. But Katie listened as Jesse answered *Mamm*'s questions.

"*Yah,* I told Norman what I had to say."

"Mabel didn't accuse him of anything?"

"*Nee,* and I don't know why. She acted like nothing had happened. She was all smiles when I got there, and she stuck up for him the whole time. She even said she'd fallen by accident. Norman did admit they'd been arguing, and he may have gotten a little loud. But that he was trying to catch Mabel from falling, and that's where the marks on her arm came from."

Mamm's soft sobs came next and were followed by silence.

"Can I open my ears now?" Carolyn whispered.

"Yah." Katie smiled faintly. "Everything's okay, I think. For now."

CHAPTER THIRTY-FOUR

Ben parked his bicycle beside his *daett*'s barn. Dusk fell early now, but he had lights on his bicycle and a flashlight so he figured he'd be okay. More than a week had passed since he'd been at Katie's for Thanksgiving. The *Englisha* people were beginning to put up their Christmas decorations in their living rooms, but he hadn't paid a lot of attention while driving past the houses. His mind was occupied with other things. It was time he made another trip to see Bishop Miller. He couldn't make things worse for Katie, could he? How could a simple talk harm anyone? And it might help.

Someday this legal mess would be over, and things could settle down to normal. Until then, there was little any of them could do about the situation. Katie had her meeting with the school board members last week, and Ben wanted to ask his *mamm* how things had gone. He should have gone over to see Katie sometime this week, but he'd been afraid of making things worse. Katie claimed he wouldn't, but he wasn't convinced.

"It's good to see you, Ben!" his *mamm* hollered from the front porch, interrupting his thoughts. "We just finished supper."

"I'll be right in," Ben hollered back. His *mamm* was waiting for him when he came up the steps.

"Have you had supper?" she asked.

Ben nodded. He'd made sure he'd eaten beforehand. He knew *Mamm* would be tempted to invite him in otherwise. Bishop Miller might not say anything about his eating at home, but why run the risk? He had pushed things far enough by spending Thanksgiving at the Mast's place. He was thankful his *daett* allowed him the use of Longstreet and the buggy during his visits to the farm.

"We're having devotions," *Mamm* told him, seeming to read his thoughts. "You can stay for those, surely?"

Ben answered by following *Mamm* inside and taking his usual seat on the couch. He gave a quick smile and nod to his siblings. *Daett* read the Scripture, and Ben listened to the familiar words from Luke, chapter 14: "And he put forth a parable to those which were bidden . . ." The text was a parable about a man who was invited to a feast. This didn't relate to Ben's situation. He'd hoped the selection would perhaps be a message to him from heaven to give him direction, but it didn't seem to be.

Daett finished reading and closed the Bible.

Ben knelt along with the rest of them as *Daett* prayed, asking for safety and blessing on all of them and thanking *Da Hah* for all the grace already given. When they stood up, Ben followed *Mamm* into the kitchen.

"Have you heard anything about Katie and the situation at school?"

Mamm's eyes grew large. "Don't you know?"

Ben frowned. "I haven't stopped by to see Katie this week. I'm afraid I'm making enough trouble for her as it is."

Mamm smiled sadly. "You're probably right, Ben. The school board is letting Katie go after Christmas. I'm sorry to be the one who has to tell you such bad news."

"Is it because of her relationship with me?"

Mamm shrugged. "Partly, I suppose. But there are other reasons. There always are."

Ben moved toward the door. "I'm going to speak with Bishop Miller right now. I told him I wasn't going to testify at the trial, why wasn't that enough?"

Mamm touched his arm. "Ben, these things have to run themselves out. People will get over it."

"But Katie's being let go. How is she going to get over that?"

"I don't know, but Katie's not the only one who has trouble in the world. You're looking at going to jail again if you don't testify."

"I know," Ben said. "I'm ready for that, if it happens." He retreated to the living room. He nodded to *Daett,* grabbed his coat, and went out the front door. It might not do much *gut* to stop in at Bishop Miller's now, but he would have to try. Getting Longstreet out of the stall, he threw the harness on and led him out toward the buggy. Twenty minutes later he pulled into Bishop Miller's lane. The bishop and his *frau* were sitting in the living room with the gas light burning bright in the window. Laura retreated into the kitchen when he knocked on the door. She could have stayed to listen for all he cared, but perhaps Laura was tired of listening to all the troubles brought to her husband's ear. Bishop Miller, on the other hand, had to listen whether he wanted to or not.

"*Gut* evening, Ben," Bishop Miller said, answering the door and motioning him inside toward the empty rocker.

Ben nodded. "*Gut* evening." He took the seat the bishop offered.

"So what's wrong now?" Bishop Miller wasn't wasting much time getting to the point.

Ben's face was grim. "It's Katie I'm concerned about. *Mamm* says she's being let go from her school teaching job and partly because of me."

Bishop Miller grimaced. "You aren't all to blame, Ben. But you do bear some of it."

"I said I wouldn't testify. Doesn't that count for something?"

Bishop Miller shook his head. "The best thing you and Katie could do is stop seeing each other until you get yourself straightened out with the community and the church. But neither of you seem willing to do that."

Ben leaned forward. "So Katie could keep her job then? If I didn't see her again? At least until the trial is over?"

Bishop Miller didn't say anything for awhile. He stared out the living room window into the darkness. "I don't think that will help much since there are other issues involved. Questions about Katie's judgment. I suppose it couldn't hurt though, so *yah,* maybe you should stay away from her. For the *gut* of both of you, but especially for Katie."

"What a royal mess," Ben muttered.

"The way of the transgressor is hard, Ben." The bishop's voice was sorrowful. "And many innocent people are usually affected. You should have thought of that sooner."

"You don't have to rub it in, Bishop. I already know."

The bishop didn't back down. "Few people learn it well, Ben — except when they're in the trouble."

Ben hung his head. "*Yah,* I suppose so. But can't you do anything for Katie? I'm willing to do my part by staying away from her. And by not testifying in court even if I have to go to jail. Is there anything else that can be done?"

Bishop Miller cleared his throat. "I can't promise anything, Ben." The bishop paused before asking. "How's the condition of your own soul? How are you with *Da Hah,* to say nothing of the church? We still hope that you will join us someday. Even with what you've been through."

Ben kept his voice even. "I'd best not speak on those things now. My actions will have to speak for me. That seems to be the way things are these days."

Bishop Miller nodded. "Just remember, your soul is your first priority, Ben. Take much thought about that matter and consider well changing your ways. We never know how much time we have to make things right, do we?"

"I *have* changed, Bishop," Ben said. "And Katie has played a large part in that. But I'd best not go into that. There will be plenty of time later — once this is all straightened out. I won't take up more of your time. Thank you."

Bishop Miller's smile was thin. "I'm here for what needs saying. And I'm glad to hear you've worked on getting right with *Da Hah*. Would you be going over to see Katie now?"

Ben didn't hesitate. "*Yah,* and I will tell her we must stay apart. Until . . . well, I don't know when. And I won't disgrace the community at the trial, I promise."

"These are *gut* choices, Ben. But right now you must live them and not expect to reap benefits right away. I am sorry that things have come to this point, but they have."

"Goodnight." Ben left. As he guided Longstreet out of the lane, he noticed that Laura was back on the rocker. He almost waved to the two of them but decided not to. From now on he must stay out of the sight and mind of his people until his ordeal was over. He had done enough damage already — to himself, to *Mamm* and *Daett,* and, above all, to Katie. Ben drove north to the Mast place, pulled in the lane, and tied Longstreet to the hitching post. The lights were still on in the house, and Ben walked up the sidewalk and onto the porch to knock. Carolyn opened the door, gasped, and vanished without welcoming him in.

He took a step backward as footsteps sounded inside. Katie jerked the front door open. She looked like she was going to fly into his arms, but she stopped herself in time. "Oh Ben, I've been so hoping you would stop by!"

"Katie . . ." He touched her hand. "Can you go for a short ride with me?"

"I want to talk with you for hours, Ben. I have so much to tell you."

He tried to smile. "Can you come, please?"

"Let me get my coat." Katie disappeared for a moment, returned with her coat on, and followed him out to his buggy. He was untying Longstreet and ready to climb up on the seat beside her, when he changed his mind. They might as well stay right here in the driveway. Retying Longstreet, he pulled himself up into the buggy and slipped in next to Katie. She found his hand in the darkness.

Ben couldn't keep the tremble out of his voice. "*Mamm* told me about the school board letting you go. And I went over at once to speak with Bishop Miller. He's telling me the best thing I can do is stay away from you until this gets straightened out."

"Is this how you feel, Ben?" Katie whispered.

"Of course not!"

"Ben, this is so hard."

"I know, but there's no other way."

"I need you, Ben. I need your comfort and support."

"I'm only harming you, Katie. Please . . . I love you too much to continue harming you like this. We can't see each other until this is over — the school thing and the trial problem. We simply can't."

Tears spilled over her eyes. "And when will that be? Will you go back to jail again?"

"I don't know, Katie. But you shouldn't bare my shame with me. It's not right."

"Surely it won't be long, Ben. I'm going to miss you terribly."

"Katie, please . . . I love you."

She leaned toward him and sobbed on his

shoulder. "I can't stand this. You know I can't."

He stroked her face in the darkness. "It'll all be over with before long, Katie. I know it will." He drew away from her, pulled open the buggy door, and climbed down. He reached up to help Katie out, keeping her hand in his as they walked up the sidewalk and onto the porch. At the front door, they embraced, and then parted. There was so much he wanted to say. That he loved her so much. That he never wanted to leave her. But he knew it was best if he kept silent. He gave Katie a short kiss, then turned to leave.

Before he got into the buggy, he banged his fist against the frame. He had been so very stupid to ever mess up his life this way.

He headed Longstreet toward home and once out of sight of Katie's house, he yelled at the top of his voice. Wordless yells of agony coming from the depths of his soul. Why had he ever done what he did? He'd once had all of this handed to him on a silver platter, only to see it slip away from his fingers. What a fool he'd been.

CHAPTER THIRTY-FIVE

Less than two weeks before Christmas, on a Saturday morning, Katie woke before Jesse called the boys for the early chores. She dressed by the light of the kerosene lamp. She wanted an early start on this wild expedition of hers. She really needed this break in her routine right now. And surprisingly, *Mamm* had agreed without a word of complaint. No doubt everyone could see that she needed a day away — something to break this depression that hung over her.

Of course, a day to the beach might not accomplish that, but it couldn't hurt. And this close to Christmas, with winter coming on, no one from the community would think ill of her for going. And she'd stay along the beaches in the wildlife areas, even though the populated tourist beaches would be empty of sunbathing *Englisha* in the wintertime.

Tiptoeing downstairs, Katie found *Mamm*

in the kitchen, leaning over the cookstove. Katie whispered, "What are you doing up already?"

Mamm smiled in the dim light of the lamp. "Thinking of you, I guess. And I couldn't sleep. Katie, I so hope you don't let this get the best of you."

"I'm trying, *Mamm.* But I need to get away for the day."

"I know that." *Mamm* sat down on a kitchen chair. "Should someone maybe go along with you? It's not *gut* to sorrow alone, Katie."

Sure, Ben could come along. The words almost slipped out of Katie's mouth. That's where most of her bitterness was coming from. She couldn't understand how Ben's staying away was going to help things, even if Bishop Miller insisted. The bishop could be wrong.

"Let me wake Carolyn and ask her to go with you?" *Mamm* offered.

"Okay." Katie gave in at once, finding a chair to sit down on. Waves of exhaustion were sweeping over her already, and the day hadn't even begun. That's how things had been going lately. Just getting through each school day was hard. Time spent forcing smiles for everyone and pretending everything was okay. Then the practicing and practicing of the Christmas program. When the day was over she'd almost collapse behind her desk the moment the last student was out of the schoolyard.

Carolyn would be overjoyed with the invitation, Katie knew. She'd seen the longing in her eyes last night when Katie told *Mamm* of her plans. Maybe that was why she was giving in so easily. Bringing a little happiness to someone else's life might brighten her own. And it wouldn't cost much more either.

Carolyn, with her happy chatter, would be a joy to have along. How different from Mabel, her younger sister was. Of course, the relationship with Mabel had been poisoned from the beginning with Ruth Troyer's maneuverings for Jesse's hand. And when *Mamm* had won, Mabel had never completely come over to their side.

It was all a shame really. Just like this whole mess at school was a shame. Enos Kuntz had stopped by yesterday. For a friendly chat, he claimed, and to show there were no hard feelings on his part. The parents had all been contacted, Enos told her. And the support was overwhelmingly behind the decision of the school board. For the sake of the community and even for Katie herself, Ruth Gingerich would take over after the Christmas holiday. Ruth at least had the decency not to show up at the school so far. And she probably wouldn't. Apparently there were limits even for Ruth.

Katie jumped when Jesse hollered up the stairs to call Leroy and Willis. He looked surprised when he came through the kitchen and saw Katie, but he didn't say anything as he got his coat and went outside. Leroy and Willis came tramping down the stairs minutes later, and they also didn't have anything to say. Katie had figured out that men didn't talk much in the mornings.

Mamm reappeared and began bustling about preparing breakfast. There was no comment on the fact that Katie hadn't moved an inch since she'd left to awaken Carolyn.

But *Mamm* had noticed, Katie knew. She'd seen the concern flash briefly in her *mamm*'s eyes. Clearly *Mamm* had a good reason for wanting someone along with her today. Katie should, in fact, probably stay in bed all day instead of roaming out on the roads.

Katie still hadn't moved when Carolyn arrived, rubbing sleep from her eyes. Her face was glowing though. "I can go along? Oh, Katie, thank you, thank you! I didn't dare ask last night, you looked so troubled. I thought you wanted a day alone."

Katie tried to smile. "Maybe you can cheer me up."

Carolyn's face fell. "I'm afraid I'll be looking at the beaches and the sand."

"That's okay," Katie said. "I'm glad you're coming along."

"Oh good! When can we start then?"

"Breakfast first." *Mamm*'s voice was firm. "And Katie has to get Sparky ready. Maybe you can help me with the food while Katie goes to the barn."

Carolyn bounced around the kitchen as Katie left. She wouldn't be much help to *Mamm* this morning, but Carolyn would be a joy to have along. Already Katie's spirits were being lifted. Outside, the dawn was breaking, with crisp, clean air blowing across the lawn. She should have grabbed her coat, but the shock of cold felt *gut.* If she ran, she'd be inside the barn before the shivering began. She took off across the grass and burst into the barn.

Leroy looked up in surprise, a bucket of feed in his hand. "What's your rush?"

"You don't have to be so grumpy." Katie brushed past him.

He shook his head and kept working.

Katie took Sparky from his stall and threw the harness on. As she pulled on one of the straps, it tore. With a groan, Katie called to Leroy. "Will you come help me?"

Leroy came at once, and he had a new hole punched in the strap in minutes. "That'll hold for the day," he said.

"Thank you," Katie said, leading Sparky outside where she tied him to the hitching post. She would put him in the shafts when Carolyn came out with her. Katie glanced up at the sky. The bright stars were almost gone, and streaks of dawn were breaking in the sky. It promised to be a beautiful day. Just what she needed. She went inside where *Mamm* and Carolyn were putting together a picnic lunch for the trip.

"Can I help with something?" Katie offered.

Mamm waved her arm. "Sit down and eat, both of you. I have everything ready."

"Apples? Shall we take apples?" Carolyn asked from the counter, holding open the picnic basket. "That's my last decision, and then I'm done."

"Take them." *Mamm* didn't wait for Katie to answer. "And a knife to cut them with. Katie likes to cut her apples into pieces."

"I know that." Carolyn grabbed a knife from the drawer, placed it in the basket, and slammed the lid shut. She bounced down on a kitchen chair. "How long will it take to drive out to the ocean, Katie?"

"I've not been there since I was a little girl. I don't really know," Katie said, scooping some eggs onto her plate.

"Will we be back before dark? *Daett* probably doesn't want us out late on a Saturday night."

"I'm sure Katie will be back in plenty of time." *Mamm* answered for Katie. "My you are a chatterbox this morning, Carolyn."

"It's not every day I get to ride around with Katie!" Carolyn bounced up and raced for the washroom door. "Aren't we ready to go?"

"What about the dishes, *Mamm*?" Katie got to her feet. "We should at least help."

"Throw them on the counter, and then you're gone," *Mamm* declared. "No washing on this special morning."

Carolyn raced back to grab the picnic basket, and she and Katie were out of the door in no time. The men passed them in the yard as they came in for breakfast.

"Have a *gut* time, and be back before dark," Jesse told them.

"We will," Katie said. Well, at least she could agree to be back before dark. Having a *gut* time, might be more difficult.

They arrived at the buggy and Carolyn held up the shafts. With Sparky securely attached they were soon on their way, driving north of Dover, Katie having no desire to get snarled up in the Saturday traffic by driving closer to town.

"Can I drive?" Carolyn asked.

Katie handed over the lines at once. Anything that added to Carolyn's joy made the day lighter for her too. So did the bright sunlight and the smell of the ocean that greeted their senses an hour or so later.

"There's the ocean!" Carolyn hollered in Katie's ear, nearly letting go of the lines. "Where can we park?"

Katie looked around. "Over there by that tree. That looks safe enough."

Carolyn steered Sparky in that direction, and they bounced through a shallow ditch. Katie jumped out with the tie rope in her hand. When Sparky was secure, she joined Carolyn, who was staring out over the choppy waters. Carolyn gushed out, "Thank you for bringing me here, Katie. Thank you, thank you, thank you!"

Katie patted Carolyn's arm. "Run on. I'll be along in a minute."

Carolyn did that, taking off like a rocket. Katie made sure everything was secure and then followed her, noting the sand moving under her shoes. If the day warmed up enough, she would take her shoes off, and she might even run in the sand. She would forget about school in the wild splash of the waves. And she would not once think of Ben even — just the glorious ocean, the smell of salt, and the hope that if *Da Hah* could make something this *wunderbah,* He could also take care of her during this difficult time.

Katie sat down and pushed her hair back under her kapp. This was going to be a great day! A minute later, to her own surprise, she stood up and at first walked and then ran along the beach. She ran until she was exhausted, the wind over the water blowing through her hair. She could feel the tension oozing out of her muscles. Soon Carolyn caught up with her and took her hand. They ran until they could go no further, then they both flopped on the sand in their dresses.

"I wish I could be out here every day," Carolyn gushed. "The waves call your name. They speak of lands far, far away."

Katie laughed. "You're quite a poet, Carolyn."

"It's the ocean pulling the words out of me!" Carolyn giggled. After awhile she looked over at Katie. "Is your heart healing, Katie?"

Katie sat up and grabbed Carolyn in a tight hug. "*Yah,* of course. I'll be okay. *Da*

Hah will see me through this."

"He always does." Carolyn looked very wise as she wiggled out of Katie's grasp. "Shall we run again?"

"I think I've run about all I can for awhile," Katie said. "But you go on, and I'll watch."

Carolyn did, her figure soon small in the distance before she turned and raced back. Katie stood and led the way to the buggy. She got out the picnic basket, spread the blanket on the sand, and laid out the food they'd brought along. Carolyn bowed her head in thanks, and Katie did likewise, glancing up to see Carolyn already reaching for a sandwich.

"Thanks for coming with me, Carolyn," Katie said. "I like having you around."

"Anytime!" Carolyn mumbled, her mouth full.

Katie unwrapped her sandwich and ate slowly as she watched the waves slide onto the shore. She would remember this day for a long time, she decided. This peaceful balm would heal much that hurt inside, giving her strength for the journey ahead.

CHAPTER THIRTY-SIX

The night of the Christmas program found Katie sitting in the front row of the large classroom. The school desks had been pushed aside and replaced with rows of benches unloaded from a wagon parked outside. Up to this point, Katie had survived the stress of the past few weeks. The trip to the beach had certainly helped, followed by Carolyn's frequent happy outbursts at home over the day they'd spent together. Now, in just a little more than an hour, the Christmas program would be behind her. Katie could barely wait. Skeptical glances had been coming her way all evening from several of the parents, apparently wondering whether the program she'd prepared would somehow be tarnished by her reputation.

Gas lanterns hissed as they hung from the ceiling above her, and snow was beginning to fall outside. A few flakes already hung on the darkened windowpanes. The murmur of the gathered crowd rose and fell around Katie. Well, she'd done her best, and now the moment of truth had arrived. The children had practiced over and over every afternoon since the program was planned. Carolyn had even come over to help several times since she'd been the architect of the program. Maybe that's why the evening had a prayer of a chance — that and Carolyn's ever-cheerful presence.

What would she have done without Carolyn? Katie had no idea. Ever since the Saturday at the beach, Carolyn had gone out of her way to spread good cheer and hope. No doubt this was *Da Hah*'s way of looking out for her. It almost brought tears to Katie's eyes.

Would Ben show up tonight? Katie wondered. The thought sent a sinking feeling to her stomach. Ben's staying away was not doing her a bit of *gut*. All it had done was leave her heart cold and wounded and struggling along on its own.

And now on Sunday mornings Mahlon Bontrager was making eyes at her from the men's bench. Maybe he thought with Ben gone, the coast was clear? Surely she hadn't given Mahlon encouragement, had she? She'd tried to comfort him over the loss of his *frau,* Lydia. And they had chatted like friends at Mabel's wedding. But that hadn't meant anything to her. Mainly she had wanted to get through the day, smarting as she was from Mabel's rejection. But the situation was becoming obvious enough for *Mamm* to notice. Last Sunday she'd approached her in private and asked, "Is Mahlon Bontrager showing interest in you, Katie?"

"How would I know?" she'd snapped.

Mamm had persisted. "He looks interested to me."

Katie had shrugged. "Well, I'm not interested in him."

Mamm had let the subject lie, but the implication had been clear enough. *Mamm* thought Katie ought to show an interest in Mahlon . . . or at least consider the option. *Mamm* would certainly be happy if she did.

And *Mamm* did have her own life as evidence that a woman could fall in love later even if not right at the first. Twice that had happened. First with Katie's *daett* and then with Jesse. Mahlon would fit that mold like a button fit a buttonhole. Maybe she ought to give in? All it would take would be a few smiles sent in Mahlon's direction, and he would be paying a visit on some Saturday night, even overlooking the mess she was in

413

from the school board firing.

Katie jerked herself out of her thoughts. Carolyn was pulling on her arm, whispering in her ear above the murmur in the room. "It's time to start, Katie. You look like you're in another world. Cheer up. It's going to be great."

Katie smiled as she stood. She motioned for the schoolchildren to come forward, and the crowd quieted. "It's time to start," Katie began a bit nervously. "If everyone could find a seat, the children will show you what they've worked on so hard."

Katie sat down, certain that her face was as red as a beet.

"You did fine!" Carolyn squeezed her arm beside her.

The first-graders were all looking at her, and Katie nodded. They jumped up, nearly falling over each other, but they made it to the front without any further mishaps. They lined up like they had drilled so often and seemed to relax. Johnny led out in his strong voice, singing the song by John Morrison, "To Us a Child of Hope Is Born . . ."

The others soon joined in — three girls in new dresses their *mamms* had made just for the occasion. Their voices didn't carry as far as Katie had hoped, but they were as cute as buttons. Even the grins on Johnny and Pete's faces managed to look joyful instead of silly. Ray Mast's son, Troy, opened his mouth wide, singing with all his might. Despite his *daett*'s vote against her, Katie thought, Troy was the cutest little boy in her class. When the song was completed, Johnny moved the program into its second part by quoting from the second chapter of Luke. "And Joseph also went up from Galilee, out of the city of Nazareth . . ." Johnny even said the big words better than he ever had before, completing all of his verses without a mishap.

The others did almost as well, but it didn't really matter by then. Katie could feel the mood in the room turning decisively. The first-graders were winning everyone's heart. Carolyn was wiggling with delight by the time all five finished with their parts and sat down again.

The two eighth-grade girls went next with their poems, making a striking contrast to the little first-graders. Katie was ready to lean over and kiss both of Carolyn's hands in thanks, but such a display would be completely out of the question. Carolyn would be getting a hug though, right after the program was over. There was no question about that.

By the time the program wound down

nearly an hour later, Katie knew her face was glowing.

"That was the best ever," Carolyn whispered, confirming Katie's suspicions.

Katie rose to join all the schoolchildren for the last scene, a rousing rendition of "The Praise Song," sung to a fast *Englisha* tune.

"Oh, *Gott Vater . . .*" they sang together with the adults soon joining in.

Even Bishop Miller had a smile on his face as he sang along. That had been Carolyn's last stroke of genius. The young folks sang this version in the Sunday-night hymn singings, but no teacher had ever used it at a school Christmas program.

Katie glanced over at Enos. He didn't look happy, but at the moment she didn't care. She'd been through enough suffering because of him, and she was getting ready to face even worse in the days ahead. Enos had her forgiveness, but that didn't mean she had to like him right now.

Katie caught Mahlon Bontrager's eye on the back row. He looked quite impressed, and she glanced away at once. It would be so easy to encourage him, to give in to what everyone would approve of. She was getting pressure not only from *Mamm,* but from the entire community who thought she needed a serious repair job to her reputation. Who better for the task, they were probably all thinking, than widower Mahlon Bontrager?

And Mahlon was a decent man and pleasant to be around. But she wasn't ready to think of him as her husband. Her love for Ben was still strong. Why else would his absence be hurting this much?

The song ended, and Katie headed straight for Carolyn, giving her a hug right in front of the whole room. Katie whispered in her ear, "You're an angel, Carolyn. Did you know that? I can never thank you enough."

By then everyone was busy chattering up a storm, obviously impressed with the program.

"You give yourself too little credit, Katie. You're a *gut* teacher," Carolyn said.

"Well, not everyone thinks so," Katie said. "Glad I have you in my corner, though."

"You'll make it through." Carolyn patted Katie on the back. "I know you will."

Katie nodded and turned to meet *Mamm* as she approached. They embraced, and *Mamm* whispered, "That was so *gut,* Katie."

"Thank Carolyn. She helped plan it."

"*Yah,* I know." *Mamm* turned to give Carolyn a hug. "Both of you did so well."

"Thanks for the praise!" Carolyn said as

she moved aside as more parents approached. Apparently Carolyn had endured all of the limelight she could handle. *Mamm* stayed, though, to shake hands with Ben's parents, Leon and Lavina, who were the first in line.

"That was so *gut*!" Lavina said, clasping Katie's hand with both of hers. "You've done such wonders with Noah on his schoolwork. He just loves you as his teacher."

"Thank you," Katie said, sealing her lips so as not to ask how Ben was doing. She didn't dare ask right here in front of everyone.

"*Yah,* you did *gut.*" Leon offered her a smile before they moved on.

The line moved forward with Katie greeting parents and telling them how well their children were doing. And they told her how much their children loved her as their teacher. Had the tide turned? Was a miracle happening right in front of her eyes? Had Carolyn's help in producing such a *wunderbah* Christmas program changed their minds about firing her after the holidays? Did she dare hope?

Only Enos and his *frau* stayed away, hanging around in the back of the school. Clearly they weren't pleased with how things had gone tonight. They must have hoped she'd make a dismal failure of herself and seal her own doom. Well, she wasn't sorry to disappoint them. The Kuntz family deserved this.

As the crowd began to thin, Ruth Gingerich pushed her way through, a thin smile on her face. This was the first time Katie had seen Ruth since the news hit the community of Katie's firing.

"*Gut* evening," Ruth greeted her, still smiling. "That was a *gut* program tonight."

"Thank you." Keep breathing, Katie told herself.

Ruth shifted on her feet. "I hope there are no hard feelings between us about the rest of the term. I want you to know I had nothing to do with it."

Katie forced a smile. "I know."

"Katie, if you take my advice, you'll dump that Ben Stoll and get yourself a fresh start. That's the only way out of this."

Katie shook her head. "*Nee,* I can't do that."

Ruth moved on, looking more sympathetic than Katie had imagined. She must be in worse shape than she thought if Ruth's sympathies were stirred. Ruth left with one last concerned look over her shoulder.

The room was emptying quickly, and Katie was preparing to leave when a man cleared his throat behind her. Katie jumped and whirled around.

"*Ach,* don't let me bother you." Bishop Miller offered her his warmest smile. "I just wished to add my thanks for the evening, Katie. You did great considering you aren't coming back after Christmas."

Could that maybe be changed? Katie wanted to ask. But even the bishop didn't meddle in school affairs, and she would only embarrass herself.

"Thank you," she offered instead.

"I also want to tell you how much I appreciate you and Ben taking my advice," Bishop Miller continued. "Jesse told me Sunday that Ben's staying away."

"That was more his decision than mine," Katie admitted.

Bishop Miller nodded. "And that's how it should be, Katie. The man must lead, even when the way is hard."

Katie looked away. She didn't agree, but there was no sense in a protest. It wouldn't change anything.

"I'm hoping Ben will stay true to his word when the trial comes up." Bishop Miller looked sharply at her. "You pray for him, Katie. That's what the young man needs. And courage."

"I do pray for him," Katie said. "More

than you know."

Bishop Miller nodded. "Then *Da Hah* will surely answer. Thanks again for the program. That was quite an up-building exercise for our young students."

Katie watched him take his *frau*'s hand and walk out the door. It was then that Katie began to gather up her own things. Taking one last look around, she wiped away the tears before turning out the lights. Waiting a few moments for her eyes to adjust, Katie found her way to the back of the school.

"Goodbye," she whispered into the darkness. "Goodbye, sweet schoolhouse. Take *gut* care of yourself."

CHAPTER THIRTY-SEVEN

As if the weather were making an attempt to spread good cheer and the Christmas season's spirit far and wide, the storm that brought in the snow on the evening of the Christmas program continued the following day, and snow was still falling on Christmas Day. Katie sat at the kitchen table warming her hands with a cup of hot chocolate. Carolyn was outside playing with Joel in the snow. The two seemed boundless in their energy. Katie had wearied after a few hours and left them to their snowmen with carrots for noses and red beets for eyes. Both items had been brought up from the basement root cellar, the use of which *Mamm* had allowed with a smile on her face. *Mamm* was glad Katie wasn't moping around all day in her room, so a few vegetables were worth contributing to the cause.

Mamm could have asked some of Jesse's sisters over for Christmas breakfast, but after Mabel turned *Mamm* down, the heart had gone out of the plan. That and the shame they were all bearing over Katie's firing from the schoolteacher job didn't make for a festive atmosphere. Jesse even looked troubled this morning, as if the full weight of what had happened was settling in. *Mamm* had still fixed the full Christmas breakfast of pancakes and eggs with ham and bacon. But that was long past now, and the dishes were washed and put away. Jesse was with *Mamm* in the living room, talking in low tones, perhaps about the loss of her job and the humiliation she was suffering, Katie thought. She settled into her chair. The long afternoon stretched out in front of her, and the dark thoughts she didn't want to face were pushing in. Tomorrow they could come, she told herself, but today she was going to keep them at bay.

Leroy and Willis had left for a youth social not twenty minutes ago. They'd be playing games and pulling taffy at Bishop Miller's place. She could have gone, but she couldn't muster up the courage. *Yah,* she would have to face people eventually, but putting it off for now seemed the easiest and wisest choice. If she showed up looking anything but cheerful, that would only remind everyone of her fall.

Katie's concentration was broken as Carolyn and Joel went racing past the house, sounding as if they were running toward the road. Someone must be coming. Someone they knew well enough to invoke such a welcome. Katie leaped up and set the hot chocolate aside before dashing to use the mirror. She pressed a few stray hairs back under her *kapp* and straightened her dress. Whoever had arrived would have to accept her the way she looked.

Mamm was out on the front porch when Katie came into the living room, and Jesse was nowhere in sight. A quick glance out the window revealed Mabel climbing out of Norman's buggy. Jesse was holding the bridle of her horse, while Carolyn and Joel were crowding around and hanging on to Mabel's hands. Norman wasn't with her.

Mabel's head bobbed up and down a few times, as she said something to Jesse. He tied her horse to the hitching post and followed Mabel toward the house. *Mamm* met Mabel at the bottom of the steps, giving her a big hug,

What should she do? Katie wondered. Meet Mabel at the door or flee upstairs? Mabel couldn't have *gut* things to say to her. Not after avoiding her completely at the school program. It would be easier if she were out of sight, Katie decided, making a dash for the stair door. Thankfully the family had stopped to talk while on the porch. She made it halfway up the steps before the front door opened.

Slipping inside her room, Katie walked to the window to look outside. Norman's horse, Bonnie, stood at the hitching post, her head hung low. So Mabel must have driven her hard coming over. What had made Mabel change her mind? She'd refused, after all, to come for Christmas breakfast.

"Katie!" *Mamm* called up the stairs.

Now what? Katie thought. Was *Mamm* going to rebuke her for running away? It wasn't as if Mabel came to see her. With a sigh, Katie came away from the window and headed downstairs. *Mamm* was likely correct. She had to face the world someday, uncomfortable though it was.

Jesse was standing beside a weeping Mabel, when Katie arrived at the bottom of the steps. Carolyn and Joel had vanished. *Mamm* had her arm around Mabel's shoulder, pulling her tightly against her. Katie halted. Was Mabel having trouble with Norman's anger again? It was too awful to imagine.

As if she needed convincing, Katie heard the fury in Jesse's voice.

"We're leaving right now. As soon as I can hitch up my horse."

"Jesse . . . *nee* . . . maybe you should wait," *Mamm* pleaded.

Jesse ignored *Mamm* and disappeared out the washroom door.

"Oh, Mabel!" *Mamm* wrapped her arms around her daughter's shoulders again.

Katie stood frozen in place. What was she supposed to do? *Mamm* had called her, but this was none of her business. Beginning to retreat, *Mamm*'s voice stopped her. "Mabel wants to talk to you, Katie."

Why? Katie almost asked.

"I want to tell you again how sorry I am, Katie." Mabel answered the unspoken question teary eyed.

"You came here to tell me that?" Katie asked.

"*Yah,* and because I have nowhere else to go," Mabel said, breaking into fresh sobs.

Mamm pulled Mabel's dress collar down to reveal black-and-blue marks. "And there's more in other places."

Mabel looked away, tears streaming down her face.

Katie stepped closer to hold Mabel's hand. "I'm so sorry, Mabel. I never thought things would go this far."

"Neither did I." Mabel was staring out of

the window. "*Daett* will be ready to go in a few moments. I want you to come with us, Katie. To stay with me while *Daett* talks with Norman."

"But . . . Mabel . . . Norman doesn't like me. What good can I possibly do?" Katie asked, her heart racing.

A slight smile played on Mabel's face. "You're wise in ways I'm not. It would be a comfort if you came along. Would you come just for that reason?"

Please do! Mamm mouthed from the other side of Mabel.

Katie nodded even though her heart sank at the idea of facing Norman. He would have nothing but scorn for her very presence.

"Come." Mabel pulled on Katie's hand. "Get your coat. I'm sure *Daett* is ready to leave by now."

Mamm dashed to the closet for Katie's coat and handed it to her. "*Da Hah* go with both of you. I hope Jesse is making the right decision."

"He is." Mabel's face was set as they went out the front door. "Because what I'm doing sure isn't working."

Jesse had his horse hitched by the time they arrived at Norman's buggy. He untied Bonnie and threw in the lines when both women had climbed up. Mabel took them and waited until Jesse had driven forward, before following.

"How bad is it?" Kate asked, stealing a glance at Mabel. She remembered the rage on Norman's face that long-ago night when he'd said he didn't want to see her anymore. She couldn't imagine facing that repeatedly. How in the world was Mabel managing?

Mabel whimpered as if she had heard the question. "Frightening . . . terrorizing. Tiptoeing around the house. I've had enough of it. I'm not going to live like that anymore!"

"You're leaving him?"

"*Nee,* our people aren't like that, you know, and neither am I. I wouldn't so disgrace *Daett.* But something will have to change."

"And what can *Daett* do about it? That family . . ."

"I told *Mamm* the real reason why we didn't come to breakfast today." Tears were running again. "I was trying not to provoke Norman. But it did no *gut.* He wanted me to say what a lousy Christmas program you had put on at the school, Katie. When I wouldn't, he came after me. I fell over the kitchen chair, and he used his foot on me. So we didn't go to his parents' place either this morning. I locked myself in the bedroom until he cooled down. Then I came over here."

"Oh, Mabel!" Katie could picture Norman angry, but not what Mabel was describing. None of their people acted like this. At least not that she'd ever heard of.

"He's always sorry afterward." Mabel choked back a sob. "And I suppose Norman thinks I've just gone home to cry on *Daett*'s shoulder. That idea doesn't bother him too much. It seems to make him feel less guilty now, I think, if someone knows what's going on."

They drove in silence, with Katie looking out over the open fields at the freshly fallen snow. *Da Hah*'s world was so clean, so white, so washed of dirt, and yet inside the hearts of men and women such awful things dwelled. It was a mystery really, and Katie shivered.

Mabel followed Jesse into the driveway of the small farm she and Norman had purchased. Jesse stopped by the barn and jumped out to tie his horse. He came over to Norman's buggy. "Do you want to come in with me, Mabel?"

"*Nee*, I'll wait with Katie."

"It's just as well," Jesse said. He then went up the porch and into the house without knocking. Katie saw no sign of Norman through the living room window, but Jesse would find him. He was probably hiding in the basement in shame. And he *should* be ashamed.

Katie kept her eyes on the house as long moments past. At least there was no shouting coming from inside, so Jesse was controlling his anger. Though Norman was getting the full load, unless she missed her guess.

Mabel began to fidget when the front door opened and both Jesse and Norman came out. Neither of them said a word to the women. They marched to Jesse's buggy and got in. Jesse turned the horse and buggy around, and they drove down the driveway.

"I wonder where they're going?" Mabel asked, craning her neck to watch the retreating buggy.

"Norman looks like he's seen a ghost," Katie said much too gleefully, she knew, but she couldn't help it.

"He's a coward at heart, Katie. He can only handle defenseless woman." Mabel got out of the buggy, and Katie followed to help her unhitch Bonnie. Mabel was trembling by the time they had Bonnie in the barn, and Katie took her arm to lead her sister into the house. Once inside, Katie seated

Mabel on a kitchen chair and asked. "Have you had breakfast yet?"

Mabel shook her head. "There wasn't time. And I didn't feel like it, anyway."

"Then you sit right there while I fix you something."

Mabel grunted a protest, but stayed seated while Katie fixed bacon, eggs, and toast. As the bacon was frying, Katie added pancakes to the list. She might as well go all out, and give Mabel some semblance of a proper Christmas breakfast.

When the food was ready, Mabel ate without speaking, still fighting tears. They didn't even bother with praying over the food. There were other things which needed prayer much more right now. Like Jesse and Norman — wherever they were. And for the success of Jesse's mission — whatever that was.

"You are too kind to me." Mabel broke into sobs when she finished eating. "And after all the nasty things I've said about you."

"It's okay." Katie led Mabel to the couch and wrapped a blanket around her. "Where's the furnace? In the basement?" The house seemed cold for some reason. Neither Norman nor Mabel must have been paying attention to the fire all morning.

"*Yah* . . . the basement." Mabel pointed. "There's fresh wood, I think. I saw Norman stock a supply before the snow began."

Katie found the basement door, and at the bottom of the steps the furnace seated off to the side. The fire was almost out, but the furnace still had enough coals to get things going again. When she finished and went upstairs, Jesse's buggy was pulling into the driveway. After watching the two get out of the buggy and Jesse tie up the horse, Katie made a rush for the front door and opened it for them.

Norman wasn't looking at her — or much else for that matter. He still looked quite pale.

"Bishop Miller's *frau* will be over to fix supper for you," Jesse told Mabel. "And none of this will be happening again. Bishop Miller and Laura will be checking in on you." Jesse paused then added, "Often!"

"Thank you, *Daett*." Mabel grabbed Jesse and hung on to his neck until he loosened his daughter's hold.

"Just listen to what Laura tells you," Jesse said. "Bishop Miller will deal with Norman, but you are not to hide anything from now on. Laura is going to stop by at least once a week, maybe more than that. And you are to tell her *everything*, Mabel. Laura will check your story if she has to. Do you understand, Mabel?"

Mabel nodded.

Jesse turned to Norman, but he said nothing. Then Jesse said to Katie, "It's time we went home, Katie."

As they climbed into the buggy, Katie asked, "So you went to Bishop Miller's?"

"Yah." Jesse slapped the reins and offered Katie nothing more.

CHAPTER THIRTY-EIGHT

Three weeks after New Year's Day, on a cold Tuesday morning, Katie drove toward Dover. Joel had begged to ride along this morning since he was off from school, but with where she was going, that was impossible.

Katie let her mind drift to thoughts of Ruth Gingerich. The woman had fallen on an ice patch outside the schoolhouse door last week and fractured her hip. That was a tragedy indeed, and now the school was without a teacher. It served Enos Kuntz right, Katie thought, having to scurry around the community to find a replacement. Obviously Enos was having trouble finding one on such short notice or school would already be in session again.

Katie pushed thoughts of Enos and teaching from her mind as she approached the white-pillared porch of the Kent County Courthouse. There were more important things on her mind this morning. Ahead of her someone had scraped the wide steps free of snow from the last snowstorm and salted them. There hadn't been a thaw since Christmas, with winter dragging on. *Like my life,* Katie thought. She shouldn't even be here really. But how could things get much worse? So here she was, coming in to see how Ben's appearance in court went. Not seeing Ben in so long had torn at her heart. So when she ran into Ben's *mamm,* Lavina, at Byler's last week, the words had just come out. "When will the trial start that Ben's supposed to testify at?"

"Next week," Lavina had said. "And Ben's testimony is scheduled for the second day."

"Are you going?"

Lavina shook her head. "Ben asked us not to come."

It made her feel better in a way that Ben was also keeping his parents at a distance. It meant she wasn't the only loved one who was being kept from his life. Ben must wish to spare all of them the shame of former actions and his current ordeal.

And fresh shame would come indeed, if Ben returned to prison. Enos would see to it that people were reminded that Ben was only suffering for the sins he'd committed in the past. And no honor was in order for willingly accepting ill that came from one's wrongs.

Katie had decided she wanted to be here to share in Ben's shame if necessary. Weren't *Mamm* and Jesse standing with her in the shame she'd brought on the family? The first Sunday after the Christmas break when school began again hadn't been a pleasant experience. Whispers among the women stopped when she walked up and began again when she walked past.

All that had stopped last Sunday, though, when Norman gave his confession in front of everyone after the church service. Bishop Miller asked all the church members to stay behind, and then stood to announce that one of the members had been found in grievous sin for abusing his wife. "One is to love one's wife, even as Christ loved the church and gave Himself for her," Bishop Miller had said. "While women are to give in to their husband's leadership, just as the church gives in to Christ, the husband is also instructed to cherish and love his wife. We will not have husbands abusing their wives in this community. I will not tolerate such sin and will deal harshly with any such cases. So this morning brother Norman will give us his heartfelt confession, asking forgiveness from both *Da Hah* and his church. My *frau,* Laura, will be keeping in touch with Mabel on a weekly basis, and I will be speaking with Norman and praying with him at those times also. If this does not stop the sinful actions, further measures will be taken."

The room had been silent when Bishop Miller finished. No one doubted the bishop's word, but this was a shock indeed. One of the Kuntz family was abusing his *frau?* She shouldn't have taken such delight in Enos's humiliation, Katie reminded herself. The poor man had sat there, so red in the face she'd thought he might burst out in tears. The Christian attitude was for her to pray for him, but she was quite weak in faith apparently. As Norman got down on his knees to beg forgiveness, she felt a shiver of delight run up and down her back. This was quite an evil and sinful thing, no doubt, but she felt it anyway. She would surely have to pray for mercy herself before long.

Katie pushed the thoughts of Enos and Norman Kuntz aside and slipped through the huge double-door entryway of the courtroom. Ben was sitting near the front row. Katie stayed out of sight, using the back of a huge, overweight man as a shield. Ben turned and looked around. Maybe he sensed her presence, Katie thought, another thrill running through her. More than likely though, Ben was longing for a familiar face but finding none. Perhaps she should show herself. But *nee,* she'd better not. It might rattle Ben, and he didn't need distractions right now.

Two rows of seats full of men and women sat off to the side. In front of the huge judge's bench were two long tables on the left and right. Men and women sat at both of them, all of the people older looking except for one young man. He must be the defendant, Katie figured. The man accused of shooting Ben. While Katie was studying the back of his head, a uniformed officer — the bailiff — stood up in the front and called out, "This court of Kent County is now is session. All rise . . . the Honorable Judge Newton presiding."

A black-robed judge appeared from the side door. The people in the courtroom were already halfway to their feet by the time it dawned on Katie what the man had meant. Katie leaped up. She was clearly out of familiar waters in this *Englisha* courtroom.

Katie sat down again when everyone else did. People began moving around in front of the courtroom, and a man stood up to speak. Katie strained to hear what he had to say.

"Your honor," the man said, "if it please the court, the prosecution has two final witnesses to present."

"Proceed, counselor," the judge ordered from his lofty perch.

"I call Mr. Bennett Slocomb to the witness stand, Your Honor."

A man seated beside Ben rose and headed for the witness stand. When he was seated, the bailiff approached him. "Please raise your right hand, Mr. Slocomb."

When he did, the officer continued, "Do you swear to tell the truth, the whole truth . . ."

The officer's voice eventually came to an end, and Mr. Slocomb said, "I do."

"You may proceed with your questions, counselor," the judge ordered.

Katie leaned forward to listen to the answers.

"I'm a neighbor to the Stoll family. I live close enough to see across the fields. On the night of August twenty-eight, I heard a gunshot and went outside to look around. The gunshot came clearly from the direction of the Stoll residence. I was sitting in the living room, which is on the same side as the Stoll's farm. I ran back in to get my own gun out of the cabinet, telling my wife to call 911. I then ran across the field toward the Stoll's farm. I stayed along the road the whole time. When I came up to the small piece of woods that lies along the side of the road, a car started up and roared out of the woods past me. I saw the make and model and color clearly."

The counselor asked Mr. Slocomb, "Can you state the make and model?"

"Yes," the answer came. "A Chevy Malibu, dark blue. And no, I didn't see who was inside."

"Are you sure, Mr. Slocomb?"

"Yes. My wife once drove a Chevy Malibu, so I'm quite familiar with the car."

"Did you see any other identification on the car?"

"Yes, I caught part of the license plate — UYI 2. But that's all."

The counselor now produced a record of a car in the defendant's name, matching the partial license plate number given by Mr. Slocomb, he said, entering the items into evidence. The attorney turned on his heels. "That's all, Your Honor."

Katie watched as another man, another lawyer from the other side presumably, approached Mr. Slocomb. More questions came fast and furious.

"How is your eyesight, Mr. Slocomb?"

"How could you be sure of what you saw if it was dark?"

"Doesn't dark-blue blend in with the night?"

"When did Mrs. Slocomb own this Chevy Malibu?"

"Doesn't that make one see the familiar in the unfamiliar? Are there not, after all, several models of cars quite similar to the Chevy Malibu?"

"How could you see the license plate number in the dark, Mr. Slocomb?"

The neighbor was standing up well under the barrage, Katie thought. And answering the questions in a confident voice. If she were on the juror panel, she certainly would believe the man.

The questions eventually wrapped up without Mr. Slocomb being found in any inconsistency. He looked a little rumpled though as he returned to his seat.

Ben was called next.

Katie's heart pounded as she watched Ben walk up and take his seat in the witness stand. How was this going to go? Ben said he wasn't going to testify? Had he changed his mind?

The bailiff approached him, and when Ben was asked to promise to tell the truth, the whole truth, and nothing but the truth, he simply replied, "I affirm," and the judge nodded.

Stepping up the first counselor began his questions.

Ben answered the most basic ones, such as stating his name and address and even answered some other general questions about the night he was shot. But when he was asked specific questions that he couldn't in good conscience answer, he replied, "I can't answer that question, sir."

"Is it because you cannot remember, Mr. Stoll?"

"No sir. I cannot answer for reasons of my Amish faith."

Neither the judge or the lawyer looked that surprised. A flurry of activity continued in which Ben was ordered by the judge to answer the counselor's questions. Ben continued to refuse, citing his religious convictions.

Finally the judge said, "I've had enough of this. You have been served a subpoena, Mr. Stoll, and you will either answer the questions or I will hold you in contempt of court. If cited for contempt, you'll be held in the county jail until you choose to cooperate. What will it be?"

"I cannot answer the questions because of

my Amish faith, Your Honor," Ben repeated.

The judge pondered for a moment before asking. "Does the prosecution wish to continue without this witness?"

"We do," the answer came.

The judge looked to the other table. "Does the defense wish to question the witness on what he has testified to so far?"

The lawyer stood. "We do not, Your Honor."

"Then I sentence you to contempt of court. Bailiff, take him away." The judge motioned with his hand.

Ben stood and was led out by a court officer.

Katie sensed that maybe he'd caught sight of her before she could duck behind the huge man again. When she looked again, Ben had disappeared through the side door, and the two lawyers were huddled in front with the judge and speaking in hushed tones.

When they finished, another witness was called, but Katie had seen what she'd come to see. She left the courtroom and returned to her buggy.

She pulled off Sparky's blanket, stored it in the back of the buggy, untied the horse, and climbed into the buggy. Nothing had been accomplished, she told herself. Ben had been marched off to jail again — for how long was anyone's guess. Though Ben was in more trouble with the *Englisha* authorities, at least he had kept his promise to Bishop Miller. That was a *gut* sign, surely.

Though the thought of not seeing Ben for a long time depressed her, she had at least seen him today for a few brief moments. Coming had been the right thing to do.

CHAPTER THIRTY-NINE

Two evenings following the court trial, Katie was seated on the couch in the living room. The supper dishes still sat on the kitchen table needing attention, but *Mamm* and Carolyn weren't moving either. A hushed silence hung over the house, each of them lost in their thoughts. Jesse had completed the reading of the evening Scripture — a portion in Ephesians, chapter 2, beginning with "But God, who is rich in mercy, for his great love wherewith he loved us . . ."

Katie wondered what the love of God had in store for her next, now that Ben was in jail. Somehow God's love would make something *gut* out of all this. *Mamm* gave her a weak smile from across the room, so she must be thinking similar thoughts. They were all troubled again tonight knowing they were helpless to do anything about Ben.

Katie's head jerked up at the sound of

buggy wheels turning into the driveway. *Mamm* jumped up to look out the window and gave a little gasp. "It's Enos Kuntz!"

"I wonder what he wants." Jesse said, laying the Bible aside.

"I don't know." *Mamm* glanced toward Katie.

"Neither do I, but it can't be anything *gut,*" Katie said, throwing up her hands in puzzlement.

"It's surely not about Mabel?" Jesse said as he stood.

Mamm's face went white. "No, it couldn't be. I hope not!"

"I think we'd better scatter," Leroy said to Willis from his chair by the stove.

Jesse nodded to the two and asked them to take Joel with them. Leroy led the way upstairs.

Katie looked at Carolyn and whispered, "Come to my room. We can stay together until he leaves." Carolyn looked quite grateful, and the two crept up the stairs. They stood by the bedroom window that looked out over the yard. Enos was now out of his buggy, nodding and speaking with Jesse.

"I don't think it's about Mabel," Katie offered. "That doesn't seem right. Bishop Miller would come over if there had been another incident. Plus, I think Norman has learned his lesson."

"Mabel has been looking a little happier on Sundays," Carolyn allowed. "But she still won't come home for a visit." Carolyn gave Katie a wise look. "I know because I heard *Mamm* ask her."

"It'll all come in due time," Katie said, trying to smile but the attempt quickly faded. "Look, they're coming into the house."

Both of them ducked behind the drapes even though the men had their heads down.

"It must be *gut* news then," Carolyn whispered.

Katie snorted. "How could Enos Kuntz be the bearer of *gut* news?"

"I don't know, but I still hope it's *gut* news," Carolyn said.

Carolyn was trying to be her usual cheerful self, Katie knew, and she shouldn't dampen the girl's spirits.

"Katie!" *Mamm* called up the stairs.

Carolyn gave Katie a startled look. "It's about you! Be brave and strong."

Katie set her face into neutral lines and took her time going down the stairs. *Mamm,* Jesse, and Enos were waiting in a circle when she arrived. Jesse didn't look upset, but *Mamm* was looking away.

"Enos wishes to speak with you," Jesse said.

Katie turned to face Enos. *"Yah?"*

Enos blurted out the words without further ado. "You know that teacher Ruth has fallen on the ice outside the schoolhouse and is laid up at home . . ."

Katie didn't hesitate. "I was sorry to hear that. Is she okay?"

Enos nodded but added, "Other than having to heal up, which may take some time."

"I'm glad it's not worse," Katie stated.

Her words seemed to give Enos fresh courage. "The school board is asking you to consider coming back, Katie, and filling out the rest of the term. Ruth is expecting a child in the late summer, she has told us, and with the trauma of the fall, she doesn't think she can complete the year."

Katie stared at the blank wall. Had she heard correctly? She was being asked to return to her job? But what was different now? Had Enos changed his mind? Or was he giving in to the wishes of the others? Perhaps he planned to make trouble for her later even if he were being forced to ask her to return now?

"And you?" Katie asked. "*You* are also asking me back?"

Enos hesitated and then cleared his throat.

"It seems I may have been mistaken about you, Katie. Bishop Miller feels we have been . . . perhaps . . . well, too hasty in judging you. I hope . . . you can forgive us . . . well, me, for my rash opinion. And we have heard about Ben and his willingness to endure jail rather than testify." Enos was sweating now and visibly uncomfortable.

"I'm sure Katie will accept your offer," Jesse spoke up. "She hasn't taken on any other job so far, and she's not that busy around the house. Emma and Carolyn can handle things well enough."

Jesse was trying to make things easy for her, and Katie appreciated it. Being asked back was a great honor, one she had never dared imagine would happen. Now it was her place to offer Christian forgiveness — even to Enos Kuntz.

Katie offered her hand. "I'll be glad to come back on Monday morning. I'll want to meet with Ruth to see where she's at with the lessons."

"That won't be necessary." Enos fumbled in his pocket and produced several sheets of paper. "Ruth sent these along. They may not be exactly accurate, since she's going from memory, she said. But this is where she believes everyone is in their lessons."

Ruth probably didn't wish to see her after

this humiliation, Katie surmised as she took the papers from Enos's hand. Or maybe Ruth was too ill to go out or have company. Katie reminded herself to not imagine the worst about someone.

"I'm glad this is straightened out." Jesse was all smiles now. "And in the future, if there are problems with Katie's schoolwork, perhaps you could come to me before anything drastic is done."

"Of course," Enos said. "There's no reason why not. You are, after all, her *daett.*"

"I hope all is going well with Norman and Mabel." Jesse was obviously driving home his advantage.

Katie hid her smile. It was high time someone stood up to Enos.

"*Yah,* of course." Enos's face was turning red.

Seeing your son making a knee confession in front of church wasn't the most pleasant experience in life, Katie thought. But neither was being fired from her teaching job.

"Well, I should be going." Enos was retreating toward the door.

Mamm rushed over to open it for him.

"Goodnight, now," Jesse called after him.

Enos didn't look back as he headed toward his buggy.

Mamm stayed at the door and watched

450

him go. She glanced over at Jesse, who was standing in the kitchen doorway. "You should have walked him to his buggy. His feelings are hurting right now."

"I suppose so," Jesse allowed. "But he'd feel worse if I showed him pity. At least I would."

"I expect you're right," *Mamm* said just as a police car turned into the driveway. *Mamm* gasped. "Now what?"

Jesse rushed over to stand beside *Mamm* just inside the front door. Katie hurried over to the window for a look. The police car had stopped beside Enos's buggy moments before Enos took off.

"Do you know what this is about, Katie?" *Mamm* asked.

Nee, of course she didn't, but the words froze in her mouth. She looked out again and — and it couldn't be! And yet it was. Ben was in the police car! But he was supposed to be in jail. And yet there he was speaking out of the police car window to Enos.

Mamm and Jesse were silent as they watched the scene. Katie couldn't see whether Enos responded to what Ben was saying or not. Likely Enos was too much in shock for anything but staring. Here Enos had just faced the great humiliation of having to hire her back on as a schoolteacher, and now Ben Stoll was being driven to her house in a police car.

Apparently *Da Hah* was piling things on Enos Kuntz's plate thick and heavy. But why was she thinking about Enos when Ben was out there? With a shriek, Katie raced out the door, and sped across the lawn. She leaped into Ben's arms right after he climbed out of the police car. Let Enos think what he wished! she thought.

"My, my, what a welcome!" Ben held her at arm's length. "It's so *gut* to see you."

"And you!" Katie gave Ben another hug. She caught sight of Enos's buggy disappearing out the lane but didn't care. "How is it that you're here?" she asked Ben.

The officer driving the police car cleared his throat behind them. "Um, I'd best be going, young man. Take care."

"Thank you for the ride," Ben said as the officer left, following the tracks Enos's buggy had left in the snow.

Katie kept holding Ben's hand. "You still haven't told me how it is you're here."

"Shall I leave?" he teased.

"Ben, stop it! Tell me right now!"

"It's very *gut* news." His eyes twinkled. "Can we go up to the porch where your *mamm* and *daett* are? I'm sure they'll want to hear for themselves, and that way I don't have to say things twice."

"Of course!" Katie led him by the hand across the lawn.

"What did Enos want?" Ben asked as they approached the house.

"Ruth Gingerich broke her hip, and Enos asked me to come back and finish the teaching for the school year."

"That's great!" Ben's eyes shone with happiness. He stuck out his hand to greet Jesse. "*Gut* evening, Jesse."

"And *gut* evening to you," Jesse said. "It sounds as if Katie was just filling you in on the evening's news."

"*Yah,*" Ben said with a smile. "That's a sudden turn of events. And *gut* evening to you too, Emma," Ben said, turning toward Katie's *mamm.*

"And you . . . being here tonight . . ." *Mamm* shook Ben's hand. "What a surprise. We were not expecting this."

"Neither was I. The sheriff came in this afternoon and told me the judge was letting me go."

"Really?" Jesse asked. "And did he say why?"

"The sheriff didn't, but the prosecutor told me. Turns out the jury brought back a guilty verdict after lunch today. Enough other evidence had been presented, I guess. And I think the prosecutor pulled a little trick on the defense by having me refuse to testify in front of the jury. It was obvious why I was refusing, and this added to the belief that the accused shooter was guilty. At least that's the theory. There's no further need for my testimony."

"*Da Hah* has His ways!" Jesse exclaimed. "And we must not question even when things get difficult. But at least you did what you needed to do. No one can hold anything against you for how you handled this situation. I'm sure Bishop Miller will feel likewise."

"Thank you." Ben glanced away. "That means a lot to me."

There was a tear in Ben's eye, and Katie reached over to squeeze his hand. "Have you had supper yet?"

Ben shook his head.

Mamm gasped and exclaimed, "Then we have to fix something for you right now! There's still leftovers in the kitchen. Come, Katie, it won't take much to throw something together."

"*Daett* will entertain you until then," Katie said, letting go of Ben's hand. "Will that be okay?"

"Anything will be okay after where I've

been these past few days." Ben sighed as he followed the others into the house.

"So what are your plans now?" Jesse was asking as the two men settled in the living room and Katie and *Mamm* left for the kitchen. Katie didn't hear Ben's answer, but she could guess. Ben would be reporting to Bishop Miller, perhaps even tomorrow. And if things went well — and there was no reason for them not to — Ben would be in church on Sunday. And he'd bring her home that night in his buggy pulled by Longstreet after the hymn singing — if he'd moved back in with his parents by then. If not, by the next Sunday. She might even go help him bring his things back from town if there was time now that she was resuming her teaching job.

"You certainly look happy, Katie," *Mamm* said, her face beaming.

"I should be!" Katie said. "Can you believe all that has happened tonight? Pretty soon I'll be jumping up and down like Joel does."

"I might even join you," *Mamm* said. "I'm so glad things are working out for you, Katie."

"Then you approve of Ben and me?" Katie asked as she motioned toward the living room.

Mamm didn't hesitate. "I think I see *Da Hah*'s hand at work, that's all I can say. And you've stayed true to the man, Katie. That means a lot."

Katie grabbed *Mamm*'s arm and squeezed it before she calmed down. The two hugged each other for a long moment before rushing around the kitchen to prepare Ben's supper.

CHAPTER FORTY

During the second week in February, once things at the school had settled down to a routine again, Katie set out with Sparky for a visit to the ailing Ruth Gingerich. She soon pulled to a stop beside Albert and Ruth's house, where they had set up housekeeping after their wedding. Hopefully Albert wouldn't be home yet from his construction job since it was early in the afternoon. Katie had made a point of coming right after school even though a stack of papers still needed checking and were sitting on her desk. Tomorrow she would just have to work extra hard.

Mamm made a point yesterday of reminding her that Ruth needed a visit. It would be displaying a Christian attitude for her to stop by while Ruth was healing from her broken hip. Last week *Mamm* had been over herself, taking along a cherry pie and loaf of bread.

According to *Mamm*, Ruth would be glad to see her, but Katie was skeptical. Too many things had happened in their past for ill feelings to blow over. And yet *Da Hah*'s ways were great, and she shouldn't doubt the power of His hand. Look at what He'd done for her and Ben!

On Sunday evening she'd been driven home again with Ben in his buggy, leaning against his shoulder for the drive and stealing a quick kiss before he left the house near midnight. Ben was sparing with his kisses, even though he enjoyed them as much as she did. He was only trying to do the right thing, she reminded herself.

Leaving Sparky tied to the hitching post, Katie approached Ruth's house and knocked. A faint voice called out, "Come in!"

Katie pushed open the door and was greeted by the sight of Ruth propped up with pillows on a couch.

"Hi," Katie said as she halted in the doorway.

"Oh, it's you, Katie." Ruth was smiling at least. "Come in and sit down. I'm glad to see you."

Katie hesitated. "I just thought I'd stop by for a minute. *Mamm* said you were doing some better last week. I'm sorry for what happened."

Ruth waved her hand toward the rocker. "Sit down, Katie. You don't have to feel sorry for me or explain yourself. I'm the one who should do that."

Katie obeyed, taking the offered seat.

Ruth paused to pat her injured hip with one hand. "This is nothing but *Da Hah*'s judgment. Something I needed to bring me to my senses, Katie. If you hadn't come over to visit, I would have stopped by the schoolhouse to apologize the first chance after I get on my feet."

"But you mustn't speak this way," Katie protested. "We can't know how *Da Hah* judges."

Ruth shook her head. "On this one I'm right, Katie, so don't say I'm not. Albert has told me I'd better come over and apologize before *Da Hah* strikes me with something worse. That's what Albert said once he found out what all was going on. I can only say how ashamed I am of myself, Katie. It is only *Da Hah*'s mercy that I didn't kill myself on that ice spot. Thankfully, one of the children was still there to call for help. As overweight as I am, it took three ambulance workers to get me onto the gurney."

"Everyone has their faults," Katie offered.

Ruth ignored her. "I've never been so embarrassed in my life — at least that I can remember. Between that and the pain, I begged *Da Hah*'s forgiveness right then and there. I saw clearly what this was. The smiting hand of *Da Hah*. I told Enos Kuntz the same thing that very afternoon. That he had best get things made right with you before he was also smitten down. *Yah,* I said that, even though I knew seeing his son Norman on his knees in front of church had already put gray hairs on the man's head. Yet all the time my turn was coming, and I was too blind to see it."

"I still don't think you're seeing this correctly," Katie interrupted.

Ruth paid her no attention. "I'm also sorry, Katie, for my part in running down you and your *mamm*'s reputation. I let jealousy enter my heart all those years ago when your *mamm* won Jesse's hand instead of me. That was very wicked of me, and it wouldn't have worked anyway. I can tell that now. Jesse Mast and me? *Ach!* Albert's so much better suited for me. But I was too blinded by my own wishes, I suppose. I hope you can forgive me as your *mamm* forgave me last week."

"*Yah,* of course," Katie whispered. No wonder *Mamm* had told her to stop by if this was how her conversation had gone with Ruth. Yet *Mamm* hadn't breathed a word, no doubt wanting her to hear the words fresh from Ruth's mouth.

"I asked your *mamm* please not to tell you what I'd told her," Ruth confirmed Katie's thoughts. "And from the look on your face, she didn't."

"*Mamm* only suggested that I stop by. That's all."

"You are *wunderbah* people. I'm sorry it took this to open my eyes — that and Albert's words. You should have heard what he had to say, the poor man, when I told him the whole story after my fall on the ice. He had no idea what his *frau* was capable of. Albert is so innocent in some ways, but he sure has a pure soul." Ruth paused to wipe away a tear before continuing. "And poor Mabel. I'll have to visit her when I can ride in the buggy again. Here I led her into such sins over the years. Turning her against your *mamm,* and probably helping her along with her marriage to Norman. How poor Mabel has had to suffer because of what I've done."

"But it's going better now, isn't it?" Katie asked.

Ruth smiled. "*Yah,* from what I've heard." Ruth sobered again. "But no woman should have to go through that. Mabel told me what happened, and I couldn't believe Norman was capable of such things. Then when Mabel showed me the bruises I got angry, blaming Norman for all of it. All the time not seeing my own part in pushing them together. Thankfully Mabel asked for and received help even before *Da Hah* passed His judgment on me."

"I don't think you should be so hard on yourself." Katie stood up. "Are you coming along okay with your injury? May I get you anything right now?"

Ruth sighed. "I'll be well enough to get out of the house in a couple of weeks or so, the doctor claims. And I can't wait. It's awful being cooped up in the house and having other people tend to me all the time. Thankfully poor Albert has been kept in decent food. People have brought in so much or he would have starved by now."

"Is there anything I can do?" Katie asked again. "I can't stay long, but I could help with some housework perhaps or maybe dinner."

"You'll do no such thing." Ruth waved toward the couch again. "Sit down and tell me about school. And about Ben of course. I hear things are going well between the two of you."

"*Yah!*" A smile crept over Katie's face as she settled onto the couch again. "I get to see Ben every Sunday now. And he's back home with his *mamm* and *daett,* for which everyone is very thankful."

"So Ben's made peace with the faith?"

Ruth as usual knew more than she should know about people, but her apology had been sincere so Katie overlooked it. Besides, Ruth would always be interested in other people's lives. It was part of who she was. She meant no harm. "*Da Hah* has been faithful in that area. I thought way back when, that I could perhaps help Ben by taking the trip to Europe and bringing home interesting stories about our faith's fathers. But what Ben really needed was to meet *Da Hah* for himself. Which he did in the strangest of situations — through the times he served in the *Englisha* jail."

Ruth nodded. "*Yah,* each of us are reached in our own way. *Da Hah* knows I needed a *gut* bounce on my backside to knock some sense into me. So I don't belittle anyone's way back to the right path. Tell me, how's school going?"

"As *gut* as can be expected, I suppose. I've never been through the winter blues before, this still being my first year. But with a hint of spring in the air, the children are hard to keep inside. The playground is still a little muddy, so they make do the best they can with board games."

"How well I know." Ruth groaned, moving her hips to a more comfortable position. "They'll be outside before you know it though, and everything will be back to normal. All things come to an end, as they say."

"May I get you another pillow?" Katie asked, as Ruth groaned again.

"Maybe that would help." Ruth adjusted herself. "You can get mine in the bedroom — the one on the left."

Katie hurried in and returned with the pillow. Ruth lifted herself up high enough to slide the pillow in, flopping back down again. A wry expression crept across her face. "At least I've lost some weight through this accident — weight that I plan to keep off. Over Albert's objections, I must say. The man says he likes me just the way I am."

Katie smiled, thinking she should be leaving soon.

Ruth seemed not to notice, chattering on. "So will young Ben be joining the baptismal class this spring? It's coming up in April, isn't it?"

"*Yah,* he's planning on it," Katie said.

464

"And soon wedding bells will be ringing, if I don't miss my guess." With that, Ruth laughed with glee.

Now Katie was sure she was turning red, which made Ruth laugh harder, knowing she had hit home on that one. The truth was that Ben hadn't officially asked her to be his *frau,* but surely he would soon. Maybe after he began the baptismal class. Ben probably thought he should make his decision plain before he asked her for such a serious commitment. The truth was, she would have said *yah* if he had asked her weeks ago.

Ruth still wasn't through chuckling. "Well, it's *gut* to see the two of you coming along so well. Bishop Miller had nothing but nice things to say when he stopped by last week with Laura. Seems like Ben was on his mind, which isn't surprising with how much trouble Ben caused the community. It must have been a relief to get that one off the bishop's mind."

"I'm sure it was," Katie agreed, getting to her feet. "Well, I really have to be going, Ruth. And I hope you get completely well — and very soon. I'll be looking for you at church services then."

"It can't come too soon, believe me."

"Goodbye for now," Katie said, as she

made her way to the door.

How strange things were turning out, Katie thought. The ground underfoot was becoming more solid each day. Even Mahlon Bontrager had gotten the message now that Ben was coming to church and taking her home in the evenings. Mahlon had asked Millie Schrock — who was twenty-nine or so — home on Sunday evening for the first time. And from the reports the schoolchildren had whispered between themselves later that week, Millie had been spotted at the sewing still blushing.

At her age, Millie might have wondered if she'd remain an old maid. Having the attentions of a decent man like Mahlon would make a woman blush. It was all for the best, really. Katie had done the right thing sticking it out with Ben. Katie climbed into the buggy and turned Sparky toward home.

CHAPTER FORTY-ONE

It was a Sunday night in early April. Katie met Ben at the front door with a smile. As they stood at the door, the soft light from the kerosene lamp inside played on Ben's face. *Mamm* and the rest of the family were already in bed. Katie reached over to take Ben's hand. "What's it going to be tonight?" she asked. "Strawberry pie or cherry? With ice cream, of course."

"Why not both?" Ben said with a gleam in his eyes.

Katie faked a glare. "I do declare! That's all you come here for on Sunday nights . . . to eat."

"*Yah.*" Ben walked inside and plopped down on the couch. "Why else would I be here?"

Because of me, Katie almost said, but she rushed into the kitchen before Ben saw her blushing face. Why did she still get red-faced around him after all this time? Perhaps because tonight had been so special driving home. The spring weather was bringing everything alive, so they'd driven home with the buggy doors open. The peepers had been croaking in the pond along the road, and the crickets shrieking in the trees. Ben had been in a playful mood, and she'd enjoyed his chatter to the fullest, snuggling up against his shoulder with the buggy blanket at their feet. *Yah,* tonight was extra special. Things were finally going well, and enough time had passed that it seemed things might stay that way.

Katie paused in the kitchen to slide two pieces of pie — strawberry and cherry — onto a plate. She then scooped the ice cream on top and returned to the living room.

Ben took the plate eagerly and began eating. "Where's yours?" he finally asked.

"I don't really want any tonight," she said.

"That means more for me!" Ben said with a laugh.

Katie smiled and then turned serious. "Ben, do you ever think back to what it used to be like not so long ago for us? About the experiences we've had? And what may lie ahead?"

He sobered as he paused between bites. "Sometimes. But tonight I'm thinking about you, Katie."

"Oh, Ben!"

"I do that more than I should sometimes."
He lowered his head. "Katie . . ."

She waited as he seemed to search for
what to say. Would tonight be the night? Was
he going to ask her to be his *frau*? She tried
to keep breathing. She mustn't jump to
conclusions. Still, it seemed like maybe it
could happen. After all, Ben was taking life
far more seriously now. He'd been attending the baptismal class for several Sundays
already. But tonight . . . could it really happen?

His fork trembled and his voice was low.
"Katie, I've been wanting to ask you . . .
about something . . . important."

She met his gaze. "*Yah,* Ben?"

He looked away. "I know I'm unworthy of
you, Katie. But I want to . . . to marry you
if . . . if you'll consent, of course. Would
you be my *frau* come the wedding season
this fall?"

The words gushed out as quickly as her
tears of joy. "Ben, of course! I accept. I'd be
glad to marry you this fall."

A smile crept across his face. He moved
closer, the pie plate still in one hand, and
reached up to touch her face.

She took the plate from his hand and set

it on the floor. Then she wrapped both hands around his neck and kissed him.

"You really will be my *frau*?" Ben asked, long moments later.

"Of course, you silly." She kissed him again.

Ben turned serious. "I want to thank you for standing by me like you did. I never told you, but I thought my heart would burst with joy when I caught sight of your face that day in the courtroom."

"So you did see me then?" Katie snuggled tightly against him.

"How could I not see you? Your presence filled the entire place."

Katie laughed. "You'll really have to tone down all this talk. I'm just plain old Emma Raber's daughter, Ben, just in case you've forgotten."

"The girl everyone overlooked . . . except me." He stroked the stray hairs hanging on her forehead.

"Now don't get so full of yourself, Ben."

"Isn't that what you liked about me?"

She touched his face with her fingers. "I liked what I saw in you. I saw a man who charmed my heart. But I never thought it could really happen — that you would notice me."

Ben laughed. "So tell me, what was with

all the plainness, the drab dresses you used to wear, the hiding behind people at the youth gatherings, the sober face? What was that all about? Were you pretending? Testing me? Seeing if I'd notice?"

Katie rested her head on his shoulder. "*Nee,* I'm afraid not. It was all quite real. And I'm still plain, Ben. I'll always be. I was brought up that way."

Ben grinned. "And with a heart of gold. Maybe that's what shines on your face, making the beauty outside even more beautiful."

"Careful now, Ben," Katie teased. "I'll be getting old before too long."

He regarded her steadily. "Maybe it's best you don't know how beautiful you are, Katie."

"Hush," she said, kissing him again.

Ben stroked her cheek. "Don't believe me? Just look how Mahlon Bontrager was mooning over you when I came back."

Katie laughed. "How do you know about Mahlon?"

"Because I was watching you, and so was he. I'm not blind, Katie."

"You never had anything to worry about." She glanced up at his face.

He smiled. "Katie, one more thing. Can you tell what they're thinking of me in the

471

community? Have you heard any . . . any more complaints?"

Katie sat up straight. "Of course not! You've suffered enough for what you did wrong. And you chose jail time to uphold the community's beliefs."

Ben shrugged. "I think they're accepting me because of you more than anything."

Katie laughed. "Because of me? Ben, you're wrong."

"I don't think so. The love of a *gut* woman helps, Katie." Ben kissed her on the cheek.

They both sat quietly, perfectly content.

Ben reached down, picked up his plate, and finished off the pie. He looked at her, smiling. "So tell me how the program for the last day of school is coming along?" he finally asked.

Katie sat bolt upright. "Oh, Ben! I've plumb forgotten there was to be one. Just like I forgot the Christmas program. What's the matter with me?"

Ben laughed. "Nothing is the matter with you. Do you need my help planning it?"

"You? But you don't have time. Carolyn helped me for the Christmas program. I'm sure she'll have *gut* ideas again."

"I have a very *gut* idea. Shall I tell you?"

"*Yah,* please do."

"Have the children reenact your trip to

Switzerland — some of the highlights perhaps. Things that stood out to you. The adults would love it, and the children would learn a lot about our faith."

"But I've already told my story to the women at the sewing."

"You haven't told it to the men or to me. Not in that way, at least."

Katie thought about it for a moment. "I don't know, Ben. You really think they'd like it?"

"They'd be charmed. And it would wash away the last doubts anyone might have on whether they should have hired you back."

Katie tried to collect her thoughts. "Well, maybe."

Ben continued. "I could stop by after school some days, and give you suggestions the brilliant Carolyn might miss."

"*Yah,* let's do it! We can begin this week already. You can stop by whenever it suits you. And I'll tell Carolyn about it tomorrow evening so she can start planning."

"They'll be plenty of time, I'm sure. And here's the bonus — I'll get to see you more often!"

Katie leaned against him. "Ben, this is so beautiful. All of this. You being here with me, loving me enough to ask if I'd be your *frau* this fall."

Ben appeared embarrassed. "Now you'll have me turning red. Shouldn't we begin planning for the wedding soon? It'll be here before you know it."

"We have all summer for that, Ben. Right now I just want to enjoy you. I don't want this night to end."

"Me neither."

"Where are we going to live, Ben?"

Ben didn't hesitate. "There's a little place not far from *Mamm* and *Daett*'s place. It's for rent right now. I'd have to take it before the wedding, perhaps begin to live there by myself . . ."

Katie's face glowed. "So you've already been thinking about it — before you even asked me?"

Ben laughed. "*Yah,* I couldn't help myself, Katie. But I wouldn't make the plans, not without your consent."

"That's a very smart decision, Ben Stoll." She glanced at his empty plate he'd put back on the floor. "Would you like more pieces of pie?"

"*Nee,* I have to go. It's close to midnight already."

Katie followed him to the door. "I can't believe this is really happening. It hardly seems real. It's like I'm dreaming."

"Then don't wake up, dear," he whispered.

Katie pulled him close and lingered in his arms.

Ben soon pushed away and slipped out into the night. Katie watched as his buggy lights came on, and Ben guided Longstreet down the lane. Not until they had vanished from sight, did she close the door. After putting the pie plate in the kitchen, she went to her room and looked out the window. There was nothing in sight except the twinkling of the stars overhead.

"Thank You, dear *Hah*," she whispered toward the heavens. "Thank You for everything. And for everything which is still to come."

EPILOGUE

Five Months Later

Fall arrived in full force, and after a final rush of wedding preparations, Katie was married. And to Ben Stoll! She pinched herself to see if it was a dream, even though people were still standing around talking with them. The wedding had just been that morning, and now the hymn singing was over. A long line of well-wishers were coming past the corner table to shake hands. Katie stood beside Ben, glancing up at his face every chance she had. The moment when she'd promised to be his *frau* was now hours past, but the glory wasn't fading away.

They'd been married here at Bishop Miller's place, where *Mamm* had said her vows with Jesse and where Mabel had begun her married life. In every way now, she was one of them. And so was Ben now that his baptismal vows had been said last month. The *wunderbah* "last day of school" pro-

476

gram Ben had helped direct had been months ago. Life couldn't be happier.

Outside, the moon had risen, its full globe visible through the open pole barn door. Soon the couple would be riding in the buggy behind Longstreet to their new rented home where Ben had been living since late May.

Ben was busy talking with his *mamm* and *daett* right now. On the other side of Katie, Carolyn slipped away, following Marlin Stoll outside. Carolyn had been such a beautiful bridesmaid today, but now she probably wanted a few moments alone with Marlin. He was one of Ben's relatives from Lancaster. Carolyn had never met him before today, but she was smitten from all indications. She'd been stealing sideway glances at the young man for most of the day. Katie smiled. How neat would that be if Carolyn met her future husband at her wedding?

Brenda, Ben's eldest sister, had been the bridesmaid chosen from his side of the family, and now she slipped over to shake Katie's hand. "It's been a great day, Katie. And I wish the absolute best to the both of you. You deserve each other."

"*Yah*, we probably do," Katie said with a laugh.

"*Nee*," Brenda hastened to correct, "I

meant that in the best way."

Katie nodded. "I know. Thank you. You've been so sweet today."

"Take care of Ben, then."

"You know I will."

Ben's *daett* was moving closer to Katie now, offering to shake her hand. She took it with a big smile. "Thanks for raising such a great son, Leon."

A tear formed in his eye, and he didn't wipe it away. "I think you had a lot to do with that, Katie. You'll make Ben a *wunderbah frau.* I appreciate you so much."

"Thank you. I'm very happy to be a Stoll now."

Leon turned to Lavina, who had just given Ben one last hug. "It's all true, isn't it, *Mamm*!"

Lavina gave them both a big smile. "I didn't hear a word you said, but I'm sure it's all true. At least if you're saying *gut* things about Katie."

Katie gave Lavina a tight hug. "Thank you both for bringing up such a nice son."

Lavina was making no effort to hide her tears. "He's a very precious boy to us."

"And he's a precious man to me," Katie assured Lavina.

"*Mamm,* stop saying such things," Ben interrupted. "Someone will hear you."

Everyone laughed as Ben's parents moved on.

Bishop Miller and his *frau* were next in line. They must have heard what had been said because the bishop stuck his hand out to Ben. "It's *gut* to hear parents praising their children. And in this case, I must say it's well deserved. I'm glad to have all of you getting along so well."

"Thank you," Ben told him.

"You're too kind, I think," Katie said as she shook his hand and then Laura's. "Thank you for marrying us, Bishop Miller."

"It was a great honor," Bishop Miller said. "A great honor indeed. And I have a request for you, Katie, since you're the school-teacher again this year. Could you get everyone together from last term and repeat that "last day of school" program? I know some people who would love to see it."

"I'm not sure," Katie replied. "The children may have forgotten by now, and the eighth graders aren't in school any longer."

Bishop Miller leaned closer. "It's for the minister's meeting we're having around Thanksgiving. Could you have it ready by then? Surely, Katie, the children know it well enough. Even if it's only half as *gut* as it was the first time, I'd be happy."

Katie tried to collect herself. "You want us to give the program for the ministers?"

Bishop Miller's eyes twinkled. "And for their wives so you wouldn't just be looking at long beards, shall we say? Think about it, Katie. It would be quite *gut* for everyone. This would put in a nice word for the progress of our school — educating our children in the ways of the forefathers."

Ben interrupted, taking Katie's hand. "Of course we'll get the program ready. Katie, I'll come up after work and help you prepare. And maybe Carolyn can stop by during school hours. She was also involved in planning it."

"That will be *wunderbah!*" Bishop Miller was all smiles. "And I'm glad to hear that there's been no more trouble from the people who were after you, Ben. We've been praying all summer for your safety. Maybe things have blown over by now?"

"I sure hope so," Ben said, adding quickly, "Since I didn't testify, they've sort of cooled off, it seems."

"*Da Hah* be praised!" Bishop Miller said. "And the best of wishes to your married life together. May it be all *Da Hah* desires."

"Amen!" Ben agreed as the bishop and Laura moved on.

"Do you know what you've just committed us to with that school program?" Katie whispered out of the corner of her mouth.

"It's an honor to do it for the bishop, and you're my *frau*. You have to obey!"

"Ben Stoll! You're a rascal!" Katie whispered back with a giggle.

"That's why you love me."

She made a face at him, and Ben laughed, turning to shake hands with the next person in line. His Aunt Rosemary and her husband lingered for a long time, wishing them well and telling them stories of the earlier years of their marriage — about their misunderstandings over cooking and child training. They apparently expected Ben and Katie to have some of the same experiences.

It might happen, Katie thought, but at the moment all that paled to what they'd been through already. And Bishop Miller had been correct with his surmising about the further trouble Ben might have been in since the trial. She also had prayed much this summer, but Ben was sure both he and the community were out of danger. And there had been nothing to indicate Ben was wrong. Indeed, *Da Hah* had been with them, and He surely would continue to be there offering His aid.

"Thanks for the advice." Katie smiled as Ben's aunt and uncle turned to leave.

"You'll make it, so don't worry," Rosemary assured her. "I can see you're quite in love with each other."

"That we are," Ben said.

Katie turned to face the next people in line.

"Margaret and Sharon!" she gushed, "Thank you for coming!" Katie hugged both of them. Ben looked nervous for once as he shook their hands.

"We wouldn't have missed your wedding for the world," Margaret offered for both of the women.

"It was such a solemn ceremony this morning," Sharon said. "It almost brought tears to my eyes."

"And you're obviously so in love," Margaret cooed. "I can see it in your eyes. And he's handsome too. How did you catch him, Katie?"

"She chased me down with her buggy," Ben offered.

Both Margaret and Susan laughed.

"He's witty too," Katie said. "He'll keep me entertained through the easy times and the hard times."

"I'm sure he will, so be sure to take good care of him," Margaret said. Then the two girls moved on, giving a quick wave over their shoulders before blending into the crowd.

"You pick such decent friends," Ben said.

"You're just trying to build up your own stock because I married you," Katie shot back. "But they are *wunderbah.*"

Ben turned to shake hands with Jesse and *Mamm.* "You have a great daughter, Jesse. Thank you for allowing me to marry her."

"It's an honor, Ben," Jesse said, giving Ben a firm handshake. "And the best to you and yours. Take care of Katie now."

Mamm hugged Katie close and tears began to fall. "Oh, Katie, I'm going to miss you so very, very much. The house will seem empty and cold."

"Now, *Mamm,*" Katie comforted her. "Time moves on, and it won't be that bad. You still have four children at home. We'll visit often . . ."

"You do that!" *Mamm* wiped away her tears and shook hands with Ben. "I wish both of you the best. And you're getting a very *gut frau.*"

"I know," Ben said. "The absolute best. And don't worry. I'll see to it that she makes it home often."

Jesse and *Mamm* moved on. Behind them Mabel appeared with Norman following her. Behind the two of them were Enos and his *frau*. Katie really had no desire to see Norman or Enos, but one had to be charitable, especially on one's wedding day. And Enos was now decent to her whenever she had dealings with him as the head of the school board.

Mabel shook hands with Ben, and turned to give Katie a hug. "You looked so gorgeous today. You're a *wunderbah* sister, and I love you so much!"

"And I love you, Mabel," Katie said, their hug lingering. "Thanks for all the help you were with the wedding. *Mamm* and I couldn't have done it without you."

Mabel patted her rounded stomach. "You exaggerate as usual, Katie — at least when it comes to me. But I'm glad I could help before I got too big."

"Is the baby doing okay?" Katie whispered.

Mabel glowed and nodded.

Katie turned her attention to Norman, who was chatting with Ben. He looked quite nervous, but he managed to smile as he shook her hand. "Katie, I think I need to apologize about something."

Katie waited. She couldn't remember Norman doing anything against her lately, but apologizing would be a *gut* exercise for him — whether it was needed or not.

Norman hung his head. "About our wedding . . . or at our wedding, I should say. I shouldn't have objected to you being Mabel's bridesmaid. It was mean of me. And I hope you can forgive me."

"Oh!" Katie searched for the best words to say. "That was a long time ago, but *yah,* of course I forgive you."

"Thank you." Norman looked appropriately humble as he moved on. Mabel took his hand as they disappeared into the crowd.

Katie looked back to face the equally nervous Enos Kuntz. He extended his hand, and Katie shook it. Enos seemed to search for what to say. "It's a *gut* day for you, Katie. And I'm glad things turned out okay. And, *yah,* we appreciate your teaching. Abram's doing quite well."

"He's improving every week," Katie said. "And I suppose everything turned out for the best."

Enos muttered something and moved on. His *frau* shook hands with Katie, not saying anything. She was a quiet woman and always had been, Katie thought. She must be or she'd have given Enos Kuntz a piece of her mind a long time ago.

"They're nice people," Ben whispered in her ear.

Katie pinched his leg. "Stop it. This is a

serious moment."

He looked away to keep from laughing.

Katie felt she would soon do the same herself if Ben didn't stop teasing. So much happiness was rising up inside her she thought she might burst.

The line finally came to an end, and people left for home. Bishop Miller came to push the pole barn doors shut as the couple walked outside. Willis had Longstreet hitched to Ben's buggy waiting in the front yard.

"You didn't have to stay around so late," Katie protested even as she smiled.

"It's with my pleasure and best wishes," Willis said, slapping Longstreet's neck in delight.

Ben gave Katie a hand to help her into the buggy, and they took off. He drove slowly out of the lane, holding the lines gently. Once on the road, he bent his head sideways to kiss Katie, and his hat fell to the floor. Katie giggled, picked it up, and threw it behind the seat.

"I have to see to drive," he muttered, as she kept pulling his head toward her.

She let go, but snuggled up to him as Ben drove faster. The moon now hung high in the sky, the hour close to midnight. Katie didn't care — even if they had to get up early tomorrow morning to help clean the pole barn at Bishop Miller's. This was a day she wanted to remember for the rest of her life. There would never be another man in her life other than Ben. How could there be?

Ben pulled into their driveway, and Katie helped him unhitch. She waited by the buggy until he returned from putting Longstreet in the barn. Together they walked toward the house, hand in hand. Someone had been here and left a kerosene lamp burning on the living room desk. The warm light crept through the window, welcoming them home as Ben opened the front door.

DISCUSSION QUESTIONS

1. Should Katie have been more cautious in her acceptance of the offer from the chairman of the school board — Enos Kuntz — to become the new schoolteacher?

2. How well do you think Katie handled Ruth Troyer's unexpected visit to the schoolhouse?

3. Should Katie have accepted Norman Kuntz's attentions when he asked to drive her home from the hymn singing?

4. Should Ben have testified against his former comrades-in-crime? Why or why not?

5. Was Katie wise when she agreed to accompany Willis to the hospital for a visit with Ben?

6. Do you think Mabel was in love with Norman when she interfered with his relationship with Katie? What other motives might she have had?

7. When Norman came to the schoolhouse, should Katie have promised never to see Ben again?

8. When does Katie really understand that she still loves Ben, and that *Da Hah* will restore their love?

9. Would Katie have forgiven Norman for his explosion of anger, if he'd asked? Would it have made a difference in their relationship?

10. How well does Katie do with her struggle to accept Norman as family once it becomes apparent that Mabel intends to marry him?

11. Should Ben have agreed to testify against the shooter? What do you think of the community's request that he refrain?

12. What do you think of the ministry's

request that Ben separate from the community?

13. What did you discover about restoring broken relationships and healing wounds?

14. What do you think the main theme of *Katie's Forever Promise* is? Why?

ABOUT THE AUTHOR

Jerry Eicher's bestselling Amish fiction (more than 500,000 in combined sales) includes The Adams County Trilogy, Hannah's Heart series, The Fields of Home series, Little Valley series, and stand-alone novels. His nonfiction includes *My Amish Childhood* and *The Amish Family Cookbook* (with his wife, Tina). After a traditional Amish childhood that included living in Honduras, Jerry taught for two terms in Amish and Mennonite schools in Ohio and Illinois. Since then he's been involved in church renewal, preaching, and teaching Bible studies.

The employees of Thorndike Press hope you have enjoyed this Large Print book. All our Thorndike, Wheeler, and Kennebec Large Print titles are designed for easy reading, and all our books are made to last. Other Thorndike Press Large Print books are available at your library, through selected bookstores, or directly from us.

For information about titles, please call:
(800) 223-1244

or visit our Web site at:
http://gale.cengage.com/thorndike

To share your comments, please write:
Publisher
Thorndike Press
10 Water St., Suite 310
Waterville, ME 04901